From Genera...
the Great S...

The Bouchard family line was established by Lucien, a proud Frenchman of noble lineage and lofty ideals, who fled the horrors of the French Revolution to settle in what was then—in the 1790's—an isolated corner of America . . . the rich land along the upper reaches of the Alabama River, ancestral homeland of the Creek Indians.

Nearly one hundred years later, his memory lives on, though his Southern homeland has seen the bloodshed of Civil War, the travail of racial hatred, and the horrors of occupation by Northern troops and carpetbaggers. As the steel rails of modern life extend like tentacles down into the heart of old Lucien's dominion, his values endure, as his descendents struggle to preserve their beloved sanctuary, called Windhaven Plantation.

Having fought off the marauders who threatened to destroy Windhaven, Laure Bouchard Kenniston must now fight an even greater enemy to her family's future. Dire poverty and personal tragedy threaten to destroy the family unity she has so carefully built. But Laure is determined that the bonds of the Bouchard clan—no matter how they may be strained—shall never again be broken.

*   *   *

"The Bouchards are a memorable clan, larger than life."

—Donald Clayton Porter, author
of the *White Indian* Series

Also in the Windhaven saga from Pinnacle Books

Marie de Jourlet

WINDHAVEN'S GLORY

™ Created by the Producers of
Wagons West, Daimyo,
The Australians and
The Kent Family Chronicles

Chairman of the Board: Lyle Kenyon Engel

PINNACLE BOOKS NEW YORK

ATTENTION: SCHOOLS AND CORPORATIONS

PINNACLE Books are available at quantity discounts with bulk purchases for educational, business or special promotional use. For further details, please write to: SPECIAL SALES MANAGER, Pinnacle Books, Inc., 1430 Broadway, New York, NY 10018.

This novel is a work of fiction. Names, characters, places, and incidents are either the product of the author's imagination or are used fictitiously. Any resemblance to actual events or places or persons, living or dead, is entirely coincidental.

WINDHAVEN'S GLORY

Copyright © 1985 by Book Creations, Inc.

All rights reserved, including the right to reproduce this book or portions thereof in any form.

An original Pinnacle Books edition, published for the first time anywhere.

First printing/July 1985

ISBN: 0-523-41890-6
Can. ISBN: 0-523-43507-X

Printed in the United States of America

PINNACLE BOOKS, INC.
1430 Broadway
New York, New York 10018

9 8 7 6 5 4 3 2 1

I dedicate this book to all my loyal readers who, like the Bouchards, have faith in God, the unconquerable integrity of our great country, love and devotion to family, and a steadfast belief in the eternal tenets of humanity, justice, and honor that gave America birth.

Acknowledgments

Careful students of Alabama history may note similarities between one of my characters, Boxcar Pete, and the real-life Morris Slater, known as Railroad Bill, who appeared in Alabama at a slightly later date than 1883, but whose life was a legend in many of the same ways as Pete's.

Information in this book about the U.S. Trapdoor Long Range rifle is taken from *Flayderman's Guide to Antique American Firearms*, third edition (DBI Books, Inc., Northfield, Illinois). The author is grateful to the publishers of this volume, as well as to Mike Zarbock, assistant store manager, Fox Valley Rifle Range, Inc., Dundee, Illinois, for drawing her attention to the book.

The author is also indebted to Dr. Edward Wolpert of Michael Reese Hospital, Chicago, for supplying vital data on diseases of the mind, and to Dr. Robert McKenna, Department of Psychiatry, Northwestern Memorial Hospital, Chicago, for information about transient amnesia.

The author acknowledges, too, her indebtedness to Lyle Kenyon Engel and to members of his Book Creations staff—Philip Rich, editor in chief, who shaped and refined this book with sensitivity and insight; Pamela Lappies, a gifted editor whose skillful revisions and contributions of ideas and incidents immeasurably strengthened the text; Laurie Rosin, whose ability to spot extraneous elements streamlined and focused the story; and Marjorie Weber, whose keen eye for detail has added consistency and realism to the Windhaven series.

Finally, the author expresses her thanks to Fay J. Bergstrom, her transcriber since 1977, whose impeccable services have freed her from the bondage of the typewriter.

Marie de Jourlet

Windhaven's Glory

The Windhaven Families

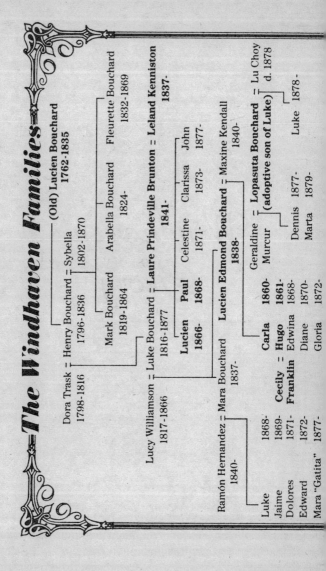

(Old) Lucien Bouchard
1762-1835

Dora Trask = Henry Bouchard = Sybella
1798-1816   1796-1836   1802-1870

Mark Bouchard   Arabella Bouchard   Fleurette Bouchard
1819-1864   1824-   1832-1869

Lucy Williamson = Luke Bouchard = Laure Prindeville Brunton = Leland Kenniston
1817-1866   1816-1877   1841-   1837-

Lucien   Paul   Lucien Edmond Bouchard = Maxine Kendall
1866-   1868-   1838-   1840-

Celestine   Clarissa   John
1871-   1873-   1877-

Geraldine   Lopasuta Bouchard = Lu Choy
Murcur   (adoptive son of Luke)   d. 1878

Dennis 1877-   Luke 1878-
Marta 1879-

Ramón Hernandez = Mara Bouchard
1840-   1837-

Cecily = Hugo   Carla 1860-
Franklin   1861-

Edwina 1868-
Diane 1870-
Gloria 1872-

Luke   1868-
Jaime   1869-
Dolores 1871-
Edward 1872-
Mara "Gatita" 1877-

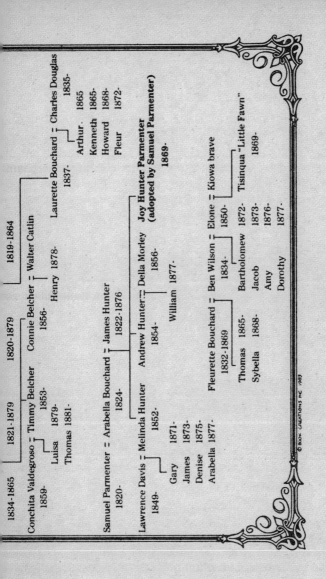

1834-1865 1821-1879 1820-1879 1819-1864

Conchita Valdegroso = Timmy Belcher
1859-   1853-
  Luisa 1879-
  Thomas 1881-

Connie Belcher = Walter Catlin
1856-
  Henry 1878-

Laurette Bouchard = Charles Douglas
1837-   1835-
  Arthur. 1865
  Kenneth 1865-
  Howard 1868-
  Fleur 1872-

Samuel Parmenter = Arabella Bouchard = James Hunter
1820-   1824-   1822-1876

Andrew Hunter = Della Morley
1854-   1856-
  William 1877-

Joy Hunter Parmenter (adopted by Samuel Parmenter)
1869-

Lawrence Davis = Melinda Hunter
1849-   1852-
  Gary 1871-
  James 1873-
  Denise 1875-
  Arabella 1877-

Fleurette Bouchard = Ben Wilson
1832-1869   1834-
  Thomas 1865-
  Sybella 1868-

Elone = Kiowa brave
1850-
  Bartholomew 1872-
  Jacob 1873-
  Amy 1876-
  Dorothy 1877-

Tisinqua "Little Fawn"
1869-

© BOOK CREATIONS INC 1983

Prologue

It was early July in the year 1883, and intense heat and lack of rain throughout the South had wrought havoc with the major crops. Indeed, the country's agricultural economy had not improved after the previous year of poor harvests, rising farm costs, and falling prices for crops. Yet fortunes were still being made in land speculation. Railroads were growing, major industry was expanding. Wherever a traveler went, from the thriving city of Chicago to the port of New Orleans, from the rustic hamlets of Maine to the poverty-stricken villages of Mississippi, there was hopeful talk. The next year was the Presidential election, and Chester A. Arthur, a colorless man who had succeeded to the nation's highest office after the assassination of President James Garfield, would perhaps have a challenger more worthy and more interesting than himself.

In the little town of Sylacauga, sixty miles north of Montgomery, Pete Robbins, the thirty-five-year-old son of a white plantation owner and a black slave mother, was weeding the vegetable garden on his fifty-acre plot of land. He and his younger brother, Jed, had been working from sunup to sundown to raise produce this summer. The cotton market had reached its lowest ebb, and the two brothers were growing vegetables and could not hire anyone to help.

Jed Robbins, hoe in hand, turned to Pete in the next row and said, "Don't seem right, Mama lyin' out back of the cabin with no gravestone over her. Dammit anyway, if only we could git one able man round here to help us work, we could go to town and see Mr. Upshaw, the stonemason—"

"I know that, Jed." Pete Robbins was over six feet tall, sturdily built, with thick sideburns and a stubbly black beard. Like his brother, he was light colored. Only the slight kinkiness of his closely cropped hair and his broad nose hinted at the black blood in his veins. "The way these weeds are growin', we leave 'em alone for one day and we'll have nothin' else in the garden. Mr. Upshaw stays late, I happen to know. Directly after we've finished weedin' out these tomatoes, you and I'll go see him and do right by Mama. Don't you fret any, Jed boy."

"Hard not to, the way things been goin'," Jed broke in fiercely as he savagely thrust the hoe down near one of the tomato plants. "First, the cotton market dries up so we have to grow vegetables, then poor Mama's carried off. And all the while that Sheriff Tom Bixton is breathin' down our necks, tryin' to catch us makin' a mistake so he can lock us up."

"Well, he can't lock us up for nothin'. It has to be done legal, Jed, don't forget that." Pete continued earnestly. "You rile too easy, man. Don't you think I know what Bixton's up to? Only, if we get riled, he'll nail us makin' some fool mistake. But Mama got this land fair 'n' square when the Freedman's Bureau gave her the fifty acres and a mule. And no sheriff can take it away just because he don't like us. Don't forget that, Jed."

"I don't want trouble any more 'n you do, Pete," Jed sighed. "When I marry Dottie in a coupla weeks, I

2

want everythin' to go right for us. Time you got yourself a wife, too, Pete, seein' as how you're older 'n I am.''

Pete threw back his head and laughed heartily. ''They's time enough for that. Anyhow, once you bring Dottie here to our cabin, I'll have to get busy buildin' another room. You young honeymooners will want some privacy. Sure would be nice to find a couple extra hands to do that along with the fields, but we've gotta make do with what we've got.''

''Seems to me,'' Jed scowled, ''folks round here owe you for all you've done. You know you've given produce to plenty of poor folks, white and black, and haven't collected yet. Least they could do is spare us a few hours of their time.''

''We don't want no favors from no one. What we can't do ourselves, we'll do without,'' Pete said firmly. ''The Lord God's been mighty good to us, while lots of folks are starvin', especially colored folks. I figger it's our lot to help them what don't have enough. That's what Mama always taught us, and that's what I intend to do. Now let's hurry up and get this hoein' done so we can go to Mr. Upshaw and arrange for Mama's gravestone.''

''All right, all right, I know you've got a better head on you 'n I've got, only it don't seem fair somehow,'' Jed grumbled as he resignedly shrugged and resumed his work.

But Pete turned, for he had heard the sound of a horse and buggy coming from upriver. ''Uh-oh,'' he said under his breath. He called back to Jed, ''We got visitors. Looks like the sheriff's rig.''

The younger mulatto cursed as he hurried into the small but comfortable cabin that he and his brother had built. "I think I'll let you handle this," he said to Pete.

The sheriff's buggy halted about fifty yards away, and two men jumped from it and approached them. "Robbins, I got law business with you. Concerns your brother, too, so git him out here!" Sheriff Tom Bixton sneered. The middle-aged sheriff was stocky, with a narrow forehead and a shaggy dark brown beard. He turned his cold blue eyes to the house and back to Pete.

His gawky deputy, Len Stuart, ventured a genial nod at Pete Robbins and mumbled, "Afternoon, Robbins."

"What's the matter, Sheriff?" Pete asked. Out of the corner of his eye he could see Jed emerging from the cabin, holding a shotgun behind his back. Pete groaned under his breath, sensing what his brother intended.

"You, Jed, git yourself over here!" Bixton bawled. "What I got to say's meant for both of you Robbins niggers!"

"No need to stir a ruckus, Mr. Bixton," Len Stuart softly protested. He had spotted the shotgun Jed carried.

Bixton whirled around. "Look you here, Len Stuart, you're my deputy. I made you, and I kin replace you, sure as shootin'! Just you keep your mouth shut." Then, turning back to Pete, he ceremoniously withdrew an official-looking document. "This is a lien of forfeiture on your place, boys. That means it ain't your place no more."

"Now just a minute, Sheriff," Pete objected. "This property's ours, free and clear, and we've paid all our taxes."

"Now, that's a goddamn lie, Robbins." The sheriff uttered a cynical chuckle. "Do you think the county recorder of deeds would put out a delinquency judgment for unpaid back taxes if they'd already been paid? It's

4

in the record books in the county office there, in black
and white—''

"You mean, it's white against black, don't you,
Sheriff Bixton?'' Jed Robbins retorted.

Pete cast another frantic look at his brother. "Look
now,'' he said in a more conciliatory tone, "our mama
died in her sleep last week, and my brother is just a
little outa sorts. Let's look into this mix-up tomorrow. I
know this plot of ground is ours. Maybe he's made a
mistake.''

"Mebbe you've made a bigger one, nigger, calling
me a liar. I wouldn't be out here if I didn't have the law
on my side. Anyway, I ain't here to argue with neither
one of you. My deputy 'n' me, we're here to see you
take your things out of that cabin 'n' be on your way—
where, I don't much care.''

"I can tell that, Sheriff Bixton." Every fiber of him
cried out to raise his hoe and beat in the sheriff's head.
Instead, he spoke carefully, with a measured rhythm.
"But don't you see, Sheriff, there just might be a
mistake. Like I say, I've got the receipts back in my
cabin about the taxes. Why don't you let me take them
in to Mr. Paxton and we'll see what the problem is?''

"Because this here paper says you got to git. You
want to land in jail, you just keep standin' here under
the hot sun arguing.'' Sheriff Bixton turned to his deputy. "Len, you go with the Robbins boys into the cabin
and see they clear out their stuff nice 'n' peaceful-like,
understand? And don't let them take the rest of the
afternoon.''

Bixton smiled. He was not concerned about what Pete
and Jed Robbins would learn when they visited the
county recorder of deeds. He had bribed John Paxton to
falsify the records. This land was far too good for
niggers. He'd turn a tidy profit selling their produce.

It was Jed who brought matters to a head. He swung the shotgun in front of him, crying out, "It's you who's gonna get off this land, Sheriff, not us!"

"Now, look here, boy. We don't want no violence over this matter. You brothers never broke the law before. I can't understand why you'd be wantin' to oppose me now. The law *is* on my side, you know."

When Jed stepped closer to the sheriff, Pete put out a restraining arm and said, "Cool down, Jed. Won't do us no good to argue with the sheriff here. We can prove that we're right."

"Listen to your brother, Jed. Opposin' us won't do you no good. Now, just git your things, and—"

The sheriff's words froze as he saw Jed reach down toward his shotgun. Bixton swiftly drew his revolver from its holster and fired point-blank. Jed Robbins dropped the shotgun and, with a gurgling cry, stared blankly down at the spreading red stain on his chest, then fell heavily to the ground.

"Oh, sweet Jesus, no!" Pete moaned. With demonic fury he sprang at Bixton, wrestled away the sheriff's revolver, and fired. Bixton sank down on his knees, rolled over onto his back, and lay with his widened eyes staring up at the relentless sun.

Stunned by the swift and savage action before him, Len Stuart could not move. Without hesitation, Pete gripped the revolver by the barrel and struck the young deputy on the left temple. Stuart fell unconscious.

Pete lowered the revolver, his face haggard, his body bathed in sweat. "Oh, sweet Jesus," he repeated. He knelt down before his brother to see whether there still might be a flicker of life left in Jed's body. There was none. With stinging tears he remembered Dottie, Jed's fiancée, and the future they had planned together. "It's all over now, Jed. It's all over now."

The shock of what he had done temporarily staunched his grief. He had committed the unpardonable crime of killing a white man—worse, a law officer. Within the twinkling of an eye, all his hopes and dreams for respectability, perhaps even marriage, fled. From now on, he would be a hunted man.

He forced himself to plan what he must do. Hurrying into the cabin, he fetched several lengths of rope. Squatting down, he hog-tied the unconscious young deputy. Then, tearing a strip from the man's shirt, he bound his mouth so that his cries would not be heard. *I must have time to escape,* Pete thought. There was nothing left now but survival.

But first he must bury his brother. There could be no funeral service, no gentle eulogies spoken over his grave.

Once again he returned to his cabin and brought out a heavy shovel. Jed would be buried next to their mother's freshly turned grave. After an hour of digging, Pete covered Jed with earth, using his own bed sheets for winding sheets. Then, taking dry twigs and a small piece of cord, he made two crosses and thrust one into the earth at the head of each grave.

"Lord Jesus, take their souls and grant them mercy. Forgive my brother for what he felt he had to do. He had pride, and he was hot-blooded, as young folks are, sweet Jesus. You know how a man can be provoked until it don't seem he can do nothin' except fight back. Look down on me, a sinner, and let me make something useful of my life. Let me help the poor folk that are treated the way Mama and Jed and I have been. I swear to You, I'll try my best, my sweet Lord Jesus. Amen."

His voice broke, and tears flowed down his cheeks. Steeling himself, he returned to the cabin for his squirrel rifle. It was a long-barreled gun, and he had lovingly honed and polished the stock so that it fitted comfortably against the crook of his shoulder. From an old worn purse he pocketed all the cash he had, and a small sum it was. He gave the narrow cabin one last look and walked out.

Old Dan, the spavined eighteen-year-old gelding, was placidly munching from a sheaf of hay. Dan did not have the strength to pull a plow, but he had been with the family for years and had earned some comfort. Now he was going to have to do one last chore.

Pete mounted the gelding, soothing him and patting his neck. "Won't take you far, boy. Won't take you far, I promise. You've just gotta get me to the railroad so I can get shunt of here for good. Maybe someone'll take you in and feed you proper and let you rest—you've earned it."

The Clanton railroad station was deserted, but there were several freight trains on the sidings. One of the engines was idling; that would be the one he would board, he decided.

"Guess this is it, Dan boy," he said, dismounting and turning to the old gelding. "Thanks for all your help." He stroked the horse's head, then turned abruptly and began to lope toward the train.

The gelding stood forlorn under the dwindling afternoon sun. Old Dan stared almost plaintively at the mulatto who clambered into one of the boxcars, pulled the door shut, and disappeared from view. A bluebottle fly settled on the gelding's mane. Dan impatiently shook it off, still staring at the boxcar. Then, very slowly, the horse began to move away and back toward his master's deserted farm.

Pete Robbins had dozed off and was wakened by a sudden jerk as the freight train started. Some two hours had passed since he had climbed into the empty boxcar, and now it was nightfall. His squirrel rifle was propped in a dark corner, next to the bed he had improvised for himself using a sack of flour and two empty gunnysacks. He took from his trousers pocket a ripe peach, which he had picked on his ride to Clanton, and began to eat it.

How strange that everything in his life should come down to this terrible afternoon! He and Jed had often thought that they would be happier in the North, where there was more tolerance toward colored people, but until their mother's death, they had not been able to consider leaving the little farm.

Pete thought of his mother. All her life she had toiled for others—her family, neighbors, anybody who needed help. And how she loved her land! "Son," she had said, "don't ever let them take your land. As long as you've got it, you've got your freedom." Pete wondered what would become of the fifty acres. After what had happened that afternoon, he knew he could never go back.

Yet if he now left the South, with all of its injustice and bigotry, he knew he would be taking the easy way out. No, instead of running away, he would stay and fight—in his mother's and Jed's memory.

He had finished the peach and flung the pit away. Then he chuckled bitterly. Greed, envy, and hatred had caused what had happened this afternoon, and he swore that he would seek revenge. He said to himself in a low, steady voice, "Dammit all, from now on I'm gonna do what I can for my own people. The rights old Abe Lincoln gave us are sure enough bein' taken away by the courts and bullies like Bixton. I've got a price on my head by now, but with the good Lord's help I'm gonna work for my people before whitey catches up with me."

The freight train was rumbling southward on toward Mobile. Pete thought it likely that he would find many other blacks there just like him—out of work, impoverished, turned out of their little farms and cabins. Well, he would help them, offer them some hope against the malevolence of the whites.

Again he thought of his mother. She had always told him and Jed stories, and one of her favorites had been about Robin Hood and his Merry Men. He smiled as he recalled the gestures and expressions she had used to illustrate the joy Robin Hood had taken in robbing from the rich to give to the poor, outwitting the stupid, unimaginative Sheriff of Nottingham.

"That's it, sweet Jesus!" he suddenly said aloud. "I could be like that Robin Hood. Things ain't so much different now than they was back then. The poor still get shoved around." He clasped his hands together and lifted them above his head. "Lord, help me do it. Let me help my people. Make the colored folks take me in, and for poor Mama's sake, maybe I can help them get what's coming to them."

At peace now, he lay back. His path was clear. He would see to it that his mother and poor Jed had not died in vain, and he was ready to spill white men's blood to do it.

Chapter 1

*A*ugust usually brought the highest temperature of the year to Alabama, and August of 1883 was no exception. Laure Bouchard Kenniston, the mistress of Windhaven Plantation, welcomed the breeze that blew across her forehead from the open window next to her bed. The gurgling sound of the Alabama River, which bordered the grounds of the plantation, was almost hypnotic, and she stretched lazily, wondering if she should try to go back to sleep. But Saturday morning was already too hot and humid, and, besides, she had much to attend to this morning—notably seeing to the comfort of her convalescing husband, Leland.

Laure thought back to the day before, when she and her eldest son, Lucien, had brought Leland home from the hospital in Atlanta, where the previous month he had undergone delicate brain surgery to remove a tumor that had so negatively altered his personality and affected the lives of everyone around him. She recalled the frightening words of Dr. Townsend, the surgeon who had performed the operation. When he had removed the growth on her husband's brain, he had had to eliminate a small portion of the healthy tissue surrounding it, and therefore he could not promise that Leland would be the same man. Certainly, she knew, it was possible that the man with whom she had fallen so

desperately in love during Mardi Gras in New Orleans—
the ardent and devoted lover whom she had married
three years before—might be lost to her forever.

Before the tumor had changed him from a responsible
businessman into an easy mark for opportunistic sales-
men and gamblers, Leland had been Laure's source of
strength. In contrast to her former husband, the late
Luke Bouchard—a man of the soil and upholder of the
Bouchard legacy as represented by Windhaven Plantation—Leland Kenniston was an urbane, well-traveled
gentleman, though always supportive of Laure's responsibility to Windhaven. Even when she and the children
had joined him in New York and taken up residence in
a fashionable brownstone on Gramercy Park, he had
repeatedly expressed concern that the plantation be left
in competent hands.

Their life in the city had been so fresh, so exciting
until the horrible events of the past year had forced
Laure to return to the plantation—damaged in raids by
enemies of the Bouchards—and then to watch her husband be transformed first into an arrogant, impulsive
man, then into a helpless invalid.

The surgeon's warning still troubled Laure. She had
not truly relaxed since the proposed operation had first
been described to her. But now that Leland was home,
alive and apparently well, things seemed a little better.
Laure's younger children—Paul, Celestine, Clarissa, and
John—had warmly welcomed their stepfather and had
helped him to settle into his temporary bedroom on the
first floor.

Laure threw back the bed sheet and quickly rose from
her bed, eager to see her dear Leland's face and to
make him comfortable. She scurried into her dressing
room, chose a pale pink summer dress, and laid it on
her bed, hoping that it would please Leland. After

washing her face and brushing her honey-blond hair, she smiled into her mirror. Though she was nearing forty-three, her skin was still soft and smooth. Her luminous green eyes and sensuous mouth still pronounced her a desirable woman, and her slender figure belied her age.

She chided herself for her vanity, then swiftly dressed and went down to the kitchen, where the cook, Amelia Coleman, was preparing breakfast. Her husband, Burt, one of the plantation supervisors, had already gone downriver to the plantation he looked after for Andy Haskins, a family friend.

"Good morning, Laure!" Amelia greeted her with a smile. "You'll be wanting breakfast—"

"Just coffee and perhaps some corn bread if you've any left from last night, Amelia," Laure replied. "Then I'll see if Leland's up, and take breakfast to him on a tray."

"Of course." Amelia sighed. "That poor man. I hope he's better today."

"So do I." Laure smiled, trying to mask her uneasiness. "Dr. Townsend said Leland must get plenty of rest and quiet."

"Well, if I can do anything, all you have to do is tell me, Laure," Amelia volunteered. "I know it must be terrible for you."

"The last thing I need is to start pitying myself, Amelia. My primary concern must be for Leland and straightening out the plantation's affairs. Will Burt come back today?"

"He plans to, Laure," Amelia answered. "He knows you and Mr. Kenniston are back and are wanting to talk to him about the crops and such."

"Good." Laure seated herself at the kitchen table, and Amelia brought her a generous wedge of corn bread with butter and honey, and a piping-hot cup of strong black coffee laced with chicory.

When Laure had finished her simple breakfast, she thanked Amelia and went down the hallway to check on Leland. He slowly turned his head as she entered the room. His once-dark hair was now completely gray, Laure observed again, and his face was a mass of wrinkles. A slow smile of recognition lighted Leland's face, and he said, "My darling. I'm glad you're here."

"Did you have a good, long sleep, Leland dear?"

"Yes. I just woke up a few minutes ago."

"That's good, darling. Let me fluff up your pillow. Would you like some breakfast?"

"Well—perhaps a little coffee, and some fruit."

"I'll bring a piece of melon and some corn bread," Laure said cheerfully.

Leland put his hand on hers as she arranged his pillows, helping him sit up. Staring into her eyes, he said in a low, hoarse voice, "I owe you so much. I've been a terrible—"

"I will not listen to such talk, Leland!" she interrupted firmly.

He closed his eyes for a moment. "I've made such stupid mistakes," he said, referring to his imprudent spending and gambling resulting from his tumor. "I don't know how I could have done those things."

She put two fingers over his lips and shook her head. Then, to soften the gesture, she leaned over and kissed him on the cheek. "Who hasn't made mistakes? Remember we've had good times together, and we'll have them again. You're not to feel guilty about anything—please promise me you won't."

"I—I'll try. I don't deserve you, Laure."

Tears formed in his eyes, and Laure's heart was wrenched. Too moved to reply, she rose, crossed to the door, and said airily, "I'll be back in a jiffy with your breakfast."

Outside his door, the tears spilled down her cheeks, and she wondered how she would endure watching Leland struggle to overcome his helplessness.

When she returned with his breakfast, she set the tray on his knees, then drew up a chair. She tried not to watch too closely as he ate, but she did happily observe that he had no problems in so doing. Dr. Townsend had warned that some human functions might be forgotten when healthy brain tissue was surgically removed. She had dreaded that Leland might have to learn to do simple things all over again.

She forced herself to talk of pleasant, inconsequential things, such as the way the girls had helped out during her absence and John's latest misadventure. If the weather held until the beginning of next week, as the *Advertiser* had predicted, they might have an outdoor picnic with all the children. "Paul will like that, Leland dear. You know, I've been worried about him recently. He has seemed so lonely."

She had no sooner finished the sentence than she knew that it had been the wrong thing to say. Leland put down his cup of coffee and closed his eyes. In a distant voice, he murmured, "It is my own fault. If we were back in New York, Paul would still be with his friends. I did this to you. . . . I don't know how you can ever forgive me."

"Oh, please, darling, you break my heart when you talk like that!" Laure almost sobbed, reaching out to touch his hand. "I love you, I'm your wife, you've done such wonderful things for all of us. All you have to do now is rest and get well—that will be my happiness. Please promise you won't apologize again."

He did not reply, and she saw tears edge from under

his closed, quivering eyelids. Finally she rose and said as cheerfully as she could, "Well, I think it's time for me to see what we can plant next year. We don't want anyone to go hungry at Windhaven Plantation."

He held on to her hand and seemed reluctant to let it go as she stood looking down at him, her eyes blurred with tears. "Maybe it was destined for me to become a farmer," he said distantly. "Yes—that's it! I'll work at it, I promise you. I'll pull my own weight here. God bless you for sticking by me, Laure."

"I'd be a fool if I didn't."

Not trusting herself to say more, she bent and kissed him and then left the bedroom, closing the door behind her. Back in the kitchen, she covered her face with her hands and silently wept.

In spite of the disturbing talk with Leland, Laure was able to compose her thoughts and consider her next most pressing concern—the welfare of Windhaven Plantation. Ever since she had returned from New York in January after the plantation had been attacked by unknown raiders, she had realized that the income from crops alone could not sufficiently provide for her family. Then a subsequent attack, the work of bigoted townsfolk who hated the Bouchards as "nigger-lovers," had destroyed the dam, causing land and crops to be flooded with polluted water. An epidemic of typhoid fever had put the plantation even more deeply into arrears, for none of the livestock on the plantation could be sold.

Laure went to her upstairs study now, intending to list possible ways of bringing additional revenue to the plantation. It was useless to think of increasing production, even though the land could yield it, because the average price paid in New York for cotton was only about fourteen cents per pound; no money could be made, even in volume.

Ideally, Laure thought, she should buy more live-stock; cattle and hogs were one way to forestall bank-ruptcy, even if they didn't bring in a great deal of money. Unfortunately, she did not have the capital to make even this kind of investment right now.

Laure put down her pen and went to see if Burt Coleman had returned from the Haskins property; he might have a solution for Windhaven's plight.

She also hoped to find Benjamin Franklin Brown, another supervisor on the plantation and a graduate of Tuskeegee Institute.

As Laure emerged from the back entrance near the kitchen on her way to the fields, Burt was returning from the Haskins property, riding his spirited roan mare along the grassy path leading to the large stable just behind the red-brick chateau. An eighteen-year-old black youth, whom Ben had hired two weeks before, hurried up to take the reins of the mare as Burt dismounted and strode over to greet the mistress of Windhaven Planta-tion. "A good day to you, Mrs. Kenniston! I'm mighty glad you're back. And I hope your husband's better."

"Thank you so much, Burt. Yes, the surgery appears to be a success," Laure responded with a smile.

"So you're going to stay here now, Mrs. Kenniston?" he asked as they headed toward Ben Brown, in a nearby field giving instructions to two workers.

"Yes, Burt, indefinitely. That's why I want to go over a serious financial problem. I have to know what direction to take so this land can provide a living, not only for my family but for our tenant families."

"Ben and I will do everything we can to make that possible, Mrs. Kenniston," Burt solemnly assured her.

Ben Brown, having seen them approach, finished

talking with his co-workers and came forward to meet
Laure and Burt. "Good to see you again, Mrs. Kenniston!" he said amiably, touching the wide brim of his
straw hat.

"Thank you, Ben. I'm glad to be here."

Burt spoke up. "Ben, Mrs. Kenniston wants to ask
about our cash crops and plan for next year's planting."

"Well," Ben frowned, "there's not much to tell.
While you were in Atlanta, Mrs. Kenniston, I bought a
fine rooster and some good hens, and one of the tenant-owner families, the Gregorys, are taking charge of the
chicken coop. We ought to have plenty of eggs and
chickens to sell by September."

"That's some help, certainly," Laure replied.

"You've also got a few acres planted in cotton,"
Burt added. "The price went up some this month, I'm
glad to say. You'll harvest about a hundred bales this
year, and that'll give you a few dollars on the credit
side of the ledger. But I'm not counting on the price
staying up—the market just isn't there. Cotton won't be
any kind of money-maker for a while."

"I feared as much." Laure sighed.

"I'd really like to see us get another bull and two
good heifers," Ben put in.

"I would, too, Ben, but I doubt we can afford such a
purchase right now," Laure replied.

"Well, it's possible that you'll make enough with the
poultry to be able to," Burt said. "And we have some
good vegetables started. With the dam rebuilt, the irrigation's working just fine, and there's a reservoir of
water in case of a drought later this summer."

"There'll be enough food for the table, Mrs. Kenniston," Ben assured Laure. "And the tenant families are
hard workers. They'll make out."

"It's a pity I won't be able to pay them much of a

year-end dividend,'' Laure said. ''They've been so patient.'' She shook her head. ''I'll be frank with both of you. My husband's New York importing and exporting business cannot be counted on for extra income.'' She found herself trembling as she spoke of her husband's debts, yet she was relieved to be speaking candidly and openly, sharing the burdens of her heart with sympathetic auditors.

After pausing to collect her thoughts, she added, ''I still have a part interest in the Brunton & Alliance Bank of New Orleans and am assured an annual income from it. Of course, since last year's recession the dividends have dwindled, but I'm hoping that by November I'll have a check from Mr. Kessling, the bank's new president.''

Both men nodded silently, each understanding her plight and admiring her courage and optimism.

''I'll try to spend as much time here as I can with Ben,'' Burt put in. ''The workers on Andy's land are doing just fine, so they really don't need me. I'll see if Ben and I can come up with some new crop for next year, to make things the same as they used to be for you, Mrs. Kenniston.''

''God bless you both. And now, let's visit our neighbors,'' Laure said. She knew things would never be the same for the families of Windhaven Plantation, including her own. Even if Leland's physical recovery were complete, it would be difficult for him to return actively to business, for he had become virtually penniless through his ill-advised speculations of the past year.

She began to walk toward the cottages at the easternmost boundary of Windhaven Plantation, where the tenant families lived—the Gregorys, the Wests, the Larsons, the Mendicotts, and the Munroes. She needed to reunite with the tenant families—to feel wanted, to feel that there was purpose for her returning here to Windhaven Plantation.

Following her visit with the tenant families, Laure felt revitalized. All had enthusiastically welcomed her, and when she had started to speak of her financial problems and her obligation to them all, Louis Mendicott had boldly spoken up: "Beggin' your pardon, ma'am, but we're all in this together. We don't much care if we're not wealthy, so long as we're together and have food that the Lord provides. We'll get along just fine, Miz Laure. You just taken care of Mr. Kenniston. When he's well enough to come out, we'll have a barbecue, with a fiddler and such, to welcome you both back."

His words had brought tears to her eyes.

As she started up to her bedroom, thinking of having her belongings moved downstairs to the guest room next to Leland's, a hoarse cry broke the silence, chilling her blood. She hurried to the downstairs hall and opened the door to Leland's room. A small snack prepared by Amelia lay untouched on the night table beside him, and his eyes were wild and glassy. His lean fingers clawed at the sheets in an attempt to pull himself up from his bed. "Laure! I'm glad you came! Please help me." His voice was hoarse and unsteady.

"Of course, my darling." Laure helped reposition her husband. "What is it?"

"The trunk—the small one I brought from Europe. There's something in there I wanted to look at."

"I'll get it, my darling. Just lie back and rest. You mustn't get yourself overexcited. I'll be back directly, I promise."

She glanced back as she left the room, at the once-vital man who now lay as helpless as a babe. *Oh,*

Leland, you must recover, you must! she thought as she quickly turned away, hoping he had not seen the pity in her expression.

The cloth-covered trunk was in the downstairs guest room Laure was thinking of moving to. She gripped one of the rope handles with both hands and pulled at it. It was heavier than she had thought, and she uttered a soft groan, pulled once more with all her might, and when she could not budge it, burst into tears. "I can't even do this for him," she lamented.

There was a sudden knock at the door. "It's Lucien, Mother. May I come in?"

Laure dashed away the tears with her hand, then called, "Oh, yes, Lucien, please!"

Her tall blond son entered and saw her standing beside the trunk, her eyes swollen with tears. He closed the door. "Mother, what's wrong?"

"I—I'm fine, really," she sniffled. "I was just trying to bring this trunk into Leland's room. There's something in it he wants to look at, and—"

"I'll do it for you, Mother." He came to her, put his hands on her shoulders, and said, "Go ahead and cry, Mother, it's good for you. Put your head on my shoulder and don't hold back."

Her green eyes widened, for Lucien's voice had the firmness of a man's, a firmness she had known in the man who now lay helpless in the next room. She bowed her head on Lucien's shoulder and sobbed. He put his arms around her, murmuring, "I'm here, Mother, and I'll do all I can to help."

At last she recovered and straightened, moving away slightly. "What must you think of me, feeling sorry for myself when poor Leland lies in there suffering so?"

"Mother, let me help you with the trunk. And then I want to sit down and talk to you."

She stood aside as Lucien took the rope handle with both hands and drew the trunk easily toward the door, which Laure opened for him. She went down the hall into Leland's room, Lucien following behind her.

"Thank you, son," Leland murmured as Lucien drew the trunk alongside the bed. He turned to look at Laure, and a shadow crossed his face, for he saw that she had been crying. To ease the tension, Lucien hastily spoke up.

"I'll open the trunk for you, Father. Tell me what you're looking for."

"That's most kind, Lucien. There should be some papers in a leather case, and a book that I bought in London. I read it when I was a young man, nearly twenty-five years ago." He passed a weary hand over his forehead, frowning as if trying to search back in his memory. "It's very romantic—and you know I'm a romanticist." He laughed softly.

"I'll get them for you, Father." Lucien opened the trunk, searched in it, and found the leather case, which he handed to Leland. Then he pulled from the trunk a bound volume of Tennyson's *Idylls of the King*.

"That's the book—yes. He's a great poet, you know. The English do a few things well, I'll give them that." Leland tried to make his voice sound bantering as he took the book from Lucien's hand and set it on his lap atop the leather case. "Thank you both very much. I—I'd like to go over these papers."

"Don't sit up too long, darling. You must get your strength back. It's wonderful that you feel better and want to occupy your mind, but you mustn't overdo it," Laure warned.

"I shan't, don't worry. Please, I'll be all right." He gave her an imploring look, and she forced a smile to her face.

"Try to nap, Leland dear. I'll look in on you later."

When they left Leland's room, Lucien accompanied his mother back to hers. He closed the door behind him and said directly, "Mother, I know what you must be going through now. But I don't want you to have to worry about me. I honestly think the best thing for me now is to go out and find a job, something where I can be of help and can use what I've already learned from my schooling in Ireland. I want to earn money so that I can help out here and do my share. I don't know what career I want to pursue for the rest of my life, but if I can get a job that will interest me, it will be a start."

Laure burst into tears, and once again Lucien took her in his arms and let her put her head on his shoulder. "Things will be fine, Mother, you'll see," he murmured gently.

Chapter 2

Sunday was a peaceful day, and Leland Kenniston seemed much more cheerful, or at least so far as Laure could discern when she took breakfast with him in his room. She had told the children that she would join them afterward for coffee and some of Amelia's wonderful corn fritters, not wanting them to feel that she was neglecting them in her anxiety to look after their stepfather's well-being.

Indeed, this intimate sharing of a meal with Leland somewhat eased her worries, for there were flashes of his old self. He was greatly pleased that she had moved into the adjoining guest room, and several times he looked at her ardently and paid her a gallant compliment, as he had done when he was courting her. When she leaned over to kiss him, he reached up, took her by the shoulders, and kissed her tenderly on the mouth.

The kiss surprised and touched her. Now, more than ever, she needed her husband's loving reassurance. She vowed that she would do everything possible to restore his health, for she yearned to have him back as her lover and companion.

And so, when she joined the children at the breakfast table, she was in a far more radiant mood than she had been earlier. Her spirits were so buoyed, in fact, that she failed for some time to observe that her son Paul seemed more withdrawn than usual. Indeed, Paul had his reasons for glumness: To him, life at Windhaven Plantation was boring. The days had become a dreary round of working in the fields and studying his books. He yearned desperately to return to New York, the grandest city in the country. There, around every corner he could find exciting things to do and places to see; here, in the South, he could see nothing but fields of cotton for miles on end. And he was tired of working in those fields alongside Burt and Ben. What could they teach him to help him get ahead in life? All they cared about was growing cotton—and Paul would never have to look at cotton once he was an adult; he would make sure of that.

"Paul, dear, you're not eating your food." His mother's voice jarred him out of his somber meditation. "Is there anything wrong? We'll be late for our visit to Dalbert and Mitzi's if you don't finish up soon. I promised them we'd arrive before noon."

Paul hated going to nearby Lowndesboro, where Dalbert and Mitzi Sattersfield lived. He felt a complete stranger to the place. The other boys his age were country bumpkins who had never been anywhere.

"Paul?" his mother asked again.

"I'm hurrying," he said. He dug into his fritters, which by now were cold and unappetizing. *I hate this place*, he thought. *I hate it*.

The next morning, Leland woke well before anyone else. The early light of dawn cast a grayish pallor over everything in his room. He turned slowly onto his side and stared out the window, which faced Pintilalla Creek. The sky was clear, the scenery pleasantly rustic and soothing. He sighed wistfully. He had prayed the night before, when Laure had left him, that he might regain all his strength and vitality. He had to begin to live a useful life. Laure was too charitable when she told him that his mistakes did not matter. No, he had to be worthy of her unconditional love. Now he saw himself only as a useless parasite.

He even considered his own appearance to be offensive. Laure had seen to it there was no mirror in his room, but yesterday he had struggled out of bed and gone to the mirror in one of the other guest rooms. Looking at himself for the first time since the operation, he had grimaced and closed his eyes, then forced himself to look again, shaking his head despondently.

As he lay on his bed now, waiting for the others to rise, he remembered what Dr. Townsend had told him. Yes, the surgeon had said, the operation had been successful. But he had not pointed out to the patient any of the lingering consequences, or predicted when he might begin to regain his strength.

The anguish of the past returned, and he surveyed his life like some stranger staring coldly at the record of his accomplishments and failures. It was not a heartening picture, and he finally closed his eyes, wishing he could fall asleep again. But sleep would not come, and he sighed in utter frustration and self-loathing.

He had become a hindrance, an old man forcing a beautiful, vital woman to sacrifice herself like the lowliest nurse in a hospital ward. It was wrong! He resolved to do everything in his power to make Laure happy and to change the grim circumstances of her life.

Later that morning, Laure found reason to be cheerful when an animated Leland warmly greeted her as she came into his room to inquire after his night. He told her that he had slept well and that he would like to have breakfast with the family. Smiling happily, she hugged and kissed him, then hurried off to the kitchen to ask Amelia to prepare a special breakfast.

Before Leland joined them at the breakfast table, Laure tactfully reminded the children that their stepfather was recovering from a most difficult operation and that they must not show their surprise if he acted differently from what he had been in New York. "You see, my dears," she explained, "brain surgery saps a great deal of your strength. Try to make him feel at ease, and I'll be ever so grateful to all of you."

Little John, who could hear from his mother's tone how seriously she meant what she said, solemnly nodded, his brown eyes very wide and attentive. Seeing this, she caught him up to her and gave him a hug and a kiss. "You can be such a darling when you want to, dear John!"

She looked at all of them and sighed. How lovely Celestine was becoming, Celestine who had inherited her golden hair and gray-green eyes and already had the poise of a personable young woman, despite being only twelve. And Clarissa, just two years younger, was going to be a beauty. As for little John, he was her joy, still childlike enough to amuse her, even when she was worried about his occasional tantrums and frequent sulks. As for Lucien and Paul, as the eldest, their futures had been drastically altered by the unfortunate economic circumstances of the family. Well, that could not be helped, but the boys must be told that she would do all she could for their well-being.

She went to Leland's bedchamber to make sure he was ready and found him coming down the hallway toward her. He wore a shirt and plain cotton trousers, his feet thrust into a pair of slippers. This costume suggested the invalid, and the pallor of his face heightened the impression, momentarily disconcerting his wife, especially after his lively demeanor of fifteen minutes before. To ensure he would detect nothing in her manner that suggested her alarm, she gaily declared, "It's just beautiful outside, Leland. We might even think of having supper out in the courtyard. It would be like a picnic for the children."

"That would be very nice," he agreed, as though he were forcing himself to display enthusiasm. Perfunctorily, he kissed her cheek, and she saw that his eyes were dull once again, as they had been yesterday, and his face was expressionless. Nonetheless, she recalled Dr. Townsend's warning that shifts of mood would occur during Leland's convalescence.

She walked beside him, ready to lend a helping hand if need be, but observed to her great relief that he was walking with a reasonably firm step today. This was a good sign, and it somewhat compensated her for his listless manner. When they entered the dining room, she was delighted when all the children piped up, "Good morning, Father!"

"Why, good morning to you, too," Leland said as he seated himself. He looked around the table, a faint smile on his face. He had not shaved, and there was a thick gray stubble on his jaws and chin, compounding the image of invalidism, the very last thing she wished the children to perceive. Laure reminded herself that here was a task she must do for him.

She turned to Leland at the head of the table and brightly observed, "Amelia took special pains to make this first family breakfast reunion of ours here at Windhaven Plantation a real treat for you, Leland dear."

"It does look very tempting, Laure," he responded.

She began to serve him from the platters sizable portions of eggs, flapjacks, and ham, and two of the very largest biscuits, which she buttered for him and then spread with strawberry preserves.

"You are trying to fatten me up," he remarked, and she laughed in her relief at his being able to make a joke. Another good sign! Now, seated with him and all her children around her, she felt proud and courageous and loving.

As the breakfast progressed, Celestine, then Clarissa, and then Lucien sought to draw their stepfather into conversation, and to an extent they succeeded. It was plain to Laure that he was making a visible effort to be cheerful. And his competent handling of knife, fork, and spoon was still another heartening sign to Laure, and perhaps why she was indulgent with little John, who, having had his first taste of coffee since he had left New York—albeit diluted with a healthy proportion of milk—demanded more.

Toward the end of the meal, Lucien turned to his stepfather. "After breakfast, I'm going into Montgomery," he said. "To find work."

At this remark, Leland frowned as if painfully reminded that Lucien was another victim of the family's reduced circumstances. But forcing a smile, he nodded and replied, "I wish you the best of luck, Lucien. I'm sure you'll have no trouble. You're alert and gifted, and you'll do very well, I'm sure."

"Thank you, Father."

But Paul, who had been withdrawn, looked up and scowled. His large blue eyes were narrowed and suspicious, for he had interpreted his stepfather's remark as an intentional slight, a sign that he was regarded as second best to Lucien. He ran a hand through his unruly light brown hair, shifted in his seat, and then reached for another biscuit, bit into it with an air that was akin to defiance, and began to chew angrily.

He glanced across the table at Lucien. Nearly six feet tall now, with blond hair, clean shaven, and widely spaced, clear blue eyes, Lucien seemed thoughtful this morning. Secretly, Paul put this down to snobbery, thinking, *He's been to Europe, he's gone to a foreign school and learned languages, he's had a sweetheart, even if she did die, and he thinks himself the big man of the family, I'll bet. If I'd had the same chances as Lucien, I'd be just as smart, I know I would.* And when Lucien happened to look up and glance at his brother, Paul's face reddened and he became seriously engrossed in the matter of spreading apricot preserves on a second biscuit.

After breakfast, Lucien saddled and mounted his horse and rode to Montgomery. Cantering along the river path, he let his mind drift back to his days in Dublin and to Mary Eileen Brennert, the Irish lass who had stolen his heart. If things had gone differently, they would have been married soon, but her death had quenched all hope for love. A stray bullet had struck her during a conflict between British troops and Irish nationalists, and Lucien had felt his own life end with hers. He had since learned that life must necessarily go on, but he held a special place in his heart for Mary Eileen's memory.

He realized that he stood on the threshold between adolescence and manhood. It was high time he proved himself worthy of his stepfather's praise.

In Montgomery, tethering his horse to a hitching post outside the *Advertiser* office, Lucien self-consciously smoothed his suit coat and trousers with the flat of his hand. He had donned a beautifully tailored suit of fine linen. It gave him the appearance of a personable, well-groomed young man ready to meet with a prospective employer.

He strode briskly into the newspaper office and laid down a nickel for a copy of the morning edition. Then, walking over to a table in the corner, he drew out a chair, seated himself, and turned to the want ads.

The young woman behind the desk—short, plump, and genial—eyed him with no little interest, for indeed Lucien was a handsome figure. At that moment, a gray-haired, lanky, bespectacled man with enormously bushy eyebrows came down the stairs to the counter and was greeted by the young woman. "Good morning, Mr. McGill."

"And the same to you, Catherine. I see we have a visitor—wonder who he is." McGill walked around the counter and approached the table where Lucien was seated. "Good morning, young man. I'm delighted to see the attention you're giving our journal."

Lucien turned, got to his feet, and greeted the intruder.

"I didn't mean to interrupt you," the man went on. "I'm Henry McGill, the *Advertiser*'s editor."

"And my name is Lucien Bouchard. I was reading the want ads, Mr. McGill. I'm after a job."

"Maybe I can be of assistance. I'm new in my post—came here from South Carolina two years ago as chief reporter—so I was in the same boat as you, you might say. Why don't we go upstairs to my office? You can tell me something about yourself." Henry McGill clapped Lucien on the back, for despite his studious appearance, he was a hearty, outgoing man.

Leading the way up the stairs and into his office, the editor showed Lucien to a chair with a wave of his hand. "Lucien Bouchard, you said your name is?" he said as he seated himself at his desk. "I've heard the name. You're from Windhaven Plantation?"

"That's right, Mr. McGill. And I know something about you, sir. I've read some of the *Advertiser*'s editorials. They're mighty sensible."

"Good common sense and the realization of it, Mr. Bouchard, is what it will take to make the South rise again. Want a cigar?" The editor gestured toward the teakwood box on his desk.

When Lucien shook his head with a murmured thanks, the *Advertiser* editor trimmed the end of his own cigar, struck a match, and puffed the cigar into life. "I'm looking forward to a new South, with scientific and industrial productivity. Those are the only things that spell more revenue for the state and jobs for the citizens."

"I share your ideas, Mr. McGill."

"Well, enough of my speech-making, young man," McGill said. "We're here to find you a job. Tell me a little about yourself."

Lucien summarized the facts of his background and education, also mentioning his stepfather's poor health and the family's finances—for something about the man caused Lucien to trust him.

"I can understand your situation," McGill said when Lucien had finished. He leaned back in his chair, puffed at his cigar until it was drawing well, then went on. "I admire your willingness to go to work. Started to work early myself—younger than you, in fact. My parents ran a small truck produce farm in South Carolina for a spell. It was hard toil, especially for a boy, but it taught me never to be afraid of honest labor. I'd guess the same is true of you—though I doubt you're looking for field work. Any idea of what you might like?"

"I just saw an ad for an assistant to an architect."

"Oh, yes, I remember that ad. Took it down myself when the gentleman came in. Fine man, upstanding citizen, very good background. Name's Nils Sonderman.

He's worked up plans for a number of the new buildings in town. Right now he's adding a wing to that run-down city hall of ours and is having the outside cleaned up, as befits the state capital. His business is growing. Yes, Mr. Bouchard, that might be worth a try."

The editor rose and extended his hand to Lucien, who came forward to McGill's desk. "It's been a pleasure meeting you, Mr. McGill," he said, his hand grasped in a firm handshake. "What you've said has given me hope. I'm going to see Mr. Sonderman and talk to him about that job."

"Wish you well, son. A good day to you, Mr. Bouchard."

Chapter 3

Following Lucien's departure for Montgomery, Laure escorted Leland back to his bedroom and helped him get settled for the day. "It's such a beautiful morning, you'll want to look out the window, dearest," she said as she guided him to a low, comfortable armchair near the window. Fluffing up a pillow from his bed, she tucked it behind his head. "Just rest now, and I'll look in on you before lunchtime."

"You're so kind to me, Laure," he said.

She kissed him on the cheek and said, "Who wouldn't be with such a wonderful husband? Is there anything I can get you? Do you want to look at the papers or your book?"

"I can reach them," he said, extending his arm and easily lifting the leather-bound volume. "Tennyson has been a great comfort to me. Did you know"—his face brightened for an instant as he turned eagerly to her—"I once tried to write poetry? With time on hand now, I might just try it again. I owe you a sonnet."

"Oh, Leland! I would be very flattered to be the subject of a sonnet. I'll tell you what, darling. I'll bring some paper and a pen and ink, in case you want to write something."

So saying, she hurried to provide the articles she had

mentioned, set them down on a taboret beside him, and then, kissing him again, left the room.

Laure headed down the hall toward the kitchen, where she knew Clarabelle, the children's nurse and her own intimate friend, was preparing a list of the supplies she and Amelia would need for preserving the vegetables and fruits that were ripening in increasing abundance. When Laure had rinsed potatoes dug from the warm soil the day before, she had noticed that the kettle they would use to stew the tomatoes had begun to corrode, and she doubted that the other women were aware of it.

As she neared the kitchen, she came upon Paul, his hands in his pockets and his face somber. "Mother!" he said, his face brightening momentarily. "Could I talk with you for just a second?"

"Of course, Paul. What is it?"

He began to walk slowly away from the door to the kitchen, and she could tell that he wished to draw her out of Clarabelle's hearing.

"All right," she said. "It seems what you have to say to me is private. Let's go into one of the guest rooms. Here, we'll be quite alone."

Once inside the room, Laure closed the door and turned to her fourteen-year-old blue-eyed son. "Tell me what's worrying you, dear. You've not been happy since you've come back from New York. You understand why we had to move, don't you, dear?" she anxiously asked.

Paul turned to his mother, fumbling for words. "I *do* understand why we had to come back here, Mother. It's only— Well, I'm working in the fields with Burt and Ben now, and to me it doesn't have any future. There's nothing exciting to it. I don't feel I'm learning anything, you see. And I know private schooling costs money we don't have, the way we had for—for Lucien."

She knew her son well enough to see that he was trying not to hurt her, yet he obviously was much troubled by the advantages his older brother had received, which intensified the rivalry they had maintained since childhood. Her son's next words confirmed that this was so.

"I *know* Lucien's older than I am, so I suppose he's got a right to have things I haven't had. Understand, Mother, I'm not complaining about that at all. It's just the way it happened."

"Yes, darling. It wasn't showing favoritism, believe me. If you'd been ready for a school like that before all this trouble happened, Leland and I would have done everything to arrange it for you."

"But Lucien already knows so much about things that are going on in the world." This time, the hurt came through clearly in Paul's voice. "He knows about politics and England's fight with the Irish and the Irish wanting to be free. I learned *something* about all that from my history class and from the books you had me read in New York, Mother. But I haven't learned it firsthand. I haven't learned *anything* firsthand. Don't you see, Mother?"

His anguish communicated itself to Laure, and she understood his complaint. He had a right to the same privileges Lucien had had, and she could see how his present existence must seem to him something of a cruel twist of fate. She wondered how young Paul had so quickly learned how dire their financial crisis had become.

"I think I know what you're feeling, Paul dear," Laure now rejoined, putting a hand on his shoulder. "We've all had to tighten our belts—and we'll have to continue doing so until the crops are sold and we get some money from our chickens and eggs."

He nodded, his face still sullen and disturbed. He could see that his mother was touched by his plight, but she had no real answer to offer him. Instead, squeezing his shoulder, she said, "You know, dear, there's nothing like work to occupy the mind and take your thoughts off your problems. I know what you've missed in New York by coming here to live, but you'll see, it'll all work out. Why don't you go out and see what you can do for Ben and Burt? Tell them you want more responsibility. I'm sure they'll do what they can."

"All right, Mother," Paul resignedly said.

"That's my lamb. You see, no situation is so bad that we can't make the best of it. And now, if you'll excuse me, I need to talk to Clarabelle."

"Of course—thank you, Mother," Paul murmured, feeling that his mother had in effect dismissed him. Disconsolate, he walked slowly down the hallway and then ascended the stairway to his room, where he changed into a pair of cotton trousers, a thin cotton shirt, a pair of work shoes, and a wide-brimmed straw hat. Pulling the hat down snugly on his head, he glanced despondently into the mirror, then left the room.

He was feeling very sorry for himself. If he were back in New York now, he and his best friends, Rachel and David Cohen, would be strolling in Gramercy Park or perhaps riding their bicycles. Would the rest of his life be like this, living on a plantation, working as a common field hand? He didn't even have a girl he could talk to, and as isolated as he was, the chances of meeting someone were slim.

But that was the way things were, and there was nothing he could do to change them. Dolefully, he let himself out the back door, wincing at the sudden contrast between the pleasantly cool house and the fiery blast of air that greeted him as he stepped outdoors. He walked to the fields.

Life was fine for his sisters, Celestine and Clarissa. After all, girls just dawdled around, got married, and then had their husbands do everything for them. But his life was a misery, and all Mother could suggest was that Burt and Ben give him more responsibility. But what could they give him besides hoeing, seeding, spading, and binding bales of cotton and hay? No matter how well you did those things, you couldn't keep improving on them; there just wasn't anything to learn after you reached efficiency.

He uttered a soft groan as he saw Burt and Ben about two hundred yards away to his left, talking with one of the tenant-owners, Elmer Gregory. Was that how he would look in twenty-five years, his skin leathery and hair like straw? He would if his days continued like this, he thought. His future seemed like a yawning chasm, ready to swallow him up. He kicked a large rock, planted his hands in his pockets, and walked toward the men.

As he approached, Burt Coleman genially called out to him, "Morning, sprout!"

The nickname aggravated Paul's troubled mood, for it was just another indication of his own lack of importance. Grudgingly, he murmured, "Good morning, Burt." Then, with a swell of bitter resentment, he burst out, "My mother said I should ask you and Ben to give me more to do so I can be more useful around here, Burt."

"Well, now, Paul, that's a reasonable suggestion." Burt drawled, surprised at Paul's vehemence. "Wanting to get ahead is a very good thing for a young fellow. Ben, what can we give Paul so he's pulling more weight?"

"I tell you what," Benjamin Franklin Brown said, and grinned affably as he approached Paul and patted him on the shoulder—a gesture the boy found irritatingly patronizing—"we could use some help in the barn this morning. Louis and Davey Mendicott are stacking bales of hay. You might give them a hand."

"I suppose," Paul grumbled. The Mendicott brothers had been at the plantation most of their lives, both marrying girls from the area. "I won't learn much by stacking hay, though, will I?"

Burt caught Ben's eye and, without Paul's seeing him, shook his head, then spoke up. "There's an old saying, Paul, that whatever is worth doing is worth doing well. A fellow gets a sense of pride from doing a good job at what he knows he has to do. It prepares him for more important things."

"I know that!" Paul looked angrily at Burt. "But everybody's treating me like a child. All I do is field-hand work, and there's never any end to it!"

"Look, Paul," Burt said in a kindly tone, "nobody is having an easy time of it. The whole country's suffering from a shortage of money. So the best all of us can do is work on from day to day and try to keep things going until the country straightens out. If you do what you have to do right now, Paul, you'll enjoy the better times when they come, because you'll have earned them, you see?"

Paul hung his head and shifted on his feet, self-consciously aware that he was being lectured like a child. By God, he'd show them all one of these days. He didn't know just how, but he would! But for the moment, he'd just have to do what he was told. "Oh, all right. I'll go help Davey and Louis." He trudged away, his shoulders slumped, his head bowed.

Burt and Ben watched him go. "That there's a mighty

unhappy youngster, Burt,'' the affable black foreman pronounced. ''Maybe I'd feel the same way myself if I were in his shoes. Sure a pity about his poor daddy.''

''Of course it is. But he's just starting his life, Ben, and it's not a healthy thing for a boy that age to start feeling too sorry for himself. He hasn't had any real hard knocks yet. That's the test of character.'' The two men stood in silence for a few moments and watched Paul dejectedly enter the barn.

Paul went toward the barn, his face set in an obstinate frown. *Help Louis and Davey with the bales of hay*—as if that were something more responsible than the chores he'd been given to do every day since the family had come back from New York.

The barn door was open, and as he entered, he saw the two Mendicott brothers busy with the bales of hay, lifting them up to a rear platform against whose edge a ladder had been placed. Louis, who was stockier than his brother, was on the ladder, taking a bale from Davey and throwing it so expertly that it sailed neatly into the left-hand corner. ''Let's see how fast we can get these things stored away, Davey, and then we'll check the horses and see if they've got oats enough. Hey, now, here's Paul!'' From the vantage point halfway up the ladder, Louis turned to gesture at the tawny-haired youth who slowly came into the barn.

Davey, seeing him also, called out, ''Hiya, Paul! What can we do for you?''

''Burt and Ben told me to help you,'' Paul said in a surly tone.

The two men looked at each other, momentarily at a loss, then Louis said, ''Well, we sure could use some help. We'd like to get this chore finished before noon.''

"What do you want me to do?" Paul asked disinterestedly.

"Well, see those sheaves of hay lyin' loose there off to your right?" Louis asked. "Shape them and pile them together until they're about the size of the tied bales Davey 'n' me are liftin' up here. Then take that heavy cord, put it under the bottom of the bale, then pull it up on the other side and start tyin', you know, like the others. Make it two thicknesses; that'll hold it. Think you can do it?"

This question irritated Lucien's younger brother even more. He snapped, "Of course I can! Anybody can. It doesn't take any brains to tie a bale of hay."

Davey eyed his brother, and simultaneously they shook their heads as Paul, his back turned to them, knelt down and began to unwind the heavy ball of sturdy cord until he estimated he had enough to tie a bale.

Paul was nettled by Louis's remarks on his not knowing how to tie a bale. It seemed yet another link in the chain that was being forged to shackle him to an inconsequential, menial post at Windhaven Plantation.

Listlessly, he looped the cord around the sheaves and tied a sturdy knot. Davey, in the act of handing up still another bale to his brother, glanced over and nodded. "That's the way, son! You know, you could sort of make a game of it, and see how fast you could do it, like you was in a race. That'd make the time go faster."

"Yes. All right," Paul retorted glumly. He bent to another pile of loose hay and began to shove it into the form of a bale, then reached for the ball of cord and measured off what would be needed to secure it.

The wooden platform at the back of the barn was about twelve feet high. The Mendicott brothers had already been working two days to pile the hay onto it, and the entire right side of the platform was consequently loaded high with bales. As Louis continued lofting bales into the farthermost left-hand corner, where there was still plenty of room, he failed to notice that the large pile of hay to his right was dangerously close to the edge of the platform. As the bales he threw thudded into place, the vibrations along the wooden projection jarred the irregularly stacked pile until at last some of these bales began to fall.

Paul glanced up and, perceiving the danger, cried out, "Look out, Louis!"

At that moment, the bales fell forward, one of them thudding against Louis's right shoulder and knocking him from the ladder.

Without thinking of the danger to himself, Paul raced forward and broke Louis's fall as he toppled from the ladder. The momentum flattened them both, with Louis atop the boy, but fortunately Paul had fallen onto a thick pile of loose hay. All the same, the wind was knocked out of him, and as Louis scrambled to his feet, Davey bent down over the recumbent youth, exclaiming as he shook Paul's shoulders, "You all right, son? You all right?"

Paul's eyes fluttered open, and he began to raise his head. "Take it easy now, Paul. Nice and slow." Davey helped Paul to sit up, aware that the boy was dazed and unsteady.

"That was a mighty brave thing you done," Louis said. "I could have been hurt real bad."

Paul looked at Louis with bewilderment. "What? I . . ."

"Don't you try to talk. Just sit and get your bearin's," Davey counseled, shaking his head in awed admiration. "You took on a mite more 'n you could handle, I daresay, tryin' to catch hold of a big bruiser like my brother here."

"I—I'm all right now. You are heavy, though," Paul admitted to Louis in a faint voice.

This remark broke the tension, and both brothers laughed uproariously as Louis helped Paul to his feet, then grasped him by the shoulders and avowed, "Man, I'm mighty grateful! You sure kept your eyes open. Lucky for me you did. Guess that'll teach me to be more careful when I'm throwin' those bales around. See, young'un, even a man can make a fool mistake and learn somethin'!"

A warm glow of pride surged through Paul Bouchard at this extravagant praise, but the feeling was short-lived. All at once he felt overwhelmed by the insignificance of the manual labor he had been performing before the accident.

Louis and Davey saw the smile leave Paul's face, and they exchanged a meaningful glance. Davey spoke up. "Paul, you've had a shock. Maybe you'd best rest a spell. I know if my brother had fallen on top of me, I'd sure feel it for a time."

"I'll be all right. Might as well get the job done since I'm here," Paul declared curtly.

"Well, if you're sure. You're man enough to make your own decisions," Louis said with a grin.

Dimly, Paul appreciated that the brothers were trying their best to make him feel good. They obviously appreciated his courageous act, and they had even praised him for doing a man's job. None of that made him feel better, however. He had, through no fault of his own, been ripped from his happy life in New York and doomed to boundless misery in Alabama. He could not accept the injustice of it all without a fight. He knew that somehow he would soon do something about it.

Chapter 4

The office of Architect Nils Sonderman was located on the second floor of a brick building two blocks east of the capitol.

Climbing the stairs to the outer door, Lucien Bouchard paused to smooth his clothes, then knocked briskly and heard a pleasantly resonant voice call out, "Come in, come in!"

The office was spacious, with a row of windows along one wall bathing with light a drafting table that stood beneath them. To the right of the table was a doorway that appeared to lead to a corridor. To Lucien's right was a door that led to a private washroom; to his left stood a magnificent walnut desk with handworked scrolls and curlicues and particularly ingenious carved drawer knobs. These caught his eye at once, for each knob appeared to be the miniature head of a dwarf, grinning ear to ear. There were two comfortable swivel chairs, behind and in front of this desk.

The man in his late thirties or early forties had risen from behind the desk. He was six feet tall, slender, and as blond as a Viking, with a beautifully groomed beard to heighten that illusion. His eyes were sky blue, his cheekbones high set on either side of a classic Roman nose, and his mouth was firm and incisive, his forehead high arching.

"Mr. Sonderman?"

"Yes. What may I do for you, young man?" His voice was soft and pleasant, with just a trace of a Swedish accent.

"I have come in reply to the ad you had in the *Advertiser*, Mr. Sonderman. My name is Lucien Bouchard."

"I see. Please, have a seat."

Put at ease by the architect's warm smile, Lucien seated himself in the chair, which he found extremely comfortable.

"Now then, tell me something about yourself, Mr. Bouchard," the architect said. "How old are you?"

"I'm going to be eighteen next March—"

"That is younger than what I had in mind," Nils Sonderman intervened, frowning. "But go ahead. I don't mean to discourage you." Again, he favored Lucien with a quick smile, and whatever anxiety Laure's eldest son felt swiftly dissipated.

"My mother and stepfather live on Windhaven Plantation, near Lowndesboro," he resumed.

The architect's eyebrows arched with surprise. "The red-brick chateau with the twin towers?"

"The very same, Mr. Sonderman."

"I noticed it when I first came here, and, indeed, when I had occasion to go to Mobile some weeks ago, I took a long look at it from the riverboat. Your chateau is a remarkable example of architecture, most unusual for Alabama."

"That, sir, is because my great-grandfather was born in Normandy. He left France in 1789 and came to Alabama. My father always said that Great-grandfather fought for justice wherever he went. He built the house in the 1830s. His dream was to build a replica of the house in which he was born," Lucien explained.

"That accounts for it! Whoever designed and built it

knew his business, I might say.'' The bearded man drew a sheet of paper from his desk. "To resume: What is your background?''

"Well, sir, I attended a private academy in Dublin for a liberal education in languages, the arts, and sciences.''

"Interesting. I'm sure in Dublin you saw some wonderful examples of architecture, particularly the churches with their Gothic motifs.''

"I did indeed, Mr. Sonderman.'' Lucien felt encouraged by the architect's positive response.

"Did you finish a complete course there, Mr. Bouchard?''

"I'm afraid not, Mr. Sonderman,'' Lucien replied after a moment's hesitation. "There was a girl I hoped to marry, and she was killed by a stray bullet fired by English troops at Irish rebels while we were walking in the park.''

"How terrible!'' The Swede's face showed compassion, and he leaned forward across the desk to study Lucien more intently. "Please accept my sympathies.''

"Thank you, Mr. Sonderman.'' Lucien breathed deeply and went on. "Another reason for not completing my schooling is that my stepfather is extremely ill. As a result of his illness, I want to earn my own keep—that's why I'm looking for a job.''

"I see. Very admirable.''

The conversation continued in this vein for several minutes, the architect putting to Lucien a number of questions about what he had seen in Dublin, then showing him some pictures of public buildings and eliciting his frank comments. Though painfully aware that his tastes were as yet uninformed, Lucien answered Nils Sonderman's questions as best he could.

At length, the architect leaned back in his chair and

said, "Well, Mr. Bouchard, I like you, and I perceive
from what you've said that you have a feeling for my
profession." The architect cleared his throat, straightened, and declared, "I'll give you a chance. I can't
afford to pay you much—only twelve dollars a week.
But I'll begin your training in the craft of the architect.
There's a lot to learn. I'll teach you everything I know,
and if you grasp it and demonstrate it, there's no limit
to what you can do, once you have passed the apprentice stage. Now then, how soon could you start?"

After the first happy flush of excitement at being
offered a job, Lucien composed his thoughts. To ride to
Montgomery every morning from the plantation and
then return at the end of the day would be taxing and
leave him very little time for himself. Besides, he knew
he would need to spend extra hours in the evening
studying all the architecture texts he could get his hands
on. After a slight pause, he expressed his thoughts.
"Would next Monday be all right, Mr. Sonderman?
You see, it's a long ride from where I live to your
office, and it would be much wiser for me to find a
lodging here in town."

"Good. Then I'll expect to see you Monday morning."

"Sir, I'm sure my mother and stepfather would be
most happy if you would visit us and inspect the interior
of the chateau."

The architect seemed genuinely pleased. "A most
gracious invitation. I will take you up on it. Thank
you." Nils Sonderman came from around the desk and
offered young Lucien his hand, which the new employee shook enthusiastically.

"Thank *you*, sir. I'm very grateful. I'll work hard
and prove myself worthy." Lucien turned and left the
office, bounding down the stairs in his enthusiasm. He
untied his horse's reins from the hitching post and,

stroking the horse's head, murmured, "Thanks for being so patient, boy. Now let's go see if we can't find a boardinghouse, shall we?" The gelding bobbed its head and nickered, and Lucien laughed aloud as he nimbly climbed into the saddle and rode on down the street toward the east, where he knew the residential section lay. There, as he recalled, one could always see signs in windows, offering rooms for rent or boardinghouse facilities.

After riding three blocks, he turned the gelding's head southward down Evandar Street, where many of the houses were older. In the middle of the block to his right he saw a sign in the window, reading, "Room and Board, Vacancy." He halted the gelding, dismounted, and looped the reins around a straggly, stunted little poplar tree near the curb. "I won't be long," he promised, stroking the horse's head again. Then, remembering, he put his left thumb and forefinger into his pocket and drew out a lump of sugar. The gelding whinnied and accepted it, bobbing its head in thanks. Lucien chuckled and strode toward the door.

Almost as soon as he knocked, it was opened by a little white-haired woman who balanced herself on a cane. Her closely set sharp blue eyes swiftly scrutinized him. "Good afternoon to you, sir. I 'spect you saw the sign. I said to myself, 'Sarah Algood, that young man wouldn't have gotten off his horse if it wasn't to come see about the sign you put in the window.' Am I right about that?"

"Yes, you are, Mrs. Algood. My name's Lucien Bouchard. I've just gotten a job in town, and I want a place to stay."

"Of course, Mr. Bouchard." Her peaked face brightened as she hobbled off to one side to let him enter, with a welcoming gesture. "So you're a Bouchard, from that big house downriver? That's recommendation enough for me, young man.''

Lucien found the elderly woman delightful, and after he had inspected the spacious room at the back with access to a yard and lovely little garden, which she proudly declared she had planted all by herself in spite of her arthritis, Lucien said, ''I'll take it, Mrs. Algood.'' He told her that he would probably move in on the following Sunday so he would be close to work on Monday.

''I'll be happy to have you, Mr. Bouchard. It's four dollars a week, including all meals. Why don't you stay and have lunch with me? How do you fancy some macaroni and cheese in a casserole?''

Lucien answered, ''That sounds fine. I'd be very pleased to have lunch with you. Allow me to pay the rent in advance.''

During lunch, Sarah Algood entertained Lucien with anecdotes of her late husband, James, who had once been a roustabout on the East Coast before coming to Alabama to live with a cousin. She had been born right here in Montgomery, and it had been love at first sight. Unhappily, she had never been able to have children, but James had not minded at all, because, as he told her, ''That means I've got you all to myself, Sarah, and that's just the way I like it.''

It amused him to see how spry Mrs. Algood was, and her flow of anecdotes did not stop until he at last bade her good-bye, thanked her, and promised to return Sunday.

Then he hurried to retrieve the gelding, mounted it, and returned in triumph to Windhaven Plantation.

Riding along the winding trail that fronted the Alabama River on his way home, Lucien was pardonably pleased with himself, for he had, on his first effort, found both a job and a most reasonable place to stay. After room and board, he could contribute eight dollars weekly to the revenue of Windhaven Plantation. Best of all, he liked his new employer and knew he would learn a great deal. It would be a challenge to apply his mind to the rudiments of what could possibly become his life's work.

The next months would bring dramatic changes—new situations, new people, and new problems to solve, transforming what would otherwise have been a drearily monotonous autumn in the rustic South into a time of growth and education.

He had crossed the Atlantic twice, received an excellent education, and met Europeans he would never forget. With such advantages, and with hard work and self-discipline, he was sure that he could forge his own path and be his own man—something he very much desired to do as quickly as possible.

When Lucien returned to Windhaven Plantation, he found his mother in the garden, tending her roses. Her back turned to him, she was carefully examining one of the largest yellow roses. She wore gloves and held pruning shears in her right hand as she scrutinized the rose, checking its petals as well as the stem to make sure that no aphids were to be seen.

"I'm back, Mother!" Lucien called as he opened the little gate and went inside.

She turned to him, her face brightening, and then exclaimed, "I suspect you've some happy news for me, dear Lucien, from the expression on your face."

Breathlessly, as Laure listened raptly, Lucien reported the momentous events of his day.

"You really have done a day's work, Lucien," she

exclaimed when he had finished. "I'm very proud of you!"

She neatly clipped off the yellow rose and presented it to him. "You deserve this—it's the largest and most beautiful of my roses, Lucien."

"Thank you, Mother." Lucien blushed.

"It would be very nice if you'd invite Mr. Sonderman to have dinner with us," Laure went on. "After what you've told me, I should certainly like to meet him."

"I've already thought of that, Mother," Lucien enthusiastically agreed. "You know, Mr. Sonderman thinks the chateau a marvelous example of architecture. He said he'd like a chance to see the inside for himself."

Laure considered. "Let's see now. Why don't you invite him for this Thursday? Amelia will surpass herself, as she always does when there's company. And it will be good for you too, dear. When he sees our historic house, he'll know a little more about your background and doubtless be even more appreciative."

"I'll ride in tomorrow and invite him." Lucien kissed her on the cheek. "He did think I was a little young for the job, but when I told him about Dublin and then commented on some pictures he showed me, he offered to give me a chance."

"I know you'll do very well. You've a quick mind, and you can apply yourself. But now, son"—her face was shadowed for a moment—"do go in to your father and tell him the good news." She hesitated a moment, then added, "It might not be a bad idea, when you invite Mr. Sonderman to dinner, to explain that Leland—"

"Well, Mother, the fact is that I did tell him that we've come back because Father was ill."

"I hope Mr. Sonderman doesn't think you were trying to play on his sympathies—"

"Oh, no, Mother!" Lucien quickly interposed. "He

never would have hired me just because he felt sorry for me.''

"No, darling, I'm sure not." She smiled tenderly at him. "Go in and change and maybe take a little nap before supper. That was a lot of traveling today in warm weather, and I certainly don't want you getting sick.''

"Oh, Mother. I've never felt better!" Lucien grinned.

Nils Sonderman drew on the reins of his brown mare to slacken its gait as he saw, just beyond him, the twin towers of the red-brick chateau. The sun was nearly setting, and the cloudless sky with its tints of red and orange made the river landscape stand out even more brilliantly. He halted the mare and leaned back in the seat of his new buggy, wanting to enjoy the view. Finding such a structure here on the bank of the Alabama River, amid a setting of live-oak, cypress, and poplar trees, and abundant, verdant shrubbery, was both startling and nostalgic for Nils. Startling because it so vastly differed from even the most luxurious mansions built in the South, many of which had imposing white Doric columns and classic portico. Nostalgic because Nils, born in Sweden, had visited great European cities, and this French-style chateau recalled those happy days of his childhood.

After drinking in his fill of the landscape and of the red-brick chateau, he took up the reins, clucked his tongue, and urged the mare on to his appointment.

The Swedish architect left his horse and buggy and walked to the door, put his hand to the ornamental brass knocker, and loudly rapped three times. It was Clarabelle who opened the door and invited him into the little reception salon just inside and to the left of the main stairway. "Dinner will be served in a half hour, Mr.

Sonderman. Mrs. Kenniston and Lucien will be here to greet you in just a moment."

"Thank you. I'm eager to meet Mrs. Kenniston. What a magnificent building this is. You must excuse me," Nils said as he took a seat and looked around him, "but since my profession is architecture, I'm sometimes too blatantly interested in other people's houses."

"I understand, sir. It *is* a very beautiful house, with so many memories to it. So many wonderful people lived here—and still do," Clarabelle loyally declared. Then she excused herself and left the room to inform Laure that the architect had arrived.

When the golden-haired woman entered the little salon a few moments later, Nils Sonderman rose to his feet and smiled in greeting. He admired her mature beauty, set off by a blue silk frock with modestly cut bodice and puffed sleeves. There was a stateliness to her, and his eyes warmed with admiration as he greeted her. "I've awaited this privilege, Mrs. Kenniston, since interviewing Lucien, who had nothing but the highest praise for his mother."

At this remark, Laure could not help blushing self-consciously. She replied, "That's most gracious of you, Mr. Sonderman. Lucien told me how much he's looking forward to beginning his job next week. May I offer you a glass of sherry before we have our dinner?"

"If you'll join me, yes, Mrs. Kenniston." Nils looked directly at Laure, a playful smile making his reply seem more intimate.

Soft-spoken though he was, the presence of this handsome, genteel man flustered Laure more than she cared to admit. For at once, and dramatically, the contrast between her ailing husband and this sophisticated man was obvious. She quickly regained her poise and retorted, "I'd be very happy to join you in a drink, Mr. Sonderman."

53

She went to the sideboard, took the cut-glass decanter, and poured about an inch of the brown liquid into two glasses, then brought one to him.

Raising the glass, he said, "To my hope that the association between your son and me will be beneficial to us all."

"I will drink to that with all my heart." Laure smiled as she raised her glass.

After a few minutes, Clarabelle came in to announce that supper was ready, that the younger children were at the table, and that "Mr. Kenniston is waiting to meet Mr. Sonderman."

"Then let's go in, by all means, Mr. Sonderman," Laure said, turning to him with a smile.

As they walked into the dining room, Laure was pleased to see her husband sitting at the head of the table, looking better than he had in some time. True, his face was somewhat wan, but his eyes were alert, and he had put on a fresh linen suit, which, Laure reflected, was a big improvement over the cotton shirt and trousers she was accustomed to seeing him in.

Leland rose as the two entered, and he offered his hand when Laure made the introductions. The Swedish architect shook hands and was shown to his place beside Lucien, who had just come back from the stables, while Laure took her place at the other end of the table. To Leland's left sat Paul, Clarissa, Celestine, and little John. The seating had been purposely arranged this way so that Laure might be closest to John. There was no doubt that the proximity of his mother eminently influenced his behavior, for he made Laure smile with pride when, acknowledging the introduction she made, he responded, "I'm glad to meet you, Mr. Sonderman," and then, even to Leland's amusement, unpredictably added, " 'Melie is the best cook anywhere in the whole wide world—you'll see!"

"I look forward to it, John." Nils gave the boy a smiling nod.

John turned to his mother and declared, "He's nice. I like him, Mama!"

"That's fine. And now that we have your approval, let us all say grace," Laure averred.

A moment of silence fell over the table, and Leland bowed his head and closed his eyes, his hands tightly clasped in prayer. Laure stole a quick glance at him and frowned, for the tension in his fingers betrayed his nervousness. *Oh, dear,* she thought to herself, *I do hope everything goes well with my poor darling tonight.*

Amelia and Clarabelle served the dinner so that everything would go smoothly on so important an occasion. A dish of fresh fruit began the supper. In honor of the guest, Laure had asked that wine be served, a light white Bordeaux.

At the head of the table, Leland was pleasant, but he seemed to lack the ability to concentrate for more than a minute at a time. His gaze would wander, and when he was involved in conversation with their guest, he would sometimes leave a remark unfinished, helplessly shrugging or gesturing with both hands as if to indicate that what had been said was enough. Laure grew increasingly distressed but tried not to show it. As for Nils Sonderman, he was extremely considerate and covered these embarrassing moments by saying gently, "Of course, Mr. Kenniston, I understand perfectly what you are saying." For his thoughtfulness, Laure was intensely grateful.

Lucien also observed his stepfather's distracted manner and the exquisite tact of his employer. He was certain that his having seen by chance the architect's advertisement for an apprentice had been a stroke of great good luck. Here was a man he could respect and who would doubtless teach him a good deal.

Nils saw to it that the children were not neglected, another indication of his praiseworthy manners as a guest. Both Clarissa and Celestine were enchanted with him, for he asked them about the books they read, praising their taste by remarking, "You are both to be congratulated on reading such mature selections, and so is your mother."

His only failure was perhaps with Paul. The boy seemed withdrawn, brooding about something, and a couple of his remarks alerted the perceptive architect to the possibility that Paul might be jealous of his older brother's newfound independence—with a new job and a place of his own in the city. Nils's attempts to draw Paul into the conversation, by careful inquiry as to his own interests, failed to bring more than a token polite response from the boy.

But with little John, Nils made an immediate friend. When served a chicken leg by his mother, John indignantly shook his head, saying that he liked white meat. At that, Nils said, "Do you know, John, you're quite right about Amelia and how well she cooks. But you see, she has given me too much chicken here, and it happens to be white meat! Let me give you a little of it."

"Oh, please, Mr. Sonderman, you really shouldn't indulge him," Laure halfheartedly protested. "It's high time John learned to be content with what's offered him." All the same, she could not help but laugh when Nils, carefully carving a section of the chicken breast that Amelia had served him, carried his plate around the table and transferred the meat to John's plate. Then, bending to the boy, he said sternly, "But now then, Master John, you must eat every bit of it! Food is never to be wasted, for there are too many people in this world who go hungry. Remember that always." With big eyes John watched the guest as Nils went back to his seat.

As dessert was served, Laure induced the architect to tell them something about his experience and travels, but the blond Swede glossed over his background, briefly describing his own education and mentioning that he was a widower, then adding only those anecdotes that would hold the children's interest.

While Nils spoke, Laure glanced at her husband and bit her lip as she saw his attention wander. He stared down at his plate, folded his napkin, and put it to one side. Then he leaned back with an air of utter weariness. Finally, in a wavering voice, he said, "I wonder if you would excuse me, Mr. Sonderman. I am recuperating from surgery and tire easily."

"But of course, sir." Nils turned to him with a sympathetic look. "I'm very grateful for the opportunity to meet you. You've a very fine son here in Lucien. I look forward to his association with me."

"Yes, he—he's a good boy. Well, then, if you'd excuse me. . . . Laure, I can find my way to my room by myself."

"As you like, darling." She watched him rise and leave the dining room. He walked slowly, his head bowed, and it seemed as if he had suddenly withdrawn into himself, as if he were oblivious to his surroundings. The way he had let his voice trail off into silence several times when Mr. Sonderman had been listening to him concerned her. Perhaps the excitement was too much so soon after the operation—that must surely be it!

After he had left, she turned to the architect. "Would you like more coffee and a cordial? There's brandy and port and some Madeira. . . ."

"More coffee, by all means. Swedes are notorious

coffee drinkers. This coffee is delicious—strong, just the way I like it. I'll also have a sip of brandy."

When Amelia brought a fresh pot of coffee from the kitchen, Laure complimented her on the wonderful meal.

"Let me add my own humble thanks, Amelia." Nils spoke up. "It was delectable. I hadn't eaten catfish before, but you prepared it so well that I must have it again. Perhaps you'd give me your recipe?"

Amelia blushed with pleasure. "I'll be happy to write it out for you, Mr. Sonderman. Here, let me fill your cup." Laure had gone to the sideboard, where she poured brandy into a snifter for the architect. Impulsively, she decided to pour one for herself, as well; her nerves were jangled during this supper. In addition to her apprehension about Leland, she had observed that Paul was still uncommunicative and glum. *Oh, dear, why must all this happen when all my attention must be devoted to poor Leland?*

Clarabelle collected John and marched him off to his room, despite his indignant protests. Clarissa and Celestine excused themselves, both blushing as Nils said a cordial good night to them. Paul mumbled, "I'm glad to have met you, Mr. Sonderman. Good night, Mother," and then stalked off.

Nils soon rose to leave, and Amelia had one of the staff bring the architect's horse and buggy to the carriage drive.

Laure and Lucien escorted their guest to the front door, where Nils turned to Lucien and said, "I'm looking forward to your joining my firm Monday. And I'm very glad to have met your family."

"I'm looking forward to Monday, too, Mr. Sonderman," Lucien said, rising and shaking the Swede's hand.

"You've been most kind, Mr. Sonderman. Thank you again for coming," Laure said.

"He's really a wonderful man, Lucien," Laure told her oldest son as they watched Nils's buggy leave. "You're very lucky."

"I know, Mother, and I'm going to make him glad that he hired me. I want to do well, earn plenty of money, and take care of things around here."

Laure smiled up at her son. "You're thoughtful and considerate, my dear, but you mustn't drive yourself too much on that score." Laure put a hand on his shoulder. "We have to be practical. I'm sure he's not paying you too much, since you're an apprentice, and even though you'll have a few dollars left over to contribute here, that alone can't meet all the expenses we have. It's not within your power to wipe away the debts, so you mustn't punish yourself by thinking it is." Laure gave her son a hug. "I love you very much, Lucien."

"I love you too, Mother." He took her in his arms and kissed her on the cheek. Then, bidding her good night, he went to his room.

Alone, Laure uttered a weary sigh. She thought that perhaps she should visit Leland, but then she decided against it. It might only annoy him if she hovered about him all the time. Besides, he must get back his feeling of independence and the ability to do things for himself. That was the only way he would make a complete recovery.

Instead, she would go help Clarabelle and Amelia with the dishes. That would give her something to do and take her mind off the vague presentiments of trouble that had beset her tonight.

Chapter 5

Leland Kenniston slowly closed the door of his room behind him and walked over to the window to look out onto the creek. The rays of a quarter moon faintly tinged the water with shimmering streaks of silver, and the foliage of the two tall live-oak trees on either side of it was similarly dappled. A light wind stirred the leaves and branches, creating the only sound of the night, save for the sudden eager chirping of a night bird seeking its mate.

He rested his palms on the windowsill, slightly stooping, as he stared at the landscape beyond him. The mood that had come over him midway through dinner was as dark now as the night outside. Oh, Lord, he had made so many mistakes, terrible mistakes. Once he himself had been a man of property and wealth and influence, but no longer.

He groaned and groped his way back to the easy chair that Laure had placed near the window. He slumped down into it, leaned back with another groan, his hands clutching the arms of the chair, his fingernails digging into the upholstery as he closed his eyes, summoning back all he could of his memory.

Now it was coming back slowly, piecemeal, and each new fragment fitted into place in his distraught mind with a terrible precision that increased his anguish.

What follies he had committed! Signing promissory notes well beyond his limits of credit, purchasing unsalable items in Europe, gambling away most of his money in a single night, and then, to top things off, going to bed with a prostitute!

He bowed his head and covered his face with his hands as he burst into choking sobs. "Oh, God, forgive me. God forgive me for what I've done to Laure!"

He rose unsteadily from the chair and groped his way to the bed. He flung himself down upon the bed, lay on his back with his arms at his sides, closed his eyes, and prayed for sleep. If he rested, perhaps sleep would drive away the specters that jeered and mocked him, pointing their bony fingers at him and accusing him of vanity and folly and stupidity. Yes, he had been guilty of those sins, and God alone knew how many more.

At the very moment Leland wrestled with his demons, Laure was in her room at her desk, writing a letter to Andy Haskins, director of the sanatorium at Tuscaloosa, where Leland's brain tumor had first been treated, telling Andy of her great concern over Leland's present behavior. To give an accurate picture of her husband's condition, she also pointed out some of the encouraging signs she had observed since Leland had come home from Atlanta:

> I really have a good feeling about what you and Dr. Townsend have done for Leland. In many ways, he seems to be improving. He takes his meals with us, for the most part, and is able to converse with the children. Just the other day he asked me for some of his papers to see if something can't be salvaged from that unfortunate buying trip to Europe. The only pressing problem, apart from my anxiety about his health and complete

recovery, is the state of our finances. The economy in the area, as you know, makes raising cotton for profit right now almost impossible.

But Lucien has found an excellent job with an architect in Montgomery, and he will start next Monday. This evening we had supper with Lucien's new employer—his name is Nils Sonderman—and I found him to be a most charming, prepossessing, and cultured man. I'm certain he can channel Lucien's talents at this important stage in his life.

And now, it's getting late. My very best wishes to you both, and may God keep you and Jessica and your children for many long and happy years. I should really welcome a visit from all of you; perhaps in the fall, if your duties permit, you might think of spending a week or two with us.

Yours affectionately,
Laure Kenniston

She laid down her pen, folded the sheets, put them into an envelope, and left them on her writing desk. Then she rose and changed into her thinnest night shift, for outside the air was sultry and humid. Disturbed by a nagging presentiment of misfortune, she knelt down by her bed and prayed. "Dear God, watch over all of us, especially my beloved Leland. Give him the will and the strength to recover. Give my son Paul peace of mind. If I have neglected him, Lord, I am truly sorry, for I did not mean it. I have the utmost faith in Thee, dear Lord, and I know that our good fortune has come about through Your blessings."

She crossed herself, blew out the lamp, and sank into bed. Outside, there was the soft cry of a screech owl in the distance, from the towering bluff. Sleep came upon her even as it sounded.

*   *   *

Lucien Bouchard was in his room, also about to write a letter. It would be addressed to Eleanor Martinson, the beautiful dancer with whom he had had a transitory affair aboard the ship that had returned him from Ireland. He had read in the *Advertiser*, in the very same issue that had contained Nils Sonderman's ad, that Eleanor's dance troupe was to begin an engagement in eight days at the Colonial Theater near the main street of Montgomery.

There was a smile on his handsome young face as he wrote, and from time to time he lay down his pen and stared out the window as if he could envision Eleanor, summon her back from memory from that exquisite night when she had initiated him into the ecstasies of love. He took up his pen and, thoughtfully choosing his words, began to write.

Dearest Eleanor:

I have just learned that next week you are coming to Montgomery, and you may be sure that I shall see you backstage. I've thought of you ever since I left Atlanta. Life on Windhaven Plantation, compared with meeting you, has been boring in the extreme. But I found a job with an architect seeking an apprentice. I start next Monday.

Now that I have a chance to learn a profession that is both honorable and profitable, my dream is that one day we can be married. I love you very dearly.

I'm looking forward to seeing you after the first performance and will dream of you until then. Your kindness and your sweetness have given me strength through the adjustments I've had to make after leaving New York.

Be assured of my sincere love—and until Tuesday, I remain,

Lucien

He addressed the envelope in care of the Colonial Theater, sealed it, then went to bed. He fell asleep with a smile on his face, for he felt that now stars had come into the heavens, and that all would be right with his world at last.

Leland awakened with a start, his heart pounding. He sat up and groped for the box of matches, found them, unsteadily struck one, and lit the oil lamp on the table beside his bed. He was still fully dressed. He walked again to the window and stared out into the darkness. The faint light of the paltry moon made the creek and the two tall live-oak trees seem like sentinel ghosts, and he turned away. His gaze fell on the trunk with rope handles, and slowly he walked toward it, opened it, and took out the book he had bought in London when he was a young man.

He sat on the edge of his bed and turned the pages. There was something, he couldn't quite put his finger on what, in this book of Tennyson's that had been sticking in his mind for the past week or two. He didn't know why, but he had to read it now. Perhaps it would explain everything. He felt that he had wakened just to read it and that he could not sleep again until he had done so.

Almost impatiently, he turned the pages, from "The Coming of Arthur" to "Gareth and Lynette," then "The Marriage of Geraint" and beyond. Vexed, he frowned and turned the pages again. Then he came upon the section "Lancelot and Elaine." And he read aloud to himself until he had reached the lines he had been trying so desperately to recall.

Abruptly he uttered a cry, his eyes fixed on the page, and he read aloud, "His honour rooted in dishonour stood/And faith unfaithful kept him falsely true."

The book dropped from his nerveless hands onto the floor. He lifted his head.

"Now I understand! Oh, dear God," he said aloud to himself. "I, who live for honor, have dishonored everything by what I've done. I believed in myself and in all I had done to bring about a happy life with Laure, but it truly has played me false. Oh, sweet God, what am I to do?"

His face was streaked with tears, and almost blindly he rose and turned to the door, then closed it behind him noiselessly so as not to waken anyone. Then he directed his footsteps toward the southern side of the chateau and onto the stairway that led to the tower overlooking the family burial ground—the bluff where old Lucien and his beloved Indian bride, Dimarte, and also Luke lay in their eternal rest.

His breath coming in painful, labored gasps, he held on to the rail and managed to climb to the top of the tower and walk unsteadily to the great window. He stood, his hands grasping the sill for support, staring into the darkness with eyes that willed a sight to be seen, a sign to be given, a message to be understood. . . .

But he saw nothing. And as he waited in that darkness, there suddenly came the mystical sound of a screech owl. For Leland, it had the eerie effect of a death knell. The tears flowed down his cheeks again as he turned away from the window.

Slowly and with difficulty, he retraced his way down the stairs and out of the chateau, and trudged to the bank of the Alabama River. He stood there a long moment, but he already knew from the screech owl's cry what he must do.

With a sob, he recalled how he had courted and won Laure. He thought of the glowing future he had believed lay in store for them and the children when he had established headquarters in New York and moved them all there.

Now there was nothing. For even if this operation of Dr. Townsend's was a complete success, Leland knew he would continue to be a burden because of the debts he had so stupidly incurred. He would never return to business and be the man of the family.

No, it would be far better for Laure and the children to be rid of him and his debts. And then, in a last flash of lucidity, his eyes brightened as he thought to himself, *The life insurance policy! That will save Laure and the children.* But with this came another concern: *It must be done with forethought. If the insurance people were to suspect that I'd taken my own life, they wouldn't pay Laure and the children. No, it must look as if I had gone for a late-night swim. Yes! It is the very best way to make amends.*

He looked a last time at the towering bluff to his left. Then, carefully, he took off his clothes, folded them neatly, and laid them down on the bank as if he were going for a swim. In only his underclothes, he walked to the edge of the bank, tested the water with a bare foot, found it pleasantly cool.

He waded out into the river. The water reached his chest almost at once, after the first foot or two of angling bank. The muscles of his jaw tightened, and then, taking a long, deep breath, he walked toward the middle of the river, his footing at once giving way, and he let the current take him as it would.

*   *   *

Benjamin Franklin Brown had risen at dawn this Friday morning, wanting to decide upon a crop that would show a profit for Windhaven by next year. He hoped that contemplating the problem while his mind was fresh might cause a solution to present itself.

Before heading into the fields, Ben decided to take a stroll by the river and check its level. There had been some reports that a thunderstorm upriver had caused the Alabama to overflow its banks and ruin crops. He did not want that to happen on Windhaven Plantation, not after all Mrs. Kenniston had had to go through already this year. It was high time the Lord smiled down on that woman, Ben thought, though he didn't mean to be passing judgment on the Almighty.

He walked slowly, glancing up at the sky and frowning. It was going to be another scorcher. But that was what you could expect in August in Alabama. He walked nearer to the river and spotted something lying near the bank. Squinting, he moved closer. There was a pile of men's clothes. What were they doing on the bank of the river? Ben kneeled down and at once recognized them as Leland Kenniston's. But what would the clothes be doing here? Had his employer taken it into his head to go swimming at this early hour in the morning? It seemed an unlikely thing for a man in his condition . . . unless, God help him, his confusion of mind after his operation had put the notion into his head. Or could it be . . .

Then his jaw dropped. *Oh, Lord, please don't let what I've been thinking be true, please don't!* Ben swallowed hard and took a deep breath. *Maybe he went for a swim and forgot his clothes—I'd better get to the chateau and ask if he's in his room.*

He hurried to the door of the chateau and then, because of the hour, changed his mind and went around the back to go in through the kitchen. He didn't want to disturb anyone, but he had to find out. Most likely Amelia would be preparing breakfast. The thought of food sickened him.

Sure enough, Amelia was bustling about in the kitchen, and she greeted him with a warm smile. "Mornin', Ben. How are you today?"

"Amelia," he said, ignoring her question, "is Mr. Kenniston up and about?"

"Land sakes, Ben, after what he's been through, don't expect him to be awake this early."

"You're probably right. I thought he might have gone for a swim."

Amelia, in the act of removing from the oven a pan of piping-hot biscuits, turned around and stared uncomprehendingly at him. "You must be joking! Whatever made you think that?"

Ben frowned. "I found his clothes folded as neat as you please on the bank of the river," he said in a low voice.

"My God, oh, no, it couldn't be," Amelia said. "You just wait here a minute. I'll go over to Mr. Kenniston's room and take a look. If he's there, we'll know everything is all right."

Ben nodded, taking a seat at the table.

A few moments later, Amelia hurried back into the kitchen, her features drawn with anxiety. "He's not there, Ben! He's gone!"

Clarabelle Hendry entered the kitchen, wearing a long robe over her nightgown. "Can I help with breakfast—" she began, and then, seeing the concern on Amelia's face and the foreman's anxious look, she exclaimed, "What's wrong?"

"Oh, Clarabelle, we're so worried!" Amelia's voice was choked with tears. "Ben found Mr. Kenniston's clothes on the riverbank. I just went to Mr. Kenniston's bedroom, and he isn't there."

"Oh, dear Lord. I must wake Laure," Clarabelle said in a hushed voice. She left the kitchen and went down the hallway to Laure's temporary downstairs bedroom.

When she tapped gently on the door, then opened it, Laure murmured something inaudible and turned over onto her other side; but then she suddenly came awake, uttered a startled cry, and sat up. "Clarabelle, what's the matter?"

In a trembling voice, Clarabelle told Laure the ominous news, and she saw her friend and employer's face become drawn with concern.

"Oh, my God. I'll put on my robe and go with you. Oh, dear Lord, please don't let anything happen to poor Leland!" Laure began to sob as she slid her long legs out of bed and hurried to the closet to don her robe and slippers.

The two women went across the hall to Leland's room, and Laure opened the door. She clapped her hands to her mouth to stifle a cry of anguish when she saw it was empty. Clarabelle tried her best to quell her friend's growing hysteria, but Laure was shaking, and her muffled sobs could no longer be controlled as she suddenly turned and clung to Clarabelle. "Last night at supper he seemed so weak and listless, and . . . and he tried so hard not to let it show."

"I know, dear. Please, Laure, you mustn't think the worst. We have to find out—"

"I know, I know." Laure wiped her eyes. "We have to find him at once. Let's get Ben and have him get some of the workers to look for Leland. Oh, Clarabelle, please, let's hurry!"

Clarabelle put her arm around Laure's shoulder, and

they went out to the riverbank. Ben was already there. When he saw the two women, he hurried toward them. "Mrs. Kenniston, I'll have two of my boys saddle up and go downriver to look for him. I'll get the Mendicott boys. They'll do a good job of looking, you can be sure of that."

"Thank you, Ben," Laure quietly said, then again buried her face in her hands.

Ben touched his forehead as a sign of respect, then hurried toward the barn. Clarabelle, anxious and silent, kept her arm around Laure's shoulders. But at this moment, Laure, shocked by the news of Leland's disappearance, was unaware of anything around her. One dreadful thought now filled her mind: *He can't be—oh, please, God, don't let it have happened! Please . . . please let him be found alive, I pray You!*

Two and a half hours later, Louis and Davey Mendicott came riding back to Windhaven Plantation, the two brothers mounted on one horse while draped across the back of another was the lifeless body of Leland Kenniston. They had found him washed up into a shallow little cove some three miles downriver, and Louis had been the first to see his body lying almost entirely out of the water on the other side of the river.

Laure meanwhile had kept an agonized and impatient vigil near the spot where Leland's clothing had been found. She was inconsolable; although both Amelia and Clarabelle urged her to return to the house and rest until there was word, she had said resolutely, "I can't—I must know the minute they get back."

And then, shading her eyes from the sun, she saw them in the distance, coming upriver. When the foremost horse drew closer, she saw that both Davey and Louis rode astride it and knew then that the very worst had happened. She uttered a desolate shriek, sank to her knees, and sobbed, "Oh, my God, my God, he's dead. . . ." She moaned softly, and as Clarabelle encircled her with strong arms, Laure whispered, "Oh, Leland . . . Leland . . . if only I had been with you." And when the two horses drew nearer, she ran up to the one carrying her lifeless husband and threw her arms around his shoulders.

Louis, biting his lip, glanced anxiously at his brother as he twisted his straw hat between his strong hands. "I'm awful sorry, Mrs. Kenniston, ma'am," he mumbled.

"Oh, Louis, where did you find him?"

"Well, ma'am, he was . . . that is, I spotted him . . . his body downriver about three miles." Louis hung his head. "I'm so sorry, ma'am."

The two men shuffled in place for a few moments, not knowing what to say, and then Davey said, "We'll help you all we can, ma'am. You want something, you call on us." Then he gently added, "We can start makin' a coffin right now, Mrs. Kenniston."

"Oh, yes . . . yes, please do." Laure found the thought of organizing Leland's burial oddly comforting, as though anything she could do to add order to the chaos of his death would help. "I'd like him to be buried on the bluff late this afternoon, a few hours before the sun goes down. That is, if . . . if it can be—" Her voice was hardly intelligible. Clarabelle held her, stroking the weeping woman's head.

It was Louis who prompted, "It'll be ready in time. That's a promise, Mrs. Kenniston, ma'am. Come on, Davey. And don't you worry, ma'am, we'll tell all the folks."

With eyes drowned by tears, she watched as the two black men mournfully led the horses toward the barn, the body of her husband slung across the first. She clung to Clarabelle as her sobs grew in intensity. "I should have been with him! I should have—"

Clarabelle remonstrated, "You cannot blame yourself for what happened; you mustn't. How could you have known that he would do such a thing—go swimming, I mean."

In spite of her confusion, Laure's mind leaped at Clarabelle's words. *That he would do such a thing? Oh, no, it can't be!* The very thought that Leland would have taken his own life cast her into a chasm of angry despair. How could he be so selfish? Did he not know how much she needed him, how much the children needed him?

Misinterpreting Laure's renewed look of shock, Clarabelle said, "He didn't suffer, Laure. The current was probably too strong."

Laure seized upon this glimmering hope that it had not been suicide. Indeed, he might just have gone for a swim, forgetting in his weakened condition and confused state of mind how fast the current of the Alabama really was. He had mentioned recently that he needed exercise to restore his strength and vigor. Oh, yes, that surely must have been it! The relief from that rationalization caused tears to come to her eyes.

Taking matters in hand, Clarabelle announced, "Come with me, Laure," and firmly guided the distraught woman back to the house with Amelia's assistance.

Laure controlled her sobs and let herself be taken back to her room. "You've been through a terrible shock. Please, Laure dear, rest," Clarabelle urged. "He's at peace now, poor man. He was a fine man, he had a good heart, and he was generous and kind—we'll always remember that."

"Yes, always," Laure echoed faintly, and then lay back, closing her tearful eyes.

Chapter 6

*L*ate afternoon arrived, and the people of Windhaven Plantation gathered to lay Leland Kenniston to rest. Davey and Louis Mendicott had made the pinewood coffin that contained Leland's body, and they carried it up the slope to the summit, to be buried near old Lucien, the first Bouchard who had left his indelible mark and immortal inspiration upon this fertile land.

Laure preceded the coffin, having donned a simple bonnet with black veil to betoken her mourning, and Burt Coleman was beside her at the left, steadying her as she slowly ascended to the top of the bluff. Lucien walked at Laure's right, clasping his mother's hand in both of his. Paul and Clarabelle followed, and behind them came Clarissa and Celestine, with John walking between them, a somber and perplexed expression on his face. Following him were family friends Dalbert and Mitzi Sattersfield, who had been summoned from Lowndesboro soon after Leland's body was found. The tenant-workers, as well as Benjamin Franklin Brown and Amelia Coleman, who carried a bouquet of roses to adorn the grave, completed the funeral procession, walking behind the coffin.

They all came to the summit, and the Mendicott brothers gently set the coffin down upon two boards, which had been laid, with ropes resting atop them, across the open grave dug that afternoon. Laure stared helplessly at the coffin as if unable to believe that this part of her life had come so abruptly and unexpectedly to an end. She looked up as tall blond Lucien stepped forward now, as if to speak. She put her hand on his shoulder, tears slowly running down her face as she stared at him. He glanced at her with a quick, tremulous smile and then began a spontaneous eulogy: "All of us who knew Leland Kenniston loved him. He was generous and thoughtful, even to the least of us, and we shall remember all these things about him that made it so easy to accept him as the head of our family. All of us prayed that after the operation he would regain his strength here and be restored to the person we so much respected and enjoyed. But it was not God's will. We shall not forget the love he had for us, and I myself, here before his grave, humbly acknowledge that I was touched by the way he showed how much he loved my own dear mother."

Laure began to sob aloud, for she had not dreamed that Lucien would assume the responsibility for speaking to the assembled friends. And yet, it seemed fitting, for it was Lucien whom Leland had sent across the seas to get an advanced education, the effects of which were only now beginning to mark his life for the future destined him.

"Let us all remember him as he was," Lucien continued, "full of ideas to surprise and delight us, a man who loved life and thereby made us love him. He is not dead truly, for he is with God, and he is in our hearts and will be always."

Laure turned to her blond son, and he took her into his arms, his own eyes wet with tears as she bowed her head upon his shoulder and gave vent to choking sobs, touched as she was by this profoundly moving tribute.

Clarabelle came forward and expressed her own feelings for Leland, who had been infallibly generous and kind to her. And then, with a whispered word to Laure, she moved to where the children were standing and took hold of young John's shoulders, for he had begun to cry and needed her comfort.

Burt Coleman and the Mendicott brothers stepped forward and grasped the two long ropes beneath the coffin. Ben Brown joined them, taking one end of a rope firmly in his hands, as did the others. Dalbert Sattersfield stepped forward to remove the two boards from under the now suspended coffin, and then, steadily and slowly, the four men eased the pine coffin into the grave. They tossed the ends of the ropes in after it, and stepped away, solemnly downcast.

Lucien stepped forward again, clasped his hands in a prayerful attitude, and lowered his head. "Oh, Lord, grant the soul of Leland Kenniston, my mother's husband, stepfather to her children, Your eternal life and redemption." Here he paused, and quiet sobs could be heard above the soothing yet disturbing noises of the river below. Then Lucien began to recite the words of the Lord's Prayer, and the assemblage joined in.

When the final amens were spoken, Laure stepped up to the grave and stood quietly for a moment. The silence that ensued was nearly total, as if nature herself had ceased her breathing in deference to the final parting of two such closely entwined souls. Her green eyes tearfully reflecting the rays of the afternoon sun, Laure looked at the bouquet of roses at the head of the grave. With what was almost a smile playing at the corners of her mouth, she reached for the roses, plucked two from the vase—one red, one yellow—and clutched them to her bosom, her eyes closed. The memories of Leland gallantly presenting her with yellow and red roses, representing passion and fidelity, warmed her heart. Then, tears coursing down her cheeks, she opened her eyes and tossed the two roses into the grave atop the pine coffin.

A sob escaped from her, and she felt two strong hands on her shoulders, turning her away from the grave. It was her eldest son, and she let him guide her toward the chateau, but not without one glance back to the final resting place of the man she had loved so completely.

Clarabelle then took John by the hand, walked slowly past the lowered coffin with him, and followed Laure and her son. Soon the entire procession had filed by the coffin and was making its way back to the house with the exception of Burt, Ben, and the Mendicotts, who stayed behind to fill the grave with the earth piled beside it.

The red ball of the August sun touched the gentle slope to the high bluff, covering it with autumnal colors, as if its hues mourned this day's end and, with it, the last moments of a life that had achieved such brilliance at its zenith, only to fall like a burned-out meteor.

Alone, Laure climbed the hill to the burial place. She stared at the well-tended graves of the first Bouchards to die here, and then she looked at the grave of her former husband, Luke. Next her eyes fixed on the newly mounded earth of Leland's grave. She fell to her knees, and clasping her hands, bowing her head, she spoke aloud. "My dearest Leland, from that first day I met you, I was enchanted by your love of life. You gave me so important a part in your life, and in many ways our union was far more than a marriage, a kind of lifetime rather, and I shall cherish it until I join you here. I only regret that I could not give you a child of your own—it would have cemented our perfect happiness beyond measure.''

She looked up at the dark sky and saw clouds drifting slowly and the edge of the moon peeping out from behind one of them. Then she turned back to Leland's grave, tears again streaking her cheeks. ''I am alone now, Leland, and I reproach myself for anything I might possibly have done to offend you. I remember how you said you needed exercise, and I pray that was why you went for a swim. If only you'd told me, I could have been out there watching you, helping. Why wasn't I there to be with you, Leland, to save you?''

She could speak no more. Her head bowed, her body shaking with sobs, she let herself dissolve into the dark night until at last the faint cry of a night bird came to her, dimly making her realize where she was and why. Slowly, she rose, crossed herself, and then turned back down the slope.

Alone in his room, Paul glumly kicked the leg of the dresser and shook his head. He moved listlessly toward the window, drew open the shutter, stared out upon the bluff, and then let the shutter fall back into place to hide the landscape. He walked slowly back to his bed, seated himself on the edge of it, then pressed his palms against his cheeks, his face morose and drawn.

He began to think of the impact of his stepfather's death. His poor mother was once again alone, alone to face the responsibilities of a dying plantation, alone to raise her children. How horrible it must be for her to lose yet another husband. And what would Leland Kenniston's death mean to him?

He sighed. Life wasn't fair. His older brother at least had a new job to look forward to, new surroundings, most likely new friends. Maybe even a new girl. He'd be in Montgomery, where there were plenty of pretty girls.

But for himself, there was nothing except the drudgery of field work. He was just another mouth to feed when the revenue of the plantation had dwindled so alarmingly.

He sprang to his feet, scowling angrily, went back again to the window, and drew open the shutter. Then he shook his head. "I've got to do something. I can't go on like this any longer—I can't! I've got to prove I can go out on my own, so I won't be a burden to Mother. I can't stay here, knowing that Lucien is doing something useful to help and that I'm not. I've *got* to make a break from this. I don't know how, but I'll find a way!"

Now he flung himself facedown on the bed and, belying his wish for instant manhood, began softly to cry, feeling frustrated, hurt, and useless.

"Mother, please try to rest. Would you like a snack?"

Laure, her eyes swollen and red from weeping, stared dully at Lucien, then shook her head. "It's very kind of you, dearest, but I don't want anything now." She tried to force a smile to her trembling lips. "I'll never forget the words that you said at Leland's burial, Lucien. You expressed everything in my heart, and not only for me, but for all of us who were there. God bless you, my dear son."

"I miss him, too, Mother. You know, I was perhaps closer to him than any of the other children, because he took me to Dublin. I won't ever forget the help he tried to give me."

"I know you cared for him, Lucien. You're a comfort to me, my darling. And it's comforting that all of us are together. With God's help we'll come out of our troubles." She squeezed his hand, then sighed. "I—I think I'll go to my room."

"I won't start my new job Monday, Mother. I want to be on hand for the next week to help out with anything you need done," Lucien offered.

"How very thoughtful, dear. But I don't want you to endanger your job."

"It'll be all right. Mr. Sonderman's a kind, sympathetic man—that's why I like him so much. He'll understand. I'll talk to him tomorrow." She wanly smiled again, then turned and went into her room.

Lucien walked slowly back upstairs to his own room, his face grave and thoughtful. He had admired his stepfather's humor and vitality. Indeed, he hoped that one day he might have as much determination and purpose in channeling his own future. *And I'm going to do it,* he thought. *I'll make you proud of me, Father.*

The following Sunday morning, a courier rode in from Montgomery, bringing for Laure an exquisite potted plant and a note of condolence from Nils Sonderman. The Swedish architect had learned of Leland Kenniston's death when Lucien came to request a postponement of his starting day. The genial man consented at once. Lucien thanked his future employer, then rode over to Sarah Algood's boardinghouse. The spry old woman was extremely sympathetic and told Lucien that his room would be waiting, no matter when he came. Before returning home, Lucien sent the telegram his mother had written to the Cohens in New York, informing them of Leland's death. He felt certain that the news would come as a terrible shock to the family who had been so involved with his family while they lived in that fascinating city.

When Laure received the plant and the note from Nils

Sonderman, she was touched by the man's thoughtfulness and concern.

At supper that evening, Laure said, "I'm going to write a thank-you note to Mr. Sonderman, and when Ben or Burt goes into Montgomery for supplies, it can be delivered to him personally. I won't forget his thoughtfulness."

It was sweltering in New Orleans this second Sunday in August, and Lopasuta Bouchard—the Comanche whom Luke Bouchard had adopted and supported while he studied the law—and his lovely wife, Geraldine, were enjoying a late and leisurely breakfast. Sharing it with them were their three children: Dennis, now six; Luke, a year younger; and Marta, who had been born in December 1879.

As Lopasuta and Geraldine were enjoying a second cup of the strong chicory-laced coffee so popular in New Orleans, there was a persistent knocking at the door, and Lopasuta excused himself, hurrying to open it. He came back holding a telegram, which he opened quickly and then uttered, "How terrible . . . poor Laure!"

"What is it, darling?" Geraldine asked, alarmed at the anguished look on her husband's face.

"There's been an accident—Leland Kenniston has died. Evidently, he drowned." Lopasuta looked again at the paper before him.

"How horrible! Oh, I feel so sorry for poor Laure," Geraldine said. "To lose another husband . . ."

"That is the way of God, my Geraldine," Lopasuta solemnly pronounced. "One day we shall learn the reason for all that has happened to us. But for now, all we can do is our best and pray for His guidance." He resumed his seat at the table. "I'd like to help her, but the best I can do is to send her a telegram of condolence and offer her financial assistance. If the Valdez trial doesn't take too long, I'll pay her a visit."

"I know how much you want to help," Geraldine murmured. "You do what you think best. Now then, Marta," she said, turning to the little girl making a wry face at her dish of hominy, "eat a little more so you'll grow big and strong and beautiful."

"Like you, Mama," Dennis piped up.

Lopasuta chuckled and nodded. "Our firstborn has a perceptive eye."

Geraldine blushed and sent him a long, loving look. Yet she too was concerned over the events that had stricken Windhaven Plantation. There had been the damaging raids, then the flooding and the typhoid epidemic, resulting in the loss of human life, crops, and livestock. Now Laure had to endure the void that her husband's death had created. It was as if a cycle of evil had been visited upon the Bouchards.

Chapter 7

*L*ucien left for Montgomery on Tuesday afternoon, the day that Eleanor Martinson and her dance troupe were scheduled to open a week-long engagement at the Colonial Theater.

Until his departure, Lucien had been at his mother's beck and call, wanting to reassure her that he would stand by in her time of greatest need. But he could not forgo his visit with Eleanor for the sake of his mother. Indeed, he had told his mother about Eleanor, told her, too, that he had proposed marriage and would be spending this evening at the theater to learn of her answer. He would never have abandoned his mother so soon after his stepfather's death for a less important event, he explained. Laure had smiled and said she understood.

He sat in the rear of the crowded theater so Eleanor would not see him. At the front, eight musicians, two with woodwinds and the rest with various stringed instruments, were assembled, drawn from the many excellent amateur players in the city.

When the lights lowered and the curtains parted, the troupe appeared, each member standing unmoving in a tableau, waiting for the orchestra's first notes. There were sixteen dancers, but Lucien's eyes singled out the tall, slim, raven-haired Eleanor. His heart quickened as he watched her beautiful heart-shaped face, the deep, dark blue eyes, dainty Grecian nose, and sensuous mouth, which he had kissed so passionately aboard the *Servia* as it had brought him back to New York from Dublin. Her classic tutu and ballet slippers emphasized the graceful fluidity and contouring of her shapely body. He trembled, remembering how she had so generously and delightfully initiated him into the ecstasies of carnal love.

As she danced, the poise, elegance, and suppleness of her movements intensified his determination to make her his wife. He hoped she would accept his proposal when he visited her backstage tonight. He could hardly wait until the program was over so that he could go backstage.

He watched, love-struck, while Eleanor danced with three other young ladies. Then the music quickened, and Eleanor, in the foreground, twirled, hands above her head, arms lifted high, the tips of her forefingers pressing together. In that swift motion, the tutu skirt lifted above her knees, and Lucien experienced conflicting emotions. On the one hand, her intoxicating beauty revived all the shipboard memories and strengthened his erotic fervor to win her; on the other, the shadow of jealousy darkened his mood. The puritanical side of his character made him momentarily wonder if, assuming she would accept him as her husband, he would permit her to display herself on the stage throughout the country before an audience of men who would, just as he did now, envision her in lascivious acquiescence to them, even though they might never meet her or see her again.

All the same, when the ballet ended, he was one of the first to applaud, clapping his palms together until they stung, his eyes glowing and shining. And as Eleanor came forward to bow with the other members of the troupe, he reaffirmed that he wanted to marry her as he had never wanted anything in his life.

After a short pause, the troupe came out again to offer an Indian wedding dance, which had no authenticity whatsoever, contrived simply to gain attention and win applause. At the end of the performance, Lucien forced himself to wait, sensing that if he were the first backstage, he might be pushed aside by other admirers.

He stood in a narrow corridor, watching over the last straggler to leave her dressing room. Then he sidled toward the still-open door, knocked timidly, and crossed the threshold.

Eleanor had gone to her dressing table and mirror, where she now sat removing the stage makeup from the delicate pale skin of her face. As she lifted her eyes, she caught sight of Lucien, whirled, and with a glad cry said, "Lucien, you really are here!"

She reached out both hands to him, and he took them in his.

Kissing her quickly, Lucien said, "You look beautiful. I've missed you so much."

"What a nice thing to say! Did you see the performance, Lucien? There were so many people out there!"

"Yes, I saw it. You were wonderful—by far the most beautiful dancer." Lucien, breathless because of his love's proximity, could wait no longer. Blushing violently, he stammered, "Eleanor, I—I meant what I said in my letter. You did get it. . . ."

"Of course I did, you silly! Oh, Lucien, isn't this all too exciting? The tour is going remarkably well. We've been written up in newspapers in every place we've performed, and—" She was stopped by the ashen color of Lucien's face. "Are you all right?"

He interpreted the fact that she had not drawn her hands away as a favorable sign. Retaining them in his, he said in an unsteady voice, "I—I want to marry you, Eleanor—and very soon!"

"Do close the door, dear," she interrupted.

"Of course." He swiftly closed the door, then went back to her.

She smiled at him and reached back with her palm to support herself on the edge of the dressing table. "Dear Lucien, I understand why you feel the way you do. But I think it's best for us to be close friends, and to see each other whenever our careers will allow. Time will tell if we're destined to be more than that."

"But you—" he began.

Swiftly, in one of those lovely fluid movements that had so captivated him during the performance, she straightened and came to him, put her soft fingertips over his mouth, and shook her head. "You really mustn't hold me to what was a beautiful episode, Lucien. It was spontaneous, and we were in need of sharing tenderness. But that's not to say it's meant to be for a lifetime."

"But I need you. I love you!" he blurted.

"No, dearest. The fact is, I'm not sure of myself right now. I've just begun this tour, which will take me all over the country. I want to see as much of this nation as I can. Please, Lucien, don't press me for an answer now. We're both young—we've our lives ahead of us. If it's meant to be, it will be. That's the way you must think of it."

He bit his lip and stared down at the floor. A mood of profound unhappiness seized him, for he knew she was right. Still, he could not help but try to persuade her otherwise. "Eleanor, I love you! Nothing's going to change that. I'll be faithful. I'll wait for you."

Eleanor shook her head and kissed him on the cheek, softly replying, "Please don't swear that and deny yourself love. I wouldn't want you to do that. And then, too, if *I* should meet someone else in my travels—''

"Oh, no, Eleanor!" Lucien burst out.

She stroked his cheek, her eyes warm and wide. "I'm very touched that you care for me so much. But you've had great sorrow recently, and it's only natural that you'd act rashly. I know about your stepfather's death, and it's had to affect you. But, Lucien, for you to try to force our friendship into a lifelong commitment is wrong! You must believe that. I wouldn't say this to you if I didn't care for you."

"Then perhaps there's hope?" he said with a forlorn look at her.

"There's always hope, my darling!" she quipped. But the smile vanished as she saw the hurt look on his face, and she cupped his cheeks with her soft hands and murmured, "We'll keep in touch but make no promises. When I marry, I want it to be for the rest of my life, and I'm sure you feel the same way. I'm just beginning to succeed in this country with my dancing, and, honestly, I don't want to give that up right now. Please promise you won't be angry with me?"

He tried to master his enormous disappointment. Finally he forced a wan smile to his handsome face. "All right, Eleanor, but I'll dream about you and pray that one day you'll say yes to my proposal." He kissed her on the cheek, then murmured, "I'll write you, and I'd be very happy if you'd write back."

"Of course. It's been wonderful seeing you."

"And you. Good-bye, then."

He kissed her again, this time on the lips, and then forced himself to turn his back and walk out the door. For several moments he stood outside her dressing room, lost in thought. He realized that nothing he could do would change her mind. With a sigh, he walked down the hall and passed a tall blond man in his midtwenties, with clear gray eyes and a well-kept, thin mustache. Vacantly, he nodded to the man and thought no more of it. But as his back was turned, he heard a knocking at a door. Something made him turn and look, and as he did so he saw the door to Eleanor's dressing room open and the dancer come out to greet the man, put her arms around his shoulders, and press her mouth to his, drawing him inside. The door closed behind them.

Lucien stood paralyzed, staring at the closed door. He did not hear the bustle of the other dancers coming out of their dressing rooms or the buzz of conversation near him. He forced himself to turn and walk slowly through the exit and into the street.

There, the night was dark and humid, and a faint rumble of thunder heralded a storm. But it was nothing compared to the storm in his heart. Anger swept through him like a white-hot flame. Such duplicity! After speaking honeyed words of caring for him, she had flung herself at this strange man as if they had been lovers. Perhaps they had! And that would mean— Oh, God, oh, God, how could she have done this to him?

He breathed in the night air, forcing himself to think rationally, though the jealous fury that filled him was slow to abate. He straightened, tilted back his head, and compressed his lips with a furious decisiveness.

Very well. If love had turned its back on him, he would do likewise. He would no longer be so dreamily idealistic about women. Rather, he would become a cynical appraiser, examining and scrutinizing their words, their acts, their promises and pretensions. Yes, that was the wisest course for him to take. And he would concentrate his efforts on his job and Nils Sonderman. Beyond that, he would gain wealth and restore Windhaven Plantation to the thriving enterprise it had been before.

He walked to the stable where he had left his horse, paid the young hostler, and then, mounting it, rode back along the river trail to the red-brick chateau.

On the following Sunday, after saying good-bye to Laure and his brothers and sisters, Lucien rode into Montgomery to take up his room at Mrs. Algood's boardinghouse and to prepare for his first day on the job at Nils Sonderman's office. By then, Lucien had made progress putting Eleanor Martinson out of his mind and was resolute about concentrating all his energy on the profession of architecture.

He arrived half an hour before the genial Swedish architect came up the stairs to open the door of his office Monday morning. "Well, now, Lucien, you're here already. That's an excellent beginning." Nils Sonderman greeted the tall, blond young man. "Come inside, and I'll show you where you'll be working."

Lucien followed his employer into the bright, spacious room. Again he admired the elegant walnut desk. "This is where Daniel Johannson works," the architect said, gesturing to a drafting table located under a long row of windows. "He'll be showing you the fundamentals of mechanical drawing. I think you'll enjoy working with him; he's very talented." Nils examined a large, translucent sheet of paper taped to the drawing board and then said, "He'll be in later. I'll show you your table. As my apprentice, you'll have a small office next to mine."

They entered a corridor, passed a long row of filing drawers, turned to the right, and faced two doors leading to adjacent offices. "Now then, Lucien," the architect said, "my office is on the left, and yours is here." They entered the smaller of the two rooms.

The Swedish architect gestured toward a chair, and

Lucien sat down. Nils perched himself on a stool near a drawing table. "I think it's an excellent idea, Lucien, for you to know something of my working philosophy as an architect. You'll find that many commissions are completely utilitarian and that you would be wasting your time and your customer's if you suggest new ideas. But once in a while you'll meet someone enlightened. Then you will be called upon to provide a plan that is practical and also fulfills the client's spiritual needs. Do you follow me?"

"I think so, Mr. Sonderman." Lucien nodded, fascinated by this discourse.

"Good! Now a number of commissions are limited by the client's financial means. You must respect these limits. For you to argue him into something that will cost him a great deal more would be contrary to our ethics. A wealthy client, however, usually will not quibble with you for a few dollars. With him you have more latitude. But you are still under constraint to achieve the most satisfying results at the least expense. When you satisfy the client, you satisfy yourself, and that is the happiest achievement of all."

"Yes, I see."

"Always the architect must strive for beauty *and* usefulness, Lucien. A house that is going to use the newly devised telephone and electricity will have wires stemming from both. When drawing up plans, you'll have to find ways to conceal the unsightly wires. Also, you'll want to give thought to the landscaping. The flower beds and lawns must be placed to provide the client with the best views from his most important windows. We also provide for shade trees. A house on a lot without trees looks barren, devoid of the privacy that a man who is buying a house necessarily demands."

"Yes, I can understand all that."

"When we come to industrial buildings, the architect's most important consideration is the load the building is going to bear. Supports must be substantial enough to hold up the weight of the floors, walls, roof, and the contents within the building."

"It's fascinating, Mr. Sonderman."

The genial Swedish architect made a deprecatory gesture with his slim hand and chuckled. "That's a general lecture, Lucien. You'll learn most everything you need to know from our working together on specific cases—and, of course, from Daniel's drafting instruction. And I'll welcome questions."

"Thank you, sir."

With a smiling nod, Nils left Lucien to his own resources and went back into the main office of his suite.

Lucien went to a bookcase by the window and brought several textbooks back to his desk to peruse. He studied drawings and blueprints. Nils Sonderman's exposition of the principles of architecture began to take hold.

That evening, Lucien returned to the boardinghouse and met the other boarders. During his introduction, Sarah Algood made him blush by referring to him in the most commendable terms. All the same, he felt very much at home there, and her warmth helped ease the possible malaise he felt at not being on Windhaven Plantation to look after his mother.

After two weeks of working with Daniel Johannson, Lucien had learned the fundamentals of draftsmanship and had a basic understanding of the most common materials used. Nils Sonderman was also extremely helpful, showing Lucien his drawings for the commissions in progress, explaining their development, and answering Lucien's questions so thoroughly and candidly that the novice felt more like a valued part of the firm than he did an apprentice.

On a warm Sunday afternoon, two weeks after Lucien had begun work, Amelia Coleman answered a loud knock on the door of the red-brick chateau and welcomed Nils, who had driven up in his buggy to pay Laure a condolence call.

"Do come in, Mr. Sonderman," Amelia said. "I'll let Mrs. Kenniston know you're here." She showed him into the parlor.

Nils seated himself on the chaise longue, but a few moments later he rose as he saw Laure enter. She wore a black cotton dress.

"I hope I haven't disturbed you, Mrs. Kenniston."

"Why, no, not at all. It was good of you to come, Mr. Sonderman."

"I want you to know how much I've been thinking about you since I heard the news about your poor husband," he finally said. "I'm very sorry."

"You're most kind. And I want to thank *you* for the lovely plant." She gestured toward the corner of the room where the plant Nils had sent now stood. "As you can see, it's flourishing. Lucien appreciated your thoughtfulness also. Please sit down."

After they both were seated, Laure asked how Lucien was doing.

"Extremely well, Mrs. Kenniston. I like your son's enthusiastic attitude toward the work. He has a future in architecture. He's absorbed a great many things in a short time, and before long he'll be contributing a few things toward the commissions I have."

"It's very rewarding to hear that, Mr. Sonderman. As you know, I've been worried about Lucien because he had to give up any further hope of continuing his education abroad—''

''I know,'' he gently interposed. ''But the technical problems of architecture—which, of course, will take time for him to learn—will, I hope, make up for that. If he applies himself, he can learn a great deal more of practical value, as well as of creativity, here rather than in school.''

''You may very well be right, Mr. Sonderman,'' Laure agreed. ''From what he tells me, you're making your firm a classroom for Lucien. I appreciate that, and so does he.''

''Mrs. Kenniston, do you happen to like Shakespeare?'' the architect asked, as if an idea had suddenly come to mind over which he was enthused.

''Very much.''

''Ah! Well, I just learned that next Saturday the Colonial Theater is going to offer a performance of *The Merchant of Venice*. Perhaps you and Lucien—and any of your other children you think might enjoy it—would like to be my guests? We could have supper beforehand at a restaurant near the theater, then go to the play. That is, if you don't think me too forward.''

''It's not that.'' Laure frowned dubiously. ''It's just so soon after my husband's death.''

''I think it would be stimulating for the mind and very worthwhile for Lucien, Mrs. Kenniston. And the change of scene would be beneficial to you, too, I'm sure. You know the story, of course?''

''Oh, yes. It's one of my favorite plays.''

''Then may we make definite plans? I'll call for you here,'' he said with a smile.

''Well . . .'' The status of her widowhood gave Laure misgivings, making her feel it would not be fair to

Leland's memory to go out on a social occasion with another man.

"I wish you would look upon me as a friend of the family, Mrs. Kenniston. Believe me, I've not the least desire to distress you," he urged.

"Very well, then. It's kind of you to offer this invitation. And I know that my son Paul will be happy to get away from the plantation and have some diversion, for he seems, more than anyone, to miss New York," Laure said.

"Then it's settled! Next Saturday at about four-thirty?"

"I shall look forward to it."

"And I as well." He took her hand and brought it to his lips, bowing his head to kiss it. "I'll bid you a cordial good evening, Mrs. Kenniston."

Chapter 8

During this first week of September, young Paul Bouchard was delegated by Benjamin Franklin Brown and Burt Coleman to help harvest the corn and melons. He did so with a gloomy face, for the Friday before he had received brief notes from his friends David Cohen and Joy Parmenter, who was the daughter of his late father's half sister. Joy lived in Galveston and had shared with Paul an enthusiasm for learning, and her letter told of her advances in the field of journalism. These cordial missives made Paul feel all the more abandoned and isolated on the plantation, which held for him no pleasurable companionship.

To be sure, he welcomed the outing to the Colonial Theater as a break in the dreary monotony of his days, but throughout the week he thought more and more of striking out on his own, just as Lucien had done, to put an end to the unending loneliness and tedium of his existence.

Yet he knew that if he showed his dissatisfaction too openly, Laure might become suspicious and take steps to stop him. So he forced himself to be outgoing, and on the evening when Nils Sonderman called for him and his mother and Lucien, who was home for the weekend, Paul tried to be enthusiastic.

The dinner was excellent, the performance competent. Paul did his best to conceal his growing unhappiness throughout the evening. Unfortunately, the young actress who played the role of Portia reminded him of Joy, for she had the same vivacity, skin tone, and hair coloring as his close friend. The similarity strengthened his loneliness and sense of isolation.

After the performance, Nils drove them home and thanked Laure and her sons for a delightful evening. When he was gone, Lucien exclaimed, "He's really a marvelous man, Mother."

Laure nodded her agreement. "With impeccable manners. So considerate." Then, turning to Paul, she asked, "Did you enjoy it?"

He tried to smile and sound cheerful. "Yes, it was all right. I guess I don't care for plays."

"Well, admittedly it's not generally considered one of Shakespeare's finest; it's still one of my favorites, though. Well, now, it's getting late. I'm for bed. The two of you had best do the same. Good night, Lucien, Paul."

"Good night, Mother," Lucien replied, while Paul only mumbled, staring at his older brother so intently that Lucien paused at the stairway and then asked, "What's the matter?"

Paul glanced around to make certain that his mother was out of earshot, then burst out in a low voice, "You think you're so smart, don't you? Everything goes your way! You've got a job. You've been to school in Ireland. You've had a sweetheart—"

"Yes, who was killed, don't forget! You haven't had that grief, and I pray God you never do, Paul. Now stop acting like a child!"

"So *that's* what you think of me. You and everyone else around here!" Paul was almost in tears in his frustrated rage. "Just wait, Lucien! I'll show everybody. I can get along just fine by myself, just like you.''

"Stop talking like that!''

'You're afraid of the truth, aren't you?'' Paul angrily interposed.

"There's no use talking to you—you're not making any sense. I'm going to bed. Good night.'' Lucien abruptly turned and went up the stairs.

Paul stood looking after him, his fists clenched, his face scarlet with fury. "I'll show everybody,'' he muttered to himself. "Just wait. I'll show them all! I'll leave, and then they'll be sorry. I'm sure not getting anywhere around this place!'' In a thoroughly wretched mood, feeling more and more sorry for himself, Paul ascended the stairs and went to his room, slammed the door, and flung himself down on his bed, where he soon fell asleep.

Early the next morning, he wrote letters to Joy Parmenter and David Cohen, revealing the unhappiness he was experiencing in his dreary life. Indeed, he tortured himself by recalling to David the happy times they had had in New York, while to Joy he wrote bemoaning the chores he was given. In both letters he expressed his fervent desire to see his friends again, though in no way did he think that was possible unless he took drastic action.

When he had sealed the letters, he asked young John West, the son of Ezekiel and Marva West, tenant-owners on the plantation, to take his letters into Lowndesboro and mail them, once he learned that John was going to drive a wagon to Dalbert Sattersfield's general store for supplies.

After his argument with Lucien, he had been thinking of running away, leaving Windhaven Plantation and its acres of corn and melons. The idea proved more and more attractive. In order to achieve anything worthwhile, he would have to strike out on his own. But to succeed, he would have to keep his whereabouts secret, so he could not be overtaken and brought back in disgrace. That would be the most crushing blow of all. No, he would leave and make a life for himself and earn money, which he would send to his mother.

After breakfast, Paul left the chateau to walk along the river, where he could be alone with his thoughts and plan a course of action. He just had to think of the right niche for himself—in a place where he would be appreciated and treated like a man. How he would leave and where he would go he wasn't quite sure of as yet, but he knew that he must make his move soon.

"Morning, Paul." A familiar voice broke in on his unhappy musings, and Paul quickly turned with a guilty expression on his face, as if he had been caught doing something wrong. Even in that flash of recognition—it was Burt Coleman—he was annoyed at reacting this way, for he'd done nothing wrong.

In a spiritless tone, he answered, "Good morning, Burt."

"Where are you off to, youngster?" Burt asked with a friendly smile. Paul was already so steeped in his own self-pity that he translated it as a rebuke.

"Just for a walk. Don't you want me to?" he countered belligerently.

"You can do as you like, but we could use your help right now. I'd appreciate it if you'd water the hogs."

"Oh, all right, if I must," Paul answered wearily.

Burt gave Paul a quizzical look. If ever he heard a sullen response, this was it. Something was eating the boy, no two ways about it. So in a conciliatory tone, he answered, "Well, now, Paul, you wouldn't want the hogs to go thirsty. They're valuable—the more so because we lost so many last year in the flood and had to spend a lot to replace them. All right?''

"No, if you want to know something, it's not all right!'' At last all the hurt and resentment Paul felt burst out. "I don't think you've got any right to order me around. I'm not a nigger or a field hand. I'm Paul Bouchard, and that's a name that means something around here.''

"Whoa now, youngster, back off!'' Burt held up both palms, a startled look on his handsome face. "I'm not ordering you around. We're all in this together. And I don't cotton to your using the word 'nigger,' which is a slur. Besides, the Negroes we've got living here are fine, decent people, and don't you forget it.''

"All right. I'm sorry,'' Paul responded truculently. "But all I get to do around here is water the hogs or bale hay, and I'm better than that! I've lived in New York, and I've traveled.''

Burt was finding it hard to control his temper. "I've known you since you were a tadpole, and I never thought I'd be hearing what you've been spouting this morning. Now, it's too bad that you had to leave New York and your school and your friends. But we all have to give up some things in life; it tests a man's character. And if you want to prove you're a man—''

"Of course I do! I'll be fifteen pretty soon, and just because Lucien's two years older doesn't mean he's the only man around here!''

"So that's it! You're jealous because Lucien found himself a job! When you're older, you'll have a career of your own just like Lucien. Till then, well, I guess you could say your career is right here, working with us. Call it an apprenticeship. We all work together to get things done. Now, I didn't mean to be harsh when I asked you to water the hogs. I said I'd appreciate it, and I would. Why don't we just let it go at that?''

"All right, I'd just have to do it anyway," Paul grumbled. His shoulders slumped, and his face dark with anger, he turned and trudged out to the hog pens. He wasn't about to take any more lectures from somebody like Burt Coleman. Burt was just a hired hand, and he himself was a Bouchard! No, he couldn't go on like this anymore.

First, how was he to leave? Walking wouldn't get him anywhere fast. He could take a horse, but as soon as he was found missing, his mother would send Ben or Burt after him. They were much better riders than he and would find him in no time. Then another thought struck him: the railroad! He'd heard that one could climb aboard a freight car with little risk of being detected, and a train would take him far away fast before anyone could discover him missing. The more he thought about it, the better he liked the idea. Riding the rails, as he had heard it called, had an adventurous, romantic appeal, especially to a boy of fourteen.

That was it—he'd board a train near Montgomery, which would take him to a place where he could find new friends who wouldn't take him for granted. He'd even find a job, make his way, without anybody else's help, and nobody would find out where he was until he was ready to come back—as a success, just like Lucien.

He leaned over the top of the hog pen and tipped the bucket into the trough. The hogs came to drink, squealing and grunting. He made a face at them. They were ugly beasts, and here he was watering them.

But now he knew what he was going to do. He turned his head to look back toward the river. He had to leave right away. There was no sense in putting it off any longer.

*　　*　　*

Paul Bouchard was relieved when his mother, at dinner that Monday evening, made no mention of Burt Coleman, and he was grateful to Burt for not having aired their differences. He forced himself to be pleasant to his brother and sisters. To be sure, it was much easier with Lucien gone for the week.

Laure, noticing Paul's amiability, sighed with relief. Perhaps her rebellious young son was at last learning to come to terms with reality.

After supper, Paul told his mother that he was going to study some books he had brought back from New York, kissed her dutifully on the cheek, and left the dining room. Once inside his room, his mind was filled with his daring plan, which he would act upon that night. He would take a horse from the stables, ride to the rail line outside Montgomery, climb into an empty car, and go wherever the train took him. The mare would find her way home, he was sure. There could be no slips, no clues left behind for anyone to find. When he had proved that he could fend for himself, he would get in touch with his family.

Of course he would leave a note for his mother. To let her find him gone without any explanation would be cruel.

He went to his desk and began to compose the letter. In it he explained that she was not to worry, that he was going to make a fresh start. He promised to send her letters so she would know he was well, and he asked her pardon for running away.

Frowning, he read it and reread it several times, and then added this postscript:

Mother, I just don't want to stay around here working in the fields. I can't learn a single thing from doing that, and I feel just like a field hand. Besides, I can't earn any money doing these chores. I do hope you'll understand and not be angry with me.

Your son, Paul

He had changed his customary attire for supper, but now he removed the shirt and trousers and put on some heavy trousers and a thin pullover shirt, which he wore to do his chores. He took a wide-brimmed hat out of the closet and flung it onto his bed. It was going to be hot at least for the next few weeks, and there was no sense dressing up. And it was wise to travel light, especially as he was not yet sure where he was going to go.

This done, he stretched himself out on his bed, folded his arms, and pillowed his head in them, staring up at the ceiling as he imagined his bold adventure. He did not even consider the dangers; all that was important was escape.

When he saw on the little clock on the wall that it was nearing midnight, he crept out of his room and went down the stairs to the kitchen. The house was absolutely silent; that was exactly what he wanted. He packed a little sack of provisions, carried it back to his room, and inspected it to make sure it wasn't too bulky and inconvenient to carry. The time had come. . . .

Adjusting the straw hat on his head and taking the sack of provisions, he took the envelope addressed to Laure and went back down the stairs again, laying it on the low table at the foot of the stairs where mail was generally placed. This done, he hurried out to the stable.

He went to a gentle black mare he had ridden several times before, and soothing her and stroking her head to reassure her that all was well, he saddled her. Leading the mare out of the stable, he mounted her and then headed toward Montgomery.

The moon was out, and so he had plenty of light to see the winding trail along the river. A flock of night birds settled into some of the trees on the other side of the river. Paul breathed in the air deeply. He felt free.

He thought quickly back to his planning and found no mistakes. No one could know where he was going or what route he had taken.

When he reached the outskirts of Montgomery, he dismounted with his bundle, then slapped the mare sharply on the rump. "Go home now, girl. You know the way."

The mare tossed her head, looked at the boy as he folded the reins over her, then bobbed her head, docilely turned, and trotted back toward the trail he had taken. He watched her disappear and exhaled a sigh of relief.

He looked around him. A long freight train stood on a distant siding, silhouetted in the moonlight. As he went closer, he could see from the markings on the cars that it was headed for Mobile. There was no one around. About four or five hundred yards farther east, two workers were talking, but they hadn't seen him.

He stealthily made his way to the next-to-last car, tentatively tugged on the side door, and felt it yield and roll back. He clambered up into it, carefully pulled the door to, and then lay down on his side, his cheek pillowed against some empty gunnysacks, which he had discovered in the corner of the boxcar. This was it! He was leaving Montgomery.

Within minutes he had fallen sound asleep. He was not even aware that the train had started, pulling out to begin its leisurely, long journey toward the Gulf. On his face was the hint of a smile.

* * *

With a grinding of the wheels on the track, the long freight train came to a jerking halt, and Paul Bouchard was rudely jostled. He came awake with a start, blinking his eyes, then rubbing his knuckles over them to clear them of sleep. Getting to his feet, he warily approached the sliding door of the boxcar and cautiously opened it just a crack. He was surprised to see from the position of the sun that it was late in the afternoon. He had slept for hours. Well, no wonder, with all that had happened yesterday. He wondered where he was. He knew one thing—he was hungry.

He went back to the sack he had brought with him, opened it, and took out a biscuit and a slice of ham. Then he scowled, remembering that he had forgotten to bring along drinking water. He shrugged; there was bound to be water from a stream or a river or somewhere, and he'd find it.

As he was finishing the biscuit, the huge door rolled back with a rumble, and Paul stared incredulously as a tall, bearded man, a mulatto, climbed inside, then stood in the open doorway. Seated upright, Paul shrank back into his corner of the boxcar, trying to hide himself in the darkness. But the big man saw him.

Hands on his hips, the newcomer demanded in a hoarse voice that made Paul tremble, "What you doin' here, white boy?"

"I . . . I'm going to visit some friends, mister," Paul finally quavered.

"Well, you certainly ain't travelin' in style. What's your name, boy?"

"P–Paul Bouchard, mister."

"You're right polite. You been brought up good, anybody can see that. But if you was really travelin' to visit friends, seems to me your mama woulda paid for a seat in a passenger train. You must be in some kinda trouble, boy.'' The mulatto pulled the rolling door almost shut and swung himself into the corner opposite Paul. The boy watched with trepidation as the huge man pulled out a half-smoked cigar and stuck the stogie between his teeth. ''So you're takin' to the life of the road, runnin' away from your problems, huh? That's no life for a child.''

Paul said nothing, still unsure of what to do about this new development. He hadn't anticipated there being others in the same car with him. Would this man make him go back? He had already called him a child.

''Well, no matter,'' the man said as he struck a match on the floor and held it up to the stogie, puffing it into life. ''You're gonna need a body to look after you, and it looks like that's me, don't it? Well, all right, if you can keep up with me. My friends call me Boxcar Pete, and I reckon you can call me that, too.''

''I—I'm glad to meet you, Mr. Pete,'' Paul responded tremulously.

''That do beat all!'' the mulatto boomed, tilting his head back in such a way that his laugh echoed against the walls of the boxcar. He carried over his shoulder a heavy sack, which he now slung onto the floor. ''Beats me why a fine-speakin' white boy like you would hide hisself in a boxcar. Slowest ride they is. Course it's free, one good thing about it. But a feller runnin' away, seems like he'd want to make better time. This here train's gonna mosey a long spell 'fore it gets to Mobile, you know.''

''I—I'm not running away, honest I'm not,'' Paul retorted defensively.

''Sure you is, boy.'' Boxcar Pete chuckled. ''Guess you might say I'm runnin', too, in one sense of the term.''

Paul was too afraid to ask any questions, but he couldn't help wondering what the mulatto was running from. However, his new companion apparently did not feel it important to explain.

The fact was that, since his fatal altercation with Sheriff Bixton, Pete Robbins had put distance between himself and the little hamlet where he had lived. In the intervening weeks, he had very cleverly managed to rob several houses owned by well-to-do residents on the outskirts of towns where the freight trains stopped. The money, clothing, and food that he had taken he had shared with impoverished blacks, many of whom, disrupted from their jobs by bigoted whites in various Alabama towns, still wandered forlornly like refugees, even trading their labor for food and a place to sleep.

Satisfied with his scrutiny of the trembling boy, Pete Robbins—Boxcar Pete—now chuckled again and said, "Well, boy, we'll be reachin' Eufaula some time late tonight. I got me a camp there and some right good friends. You'll be eatin' some fine grub, if you feel like it. How's that sound to you?"

"I'd like that very much," Paul replied timidly.

"You're real polite—got real good manners. But lemme tip you off right now while you're startin' this travel of yours. The folks I call my friends is colored folks, 'cause they're the ones most hurtin' in these bad times. White folks seen to that. What I'm gettin' at, boy, is that I'll stand up for you, but don't you expect no special favors."

"I—I won't, sir."

"You really got no business riskin' your life by goin' out like this on your own. Lordy, if I had me a son your age . . . You can't be more than fourteen or so, I'm thinkin'."

"I'll be fifteen in December," Paul declared spiritedly.

"Well, now, don't that beat all!" Again the mulatto, hugely amused, tilted back his head and uttered a deep laugh, which resounded through the boxcar. "All right, give you fifteen. But you're still no man, and when it comes down to a fight over grub or money or even a gal—though I s'pose you're a mite too young for gals— you won't stand a chance agin my friends, you hear now? It's agin my nature to account for anyone 'cept for my own kind, but I guess we can get along. But I'm tellin' you, just you be mindin' yourself, hear?"

"Thank you, Mr. Pete. I'll do whatever you tell me to."

"I like that. Long time since any white boy said a thing like that to me." Again the mulatto laughed, but this time in bitter irony. "Well, now, boy, might as well stretch out and snooze some. It'll be awhile before we get to Eufaula."

So saying, he put his sack to one side, stretched out on the floor of the boxcar, pillowing his head in his arms, and closed his eyes. Vastly reassured, Paul slipped down onto his back and resumed the sleep that had been interrupted by the sudden jerking halt of the freight train.

Chapter 9

When Laure went down to breakfast Tuesday morning, she found Paul's letter on the table at the front of the stairway and, with a cry of alarm, stared incredulously at the words. She could not believe that he would take such an impulsive and dangerous step without at least having discussed his unhappiness with her.

Amelia, seeing at once how upset Laure was, asked, "What's the matter, Laure? Anything I can do?"

"Oh, Amelia, Paul ran away last night. I don't know where's he's gone or what he's going to do. He's only fourteen, still so young, and knows nothing about all the dangers of mixing with rough people. Oh, Lord, why did he have to do it?"

Amelia took the letter from Laure's unresisting fingers and quickly scanned it, then shook her head. "He ought to have had more sense! Couldn't he know how much it would upset you, Laure? What he needs is a good whuppin'."

"Oh, no, Amelia. It's really my fault. I knew he was unhappy. But I never dreamed he'd do anything like this! I'd be so grateful if he just came back. I don't think I'd even scold him."

"He probably rode just a short ways away," Amelia said, trying to be helpful.

"He didn't have any money—maybe a dollar or two

from his allowance. But even so, he could have found a ride with someone.''

Laure burst into tears. She had not yet escaped the feeling that Leland's death had been caused by her negligence, and now to find her son a runaway piled the burden of guilt upon her.

''Would you ask John to hitch up the buggy and drive me into Lowndesboro? I want to go see the sheriff as soon as I can.''

''I'll do it right now, Laure.'' Amelia left while Laure searched for photographs of Paul and tried to keep her composure.

As John West drew the reins of the black gelding in front of the Lowndesboro sheriff's office, Laure looked carefully around the street, hoping in vain to catch a glimpse of her son. Quickly she resigned herself to letting Sheriff Blake do the searching.

''I'll be waiting right here, ma'am,'' the young driver said solicitously.

''Thank you, John.''

Laure walked into the office and found the sheriff seated at his desk.

''Mrs. Kenniston!'' John Blake said as she entered. ''What can I do for you?''

''Oh, Sheriff Blake, the most awful thing has happened. My son Paul has run away. You must help me find him!''

The young man, who had recently been appointed sheriff after his racist predecessor had been forced to resign, rose from his desk, walked to Laure, and taking her arm, led her to a chair. ''Please, Mrs. Kenniston, sit down and rest. I'll take care of everything. You just relax.''

''He's only fourteen, and I have no idea where he's

gone." She reached into her bag. "Here's the letter he left me."

The sheriff took the letter, read it quickly, and handed it back to her. "Has Paul ever done anything like this before, Mrs. Kenniston?"

"Never," Laure answered. "I feel so guilty."

"No need to, ma'am. Boys his age sometimes get the notion that they'll be happier somewhere else, outside of their parents' authority. It's just a stage. Does he have any friends living someplace else? Friends he might go to visit?"

Laure looked up at the young man. "Why, yes, but you don't suppose . . . I mean, they live so far away. He has a very close friend in New York, where we used to live."

"May I have his name, please? And his address?"

"Of course. David Cohen. I'll write down his address for you. And there's someone else—Joy Parmenter. In Galveston, Texas. Here's her address." She handed him a card. "But you don't really think—"

"Mrs. Kenniston, a determined lad can move pretty far when he wants to. And I've found in cases like this, where a boy hasn't left home before, that nine times out of ten he'll go to someone he knows. The world's just too big to feel comfortable in without friends." He smiled at Laure in an attempt to calm her. "Now here's what I'll do. I'll wire the police in New York and Galveston right away and have them alert Paul's friends. I'll need a description of Paul—a photograph, too, if you have one—and I'll send out bulletins to major cities in the South and East. I want you to go to the Montgomery County sheriff's office today and tell him everything you've told me. If your son has decided to hop a train—and my guess is that he's done just that—he'd have to go to Montgomery to get one. I want Sheriff

Burkholder to know of the situation. Someone might have seen Paul.''

Laure earnestly thanked the young sheriff and, after giving him one photograph and a description of Paul, hurried out to the buggy, where John West was waiting.

''John, we've got to go to Montgomery,'' she said as she climbed into the buggy, ''and the sooner we get there, the better.''

John West drew the horse to a halt in front of Sheriff Burkholder's office, jumped down, and helped Laure descend from the buggy. ''I'll be waitin' for you, Miz Kenniston.''

''Thank you, John.'' Laure smiled nervously, for her anxiety over Paul's disappearance had not abated despite Sheriff Blake's help. She had struggled to regain her self-control after Leland's funeral, but this new blow had rendered her even more vulnerable.

Martin Burkholder, a stocky man of medium height with pleasant features, a neatly trimmed walrus mustache, and thick sideburns, opened the door of his office as he saw Laure approach. ''Come in, ma'am. How may I help you?''

''Sheriff Burkholder, my name is Laure Kenniston. I come from Windhaven Plantation—''

''*Ach ja,* the famous Bouchard home! When I first came to Montgomery from Germany, I was told of your beautiful castle. And I have read about the Bouchards in the newspaper.'' Abruptly, his face became solemn. ''Forgive me, Frau Kenniston, for prattling on. I know of your grief. Poor Herr Kenniston's death was a dreadful shock. Please, sit down here. Tell me how I can be of service.''

''You're most kind, Sheriff Burkholder. I've come because my son Paul, who's fourteen, ran away.'' Laure again told the story of Paul's disappearance, this time adding the information she had been given by the Lowndesboro sheriff. "Here is a photograph of Paul, Sheriff."

"What a fine-looking boy. I shall do everything I can to locate your Paul, Frau Kenniston."

"Thank you so much, Sheriff Burkholder. I'm happy to have met you, even though it is on such a sorry errand as mine." Laure rose and offered her hand.

Martin Burkholder grasped it warmly and accompanied her to the door. "The moment I have any news about the *Jüngling*, I'll see that you have it just as swiftly as I can get it to you."

Once outside, she asked, "John, could you drive me over to Mr. Sonderman's office? I'd like to tell Lucien about Paul." Laure dabbed her eyes with a handkerchief.

The tall young man nodded, loosened the reins from the hitching post, and, as Laure got in on her side, mounted his seat in the buggy. "Paul's gonna be just fine, you wait and see. With two sheriffs workin' on findin' him, he'll turn up before you know it."

Laure smiled at the young man's attempt to console her. "I'm sure you're right."

The young black man smiled shyly in return, then drove the horse to Nils Sonderman's office building and waited patiently as Laure went up the stairs to the second floor.

As she entered the office, she caught sight of Lucien seated at the drawing table under the row of windows, so absorbed in his work that he was unaware of her presence. Laure stood watching him for several moments. The constricted look on her lovely face gave way to one of satisfaction to see him so engrossed at his task. As he laid down one pencil and took up another, he lifted his eyes and saw her standing there. "Mother! What a nice surprise!"

At this moment, Nils Sonderman walked into the office. "Mrs. Kenniston! How good of you to call!" He walked toward her. "Lucien has been laboring most diligently. He's a great credit to you."

"I wish that things were going so well for all my children."

"Is there something wrong, Mrs. Kenniston? You seem distressed," the architect said.

"I just came from the sheriff's office to tell Lucien that—well, this morning I found a note from Paul. He's run away!"

"Run away, Mother?" Lucien echoed, his eyes widening.

"It's an unkind fate that sends you so many troubles all at once, Mrs. Kenniston," Nils solicitously put in. "But I've met our new sheriff, and if anyone can find your boy, he can."

"Why would Paul do a thing like that? Where would he go?" Lucien asked.

"I'm not really sure. I was hoping you might be able to tell me."

"I have no idea, Mother. Paul has avoided me lately."

Laure pulled the letter from her bag and handed it to Lucien. "He was envious of your accomplishments, and I was so involved. I *do* wish I'd been more sympathetic to him. I might have prevented—"

"I don't think so, Mother," Lucien gently broke in. "He's been very morose ever since he came back from New York, and he felt sorry for himself. I know he didn't like some of the things I did and said. He told me as much. But don't worry, Mother. I'm sure the sheriff will bring him back safely."

"I do hope so. He's so young, Lucien, and to be by

himself, heaven knows where—oh, excuse me, Mr. Sonderman, I didn't mean to plague you with my problems!''

"You never could plague me, Mrs. Kenniston. If there's anything I can do to help, call on me any time.''

"Thank you. Well, I—I'll be going back now. Lucien, is the boardinghouse all right for you?''

"Oh, yes! Mrs. Algood, my landlady, is really a character, Mother.'' Lucien chuckled. "And a very good cook. I couldn't have done better if I'd looked all over town. I'll be coming home tonight, though, Mother. I don't want you to have to face this all alone—''

"Nonsense!'' Laure interrupted. "I'll be just fine. You stay here and concentrate on your work so that Mr. Sonderman won't regret having hired you.'' She eyed Nils Sonderman and could not suppress the blush that sprang to her lovely face. She cordially nodded to the architect, kissed her son, and assured him that she would send any news she received of his brother. Then she went down the stairs and back to the buggy to be driven to Windhaven Plantation.

It was midnight when the long freight train came to a final stop and Boxcar Pete warily slid open the door just enough to peek out. "Here's where we get off, boy,'' he muttered. "Mind you, you be doin' just what I tell you. You don't want none of those railroad guards seein' you, or they'll like as not bang you around. The Alabama and Chattanooga don't take kindly to folks ridin' for free. Hurry up now!'' He made an impatient gesture toward Paul Bouchard.

The boy collected his sack of provisions and leaped to the ground, following Boxcar Pete, who pointed to a thicket that nearly covered a slight ravine. "Crawl on your belly in there. The brakemen'll be by any second now, 'cause they gonna shift this train onto another sidin'."

Paul scrambled into the ravine, where he sprawled beside his companion. Boxcar Pete watched as a bearded, gray-haired, bespectacled brakeman carrying a lantern ambled past them and toward the caboose.

"All right now. Looks like they gonna take on water at the engine 'fore they switch off to the sidin'. But we ain't waitin' none for them to come find us."

Boxcar Pete crouched, slowly climbed out of the ravine, and moved through a thick undergrowth of weeds and yellowing grass.

"Where are we, Mr. Pete?" Paul quavered. He was terribly thirsty and remembered how stupid he had been not to think of taking along a canteen to tide him through a long journey.

"Eufaula, boy. 'Bout a hunnerd miles southeast of Montgomery. See way over there to the left? Can you make out a little light? That's a campfire. I've got friends there."

"I—I never heard of Eufaula," Paul timidly ventured.

"That's 'cause you ain't been around much, boy. Lots of colored folks work at the turpentine mill outside of town. It's purely drudgery. Awful smell, and you gets a headache that lasts all week long. And the pay's not much better than slavery."

"I—I wish I had some water. I forgot to bring some."

"Hell, that bothering you? Here—watch your step now, there's a stream in this here gully. Drink your fill!"

Soon Paul was down on all fours, his head bowed to the little stream, thirstily gulping water.

"Gosh, that's a lot better," he said as he rose to his feet.

"One thing you gotta learn, boy. Whenever you on

the road, you gotta think ahead. You oughta brought some water along. S'posin' we'd had to go on another coupla hunnerd miles, and you with no water? You'da been real parched. Lucky for you I got this here canteen to hold us between stops. Let's get to the camp. I can smell some good food.''

Indeed, the fragrant aroma of a stew had begun to reach Paul's nostrils, and suddenly he was extremely hungry.

"Get that worried look off your face, boy,'' the mulatto chuckled, slapping Paul on the back. "They's always enough for latecomers. And anyhow, they be expectin' me—I got business here.''

They finally came into a clearing. Far beyond, Paul could just make out a small frame house in the flickering light of the campfire. Around the fire sat a dozen men. One of two white men greeted the mulatto. "Good to see you, Pete! Any luck?''

"I always have luck, Jack, you knows that,'' Paul's companion averred. " 'Sides, I just come down from Montgomery, and the pickin's were real good there. You still got the job at the mill?''

"Naw.'' Jack, appearing to be in his late thirties, limped toward them. "Laid me off last week, 'counta me bein' gimpy. Said they was cuttin' down help anyhow. Didn't have that many orders.''

"You hear that?'' Boxcar Pete addressed the others in the camp. "The white folks who run things ain't only tryin' to shaft niggers—they done it to Jack here. That mill's got plenty of orders for turpentine. That was just a story they told you, Jack. Anyhow, here's thirty bucks to tide you over. I heard tell some good farmhands might be needed coupla miles downriver from Lowndesboro. You might go down that way and try your luck. You ain't got a family to worry about, so your chances are good—and, of course, you're white. If you was black, I'd have to say a prayer for you.''

"Won't forget this, Pete.'' The stocky white man pocketed the bills that the mulatto held out to him. "I'll pay you back, I swear I will.''

"No, you give it instead to some poor soul who's down on his luck. When I started this thing, I was gonna take from the rich and give to those that don't have nothin'. Like Robin Hood, remember? Now then, I smell stew.''

"Yeah.'' A tall, lanky black man in his early thirties came forward, glaring suspiciously at Paul Bouchard. "It's stew, all right. Who's this you done brung along, Pete?''

"A partner. Mind your own business.''

"Hell if I will. I knows what you're doin' for us, and we're mighty grateful, but you don't run this camp,'' the man grumbled. "Eustace, this here's a white boy. And he's been eatin' fair, from the looks of him. We oughta be able to shake him down for some cash.'' At this, a somewhat younger black approached, a patch over one eye, having been blinded in a fight with the white farmer who had engaged him to do sharecropping.

"Back off, back off, Rastus, and you too, Eustace!'' Pete stepped forward in front of Paul, clenching his right fist. "A fine thing, pickin' on someone half your size here. You wanna hassle him? You hassle me first and see how far you gets!''

"All right, all right, we ain't lookin' for no trouble,'' Rastus grumbled as he gestured toward his companion. The two blacks, casting a last hostile glance at the cowering boy, moved back to where they had stood, guarding the kettle of stew.

"I admit he ain't much of a partner, but he's alone, orphanlike, you see?'' Pete gestured with his thumb back at Paul, then let out a snigger. "So I brought him along to teach him the ropes. He be in my charge now, and you'd best leave him be—else you'll be dealin' with me. All of you understand?"

There was a grumble of assent, but Pete quickly changed the surly mood of the camp to one of jubilation as he swung his sack from his shoulder to the ground. "I got grub, clothes, and more cash, and I'm gonna dole it out accordin' to your needs, fellers," he told them. As he spoke, he took an unlit stogie from his pocket, stuck it into a corner of his mouth, rolled it to the other side, then smacked his lips. "Those of you that needs it the worst, you gets the most. Now look here, Rastus, I knows you was kicked out of your house six months back, and nobody's given you a job since. Ever stop to figger that one of the reasons is that you so mean folks is afraid to put you on their payroll? Just like the way you come on here when you first saw my partner. All right now, take this." He handed four ten-dollar bills to the man. "Oughta give you a new start—but not here in Alabamy. Go someplace new, Texas or out west where ain't many folks hate a man 'cause of his color."

"Maybe you's right, Pete." Rastus lowered his head and looked at the greenbacks Boxcar Pete had placed into his hand. "I'm mighty beholden to you. I been thinkin'—folks say Californy is a good place to be."

"Now, that's bein' smart. The next freight to Mobile leaves around dawn. Get on it—and you too, Eustace. Here's somethin' for you. You're about as bad off as Rastus here."

"Yeah, I know. I'll go where he does, and maybe we can start fresh together."

"Sure you can. Only you gotta smile. I don't mean kowtow to nobody—just show that you're friendly."

Pete turned to the others, who now came forward. Paul watched, openmouthed, as the mulatto generously handed out money, food, and clothing, keeping almost nothing for himself, until the sack was empty. Just before he had finished, the mulatto glanced over at him. "Bet you'd be wantin' a little of this yourself, boy, ain't that right?"

"Oh, no, sir, I—I don't want anything."

"Hmmph. Well, now, can't say as I blame you none. Trouble is, sometimes a feller needs a little help. We'll have some stew, and then we'll take ourselves off to find a place to sleep. In the mornin' we'll be gone."

The men in the camp shook Pete's hand, patting him on the back and offering profuse thanks for his generosity. Rastus even went so far as to dish out a plate of stew and hand it to the mulatto while Eustace, not to be outdone, piled a plate high for Paul and, slapping the boy on the back, said, "Eat hearty, boy. I helped make it myself."

Paul's mentor had seated himself near the campfire to eat his stew. Paul joined him, entranced by Pete's good nature. Finally, when the mulatto had finished his food, he rose and tossed the plate to one side. "Real good. Tomorrow my partner and me are goin' to Mobile. Pickin's oughta be real good down there. Now you all keep out of mischief, you hear? Those ornery sheriffs and deputies are wantin' to run you in or lynch you."

Then, his arm around Paul's shoulders, he urged, "Time for bed, boy. Come on, I'll tuck you in. We'll sleep under the stars tonight. Ever done that before?"

"No, sir."

"Well, there's a first time for everythin', boy. Come on now! I'll bet your mama be worried about you— don't try to tell me different. That's one reason I'm gonna see to it you get your proper sleep."

"But—" Paul began, but subsided when the brawny mulatto turned and stared hard at him. "Yes, sir," he finished meekly.

"That's better." Pete laughed. "You and me, we be gettin' along fine. Me, I had a mother once. . . ." He did not finish, his face hardening with a sudden anger. Then he led the bewildered youngster to a grassy knoll near a large cypress tree, and the two of them lay down to sleep.

For young Paul Bouchard, it had been a day full of astonishing developments, meeting people he had not dreamed existed. As for Pete, Paul had never met a man so forceful and determined, who exercised such influence over rough-and-tumble men.

Chapter 10

$\mathcal{L}$aure Kenniston sat down at her writing table. Before opening the day's mail, she wiped her brow with a handkerchief and took a sip from a tall glass of lemonade. The day was excruciatingly hot and humid, making her uncomfortable no matter how little energy she exerted. Earlier she had attempted to do some cultivating in the vegetable garden, but after only minutes of moderate activity, she had returned to the house to take up this sedentary pursuit, which could be performed in the dark coolness of the study.

She flipped through the mail, noting with displeasure that most of the envelopes contained bills, but then she singled out a familiar script, that of her longtime friend Jessica Haskins. Smiling, Laure hastily ripped open her friend's letter. Laure hadn't seen Jessica for several months—indeed, not since long before Leland's death. Perhaps the letter would bring news of an intended visit. She read quickly through the greeting, but shortly her brow furrowed, for instead, terrible, shocking news was revealed. Jessica's husband, dear Andy, was dead!

Laure gasped and covered her mouth with her hand as she read further. Andy had been horribly upset by the news of Leland's death, Jessica explained. He had so hoped that the Irish entrepreneur's surgery would have restored his health. Jessica had tried to reassure Andy that he had done all he could for Leland, the letter went on, but he could not be consoled. That night Jessica had found the lifeless body of her husband, the victim of a heart attack.

Tears came to Laure's eyes. Andy had been buried the next day, Jessica explained, and she had made arrangements with a realtor to sell their property. Unable to bear to stay in Alabama without Andy, she planned to stay with her cousin Medora in Roanoke just as soon as the property was sold. But she wouldn't leave the South without seeing Laure again.

Laure clutched the letter to her bosom and let her tears flow unchecked. How much more misery could she and her family and friends bear? Andy had been like family. So much of the past had vanished—Luke, Leland, and now Andy were gone. *Poor Jessica*, she thought. *How she loved Andy, and how she must be suffering now, a suffering I know all about*. She would go to Jessica soon, Laure resolved, for one last visit with her old friend.

The man who sat opposite Ernest Medfors's desk in the Medfors Real Estate office on the main street of Montgomery was fifty, tall, and stout, but exuded an air of health and energy. His black hair was touched with gray, as were his neatly trimmed Vandyke beard and luxurious sideburns, which gave a distinguished look to his round face. His shifty eyes were gray and cunning, particularly when they narrowed. His mouth was fleshily sensual. He leaned forward, shrewdly eyeing the white-haired realtor. "I've looked over the Haskins property downriver, Mr. Medfors, and I think it has possibilities. I take it that you'll accept a binder of five hundred dollars on the land?"

"That will be quite satisfactory. Given the right stewardship, you should turn a handsome profit; it's extremely rich land with excellent irrigation from the river. The house on the property, though small, has been well maintained."

"Yes, I noticed it seemed to be in good condition. And the land will turn a profit for me, I'm sure. You know, Medfors, the secret of staying rich is to invest your money where it will bring you good returns."

"This is prime property, Mr. Weymore. Without trying to rush you into the transaction, I can assure you that I'll have no trouble selling it if you decide against it."

"What again is the asking price?"

"Twenty-five hundred. You're paying for river frontage—good, rich soil that hasn't been worked to death from cotton and tobacco."

James Weymore thoughtfully reached into his pocket for a thick black stogie, scratched the match on the side of the realtor's desk, and lit it, puffing vigorously until he could draw satisfactorily on it. Then, exhaling a wreath of acrid smoke, which made the old man grimace and push his chair back from his desk, Weymore reached into his lapel pocket and drew out a thick wallet. "In that case, might as well get the whole thing over and done with so there won't be another buyer. Five hundred will suffice to hold the property, I think you said?"

"That's correct, Mr. Weymore."

"Here you are, then," Weymore said. "I don't want any loose ends, Medfors. I'm leaving the details to you."

Ernest Medfors took the cash, counted it, then nodded. "I'll have the title drawn up, Mr. Weymore. That will take four to six weeks."

"Right, but I want to get hold of the land quickly. I

haven't yet decided where I'll make my home, but Alabama doesn't seem to have been much touched by the war.''

"That's true. In the last days of the war, the Montgomery mayor surrendered before the city could be destroyed. The people of Alabama—with the exception of Selma, which of course was burned—were very lucky.''

James Weymore rose, took another puff on his cigar, and exhaled the strong-smelling smoke at the realtor. "I'll amble along and see what Montgomery is like.''

"My assistant will write a receipt for you.'' The realtor stood and held out his hand. "Mr. Weymore, I admire a man who makes quick decisions. You've made no mistake in this one, I can guarantee it.''

"Ha! I'll hold you to that if anything does go wrong, Medfors. I'll be back.''

"Good day, sir.''

Without even bothering to shake the realtor's hand, Weymore strode out and walked down the street. He was wearing a silk top hat, unusual in the September heat. But it befitted his overbearing personality and the aura of wealth that he adopted to impress those whom he met.

He walked slowly, stopping now and then to adjust the stogie in his mouth, sometimes removing it to blow out a series of rings. There were not too many people on the main street, but Weymore was not interested in the populace. He had his eye out only for female company, especially the less straitlaced variety. In his opinion, women were made for a man's use, and he was a man who knew how to take all and give as little as possible. But when he wished, he could be charming and suave, particularly to a woman who aroused his carnal desire. The concepts of constancy and love, however, were entirely alien to him.

He had nearly finished his cigar by now, and he threw it down and crushed it underfoot on the pavement with a vicious twist of his sole, promptly lighting another.

He had recently come from Birmingham, where he had thought to do business with a land speculator. But the man had wanted too much capital without enough collateral, so Weymore had come to Montgomery. En route, he had read in the newspaper that Leland Kenniston, the famed entrepreneur, had died. And when he had met Ernest Medfors to inquire about available properties, the realtor had revealed that this particular piece of Haskins property was not far from Windhaven Plantation, the home of Kenniston's widow.

His face brightened, remembering this. Now that he had acquired the arable land near that magnificent estate, it should be easy to persuade the Kenniston woman to sell her property to him. She would, of course, be in straitened circumstances. Besides, if the picture in the paper did her any justice, she would not be a bad acquisition in her own right.

It was highly unlikely that anyone in Alabama would know he was not a widower, that his wife had, in fact, left him. He had been careful to spread the news, even to loungers at the hotels in Birmingham and Montgomery, that his wife had died about five years before from "river fever," a disease that covered just about everything except death by violence. In the South one had only to mention river fever and people would sigh and nod sympathetically and then relate similar cases from their own families.

Getting the Haskins property was the first step in a new campaign that would be both interesting and profitable. And he needed nothing more than that in his life—along with a nice-looking woman now and then to while away the long hours of the night.

On Wednesday, September 19, Lucien Bouchard had been invited to dine at the home of a prominent Montgomery family, the Marksons—an invitation that had in reality been procured for him by his genial employer. A week before, Nils Sonderman had received a commission to build a stately mansion for Carl Markson and his wife, Genevieve. Sonderman had shown Lucien a drawing for the proposed building. Much to the architect's pleasure, Lucien had suggested the construction of a greenhouse, which would provide fresh fruit and vegetables year round for the family. Lucien had shown how the greenhouse could be situated so that one could enter it either from the outside or through the food-storage area adjacent to the kitchen. The greenhouse would extend along the south wall of the house and would therefore get plenty of sun. This simple but adroit contribution to the plan had impressed Sonderman, who had profusely praised his apprentice. When Nils had gone to the Marksons' present residence on one of the exclusive streets of Montgomery and had shown them the drawing, Carl Markson had been most enthusiastic about the greenhouse. "Please come for dinner so that my wife and I can discuss the plans with you in a more relaxed manner," Markson had smilingly averred.

"You're very kind, Mr. Markson. But in all fairness, it was my young apprentice, Mr. Lucien Bouchard, who suggested the addition of the greenhouse. He deserves the credit."

"You're a man of integrity. Bring Mr. Bouchard," Markson had answered. "Bouchard—is he related to the Bouchards of Windhaven Plantation?"

Nils had nodded. "He's the eldest son of the current

owner, Laure Bouchard Kenniston, who was recently widowed. I should be most happy to convey your invitation. I know he'll be delighted."

Carl and Genevieve Markson had been married twenty-five years. They had an extremely attractive daughter, Angela, now nineteen. The Marksons were quite concerned with finding her a suitable husband. They believed in marriage for love—their own union had been sterling proof of the happiness that comes from love—not merely financial or social advantage. As a result, they were eager to find a young man who not only met every social and financial requirement, but also sincerely loved Angela and was loved by her in return.

Doubtless, this was why Carl Markson mentioned to his wife that they would have the architect's apprentice, Lucien Bouchard, as a guest for dinner. "You know the Bouchard name," Markson said to his wife. "The most honorable one in the entire area, with an impressive history to it."

"And you think that this young man might be a potential husband for our Angela?"

The pleasant-featured, gray-haired man's blue eyes twinkled. "It's quite possible. We'll wait and see. My dear," he said as he draped his arms over his wife's shoulders, "I'll wager you have forgotten that Wednesday night marks our anniversary."

"You silly!" his wife playfully teased as she kissed her husband on the cheek. "I was waiting to see if *you* would remember. You completely forgot our third anniversary, and I had to take you to task! You dazzled me with that wonderful silver bracelet, which I still cherish."

"I remember," Markson chuckled as he hugged his wife. "This time I haven't forgotten, and there's something even nicer."

*　　*　　*

"Mr. Bouchard, this is our daughter, Angela."

"I'm very pleased to meet you, Miss Markson," Lucien said respectfully. Angela had already held out her hand, and self-consciously flushing, Lucien took it.

Angela Markson was indeed stunning. Of slightly more than medium height, she had long red hair styled in a sophisticated chignon. Her face was a classic cameolike oval, with large dark-brown eyes, a dainty nose, and an enticingly ripe mouth. She wore a blue silk frock, demure and fully cut but revealing nonetheless the voluptuous contours of her hips and thighs. Her creamy skin was embellished with exquisite rosy tones, and her voice had a kind of hushed expectancy, which those young men who had met her found devastatingly exciting with its hinted promise of erotic joy.

"A pleasure, I'm sure," she murmured throatily, giving Lucien a long look from under fluttering, thick eyelashes.

Lucien swallowed and tried not to stare. Carl Markson, smiling to himself—for he was all too familiar with the effect his daughter had upon young men—came to Lucien's rescue and, holding out his hand, exclaimed, "Mr. Sonderman tells me you're the genius who suggested the greenhouse. Genevieve and I fell in love with it. Such an idea does you credit, young man."

"You're too kind, Mr. Markson. I'm just a novice," Lucien protested modestly.

"Novice or not, it suited our fancy to a T. And Sonderman is already quite pleased with you," Markson responded jovially.

"I am indeed." Nils chuckled as he patted Lucien on the back. "I'll say also that it's most refreshing to find an enlightened client who is so enthusiastic about our humble efforts." Lucien blushed again, for being considered a part of the architect's firm was high praise.

A pretty octoroon maid entered the living room to announce dinner.

Genevieve Markson at once graciously declared, "Mr. Sonderman, Mr. Bouchard, this way to the dining room."

Carl Markson enjoyed the little luxuries of personalized service. It delighted him that the cook took particular pains in preparing an elegant repast this evening, the twenty-fifth anniversary of his marriage to Genevieve. The octoroon maid served a preliminary entrée of red snapper and then a tenderloin of beef, which their Haitian cook had prepared with mushrooms and a thick bordelaise sauce. There was sweet corn, okra, snap beans, and black-eyed peas, as well as a tossed salad. For dessert, the cook had made an impeccable blancmange, with an accompaniment of strong coffee and a bowl of fresh fruit, raisins, and nuts and cheeses, together with an apricot liqueur. Nils, who as a youth had dined in some of Europe's finest restaurants, enthusiastically praised the cook, who was induced to come out to hear these plaudits.

After the dishes were cleared, Markson turned to his wife and took out of his pocket a velvet case, which he handed to her along with a folded sheet of paper. Genevieve's eyes widened as she opened the case. Inside was a silver necklace, whose thin links showed the most exquisite filigree work, and from it hung a magnificent cabochon ruby. "Oh, my darling! It's absolutely breathtaking! Thank you, Carl!"

He rose and, going behind her, placed it around her slim throat and locked the clasp. "But you haven't looked at the other gift, my darling," he told her softly.

Genevieve unfolded the paper. It was a ballad Carl himself had composed, commemorating their years of happiness together. After she had read it, she blushed and looked tenderly at her husband. "I shall never forget tonight, dear Carl.'' And then, blushing again, she turned to her guests and apologized. ''Please forgive my neglecting you, but my husband has just enchanted me.''

''As you've enchanted me for all these twenty-five years—and will for many more to come, God willing,'' Markson swiftly replied.

All the while, Angela was sending Lucien covert glances, and when she finally caught his gaze, she favored him with a dazzling smile, which made him flush and nervously look down at his plate.

Genevieve observed this and caught her husband's eye with a meaningful gesture, so that he also could observe Angela's attention to the handsome—and socially acceptable—young man.

Chapter 11

The same day that James Weymore had put a binder on the Haskins property, Carla Bouchard, eldest grandchild of Luke Bouchard and now a resident of Paris, had opened an exhibit of her Impressionistic paintings in a small but extremely popular gallery near Montmartre, owned by Giles Vertrier.

As sundown approached, the Vertrier gallery was still crowded. The weather had been superb, without the slightest hint of rain, and thick white clouds majestically and slowly moved across the dazzling blue sky.

Not far from the gallery was a little bistro with outdoor tables under a canopy. Sitting by himself at one of the tables was a wiry man in his early fifties, with high-set cheekbones and a short, neatly trimmed beard. He was sipping a glass of Chablis and, with his other hand, reaching for a bit of Brie, which he spread upon a small piece of black bread. He observed the well-dressed men and women emerging from the nearby gallery and told himself that when he had finished his predinner repast, he must visit it. So popular an exhibit must mean an excellent collection.

A waiter in black coat and white apron approached and asked him in French, "How does M'sieu Courvalier find the Chablis?"

Henri Courvalier nibbled the edge of the black bread

to clear his palate, then sipped from his glass with the air of a connoisseur. He pursed his lips, narrowed his eyes, and then pronounced, "Good, but not great. A great Chablis is rare, indeed."

"Our little bistro has been honored to have you as our guest during the past week, M'sieu Courvalier. Will you be staying much longer in Paris?"

"Perhaps." The bearded man shrugged. "Your *patron* is an old, dear friend of mine, as you know, Jacques. When he heard that my wife had died, he wrote me the most touching invitation. *Eh bien*"—again, he shrugged—"since her death, I have been lonely and bored with my vineyards, so I've come to Paris, eager to see what is new in the world of art and the theater and literature."

The waiter nodded solemnly.

"Tell me, Jacques, what do you know about the gallery down the street?"

"A gifted new painter—an American—has work on display. I have already been to the gallery, and I tell you, the artist has learned much from our great masters. Yet there is something unique in the paintings."

"Vous dites ça?" Courvalier's eyebrows arched. "I must certainly visit this gallery. *L'addition, s'il vous plaît*, Jacques." After paying his bill, Courvalier walked down the street toward the gallery.

Upon entering, he painstakingly made his way through the throng of people who were talking and sipping champagne, blocking his view of the paintings. At last he managed to find a relatively unoccupied corner of the gallery and, stepping back, contemplated one of the works on exhibition. It was an impressive view of a Paris street on a rainy day. There were puddles of water on the cobblestones, and at the end of the street, an old, spavined horse, its head mournfully drooping, pulled a cart driven by a stout man wearing a beret, rough work trousers, and a dirty shirt, taking a load of melons to market. Henri Courvalier put his hand to his beard and stroked it while he scrutinized the painting. It was exceptionally well done, obviously influenced by Monet, possibly even Degas, and yet this work was strongly and vividly stamped with the individual mark of the painter.

Now that he saw this painting, he was glad he had come. It was all very well to make good wine and sell it at a high profit, to be wealthy and to have a fine chateau with an estate in one of the most beautiful countrysides in France; but there must be more to life than that—and art and literature were a part of it.

He moved to a second painting, of a handsome young black-haired man on a couch near an open window, who was reading while a breeze fluttered the pages of another book on the table beside him. The patterns of the furniture and wallpaper were delicately detailed, yet there was a delicious haze to the whole that was in the best style of Monet and even Cézanne. Decidedly, whoever this painter was, he was articulate and talented.

Courvalier decided to obtain a program, and he looked around to find someone who might direct him. A lovely young brunette, her dark hair in an elaborate chignon with a row of tiny curls all along her high-arching forehead, was chatting with a man whom he estimated to be of his own age, nearly bald, wearing pince-nez and neat Vandyke beard. He edged his way toward the couple and then apologetically interposed, *"Pardonnez-moi,* mam'selle, m'sieu, could you tell me whose paintings I have been admiring?"

Giles Vertrier, the owner of the gallery, chuckled and turned to the vintner. "M'sieu, I am Giles Vertrier, owner of this gallery. May I introduce you to the creator of these works that you profess to admire. Mam'selle Carla Bouchard—and you, m'sieu?''

"*Enchanté*. I am Henri Courvalier. May I say, Mam'selle Bouchard, that I am taken by surprise. I surely did not expect the artist to be either a woman or so young.''

Carla's blue eyes narrowed, and she retorted rather snippily, "Am I to assume, M'sieu Courvalier, that you think it surprising for a woman to be capable of anything other than bearing children, tending a kitchen, and being, when all things are said and done, subordinate to the male?''

"*Mon Dieu!*'' he exclaimed, bursting into laughter. "I must confess myself crushed and entirely at your mercy, Mam'selle Bouchard! I hope I did not imply so rude a comment, but the talent, the mood, the feeling for color you show in these paintings, which I've only just observed, are those of a master.''

"And now you want to placate my feelings by paying me an extravagant compliment, is that it, M'sieu Courvalier?''

Again he chuckled. This young woman was not only attractive but had a mind of her own, and he admired the way she spoke French, though of course she could not be a native of La Belle France; the accent gave her away. "I throw myself on your mercy, mam'selle.''

"Mam'selle Bouchard is an American, M'sieu Courvalier,'' Vertrier explained in an attempt to turn the conversation to a less volatile topic.

"For an American, you speak our language beautifully, Mam'selle Bouchard,'' Courvalier proffered.

"That is a left-handed compliment, M'sieu Courvalier. I have been in Paris about two years now, and it is, shall we say, my spiritual home. Since I think and talk in French, I like to think that I do not reveal my background, which happened to be on a cattle ranch in Texas.''

"*Mais, c'est incroyable!*" he breathed. "I had best not say any more, for you are sinking all my ships at your first volley. However, I wonder if I may be allowed to purchase one of your paintings.''

"That is why they are on exhibit, M'sieu Courvalier,'' Carla said, a glacial tone to her voice. Her first impression was that Courvalier was somewhat patronizing.

"Well, then, there is one of a young man on a couch reading a book. I like the feel of it.''

"Yes, that's one of mine,'' Carla admitted with a momentary frown. "To be honest, M'sieu Courvalier, I haven't yet decided whether that one is really for sale.''

"I will offer you five thousand francs, Mam'selle Bouchard,'' the vintner declared.

Giles Vertrier uttered a stifled gasp and, turning to the lovely young brunette, exclaimed, "But that's fabulous, *ma chérie*! That's as much as a Degas or a Monet or a Manet will bring. My advice to you is to accept it.''

"You may be right, Giles,'' Carla reflected in a low voice. Indeed, this offer—worth about two thousand dollars in American money—could enable her to continue her work in Paris and live comfortably. It was important to remain in Paris, since Giles was making other sales for her and her name was beginning to appear in some of the art columns of the Parisian newspapers.

"Isn't that enough, Mam'selle Bouchard?'' Courvalier innocently asked.

"Oh, yes, it's most generous! I— Very well, M'sieu Courvalier, if you're truly sincere about wanting it, I will sell it to you at the price you offer,'' Carla declared impulsively.

"*Brava, ma chérie!*" The art gallery owner applauded. Then, turning to the vintner, he declared, "You've made an excellent choice, M'sieu Courvalier. One day this investment will bring you a very fine return. Mam'selle Bouchard, in my humble opinion, is destined for greatness."

"I quite believe it. Well, now, let me write you a bank draft, M'sieu Vertrier."

"Let us go into my office." He made a subtle gesture to a clerk and then pointed at the painting. "Carla, *ma chérie*, you'll excuse us?"

"Of course. Thank you very much, M'sieu Courvalier." Carla felt a slight bit of remorse at having initially treated this generous client so tactlessly. "Let me apologize if I offended you. Americans speak their minds. I still have to learn diplomacy."

"Do not distress yourself, Mam'selle Bouchard." Courvalier reached for Carla's hand and brought it to his lips with a cavalier gesture. "It is I who should apologize. Now that I have acquired what I consider to be a masterpiece—and having met its creator—I am happy indeed that I have come here to Paris. Now then, M'sieu Vertrier, let us conclude this transaction."

Once inside the owner's office, Courvalier took out a handsome pocket cigar case and offered it to Vertrier. "I have these sent to me at my vineyard, M'sieu Vertrier. Won't you join me as a celebration for my having met so charming a *demoiselle* and acquiring such a superb painting for my chateau?"

"I'd be pleased to, sir. My clerk is wrapping your purchase, and it will be here in a moment." Vertrier held the cigar with his lips as he lit a match. Courvalier leaned toward the gallery owner to accept a light, drew on his cigar, and nodded. "Mam'selle Bouchard is remarkable. She is, I'd guess, less than half my own age, and I find myself excited by her beauty——perhaps even a little more than her artistic ability. And she has a quick mind as well. *Vraiment*, these Americans intrigue me!"

Vertrier leaned back in his comfortable chair and puffed at his cigar, examining it critically. "A superb Havana, M'sieu Courvalier. Yes, Mam'selle Bouchard is a most unusual young woman. She has learned much from our great masters, but her work has also something of herself."

The gallery clerk entered with a package. "Ah, here is my painting now, and here, M'sieu Vertrier, is your check. I shall visit you again, for I wish to see more of the exhibit at a leisurely pace. Now I'm anxious to have this painting stored in my hotel vault."

"It is a pleasure to have done business with you, M'sieu Courvalier. What hotel are you staying at, if I might inquire?"

"At the Roi-Georges near the Tuileries," the vintner replied.

"*Merci*, M'sieu Courvalier. If you are staying in Paris for any length of time, I shall send you news of further exhibitions I plan to give. And I'll let you know of any other exhibitions of Mam'selle Bouchard's work. You might be interested in attending them."

"Decidedly. I am greatly interested in Mam'selle Bouchard."

Giles Vertrier rose from his desk and smiled. "If I were not her agent, M'sieu Courvalier, I should also be interested in Mam'selle Bouchard, but I must tell you that she has *un amant* and is faithful to him. Speaking paternally, since that is my only role with her, I must add that she is a sensitive, gifted, and very impressionable young woman."

"I am not a Don Juan, M'sieu Vertrier. In fact, my

dear wife died a mere three months ago. It was loneliness that brought me to Paris, but I am not seeking the contemptible forgetfulness that taking one *maîtresse* after another provides for a man.'' Henri Courvalier's voice and face were serious

"I like you, M'sieu Courvalier." The art dealer extended his hand, which the vintner shook.

"Thank you. And if you should ever come to Bordeaux, I wish you to be my guest and to enjoy some of my best vintages. *À bientôt!*''

The young man with unruly black hair and short, wiry beard turned to stare at Henri Courvalier as the vintner left the art gallery with the wrapped painting tucked under his arm. He muttered something to himself and then strode angrily toward Giles Vertrier's office just as the proprietor was emerging. "Who was that man? Did you sell him *The Study of Poetry*?'' he demanded.

"He is a vintner from Bordeaux named Henri Courvalier, to answer your first question. Now, as to the second, yes, I sold him *The Study of Poetry*, and for five thousand francs.''

"Diantre!" James Turner swore, his handsome face twisted in a scowl. "How could you sell that one? Carla promised not to sell it. I modeled for it!''

"Of course you did. But may I remind you, M'sieu Turner, that five thousand francs will enable Mam'selle Bouchard to live quite comfortably in Paris while she continues to paint? She herself consented to the sale.''

"Very well. It's done now, but I'll have words with her.''

"Mon ami, you should be happy for your lady friend.''

"As you are, I am sure. After all, you just made yourself a very handsome commission. I bid you good evening, M'sieu Vertrier!'' The young man turned on his heel and strode back into the salon. He scowled again when he saw that his brunette sweetheart was being engaged in conversation by two elderly women and, clenching his fists, stood off to one side to wait until they had moved on. The moment Carla was alone, he came toward her. ''What the devil do you mean by selling *The Study of Poetry*, Carla? Didn't I tell you I wanted to keep that? I was the model, and it showed my atelier. To sell such a painting shows that you have no heart.''

''Now just a moment, James.'' Carla was nettled, and her eyes darkened with anger. ''Did Giles tell you what M'sieu Courvalier paid for the painting?''

''Of course he did, and I've already calculated his commission. That's crass and mercenary of you, Carla.''

''Is it? I should think you'd be happy to share this wonderful sale with me.''

''Well, I'm not.''

''In that case, I can only conclude that you're simply jealous.''

''Oh, yes, I saw that man talk to you, and I saw his fatuous look. You are very beautiful today—you always are—but don't forget he's an old goat at least twice your age.''

''Please keep your voice down, James. Other people are starting to—''

''To hell with them!'' he muttered. ''Just remember that I have genuine love and respect for you and share your artistic credo.''

''James, this is too ridiculous. You must put an end to these attacks of unwarranted jealousy! It's ruining us!''

''Pardon me, m'sieu,'' a wizened man with spectacles said as he elbowed his way past James. ''I wish to

meet this charming *artiste*. Mam'selle Bouchard, my
name is Charles Duroyer. I wanted to tell you how
much I enjoy your work and that I already have two of
your still lifes in my apartment.''

"You're very kind, M'sieu Duroyer. Thank you so
much.''

The elderly man reached for Carla's hand, brought it
to his lips, then thanked her again and walked away.
James Turner watched him with a sneer on his handsome face, then turned back to his beautiful young
mistress. "Just as I thought! An old fool makes a fuss
over you and you're swept off your feet.''

"That will do, James. I don't want to hear another
word on the subject. Now you're not only being ridiculous but insulting.''

"If that's how you feel, maybe we should go our
own ways. This seems an ideal time for a visit to see
my family in Minnesota.''

"That's the first sensible thing you've said today,''
Carla airily told him, her eyebrows arching. "A vaca-
tion will be very good for both of us.''

"So be it. There's no guarantee I'll feel the same
toward you when I come back, Carla.''

"Well, then, maybe you should marry some sweet
little obedient farm girl who will say, 'Yes, James
darling,' to every statement you make. It will be good
for your ego.''

"Damn you! You're a heartless bitch!'' His face
black as a thundercloud with rage, James turned his
back on Carla and stalked out of the gallery.

After the exhibit, Giles Vertrier took Carla to a private party in her honor, so it was midnight when she
returned to the atelier she shared with James Turner.
When she entered, she found that he had already packed
his personal belongings—as well as the twenty-some

paintings he had kept there—and had gone. On the table was a note addressed to her:

Carla,

It has been wonderful with you, but I resent the way you acted this afternoon at Vertrier's. By selling that painting, which was a testimonial to our love and our life together, you violated our relationship. I shall take the train to Le Havre in the morning and go back home. When you're ready to make amends, write me in care of my parents. Their address is on the desk. I still love you, though you may not believe it.

James

Carla stood staring out the window as she crumpled the note in her hand. She tried to analyze her feelings. Although her first reaction was one of hurt at his unjust accusation, she discovered that she was not shattered and despairing. Perhaps, then, their love affair had only been a kind of hedonistic adventure. If he thought that she would apologize to him, he would certainly have to wait a long, long time! James Turner was not the partner with whom she intended to share her life. She was grateful to have learned this when she did.

She straightened, her lips tightening. The money she had just earned would add to her independence and allow her to develop her skill. She felt exhilarated. Among the guests at the party had been two of the leading art critics of the Parisian papers, and they had been sincerely adulatory. If she could achieve such acclaim at this early age, what might she not do in the years ahead?

* * *

On Friday, September 21, Carla went back to visit Giles Vertrier. In the interim, she had made preliminary sketches from memory for a painting of the gallery itself, showing the portraits on the walls and the varied groups of visitors—herself among them as she talked with the vintner who had purchased her painting. When the art dealer caught sight of the sketch, he said, "Mam'selle Bouchard, I see you've been at work. I couldn't have recommended better therapy."

"And why do you say that, Giles?" she smilingly queried.

"It seems that M'sieu Turner has left our beautiful Paris in a fit of pique. Oh, yes, he came to me the morning after your quarrel and told me his plans. I see you've survived the lovers' tiff."

"It's not a 'tiff,' Giles. I don't like jealousy in a man, and he had been acting like a spoiled child."

"I agree with you wholeheartedly. Now let's see this. . . . Ah, I like it very much, the way you contrast the people. I can almost recognize some of them! Oh ho, I see you've captured M'sieu Courvalier reasonably well."

"You needn't look so smug, Giles." Again Carla smiled. "My including him means nothing at all—except that he *is* a striking man, and after all, his generous purchase is an investment in my staying to work with you."

"Excellent! I had hoped it would be. I'd had the fear that you might give up all for love and go back to the United States to marry M'sieu Turner."

"The fact is, Giles, if he hadn't had that flaw in his character, I was hoping that one day we might be married."

"Well, my dear, since you've already expressed your feelings about M'sieu Turner, I'm going to be an old gossip and tell you something you may not have heard. M'sieu Turner didn't leave alone for les *États-Unis*. A certain Melisande Raboutier accompanied him.''

Carla was startled at this unexpected piece of news, and her eyes widened incredulously. "I've never heard of her," she said at last.

"M'sieu Turner didn't mean for you to. Because I sold his paintings as well as yours, I learned of his affair. He's known the charming Melisande—a sculptress, and a very poor one, I might add, but who does have rich parents in Normandy—for the past two months. And I think that her parents' wealth has begun to interest him. As you know, in France the family of the bride provides a substantial dowry."

"Giles, I'm glad you told me. At first I had some second thoughts about my break with James, but now I'm not sorry at all. I can't believe he'd be so cruel! Well, now I can really get down to my work."

The art dealer chuckled. "And now I can bring you another piece of news. M'sieu Courvalier came in again yesterday at noon and discreetly—mind you, *very* discreetly!—asked if I would be kind enough to put you in touch with him. He would like very much to take you to lunch and to discuss a commission for another painting. You see, *ma chérie*, he would like a painting of his chateau in Bordeaux."

"How encouraging to be considered for such a commission! Thank you, Giles. This news is just what I need! Give him my address and tell him that I would welcome his calling upon me at his leisure."

"*C'est entendu.*"

Chapter 12

On the last Tuesday in September, Henri Courvalier sent a liveried porter from the elegant hotel at which he was staying to Carla's atelier. He had handsomely tipped the man to deliver a note to Carla and also a bottle of his own excellent Bordeaux. When he had come to Paris, he had brought along two bottles of white and three of red to give to special friends and acquaintances. What he had sent with the porter was the very finest of all his vintages, aged four years and eminently mellow.

As it chanced, when the porter arrived, the lovely young brunette was working, developing into a full-sized canvas the sketch she had shown Giles Vertrier. Startled by the messenger, Carla opened the note. It was an invitation to lunch the next day at La Marmite, one of the great Parisian restaurants on the outskirts of the city. The note asked that she send a reply with the same messenger, who had been instructed to wait. With an air of excitement, she scribbled her own note that she would be happy to accept his gracious invitation.

Accordingly, Henri Courvalier called for her the next day in a hansom cab, which he had engaged for the afternoon. His suaveness and courteous demeanor impressed her, and he was adroit enough to let her do almost all the talking while they made the long, leisurely journey to the outlying restaurant. From his lively comments, she learned that he had a dry sense of humor and was quite knowledgeable about French politics and the differences in life in the provinces compared with that of Paris. Mainly, however, he questioned her about her background and her work. Consequently, she found herself revealing much more about her life than she had planned to. She felt entirely comfortable in his company, and the weather could not have been more ideal, so that the ride through the parks and along the boulevards of Paris under a blue sky and a bright sun made this a kind of festive occasion, exactly what she needed after James Turner's importunate behavior.

When they arrived at the restaurant, Courvalier turned to the hansom cab driver. "With your permission, I will have the proprietor send a *déjeuner* out to you."

"*Mais, m'sieu, ce n'est pas nécessaire—*" the driver began.

But the vintner held up his hand and interposed, "But I wish to do it, *mon ami*. It will give me pleasure."

"That was very nice, M'sieu Courvalier," Carla observed as he led her into the foyer of the beautifully furnished restaurant. It was modeled like a private home, with two dining rooms separated by a large wall and a narrow doorway. There were luxuriously upholstered velvet armchairs, paintings on the walls, and a thick red carpet. The murmur of voices was subdued, and those already at the tables were obviously enjoying their repasts. The maître d' ushered Henri Courvalier and his lovely young guest to a table beside a window, where they could look out onto the rolling countryside, a flower garden, and the stately trees on the perimeter of the estate. "How beautiful!" Carla exclaimed.

"I thought you might like it, Mam'selle Bouchard. I am proud to say that this excellent restaurant stocks my Bordeaux, though that is not at all the reason I chose it for our luncheon. The cuisine here is impeccable, imaginative, and served with joy and intelligence—rare attributes in a popular restaurant. Now, here is the menu," her host said as he handed it to her. "They are famous for coquilles St. Jacques and cassoulet Toulousain.

"And since the day is warm, we'll have a white Bordeaux—though if you prefer the heavier Burgundy, you would not be wrong. The cassoulet is robust enough to deserve a full-bodied wine."

"You are a most delightful host, M'sieu Courvalier." Carla could not help laughing in high good humor. "But since I wish to treasure the red Bordeaux you so graciously sent me yesterday and enjoy it when I am by myself and in need of sustenance while I am working out a detail in my painting, let it be your white Bordeaux that I drink this afternoon."

He proceeded to order an exceptional luncheon, very likely the finest meal that Carla had had in Paris.

"Do you intend to remain in Paris, Mam'selle Bouchard?" he said as cordials were being served.

"Yes. To a large extent, M'sieu Courvalier, I owe that decision to you for having bought my painting."

"When I entered the gallery and saw that painting of yours, Mam'selle Bouchard, it struck me that I must have it and that it deserved a premium price."

"I'm extremely grateful."

"No, no, Mam'selle Bouchard, you mustn't be. You deserve it. My feeling is that if you remain here in Paris, you will go even farther and there will be recognition for you and others of the school with which you are affiliated. I have some little influence in my own countryside of Bordeaux, and I should like very much to arrange an exhibit of your work before winter sets in."

"You're most kind!"

"Have you ever been outside of Paris since you came to France?" He eyed her intently.

"No, M'sieu Courvalier. I've wished to go on tours to Provence and Auvergne and the Basque country."

The vintner patted his mouth delicately with his napkin and then, after a moment's thought, pursued, "You might be inspired by the landscapes in the countryside, Mam'selle Bouchard."

"You're quite right about that!" she avowed enthusiastically.

"In that case I have a proposition to make. I hope you will not think me bold in suggesting this, but I would be honored if you would accompany me to my chateau for the weekend to determine whether you will accept a commission to paint my home. Be assured, I have an elderly housekeeper who will chaperon us."

Carla tilted her head and laughed wholeheartedly. By mentioning a chaperone, he had convinced Carla that he was not simply luring her to his home in order to seduce her. On the contrary, he genuinely admired her talent. "I'll accept your invitation, M'sieu Courvalier. I very much would like to see your chateau. Perhaps I might also see how you make your superb wine—it really is superb, you know."

"I will send you home with a case of white and a case of red," he laughingly told her as he beckoned to their waiter for the check.

Carla excused herself for a moment, and Courvalier stared after her and smiled. He had never before met a young woman like her. He told himself that he would be a liar if he were to claim that he had no physical attraction to her, yet he determined in no way to show any forwardness, which might alarm her.

All the same, he was glad to hear that she intended to remain in Paris, for he wished to further their acquaintance. He had loved and respected his wife, but he could not forever remain a slave to her memory. When a man reaches his fifties, he begins to hope that there may be one unforgettable adventure to brighten the coming dark days, the inevitable finale of life.

Henri Courvalier's estate was situated a few miles south of the town of Pessac in the bucolic region of the Gironde, near the Garonne River. It was about three hundred miles from Paris, and Henri had booked a first-class compartment on the train for Carla and himself. He had sent a wire on to his majordomo to prepare the chateau for a visitor of distinction and to inform the cook that he would be expected to create culinary masterpieces throughout the weekend for the delectation of his guest. They arrived at the Bordeaux station an hour before sunset, and the vintner's coachman awaited them, driving a cabriolet drawn by a spirited mare.

The railway journey had been a revelation to Carla, and she had frequently taken out her sketch pad and drawn the steward and conductor and, when the train had stopped at a station, a distant cottage surrounded with trees. Courvalier silently watched her and appeared to be enjoying himself. For her part, Carla appreciated his ability to keep silent when she was sketching. His gracious behavior was so diametrically opposed to James Turner's that Carla felt fortunate to have met a genial man of wit who shared her interest in painting.

As the coachman directed the cabriolet into the winding road that led to Courvalier's chateau, she gasped at its picturesque beauty. He explained that his parents had built it and bequeathed it to him. Perched atop a small hill, it overlooked the rolling valley beyond. With dusk having arrived, the lights had been lit inside, emitting an enticing glow through the thinly veiled windows, making the chateau seem a magic castle within whose walls awaited adventure. It was built in Gothic style, with turrets and one large tower—much like a cathedral's—to the west, though more severe than the red-brick chateau of Windhaven Plantation. The doorway was crowned by a majestic arch. A man in red livery and a gray-haired woman, her arms folded over her black, high-necked dress, stood before it, awaiting their employer and his guest.

"I wired my majordomo, Albert, and my housekeeper, Madame Thierson, to have everything prepared in advance. I warn you, Mam'selle Bouchard, we are in for a sumptuous dinner. Last year I engaged one of Paris's finest chefs. I have instructed him to surpass himself tonight."

"The train ride and journey through your beautiful countryside have given me an enormous appetite," Carla said happily.

"I am glad you find this region to your liking. Your pleasure, if you'll permit my presumption, Mam'selle Bouchard, is of the utmost importance to me."

Carla could not help blushing and feeling agreeably unnerved by this direct compliment, so candid and spontaneous. "Thank you, M'sieu Courvalier."

When the cabriolet halted in front of the chateau, the majordomo, very grave and ceremonious, came forward to take her valise, and then he bowed low to her. Henri Courvalier introduced her to him and the housekeeper, who welcomed her to the chateau in a stiffly formal manner. Carla could not help smiling and, when the woman was out of earshot, whispered, "I don't think she approves of me, M'sieu Courvalier."

"That is her way. It was her way even with my wife. She has been with my family some forty years and still looks upon me as a little boy."

Carla was lost in admiration as he escorted her though the reception salon, appointed with magnificent tapestries and furniture. The majordomo led them to an enormous bedroom suite. "There is an adjoining bath, mam'selle, where you may freshen up. Dinner will be served within an hour—if that is convenient?"

"Yes, that's fine, thank you," Carla said.

Henri laughed, remembering how hungry Carla had said she was. "One of the joys of living—although this axiom is meager sustenance," he philosophized, "is that the pleasure of anticipation is often even more intense than that of realization."

"I must remember that," she said wryly.

"I will instruct Albert to serve dinner in thirty minutes." He grinned, then took her hand and kissed it. "Thank you for coming. You have brightened this gloomy mansion, which has been in shadows since my poor wife's unexpected death. But, please, Mam'selle Bouchard, take that as a compliment and not as self-pity."

"I do not think you are guilty of that, M'sieu Courvalier."

The vintner bowed and then turned away to follow the majordomo and give the staff instructions for the dinner to be served.

It had been a dinner worthy of remembrance, and Carla had done full justice to it. The cook had prepared cherry-glazed mallard ducks, succulently tender, with *petits pois*, cauliflower, and fine French beans.

The dessert was trifle with fresh raspberries and blackberries. Carla unabashedly asked for a second portion, and her host signaled Albert to bring it to her. When she protested that the serving was far too big, Henri laughingly responded, "What you cannot eat, I shall finish. A meal like this is to be enjoyed without recrimination or regret—like a love affair.''

Carla gave him a sidelong glance at his strange comment, not knowing exactly why he had said it. What Henri had said was true. When she and James Turner had first become lovers, she had gloried in their relationship even though letters from her parents sometimes overshadowed that enjoyment with a brief bout with guilt. Yet it was all part and parcel of being the new liberated woman in modern Europe.

Next Albert served rich black coffee and huge snifters of a Martin cognac at least twenty years old. Henri was longing for a cigar but refrained. Carla, sensing that he would enjoy one after such a dinner, spoke up. "I love the aroma of good tobacco, M'sieu Courvalier. Do smoke your cigar—I'm sure you're longing to.''

"Thank you. You are most perceptive. I confess this is one of my little sins.'' He drew out a cigar, lit it, then leaned back with a sigh of sybaritic pleasure. "I hope that my cook has pleased you tonight.''

"It was really marvelous! I'm ever so grateful to you for inviting me here. I think I needed this interlude.''

"Because of something that happened to you?'' he tactfully queried.

She nodded, her eyes suddenly downcast. Then, again with a flash of her newly won candor, she faced him and said rather airily, "Yes, because I parted with M'sieu Turner, the artist with whom I was sharing an atelier. He was the model in the painting you bought, and he behaved like a jealous little boy when I allowed it to be sold. I couldn't tolerate it. The way you've brought me here and let me sketch without saying a word, this dinner and the way you've treated me—well, I should say it has all been a wonderful cure for the temporary unhappiness I had from that business. And I *do* want to accept your offer of painting your lovely home.''

"I'm very glad. I'll do everything in my power to help you with your painting. You'll be completely undisturbed as you work.''

"I would like to start tomorrow morning if the sun is as clear and bright as it was today, M'sieu Courvalier.''

"I should like it very much if you would call me Henri.''

"Only if you call me Carla.''

"Entendu!" He laughed and held out his hand to her. She took it and shook it, and their eyes met.

She went back to her room, where her valise had been unpacked by one of the staff. Picking up her sketch pad, she seated herself by the window, pulled back the draperies, and looked out on the moonlit valley. It was so peaceful, so beautiful, a refreshing contrast to Paris's noisy, frenetic excitement. She felt at peace and knew this was because the worrisome denouement of her love affair was behind her. There would never be any reconciliation between her and James, but she found that it really did not matter so very much.

She began to sketch and became absorbed in the moon-touched landscape. There was magic here in this countryside. How many city dwellers never saw such marvels! And, ironically, many who lived in the countryside took such natural beauty for granted.

At last she put down her sketch pad and undressed to her chemise and hose and shoes, then put on the blue silk robe she had purchased on an extravagant impulse when Giles Vertrier had sold three paintings for her. James had found her stunning in it, setting off as it did her dark hair and warm, creamy skin. She stared in the mirror, scrutinizing herself. Yes, she was desirable, young, lovely. Certainly she could give great delight to the right man and share with him all those pleasures of which the poets romanticized. One thing was certain. It was not enough to be done with James Turner; she must forget him totally, for she was sure that he had forgotten her, with his other lady friend in his company. She grimaced at the recollection.

She kicked off her shoes, lay down on her bed, and closed her eyes, but could not sleep. She remembered her arguments with her brother, Hugo, when they had been in Chicago together to study, she at the Art Institute, he at Rush Medical College. How he had teased her about wanting to paint, calling it a frivolous pastime. She made a note to herself that, when she returned to Paris, she must send Cecily and him a long letter and enclose some of the enthusiastic reviews from the newspapers, which ought to convince even Hugo that she had finally found her true metier.

Her thoughts turned to Henri, a man she found so sophisticated, so considerate, so attractive. A shiver traversed her spine as she recognized her desire for him and how easy it would be to satisfy that desire. She had only to go to him—it would be her choice entirely. The thought of such freedom and control thrilled her almost as much as the thought of Henri himself.

She did not know how long she had lain there thinking, but suddenly she knew that she would not sleep this night. She rose from her bed, buttoned the robe out of modesty, put on her slippers, and then quietly left her room. When the majordomo had brought her valise, she had casually asked him where M'sieu Courvalier slept; it had occurred to her that if his suite were beside hers, his gracious behavior might have been only a foil for his true intentions. But the majordomo had said that his bedroom was the last room in the opposite wing.

The chateau was silent now. The tapers had been extinguished, and it was very dark. As she tiptoed down the long, wide hallway, her heart began to beat more quickly. She was now mistress of herself and of her own destiny.

She reached the door of the master bedroom, hesitated a moment, and then, taking a deep breath, gently knocked.

"Entrez, donc!" he called.

She turned the knob and entered. Henri was in his robe, seated at his desk. He turned, his eyes widened with surprise, and he swiftly rose. "Carla! Is anything wrong?"

"No. I wanted to see you. I—I wanted to tell you how much—how much I like you."

Even as she spoke, she had closed the door behind her very quietly, lest any servant hear.

He stood a moment, his face stricken with incredulity, and then he came toward her. *"Ma chérie, ma belle Carla!"* he sighed. He put his hands on her shoulders and very gently kissed her on the lips.

Her arms rose to embrace him, and she gave him her mouth. It was a long and passionate kiss, yet in it she perceived a tenderness and almost grateful humility.

"My beautiful one—but you mustn't feel—" he began.

She put her forefinger to his lips. "Don't talk, Henri. Love me."

Henri accompanied her back to Paris on Sunday afternoon, for he wished to visit some of the wholesalers who distributed his wines. On the train, she discussed with him the possibility of returning to the United States for a visit to her brother and his wife, Hugo and Cecily, and then to her parents.

"But if you leave Paris now," he said, "it may

interfere with your career. If you go to the States for even as little as three or four months, the critics will look for new celebrities to acclaim. You are a force to be reckoned with and must stay, *chérie*.''

''You're right, dear Henri,'' she had told him. ''And I do love Paris so, especially while you are here. Please, my darling, don't spend all your time visiting wholesalers. Save an evening for me.''

The ardent look he had given her and his soft laugh as she squeezed his hand had told her that she had made no mistake in judging the worthiness of this new friend and thrilling lover.

Chapter 13

$\mathcal{I}$t was a crisp, bright Monday in October, and Carla's brother, Hugo Bouchard, and his lovely wife, Cecily, were enjoying a free afternoon. The young couple, who had met in Chicago while attending Rush Medical College, would celebrate their second anniversary this month in their new home. Although they were only twenty-two, they had already earned reputations as dedicated and gifted medical practitioners here in Wyoming Territory.

Hugo, who had grown up on Windhaven Range, a communal ranch in Texas, had fallen in love with Cecily because of her honesty and intelligence, but she was also unusually attractive, with expressive dark-brown eyes and an exquisite heart-shaped face.

Earlier this morning, Hugo had gone into Cheyenne for some supplies. He had also picked up the mail, including Carla's letter from Paris. He and Cecily had finished the letter, then had read the newspaper clippings reviewing her exhibit. Hugo said philosophically, "Carla is finally settling down. I think her break with Turner is for the best. I just wish she could marry someone wonderful and have all the happiness I've had with you while she continues her career."

"Thank you, my darling." Cecily wrinkled her snub nose at him. "What makes me happy is that your sister is finally standing up for herself and making her own decisions instead of letting that Turner fellow lead her around like an obedient sheep.''

"I see where your analogy comes from, honey,'' Hugo joked, reaching out and squeezing Cecily's slim hand. "I only hope one day you'll forget that I was born to a cattleman.''

"You've done a very good job of overcoming that hindrance, I'll say that, my dear,'' she replied in a mock-solemn tone, then wrinkled her nose again, prompting Hugo to rise from the table, bend over her, and kiss her most satisfactorily.

"Mmm, that was very nice. I'm glad that with our second anniversary approaching, the honeymoon isn't entirely over'' was her saucy reply.

"It won't ever be over, because I'm finding out wonderful new things about you every day, honey'' was his gallant answer.

"So long as you keep finding the right words to express your contentment, we'll get along just fine,'' Cecily concluded happily.

From the outset of their marriage, their only real bone of contention had been that Cecily considered Hugo biased against sheep ranchers—with whom she sympathized—since he was the son of a cattleman. But these differences had been resolved, partly because of their friendship with Maxwell Grantham, a Wyoming cattle rancher who was exceptionally tolerant of sheep ranchers.

Hugo had first met Grantham four years before on a cattle drive with his father, Lucien Edmond Bouchard, who had been selling some of his best stock to the tall, gray-haired rancher. A relative newcomer to the area, Grantham was a wealthy Easterner who had moved west after his wife left him. Since then he had become one of the most influential cattlemen in all of Wyoming. More impressive, Grantham had invested his profits generously by founding a hospital in Cheyenne and had inspired his friends to do likewise. Hugo and Cecily realized they could better serve their patients if they lived close to the hospital, and Grantham had helped them to find a new house just ten miles from his huge spread.

Her face sobering, Cecily now said to her husband, "Hugo, you just reminded me of something Mr. Grantham said. He told us that he intends to do all he can to promote peace between the cattlemen and the sheep ranchers. I think it's high time there was an organization in this territory to bring both sides together to air their grievances and avoid bloodshed. There's plenty of grazing land for both of them."

"That's true. Besides, the days of the big drives are just about over. With all the railroads being built, the cattle breeder doesn't have to risk long, dangerous drives. I guess that's what you call progress."

"Yes, but I think we should mention the idea of an organization to Mr. Grantham." She was interrupted by loud knocking on the door.

When she opened it, she found a cowhand nervously twisting his battered, dirty Stetson between his callused hands, anxiety written on his homely, weather-beaten face. "Good afternoon, Corey."

"To you too, ma'am—I mean, Doc. Wonder if you could come out. My boss, old Mr. Blaisedale, got himself throwed from his mustang, and he's feeling mighty poorly."

"Anything broken?"

"I don't think so, ma'am—Doc—but he's limping. He had the wind knocked out of him, and he feels sort of liverish, if you know what I mean."

"I'll come right away. Hugo, be a lamb and fetch my bag, please."

"I'll not be a lamb, but I'll fetch it." Hugo chuckled at his riposte, and Cecily burst into laughter.

On the evening of this same day, Maxine and Lucien Edmond Bouchard were dining together with Ramón and Mara Hernandez on Windhaven Range in Texas. The Bouchard and Hernandez children had already left the table to go to bed or to study their homework when Lucien Edmond poured brandy for the adults.

Maxine smiled at the children diligently doing their homework. "I wish Lucien Edmond and I could bring our children together for a reunion. They seem to be flung across the globe!"

"Yes, but at least we just received a letter from Carla," Lucien Edmond said, pulling an envelope from his pocket and handing several newspaper clippings from inside it to Ramón. "Just read these! We're quite proud of Carla."

He finished serving the brandy while the Hernandezes read the clippings, exclaiming over the praise that had been lavished on their niece by the Parisian critics. As he set down his brandy snifter, Lucien Edmond said, "What pleases me most is that she has ended her relationship with that Turner fellow. Maxine and I have always been afraid that she'd sully her reputation abroad by living with a man who was not her husband."

"That's wonderful news!" Maxine exclaimed. "I really thought at one time that you were going to go to Paris and bring her home."

Lucien Edmond smiled wryly. "You don't know how often I've been on the verge of doing just that."

"I had the same urge, Lucien Edmond," Maxine admitted. "But I've begun to understand Carla better.

There was nothing for her here in Texas. You can't blame her for wanting to make a life for herself. Now we can be proud of both our grown children.''

"Yes, indeed." Lucien Edmond lifted his brandy snifter to toast his wife, sister, and brother-in-law. "Just as Shakespeare himself might say, ' 'Tis a consummation devoutly to be wished.' ''

Autumn's chillier weather had come to Windhaven Plantation. The moderate rainfall precluded flooding, and the crops had brought in some much-needed revenue—though a comparatively modest amount when compared to the imposing debts that Laure Kenniston faced. Her greater concern, however, was the continued absence of her young son Paul. It was an anxiety-ridden time, and she spent much of it praying for his safe return.

She was comforted, to be sure, by Lucien's success. By this third week of October, he had made considerable progress on the splendid new house plans for the Marksons.

Carl Markson had told Nils Sonderman that no expense should be spared. Nils and Lucien had paid several visits to the Marksons to discuss details of contracting out the actual building of the house. Soon Nils engaged a supervisor to direct the building crew. By the middle of October, the foundation was being laid, and the contractor had promised Markson that he could plan to move into the house by February.

During these visits, attractive Angela Markson made a point of engaging Lucien in conversation and revealed her growing interest in him. Earlier in the week, she had urged her parents to invite Lucien to dinner by himself, so her father had sent a messenger to the architect's office with an invitation to Lucien from Mrs. Markson.

On this Friday evening, October 19, Lucien, in a suit and new cravat, presented himself at the door of the Markson house and was admitted by his gracious hostess. "Good evening, Mr. Bouchard! How very nice you look this evening!" she greeted him. "Do come in. Would you like a glass of sherry before we dine, Mr. Bouchard?"

"Oh, ah . . . thank you very much, that would be very nice," Lucien stammered. He had just caught sight of Angela, who had entered the salon in a shimmering violet silk frock. Her eyes brightened at the sight of him, and he felt his cheeks turn crimson. He cursed himself inwardly for being so susceptible to her beauty.

"How are you this evening, Mr. Bouchard? It's so nice to have you here! Mummy told me you were coming," Angela said coyly.

"I'm very happy to be here, Miss Markson."

"Please call me Angela—my good friends do, and I surely hope you want to be one of those!" Angela ignored a quick, disapproving glance from her mother.

The mulatto maid now entered, and Genevieve asked her to bring sherry for them all. Carl Markson entered a few moments later and jovially came up to Lucien and shook hands with him. "Glad you could come, Bouchard. It's always good to have a young man with such promise in one's home."

The maid appeared with a tray bearing four glasses filled with nut-brown sherry. Markson gestured to her to serve Lucien first. He lifted his glass to his host, hostess, and their daughter, then waited until the others had their glasses before sipping his. Carl and Genevieve exchanged a warm glance, for they found the young man's manners impeccable. A few minutes later, the maid entered to announce that dinner was served.

The Markson cook had prepared a baked ham with cloves, a sweet potato pie, a dish of mixed vegetables, and ears of sweet corn drenched with butter and salt, as well as a salad. Throughout the meal, Angela expressed her admiration of Lucien's skill as an architect. Several times her leg brushed provocatively against his under the table, and when Lucien looked up at her in surprise, she offered him the most suggestive smile he had ever seen. Indeed, often during the dinner when her parents weren't looking, Angela directed a lascivious wink at Lucien, as if to say that she desired him. These bold overtures were followed by coy, schoolgirlish talk, as if to deceive her parents.

Lucien reached for a glass of water, for Angela's feverish behavior had by this time completely overwhelmed him. He did not know exactly how to react to her overtures, so he remained silent.

As soon as dinner was over, Angela asked to be excused. Carl Markson turned to Lucien. "Play billiards, Bouchard?" he asked.

"I've played once or twice, yes, sir."

"Fine! Why don't you come with me into the library? We'll have some brandy and a game. Besides, I want to have a little chat with you. Genevieve, you'll excuse us?"

"Of course, Carl. Er—might I see you for a moment? Please excuse us, Mr. Bouchard."

"Of course, Mrs. Markson." Lucien inclined his head toward the handsome matron and then walked into the living room to wait for his host.

Genevieve approached her husband and, putting her hand on his shoulder, murmured, "What do you think? Angela certainly seems to like him. In fact, *I* think she went a little too far in her admiration for Mr. Bouchard, don't you?''

"Decidedly. But you know how she is, Genevieve. At least Lucien is a suitable candidate for marriage with our daughter.''

"True. I hope she doesn't scare him away. She's so headstrong and so . . . so physical.''

"I've been thinking the same thing. We ought to persuade her to marry him as soon as possible, before she puts her reputation in danger.''

"Then it's settled. You have a little talk with Mr. Bouchard. Let him know that we would welcome him as our son-in-law.''

"Your shot, Bouchard.'' Carl Markson stepped to one side as Lucien approached the billiard table. Lucien had begun the game and had run off a dozen successful shots before missing one. Markson had then had a run of twenty-six, finally missing on a particularly difficult angle shot.

Very slowly, Lucien chalked his cue, then bent to the table, squinting at the ball he meant to send into the far right-hand corner. He angled his shot off the far left edge of the table, waited in suspense as it bounded toward the ball he had marked, but flinched as it barely grazed the ball, edging it about four inches from its goal.

"Too bad! That was a very difficult shot, Bouchard. You play very well.''

"It's a game I enjoy. The concentration and geometry appeal to me.''

Markson paused as he approached the table for his own shot. "I'd like to say something personal, if I may.''

"Of course, sir.''

"I'm sure you've noticed by now that my daughter, Angela, seems to be quite smitten with you." Markson grinned sympathetically. "My daughter is . . . shall we say, romantically inclined and quite impressionable. But she seems to have a genuine liking for your company." Markson put down his cue and eyed the tall blond young man. "I want you to know that I haven't any objection to your courting my daughter. You understand that I wouldn't let her keep company with anyone who I didn't think had a promising future."

Lucien was both startled and flattered. It was conceivable that a lasting feeling might develop, and an alliance with a wealthy family could be of inestimable benefit to his mother and Windhaven Plantation. He strove to keep his face calm and his tone bland as he finally responded, "I'm happy to say that I like your daughter very much. I certainly look forward to seeing more of her."

"I'm delighted to hear it, my boy!" Markson clapped Lucien on the back and took an expensive Havana cigar from his pocket. "Here. Enjoy it. I'll have one too before we go on with our game."

"Thank you, sir."

"Let me light it for you. Well, young man, we'll see what will happen. Mind you, you're not to do anything foolish like eloping. My wife and I want to make a real spectacle of our daughter's wedding because Angela is our only child, and we love her very much."

"I wouldn't think of going against your wishes, sir," Lucien declared, wondering if Mr. Markson would have him marching down the aisle before the evening was over.

"Then it's settled. I expect to have you as a frequent guest so that you may proceed with your courtship. Rest assured, my boy, I want you both to be sure of each other so there are no mistakes."

"Of course, Mr. Markson. As you say, it's still very early. I've only just met your daughter."

Angela had gone to her mother's bedroom during the game of billiards and had explained that she had suddenly been stricken with a dreadful headache. If her mother didn't mind, she had said, she would go right to bed.

Genevieve, instantly solicitous, agreed that a good night's sleep would cure the headache. The older woman hesitated a moment. "Angela dear—you seem to like Mr. Bouchard a good deal."

"Oh, I do, Mummy!" Angela exclaimed with a beaming smile. "He's polite and nice, and he's awfully handsome and distinguished. You and Daddy like him, too, don't you?"

"Very much indeed. Now you go to bed, darling, and get your proper rest."

"I will, Mummy." Angela gave her mother a kiss, then retired.

Once in her room, Angela took one of the bolsters from her sofa and wrapped it in a sheet. She then inserted the wrapped bolster under her covers. Going to her dresser drawer, she took out a wig the exact color of her hair and placed it at the top of the wrapped bolster. Next, she drew the sheets and covers over the form so that it would look as if she were sleeping on her side. Her mother rarely looked in on her, but it was always good to be prepared.

Her eyes sparkled and her cheeks flushed with anticipation. She slowly opened the window and clambered out onto a wide ledge, then took pains to draw the window down to within two or three inches from the sill, for in the event that her mother came into her room to make sure that she was asleep and saw a fully opened window, she might close it. Angela swung herself into a tree by the corner of the ledge and climbed to the ground, where she hurried to the stable and led a gentle black mare out of her stall. "Henny, we're going to town again." She harnessed the horse to the family buggy, then clambered up, took the reins, and drove out of the stable.

Twenty minutes later, she turned the mare into a driveway leading to a stable at the back of a stately white-columned house on Mapleson Lane. She made the reins fast to the trunk of a giant oak near the stable and then, glancing up at the sky, stroked the mare's head. "You'll be all right here, Henny, girl. You be good, and I'll give you some sugar when we get back home." Glancing back at the deserted street, she tip-toed toward the rear of the house and knocked softly at the kitchen door.

A few moments later, a tall, brown-haired man in his early forties, with prominent sideburns and a curly beard, opened the door. He was bare-chested above his black slacks and slippers, and he held a half-smoked cigar.

"Jimmy honey, I'm so sorry I was late! I had to be on hand for a dinner Mummy and Daddy were giving for some business acquaintance!" Angela exclaimed in a honeyed tone.

"I understand, doll. Come in. Did anyone see you?"

"Thank goodness, no! Oh, honey, I've been just dying to see you."

He had crushed out his cigar in an ashtray on the kitchen counter and now took her into his arms. With a little sigh, Angela melted into his embrace, closing her eyes and responding passionately to his vigorous kiss. He stroked her sleek back and lowered his hands to her voluptuously rounded hips as she arched herself, like a cat, against him. "Oh, Jimmy, honey!" she breathed after the kiss. "What you do to me! You aren't mad at your Angie 'cause she was late, are you?"

"You're here now, doll, that's all that matters. Come on. I can't wait for you either," he said hoarsely as he led her into the bedroom.

Her eyes glazed over with lust as he led her toward the bed, his wiry fingers boldly cupping the high-perched globes of her breasts. "Oh, Jimmy . . . ." she moaned. "How I've waited to be with you." Her voice grew husky as her fingers unfastened the buttons on his trousers. Under them he wore nothing, and with a lewd laugh, Angela squeezed his aroused manhood. "My goodness," she purred, "is all that for poor little me?"

"You're the only honey-gal 'round the place, Angie. You ought to know that by now." He broke off his embrace, moved to the night table beside the huge four-poster, and poured from a cut-glass decanter into two hand-blown snifters. He shrugged on a dressing gown that was draped across the bed. "I've been hearing things about you, Angie doll."

Angela began to undress, moving slowly toward him, letting her elegant dress slide to the floor over her undulating hips, then swiftly slipped off the single petticoat beneath it till she was covered only by her lacy camisole, drawers, and stockings. "What, Jimmy lover?" she said in a sultry voice.

He handed her one of the snifters as his narrowed eyes examined every lush curve of her body. Then he quickly swallowed all of his brandy, unabashed that his dressing gown gaped to show his arousal. "I heard that a young man has been calling on you. You know I'm not the marrying kind, but I don't want anyone takin' you away from me either. In fact, I might just have to talk with your young man.''

"Silly boy,'' Angela cooed as, having taken a swallow of her brandy, she set the snifter down on the night table and pressed herself against her lover, closing her eyes and shivering at the pressure of his maleness against her loins. "Did I ever say anything about marryin'? But since you've brought the matter up"—her hands traveled down his broad body, caressing, teasing him—"you know that Papa and Mama don't exactly approve of my—my 'flirtatious nature,' as Mama calls it, and they'd like nothing better than to see me settled down like a respectable wife.''

Jimmy interrupted her with a snort. "Respectable?'' he murmured, taking his big hands from where they were pressed against her buttocks to reach out and slip the straps on her camisole from her shoulders. The silken garment slipped down to her waist, baring the magnificent globes of her ripe, dark-nippled bosom, and he began to fondle them lingeringly.

"Uh-huh,'' she panted, her dainty pink tongue emerging to rub a corner of her sensual mouth as she tugged the camisole down to her ankles and stepped out of it. "This young man comes from one of the finest old families in the state, and I couldn't be more respectable once I marry him.'' She was breathing hard now as he backed her to the bed. "You don't have to worry, Jimmy. I don't think he even knows what to do with a girl. And even if it turns out he does, I'll—*ooooh*, can't we stop talkin' now? Give me what I need. . . . *Ooooh*, yes.''

Chapter 14

$\mathcal{P}$aul Bouchard's whereabouts were still a mystery to his family. Thus far, there had been no letter from the boy, and Sheriffs Burkholder's and Blake's repeated inquiries in Alabama, New Orleans, and even St. Louis had brought not the slightest lead. Had they walked along the rails in Cullman, in the northern part of Alabama, about sixty miles southwest of Huntsville, they would have found the boy—in the company of the notorious Boxcar Pete.

Within a short month, Paul had become fully indoctrinated in the ways of the road and had won acceptance by Pete's companions. The clever mulatto never stayed longer than two days in any one area and moved in what at first had seemed to Paul a haphazard way across the Alabama countryside. Pete, who had taken a liking to the boy, had soon explained, "You see, Paul, a feller like me has to keep one step ahead of the law. By now, most likely every sheriff in the state knows who I am and what I look like and would love to fill me with buckshot or string me up to a tall live oak. Ever notice when I talk to the boys I meet at the camps I don't tell 'em where I'm gonna be at such and such a time? That's just plain good sense, Paul boy. You never know, somebody new in the camp might be workin' for some local sheriff and wants to cover hisself with glory by catchin' Boxcar Pete. What the boys don't know, they can't tell.''

Paul, now looking scruffy, could never be construed as anything but white trash and therefore did not feel the risk of discovery. In the ten days since leaving Eufaula, the boy's respect for his protector had grown, especially when he witnessed the unjust attitude of many southern whites against the blacks. He had gone into a general store in Anniston to buy a loaf of bread. While he had been looking at the merchandise, a timid little black boy had come in, and the whites in the store had fallen silent and turned to glare at him. He had been even more ragged looking than Paul, and as he came up to the counter, he begged, "Please, suh, mah mammy asks, kin you trust her till mah paw gits paid next week, 'n' spare us a l'il flour 'n' beans 'n' such?''

The storekeeper, a fat, bald man, had leaned across the counter and seized the boy by the shoulders, snarling, "Now lookee here, nigger, don't you come whinin' here to me with your hard-luck story. You jist tell your mammy that I give white folks credit, but no niggers, not ever in this store, not so long as I own it, git me? Now git outta here before I whale the daylights outta you!''

Paul had wanted desperately to intercept the sobbing little boy and, if he could, hand him a loaf of bread, but the hatred and contempt on the faces of the other whites in the store had warned him off. It was the first time he had been made so vividly aware of the racial hatred of some whites for the blacks; on Windhaven Plantation, bigotry had never existed. Paul then began to perceive that there were many others his own age and younger whose lives were plagued with trouble and deprivation he had never dreamed of. For an instant, he longed to go home and ask his mother's forgiveness.

The storekeeper turned to him now and with an oily smile demanded, "Now then, boy, what can I do fer you? You look mighty low down, but at least you got white skin. Speak up, boy!" Paul had stammered that he wanted a loaf of bread, paid for it, then walked out, but not until he had heard the storekeeper loudly declaim to his cronies, "Now you see the difference: a white boy pays up and acts like a man. But not niggers. Damned if I know why that no-good ape Abe Lincoln ever thought he was doin' right when he let 'em go free!"

That night when Paul had told Pete of the scene in the little general store, the mulatto, saddened, had muttered, "Maybe you're learnin' somethin' that'll put some starch in your backbone when you grow up and can do somethin' about what's goin' on between folks who got and folks who ain't. Yessiree, maybe you was meant to run away to learn what you're learnin' now, boy."

Paul began to assist Pete in his crusade to help the poor. Inside a month's time, he had proudly become a valuable aide to Pete, who was now a veritable legend in Alabama's poverty-stricken areas. When the boy located houses of the rich and scouted them out to see whether anyone was at home, he knew he was being an accomplice to robbery. Yet the glaring discrepancies between the rich and the needy convinced him to suspend moral judgment. Many of the men at the camps had been treated just the way he felt he had been at Windhaven Plantation—they were downtrodden and contemptuously shoved aside. And so, his sympathies had begun to grow with the dispossessed and the deprived.

The week before, in the town of Demopolis, over a hundred miles west of Windhaven Plantation, Paul had seen a poster outside the sheriff's office offering a $250 reward for "a mulatto, well-built, no more than forty years of age, named Pete Robbins, better known as Boxcar Pete, for the murder of Sheriff Bixton and the assault upon his deputy. Anyone having information as to the whereabouts of this dangerous criminal should come forward and tell all he knows. Robbins is known to be armed and dangerous. If he resists, shoot him down, for he is as dangerous as a mad dog." Paul had been horrified; he was convinced that Boxcar Pete's cause was a worthy one, indeed.

And so this afternoon he went into the general store on the outskirts of Cullman to buy some cigars, beans, and a little meat. Pete had given him almost the exact change.

He entered the store and found three bearded farmers chatting. "Sure wish I could buy me some real good likker, Dan," one of the men commented. "Maybe if I get the reward on this devil Boxcar Pete, I'll be able to treat you all to some Kentucky whiskey."

"Whaddya mean?" another of the farmers asked.

"Sheriff Dunlap done told me this morning, he 'n' his men are fixin' to set a trap for this Boxcar Pete. Everybody knows he hops freight trains between Mobile 'n' the top of 'Bamy, 'n' lately there's been reports that he's been sighted up north. Well, the sheriff reckons that must mean Boxcar Pete's movin' south. So he plans to wait for him in the next town down the line from here. He 'n' his men will search every train. Dunlap figures he's bound to find him." The man bit off a chew of plug tobacco.

"But where do *you* come in on the reward?" a wiry little farmer demanded.

The man with the tobacco winked and grinned. "I'm gonna take my shotgun, hitch up my old mule, 'n' ride up to Lacon. See, Jake, that's the next stop north of Cullman. I'll hide in one of those brakeman sheds, 'n' when I see that nigger, I'll blast his head off. When I get that two-hundred-fifty-bucks reward, I'll treat you to the best likker you ever tossed down your gullet, that's a fact!''

"You sure you'll see him?"

"I'll see him, don't you worry none about that. 'Lessen he turns hisself into a dog or a rabbit, or suchlike.''

"What?'' the other man demanded suspiciously.

"Ain't you heard?'' He spat tobacco juice before answering. "Some say this Boxcar Pete can disappear 'n' make hisself a possum or snake or bear—leastways, that's what the niggers say he can do. I think he's old Lucifer hisself. No God-fearin' nigger could be so lucky after what he done to that poor sheriff back in Sylacauga 'n' robbin' white folks 'n' gettin' away with it. My shotgun'll put a stop to him fer certain!''

"Ain't you afraid of bein' tried for murder?'' his friend asked. "After all, the sheriff wants Boxcar Pete for hisself, and he'll be mad as fire if you spoil his plans.''

"The sheriff's more like to build me a monument! Besides, from what I was readin' in the paper this mornin', the government is finally gettin' back some sense about these niggers.''

"I heard!'' Jake said. "That Civil Rights Act has been declared unconstitutional. It's about time the Supreme Court woke up to what's been happenin', that's all I have to say.''

Paul quickly gave the order to the storekeeper, who brought it to the counter, then totaled the price. The boy delved his grimy hand into his ragged pocket and brought out the amount, picked up his parcel, thanked the storekeeper, and left.

"Must be buyin' dem cigars for his daddy,'' the man

with the tobacco plug commented, jerking his thumb at the departing boy.

The storekeeper scratched his head as he looked after Paul. "Never saw that kid around here before."

"Hell, Benjy, lotsa poor white trash is movin' round Cullman these days, lookin' for work, for some share-croppin'," the wiry little man spoke up. "Like as not, you'll see his pappy come in one day 'n' ask for more of those rotten cigars. Bet you don't smoke 'em yourself. They'd turn your gills green."

The three farmers burst into hearty laughter as the storekeeper scowled.

"So that's the way the wind blows, is it now?" the mulatto chuckled as he lit a stogie. "Thanks, boy, you done me a mighty good turn there. You're a big help! Those white folks don't know that I'm not goin' to Lacon at all. We're gonna head east about as far as Gadsden. But first I got me a special job to do tonight. Suit you, boy?"

"Sure, whatever you say, Pete."

A little after midnight, he and Paul clambered aboard a freight train. The mulatto patted a sack he had slung aboard the boxcar, grinned, and said, "Did all right tonight. Better 'n I hoped for. Gonna help a lot of poor folks when we get to where we're goin', Paul. And I ain't forgettin' you saved my hide by keeping your ears open and your mouth shut in that store. Yessiree, you been a big help to me, and you can tell yourself you did your part helpin' lots of down 'n' out folks who wouldn'ta had another chance."

Paul flushed at the praise and lowered his eyes. Pete's approval made him feel a good deal less guilty about being an accomplice to robbery. After all, he was

helping people who were much worse off than the
people Pete was stealing from.

By the morning of Tuesday, October 23, the freight
train Pete and Paul were riding stopped at Brewton, a
little town near the Alabama-Florida border some sev-
enty miles northeast of Mobile. Paul and Boxcar Pete
scrambled out of the car. "I know this station, Paul
boy," he told the youth. "The railroad bulls go down
the line, so we want to get out of sight. Wouldn't be
surprised at all if there's fellers here, too, lookin' to
collect the bounty on my head. Hurry up now! Stoop
down like an Injun and start runnin' in the tall grass
ahead. There's a camp about a mile from here."

Paul emulated his mentor. He thought that Pete was
one of the smartest men he had ever met. He had been
reassured of the man's goodness when Pete had commented, "I never once hurt anyone, and I hope I never
will. Just let's say I'm helpin' colored folk to have
another chance to make good. Ain't that what you're
doin' by runnin' away—tryin' to make good on your
own?"

When they reached the camp, they found a group of
some twenty blacks squatting around a fire. As Pete and
his young companion pushed through the tall grass and
came into the clearing, the men got to their feet to hail
the mulatto. "Hey, it's Boxcar Pete!" "Lawdy, we
heard the law done caught up with you up north, Boxcar boy!" "Nawsuh, ain't no whitey gwine ketch Boxcar Pete! He be doin' the Lawd's work for us poor
niggers!"

"Glad to be here, boys. Heard you was goin' through
some misery down here in Brewton, so I moseyed down
here special-like." Pete affably greeted the group as he
dropped his sack onto the ground and hunkered down,
gesturing to Paul to do the same.

"That ain't no lie, Boxcar," a squat, nearly bald black in his late forties grumbled. "We had a rough deal from the Brewton Turpentine Mill last week."

"I know. Way I heard it, you boys had three months of good hard work, all of you, then got fired. The foreman said you was troublemakers, in debt to the mill's general store."

"That's the size of it, Pete," the squat black admitted. "Only it's a lie. Old Lonnie here, he just spoke up 'n' asked the boss man couldn't we have a little more money. Hell, they was only payin' us 'bout twenty-five cents a day. And you knows yourself how sick a man gets in that dang turpentine mill. Workin' from sunup to sundown. Danny 'n' Joe 'n' Matt," he jerked his thumb back at several of the members of the group who nodded confirmation, "they all been sick a week from the smell. A man can't get the smell outta his clothes or hair, no matter how hard he scrubs."

"And when you ask for more money, that foreman gets rid of you all and hires new men at the same startin' wage you was at, right?" Pete avowed.

"Right as rain!" A chorus of angry affirmatives came from the blacks.

Pete took a plate of stew handed to him and gave it to Paul, then accepted another one for himself. As soon as he and Paul had finished the stew, Pete opened the sack and summoned the men of the camp. "Get in line, boys, and I'll divvy up the pickin's from Cullman," he announced. "Here, Frank, here's somethin' for you. And Sam, you take this."

As Paul had seen his companion do time and time again, Pete distributed the money to the outstretched hands. Then, as was his custom, Pete gave them some advice. "I say to all you turpentine workers, get out of this county while you can. That foreman blacklisted you as troublemakers. You won't work again hereabouts. Go to Texas or Californy. You could do worse than getting a job on a big cattle ranch up around Montana and Wyoming. Course, them winters is real cold up there, and they got snow.''

''Snow'd be a sight healthier than what we got here, Pete,'' Frank responded, and there was a low growl of ''You be talkin' right, man!'' from the others.

''You know, Pete, I got a hankerin' to work on a cattle ranch 'n' git away from 'Bamy,'' one young man said.

''You could do worse, son. Here's sixty for you. You know how to ride the rails, and you got my pass so's the boys out west 'n' up north'll look after you. The rest is all up to you—and Gawd, so don't forget to say your prayers.''

''No fear of that, Pete. Thanks a heap. Mebbe I'll see you out somewheres in Texas or Californy,'' the man exclaimed.

''No, I gotta stay here, no matter what the risk.''

''Hey, Pete,'' said one of the last men in line, ''I heard tell you stay one step ahead of de law because you change yourself into an animal. Any truf in dat?''

The mulatto stared at him a moment, then chuckled and replied, ''Barney, all I got to say on the matter is if them sheriffs believe that, so much the better. Well, now, boys, I'll be thankin' you for the stew and so'll my young pardner here. Good luck to all of you!''

Turning to Paul, he declared, ''Come on son, we got work to do. This sack of mine is sorta empty right now, but everything went for a good cause.''

''Yes, yes it did—Boxcar Pete,'' Paul agreed. And this time the adulatory title he bestowed on the mulatto was compelled out of his deep respect and admiration for this man who kept nothing for himself and gave everything to those who were down and out.

Late that same afternoon, he and Pete cautiously made their way back to the freight yard and, when the coast was clear, climbed into a boxcar of a train on a distant siding. "We'll mosey down to Prichard, Paul boy," Boxcar Pete told him. "I hear tell my relative, poor old Aunt Tildy, is bein' put out of her home by the sheriff. He's a skunk who wants to grab her land for hisself. Sorta reminds me of another sheriff I knew back where I started out from."

"Are you going to help her, Pete?" Paul asked.

"You betcher sweet life I am," the mulatto stoutly responded. "She's got some kinfolk down N'Awleans way, they say. I'm gonna hand her some cash so's she can get down there."

Paul turned to his companion, his eyes shining with admiration. The mulatto patted him on the back and chuckled. "Ain't a sinner, but I ain't no saint either, so don't be lookin' at me like that. I be doin' what any decent God-fearin' feller would to help a poor old soul what can't fend for herself. We'll get into Prichard come noon tomorrow, I reckon. Better catch some sleep while we can. We really been makin' tracks, ain't we, Paul boy?"

Paul agreed. Looking back, it seemed a century since he had left Windhaven Plantation. He felt momentary qualms about not having sent a letter to his mother, but too many things were happening in this new life. He really didn't have time to write a letter. He promised himself he'd do it just as soon as he could, though.

That Wednesday morning was unnaturally cold and foggy. Paul and Pete left their car and made their way through a field of rotting vegetation, the ghostly residue of a farm that had been abandoned some five years before. No one had bought the property to this day, for it was said that the land was blighted and that nothing would grow on it. "Old Aunt Tildy's shack's about a mile east of here. We'd best walk fast, 'cause the sheriff in these parts is just about as bad as they come."

They had come at last to an old ramshackle wooden house and an equally dilapidated barn. A cow was grazing in the fenced-in pasture, and a flock of chickens squabbled for grain at the back of the house. As Paul and his companion approached the farm, they could see a white-haired black woman slowly scattering another bucket of grain before the chickens. "That's Aunt Tildy, boy." The mulatto chuckled. "Sixty-eight years old!"

He hurried toward the farm, Paul keeping up with him. The boy looked over his shoulder, but there was no one in sight. He shivered as the thick fog gathering from the Gulf slowly rolled over the bottomland.

"Hey there, Aunt Tildy!" Boxcar Pete called.

"Land sakes!" The old woman dropped the bucket, a broad smile on her wrinkled face. "If that don't beat all! Never 'spected Ah'd see you!"

"That's just why we came!" Pete sidled up and put his arm around her. "Aunt Tildy, I want you to meet my pardner, Paul. Paul boy, I want you to meet the most beautiful woman this side of the Mississippi."

The old woman hooted with pleasure at Pete's words. "Glad to make your 'quaintance, chile," she said to Paul.

"I'm glad to meet you, ma'am," Paul replied.

"Mercy, ain't he polite!" she said to Pete.

"I hear tell you got miseries from a sheriff in these parts," Pete said seriously.

The old woman's smile vanished, and she bobbed her

head, then started to sniffle, reaching for a corner of her apron to dab at her eyes. "Sheriff Orban done tol' me Ah gotta git off dis here farm by tomorra 'cause Ah ain't paid mah taxes. He be lyin'."

"That sheriff'll see to it that you won't get no help round here, I 'spect."

"You's right, Pete. Mighty tough on a poor ol' woman."

"I'm gonna help you get to your kinfolk in N'Awleans, Aunt Tildy." Pete opened his sack and took out a wad of greenbacks. "Now you be packin' up, then pay somebody you trust to drive you down to Mobile for the ferry, see? When you get to N'Awleans hire a driver at the wharf to take you right where your kinfolks live. Easy as pie, Aunt Tildy."

"You mean—" The old woman stared at the wad of crumpled bills the mulatto had pressed into her trembling, bony hand. "You mean you's givin' me dis here money?"

"Sho am."

"Ah'll say prayers fo' you every night, Pete honey. Land o' Goshen, must be nigh unto three hundred dollars here."

"It's yours, Aunt Tildy. You just take care of yourself."

The old woman cried softly as she clung to her nephew's arm. "I heard what happened to Jed, and I'm mighty grieved 'bout it. The sheriff done come here, lookin' to see iffen I be hidin' you here. I'm purely pleased to see you, Pete, but I'd rest easier knowin' you was back on the road."

"You're right, Aunt Tildy. 'Sides, there's someone I want to see in Mobile. Come on, boy, we'll make tracks," Pete said to Paul, who nodded.

They made their way through the same abandoned

field through which they had come from the railroad yard. Paul trotted beside his companion, crouching so that their heads would not appear above the tall grass and rotting corn stalks. Paul half turned to look back the way they had come and saw the distant outlines of five men coming in their direction.

The brawny mulatto turned, scowling, then his eyes narrowed. "I see 'em! Look, boy, save yourself. I'll turn to the right up here. You go left. I'll try to meet you at the railroad yard after midnight."

He began to run before Paul had time to beg to stay with Pete and take his chances. The boy ran in the opposite direction, crouching very low to keep out of sight. He could not see where the five men were.

He heard their dogs now—the long, low wail of the bloodhound. He forced himself to keep running while the corn stalks whipped at his face and pulled at his clothing. He had no idea where he was.

Behind him was the sound of boots running through the rotting vegetation, and the baying of the dogs drew closer. He turned, startled, and the shocked look on his face was not at all feigned, for within a few feet of him was a fat, walrus-mustachioed man wearing the star of a sheriff. With him were four lanky, younger men, two of them dark haired, two towheaded, who were his deputies. Each of three of the deputies held a pair of bloodhounds on his leash; the fourth had drawn a revolver from his holster. Paul eased himself back as noiselessly as he could while the sound of his heart thudded in his ears. He lowered himself to the ground and stretched out flat on the ground.

"All right. Joe, Mack, Doug, turn the dogs loose. They'll find that son of a bitch if we can't!" the sheriff ordered.

The three deputies unsnapped the leashes, and six

massive bloodhounds bounded forward, sniffing at Paul, then moved off to his right and northward along the riverbank. The first three suddenly pricked up their ears and increased their loping gaits. The three others followed, howling.

"They got him!" the deputy with the drawn revolver exclaimed gleefully.

"They're the best in this county, Jim-Bob," the sheriff added. "If he's around here, they'll flush him out."

The sheriff and his companions took off after the hounds, which stopped about two hundred yards farther north from where Paul sat. The dark-haired deputy whom the sheriff had called Mack suddenly called out, "Hey, Sheriff, what's this black dog doin' there?"

Paul listened incredulously, because beyond him he could see the six bloodhounds standing near a seventh, black dog, as large as any of the bloodhounds.

Oh, Lord, it can't be! It just can't be! Paul thought, thinking of what the man at the camp in Brewton had said about Pete being able to turn himself into animals to evade capture. *It's not possible.* Yet where had that big black dog come from? The bloodhounds weren't even bothering with it. They were wagging their tails and trotting back the way they had come. *I don't believe it!* he thought again, but he was seeing it with his own eyes.

"Well, I'll be hornswoggled!" Paul heard the sheriff gasp. "I never saw the hounds act like that before. You'd think they'd have tried to take a nip out of that big black dog. Now where the hell did it go all of a sudden?"

"Beats me, Sheriff," the man with the revolver panted, for he had run back with the dogs. "No sign of it. And

I guess the hounds don't have the smell like we thought they did.''

"Hell's fire, he's probably long gone by now!" the sheriff growled. "Might as well get back to town. I'll wire down to Mobile. They'll lay for him there. I want to see that colored bastard riddled with bullet holes and stretched out on a slab. Damn the luck!"

Disgruntled, he and his deputies, who by this time had snapped the leashes on to the bloodhounds' collars, dejectedly tramped through the field and away from Paul as they returned to the town. When they were gone, Paul closed his eyes, uttered a long sigh of relief, and tried to ease the pounding of his heart by relaxing all his muscles and keeping his eyes closed. Those huge dogs had big teeth—he was certainly glad they hadn't tried to bite him. But what had happened to Pete?

When he was able, he sat up, brushed himself off, and looked around. The fog had settled in again, and he thought that this must be the most desolate, deserted place in all the world. He tried to decide which way to go to the railroad yard, where Pete had told him to wait. He decided to start out and get his bearings once he was out of the cornfield. After several minutes, he heard footsteps behind him. His heart leaped to his mouth out of fear. He swiveled, and his jaw dropped. "Pete!" The mulatto was standing there, hands on his hips, chewing a stogie.

"You—you scared me! What—how did—" Paul began.

But the mulatto took the stogie out of his mouth, waved it with an air of dismissal, and said, "I ain't gonna answer no questions, Paul boy. Now come on, let's get a fire started and have something to eat. I got me a real appetite. In my sack is a hambone with at least a pound of good meat on it and some sweet taters. How's that sound?''

Paul could only nod. He had seen what he had seen, but he could not explain it satisfactorily even to himself. He began to understand Pete's already legendary reputation, his uncanny ability to stay one step ahead of the law. And when Paul looked up at the mulatto, the unspoken awe still in his eyes, Pete tilted back his head and let out an eerily mocking laugh. It sounded as if the devil himself were laughing—or so it seemed to the wondering boy.

Chapter 15

$\mathcal{P}$ete and Paul disembarked from a freight train on the outskirts of Mobile on the last day of October, a clear, warm day. The railroad station was not far from the Gulf, and vaguely in the distance, Pete could make out a paddle-wheel ferry, which conveyed passengers to New Orleans.

It was shortly after dawn, and the railroad yard seemed deserted. Pete took Paul's elbow and led him away from the siding. Then the man turned to Paul and said, "It's time we broke this up, boy. You been a mighty good pardner, and you stood up to this hard life pretty well. But it's gettin' too hot for me, Paul boy, and I wouldn't want a nice kid like you gettin' into trouble."

This sudden declaration took Paul completely by surprise. He had felt himself totally allied to this man, whom he respected and on whom he could rely, even in the face of danger.

Pete placed his strong fingers on the boy's shoulder. "Where might you be wantin' to go?"

"Well, I—I've got relatives in Texas. . . ." Paul stammered.

"Well, if I was your daddy, I'd send you home. But if you wanna go on to Texas, I can help. See, I got friends along the railroad out that way what'll see you don't come to no harm. I'll give you a pass."

Paul watched as the mulatto took out an oval piece of leather from his trousers pocket, drew his jackknife out of another pocket, and cut a cryptic sign on the leather oval, then handed it to him. "Here it is. Now this here piece says Boxcar Pete's lookin' after you. Show this to the fellers you meet on the railroads from now on, and they won't hurt you none. All right now, shake hands with Boxcar Pete, and then it's good-bye."

There were tears in Paul's eyes as he held out his hand to the huge mulatto, who walked toward the underbrush and then, almost as if by magic, vanished from sight.

Paul knew he had about four dollars in his pocket, more than enough to pay his way on the ferry across to New Orleans, where he could find trains headed for Texas.

Once aboard the ferry, he looked back at the receding shores of the Alabama River. Once again he felt lost and abandoned, grieving for his lost friendship with Pete. The man had, after all, watched over him and taught him much he had never suspected about life.

Paul opened his little traveling sack to check on his provisions, and his eyes widened with surprise when he saw a wad of greenbacks. He found that Pete had managed to slip five twenty-dollar bills into his sack. He promised himself that somehow he would pay Pete back, because he knew the money should have gone instead to some poor person unjustly uprooted from his home.

Paul reached New Orleans early in the evening and treated himself to a meal in a shabby restaurant near the waterfront, then made his way to the railroad yard. He held Pete's leather oval pass in his palm. In a boxcar bound for Texas, he said a prayer for his friend and fervently wished the mulatto were riding with him!

* * *

Pete's pass worked like magic, paving the way along the rail line from New Orleans to Texas. He was given special treatment at every camp, cordially invited to share meals, and told which trains to take to Galveston.

A little after two o'clock on the afternoon of the first Saturday of November, Paul eased himself out of the boxcar as the freight train came to a grinding stop in the railroad yard near the large Galveston station. He decided to visit his friend Joy Parmenter. He could hardly wait to see her, a saucy, black-haired girl with whom he had always felt at ease. Paul hired a hansom cab to take him to Joy's stepfather's house, two blocks away from the Galveston General Hospital, where Joy's mother had worked as a volunteer.

"Well, here y'are, sonny," the cabdriver spoke up after reining in the horse in front of a huge stone house.

"Thank you. Here, you—you can keep the change," Paul said impulsively, handing the driver the dollar bill.

"That's real neighborly, sonny. When I saw you— your clothes and all—I wondered if you had the money to pay me," the driver admitted.

Paul blushed self-consciously, for hot water and clean clothes had not been available during his travels with Boxcar Pete. He alighted from the cab and hurried toward the door, rapping loudly. Meanwhile, the driver, out of curiosity, remained on his perch, watching.

When the door was opened, Joy stood before him, her black hair streaming down her slim shoulders. Her eyes widened, for she did not immediately recognize him. But when he doffed his cap, she gasped, "Paul! What in the world are you doing here?"

"Who is it, darling?" her mother, Arabella, called from an adjoining room.

"Mother! It's Paul Bouchard!" Joy called back. "Come in, come in, for heaven's sake!"

Arabella came into the living room, followed by her genial elderly husband. She clasped her hands together and uttered a cry. "Oh, my Lord! Paul! Did you come here all by yourself?"

Dr. Parmenter looked concerned. "Are you all right, son? You look worn out."

"I *am* tired, and I know I'm dirty," Paul answered. He was embarrassed by his bedraggled appearance.

"What this young man needs, Arabella, is a good hot bath and some solid food. I'm afraid my clothes wouldn't fit you, young man, but you can wear one of my bathrobes until what you're wearing can be washed."

"Thank you, Doctor."

"We heard from your mother that you had run away," Arabella said, shaking her head. "She must be frantic with worry. Come along, Paul—we'd best clean you up and get some good food into you."

"I—I'll see you later, Joy," Paul murmured meekly, then followed the handsome matron.

An hour later, shining clean and happily replete, Paul came out into the Parmenter living room. Arabella had put his clothes to soak, and he had donned some of her husband's undergarments, a thick belted robe, and slippers.

"Now then, tell me just what you've been up to, young man," Arabella demanded sternly. "The police have been here looking for you."

Paul took a deep breath, then began his story. He left out the details surrounding Boxcar Pete, thinking that his hostess might be scandalized. More specifically, he explained why he had run away, that he had felt ignored and useless.

"After what you've said, I can understand why you left home. But you must notify your mother that you are here now. Also, you must think of going back. We'll be glad to pay—"

"No!" Paul blurted. Then, in a softer tone, "I—I just can't, not yet. I'd really like to go to Wyoming to see my cousin Hugo and his wife, Cecily."

Arabella directed a searching look at her husband and then said, "I don't approve at all, but I'll make a bargain with you. I'll lend you some money to get to Wyoming if you'll send a wire to your mother and tell her that you're safe and sound. That way, she won't worry."

"Well, all right. Only you don't have to lend me money; I have some of my own."

"I see." Arabella frowned. She could see that Paul was a stubborn boy and could read the anguish in his eyes. When he boarded the train here at Galveston, she would see to it that the conductor would look after him until Paul reached his destination.

The next day, Sunday, the Parmenters took Paul in their buggy to town, where he sent a wire to his mother. They took him for a ride around Galveston, and Joy prattled on about her job as a free-lance newspaper writer and how she hoped that someday the editor would offer her a full-time job. Arabella looked proudly at her daughter, and Dr. Parmenter chuckled and said, "As you can tell, Paul, we're both very proud of Joy. She's a remarkable young lady."

"I know, sir. And she's also—she's also become awfully pretty," Paul stammered, flushing hotly.

"Why, Paul, what a thing to say!" Joy giggled and impulsively gave him a kiss on the cheek, making him blush more deeply.

That evening, over a leisurely supper, Joy showed him her newspaper clippings. "If I've talent enough, Paul, I want to write a novel. And maybe I'll put you in it."

"Sure," Paul said, blushing again. "I don't know what I'm going to be, Joy. That's one reason why I ran away. I have to find out about myself."

"You have to have confidence in yourself. When I started writing, I didn't think that the editor would pay me a cent for what I was doing. I just liked it, that's all. You do have to do what's best for you, though."

"That's exactly it, Joy. There was something else. When I was in Alabama, I . . . I didn't get many letters from you. I didn't think you cared anymore."

"Oh, Paul! I'm so sorry. From now on, I promise that I'll write you faithfully—as soon as you get back home safely, that is," Joy told him, shaking her forefinger at him in mock sternness.

And so, on the next day, Monday, the Parmenters took Paul to the Galveston railroad station. Before the train left at noon, Arabella took the youth into a clothing store and told him that she was going to make him a present of new clothing and would not take no for an answer.

While Joy's mother was paying the clerk, Paul found himself alone with Joy for a few moments. He stared at her, his heart in his eyes, and finally he stammered, "Joy, I was thinking that maybe, in a few years if I find a good job, we could, you know . . . maybe get together."

The lovely girl understood what he had in mind, and she liked him a great deal. But she knew that at their present ages, the thought of marriage was inappropriate. So she answered, "I'll tell you what, Paul. I promise to keep in constant touch with you and send you samples of my writing and tell you all that's happening here in Galveston. We'll be friends that way for now, and then later we'll see. Won't that be the most sensible thing?"

"I—yes, you're right. I—well, I like you a lot, Joy," he stammered.

"Mother's coming now, but here's a kiss for good luck!" she whispered, and very swiftly kissed him on the cheek and gave him a hug.

James Weymore went back to Tuscaloosa after learning from Realtor Ernest Medfors that it would take four to six weeks to close on the Jessica Haskins property. The next week Weymore returned to Montgomery and stopped at the realtor's office to check on the transaction. Knowing of his client's interest in riverfront land, Medfors had remarked, "There's a larger property in Andy Haskins's will that was left to his widow; it isn't far from the parcel you're about to acquire. When you put the binder on the first property, I contacted Mrs. Haskins and found that she hadn't decided yet to put that second piece of acreage on the market. It seems the land used to be in the Bouchard family, so Mrs. Haskins felt she first had to consult Laure Bouchard Kenniston. People around here are sensitive when it comes to land that's been in the family. They care more about family than money."

Weymore showed immediate interest. "Tell me about this other piece."

"Four hundred acres, originally belonging to a Mr. Edward Williamson, whose daughter Lucy married Luke Bouchard. That's how the land came into the Bouchard family."

"Get to the point, Medfors," Weymore snapped.

"At the end of the Civil War, all that land was confiscated. Some years after that, Mr. Bouchard managed to buy back the acreage and turn it over to Andy Haskins. Incontestable ownership. There's a house there on it, too; it's old but in good condition."

Weymore thoughtfully stroked his beard. "Is there any chance I could someday buy Windhaven Plantation?"

"I strongly doubt it, sir. Mrs. Bouchard would consider it a mortal sin to sell the property, which had been given to the first Bouchard by the Creeks and then passed on to her as Luke Bouchard's legacy."

"I understand. How far from Windhaven Plantation are these four hundred acres of Mrs. Haskins?"

"Within about a half hour's ride, Mr. Weymore."

"Very good." Weymore chuckled, and his eyes glistened with avarice. "That would give me two prime sections of riverfront land closely connected and not far from Windhaven Plantation. What does Mrs. Haskins want for the four hundred acres?" Weymore glowered greedily down at the man.

"Eighteen thousand dollars. In cash. She plans to move to Virginia just as soon as I can complete these transactions."

"All right, Medfors, I'll meet that price. I'll have a bank draft within a week." Weymore took out his wallet and laid down ten one-hundred-dollar bills. "Here's a binder. Give me a receipt."

True to his word, James Weymore appeared in the realtor's office exactly a week later with the bank draft. Jessica Haskins had been informed that the titles to both pieces of her late husband's property would be officially recorded in the office of the county recorder of deeds and that the new owner intended to take possession at once. Jessica had no recourse, although she regretted that the buyer had not been her dear friend Laure.

James Weymore returned to Tuscaloosa and managed to occupy the time until the closing on the two properties would occur. Upon leaving a restaurant, he saw an attractive, buxom young woman in her midthirties struggling with a restive horse as she was trying to get into her buggy to drive home. Gallantly, he came to the rescue, introducing himself as Jason Oliver, then soothing the horse and holding the reins until it quieted. The woman's name was Flora Alexander, and Weymore knew of her; when her husband died two years earlier, he had left her an insurance policy for ten thousand dollars.

Weymore utilized all his magnetic charm, which was considerable when he put his mind to it. Within a week after their meeting, Flora Alexander became his ardent mistress. The day after they had become lovers, he proposed to move into her little house and contribute to her household expenses—which he did most generously, as a further means of gaining her complete acquiescence.

This evening, after supper, as he gallantly turned his back so that she might undress and slip under the covers to await his lovemaking, he declared in an unctuous tone, "Flora dearest, you've changed my life. Thanks to you, I've been able to bury the ghost of my dead wife, and I look forward to the years ahead with joy and expectation."

"Oh, Jason dearest, a fine, sensitive man like you needs someone to care for him," she murmured, blushing as she felt the cool sheets caress her naked body. She had already extinguished the little lamp beside the bed. In her mind, only in the dark was lovemaking proper. At first she had been hesitant to accept a lover, but when Weymore intimated that his feelings were lasting ones, she had succumbed.

"Now that I've met you, sweet Flora, all my prayers have been answered," Weymore replied huskily as he began to undress. "You are a beautiful, exquisite woman, created to bring all manner of delight to a lonely man!"

"Ohhh, Jason!" she sighed, her flesh tingling with an almost burdensome anticipation. "Fate brought us together, didn't it?"

"Yes, my beloved. Yet I've great plans for us, Flora dear, and for our future together."

"Jason—oh, you're so good for me," Flora moaned, almost beside herself by now with yearning.

"I'll tell you a secret, darling," he ventured, his right hand slyly caressing her hip. Flora caught her breath and closed her eyes, her heart pounding wildly as she felt herself churn with longing.

"I told you when we first met that I'm an investor. Right now, I've some very important transactions going on. I'll be a very rich man soon. Only then can I talk about our future together, beloved."

By this time, Flora had to bite her lips to keep from turning to him and begging for his embrace. She was nearly swooning with desire. *Oh, why didn't he take her now?*

"One of these days, when all these transactions come to fruition, I may have to go east for a spell—but I'll be back, and then we will make plans, Flora."

"Yes, yes, Jason. I'll wait. I can't believe how wonderful . . . Ohhhh Jason."

The day before James Weymore left Tuscaloosa to take possession of his property fronting the Alabama River not far from Windhaven Plantation, Flora blushingly confessed that she was pregnant. Weymore uttered a cry, then hid his dismay by taking her into his arms. "Oh, my Flora!" he exclaimed. "It will be the very first. My poor wife could never give me one. I bless you, my darling, for this news. Now, as I told you, I have to go east, and I leave tomorrow. But I'll be back a rich man, and I'll be able to give our child everything. I thank you on my knees for this news, my darling."

In a tumult of passion, hating that they must part even for a short time, Flora gave herself to Weymore that night without restraint. In the morning, when she wakened, it was to find herself alone in the rumpled bed. She reached over to touch the pillow on which his head had rested and kissed it almost reverently.

In mid-October Jessica Haskins had written Laure Kenniston to give her the news that the two pieces of property were to be sold to a James Weymore and that she intended to leave for Roanoke with her children shortly after the first week of November. She invited Laure for a visit before she had to pack, and Laure decided to accept so that she and her longtime friend could share the warmth of their friendship one last time.

Benjamin Franklin Brown drove Laure to the Montgomery railroad station, and three hours later she was in Tuscaloosa and seated in a buggy on her way to the Haskins house.

Horatio, the eldest of the Haskins children, had seen the buggy stop at the curb and watched the driver help Laure down and then carry her valise for her toward the door. He ran to tell his mother that they had a visitor, and Jessica opened the door just as Laure was about to knock. "Oh, Laure!" she exclaimed. "How sweet it was of you to come! Here, I'll take your valise, dear."

Laure sighed as Jessica's four children came out to greet her: Horatio, Andrew, Ardith, and Margaret, all smiling and eager to welcome her. "How darling they are—and Horatio's so tall now!" Laure exclaimed. Seeing that Andrew's face fell, she hastily added, "Andrew dear, when you're your brother's age, you'll be just as tall. But you're just as good-looking right now!" At this, Andrew's face brightened with a beaming smile.

Jessica sat down on the couch beside her. "Has there been any word from Paul yet?"

Laure shook her head, her face shadowed with anxiety. "Neither Sheriff Burkholder nor Sheriff Blake has had any reply to the wires they sent. I'm terribly worried. He's not even fifteen yet. Sometimes I lie awake nights worrying that he's out in the night with no place to sleep and not enough food. Oh, dear, I didn't mean to worry you, Jessica. You've got your own troubles. How you must miss Andy!" Laure put her arm around her friend and listened as Jessica told of her adjustment to life without Andy. Both women fought tears during their talk, but their friendship served to lighten the burden each faced.

"Horatio, be a darling and bring Mrs. Kenniston a cup of strong tea," Jessica called to her son a short time later. "The pot's already on the stove, sweetheart."

Then Jessica tried in turn to console her friend. "I'm sure nothing's happened to Paul. If people see a boy all by himself wandering around where he doesn't belong, they're bound to ask questions. Some sheriff in some town will wire Sheriff Burkholder or Sheriff Blake that your son's been found, any day now!"

"I'm praying for that, Jessica. But you see, I'm worried about Lucien, too. Oh, he's fine—he's plunged himself into his new job. But Lucien has had to grow up very fast and assume greater responsibilities than I feel he was ready for, because of Leland's death."

"But I'm sure you're proud of him. I know you've written in your letters how well he's doing with Mr. Sonderman," Jessica murmured. "Thank you, dear Horatio. Here you are, Laure. Drink this. It'll make you feel better."

"I feel terrible for unloading my grief on you. *Please*, Jessica, don't go to any trouble—"

"Now don't talk like that! It's no trouble at all to console a friend." She gave Laure a hug.

"And you're a very loyal friend, Jessica." Laure leaned back against the couch, sighed, and took a sip of tea. "Just what I need. Beyond what's happening to the boys, there's my worry about money. I don't know who it was that said it was the root of all evil, but the lack of it is just as bad. The plantation means so much—there's so much history to it, and the Bouchard name is a legend in Alabama. Right now I'm responsible for the plantation's welfare, so it distresses me when things don't go well. I must make it successful once again."

"And you will. Cotton and tobacco prices are down throughout the South. Maybe if a new President is elected next year, things might be different."

"One bright side is that I have two wonderful people doing the planning and the running of the plantation—Burt, of course, and Benjamin Franklin Brown. I don't know what I'd do without them."

"Andy thought the world of Burt's ability," Jessica said. "You'll see, Laure dear, everything will be fine. We'll always stay close, no matter where we are. I'll write you from Roanoke all the time, I promise."

An hour later, Laure and Jessica and the children sat down to a bounteous supper, and Jessica did her best to brighten Laure's feelings. But for Leland's beautiful widow, the foremost fear in her mind was that the family was falling apart. She felt she must take any steps necessary to bring them back together again.

In his study late on the first Sunday afternoon in November, Nils Sonderman was seated at his desk, absorbed in thought. He took up the sheet of paper before him and read what he had written, then frowned and crossed out a word here and there. When he had substituted new words, he took another sheet of paper and copied his words onto a final draft.

For many years, Nils had secretly written poetry. Tonight he had spent a good hour composing a poem.

Though the poem resembled a sonnet. It expressed what he felt most deeply for the courageous, beautiful, and troubled Laure Kenniston.

He reread it, then stared out the window on to the empty street, seeing the live oaks and dogwoods, and he thought to himself that the time was not yet right to say aloud what he had set down on paper. Perhaps one day he would say those words to her and be well received.

He had entitled the poem, quite simply, "To Her" with good reason. The title would not betray the identity of the person who had inspired it. He read it again and nodded. It was done.

I dreamed I had been taken back in time
Unto an age of heroes aboard their great long
   ships:
The Norsemen, heralded in legend as in rhyme,
Battling with swords and axes, the call of
   "Odin!" on their lips,
And I, a scholar presently, but in that dream
   reborn
Into a Viking, rousing my comrades with my
   horn
To sail again for new shores we had not yet
   known,
Seeking the conquest of a castle or an enemy
   throne.

And then we came upon a rolling meadowland,
And there I saw you, hair as golden as the
   wheat,
Eyes as green as ivy on your castle's wall.
No longer was I warlike, venturing upon your
   mystic strand.

For, dazzled by your beauty, I knelt down
    before your feet
To pledge my love and loyalty for your sweet
    beck and call.

He rose abruptly from his desk, opened a drawer, and put the folded sheet under a sheaf of sketches. If nothing more, it was a candid and honest admission to himself of how much he admired, respected—and yes, even loved—Laure Kenniston.

Benjamin Franklin Brown called for Laure at the Montgomery station on Monday, after her weekend visit with Jessica. The two women had talked for long hours, and Laure felt considerably eased by Jessica's solace. If Andy's young widow could endure the anguish of losing her husband and still have an optimistic outlook for the future, Laure could no doubt do the same.

She would miss Jessica a good deal. Even frequent letters could never quite replace the loss of the close proximity of so dear a friend.

"Glad to see you back, Mrs. Kenniston," the genial black supervisor greeted her as he helped her into the buggy and placed her valise on the seat beside her.

"Is everything all right at home, Ben?"

"Right as rain. Oh, just as I came out to fetch you, Mrs. Kenniston, a wire came for you. Clarabelle signed for it, and I brought it along."

Laure took it with trembling hands and ripped it open, scanning the contents quickly. "Oh!" She nearly screeched. "It's a wire from Paul! He's safe in Galveston. Oh, my, he's going on to Wyoming to see Hugo and Cecily. Now I have to start worrying all over again."

She looked at Ben with tear-filled eyes. "May I ask a favor of you? Would you take me to the telegraph office before we go home? I want to wire Hugo and Cecily that, as soon as Paul arrives, they're to insist that he come back home immediately.''

"Of course, Mrs. Kenniston. You just write out what you want to say, and I'll take it in for you.''

Chapter 16

In Cheyenne, the Wyoming Stock Growers' Association had called its monthly meeting for the first Saturday of November at the town hall. Maxwell Grantham, chairman, had presided over the proceedings from the little stage at one end of the room. Now, as the meeting was drawing to a close, he was determined to address the membership on a sensitive issue of burning importance to him.

"May we have some quiet, please? I have just a few remarks to make before we close." He raised his voice, then banged the gavel down sharply. At last the restless men grew quiet. "As a cattleman, I've conducted my business honestly, without any violence or bloodshed, and I've been able to make a decent profit."

"Oh, sure, Grantham, you're rich now, and you've got it nice 'n' easy. You don't need to worry none about the goddamned woollybacks comin' into our territory," a stocky, ruddy-faced man in his early fifties called out.

"That's just what I wanted to talk about, Elston." Grantham leaned forward, a serious look on his handsome face. "I think it's time the cattlemen and the sheepmen worked out an arrangement to live in peace."

"I know where you got that line of bullshit, Grantham," Albert Elston called out angrily. "From that woman doc you're pals with. Sure, she'd stick up for the woollybacks; her aunt's got a sheep ranch over in Rawlins.''

"That's true, Elston," Grantham parried, "but Dr. Bouchard is married to Hugo Bouchard, and he's the son of a Texas cattle rancher. Now, if *he* can accept the sheepherders, all of you can." Then, almost pleading, he went on, "Look, men, it's giving Wyoming a bad name—''

Another rancher leaped to his feet and brandished his fist. "We oughta drive them woollybacks out of this territory!" he shouted. "And when we become a state of the Union, we oughta elect congressmen who'll keep the damned sheepmen out!''

The cattleman's protest was followed with hearty cheers of support from many of the other men.

"You won't be able to do that, and you know it, Trask," Grantham scornfully shouted over the voices. "They have as much legal right to their land as you do to yours. Anybody with ten bucks for a filing fee could claim a quarter section of public domain. That was only one hundred sixty acres, and even in good years a steer or a cow needs at least ten acres to graze on. I can guess that many of you had some of your cowhands file claims as homesteaders so you could get all the land you need. So when you talk about electing congressmen, I hope the people you elect have gumption enough to look into the situation and throw out those false claims of yours. Let me remind you that if violence against the sheepmen continues, you'll only draw attention to yourselves and to those claims.''

There were cries of protest from the other members. "We were here first!" "Get rid of the woollybacks for good!" "They won't listen to reason!''

"You've elected me president of this association,

gentlemen," Grantham said after the men had quieted down, "and while I hold office, I'll try to keep everybody levelheaded. It takes patience and understanding. We must sit down with the sheepmen—maybe at a barbecue—and talk out your grievances. I'm sure we could come to a reasonable understanding."

"You're a damn traitor, Maxwell! Why the hell don't you go live with the damn sheepherders you stick up for so much!" a short, sneering rancher cried out, and his words were applauded by others in the audience. "That's right—take a sheep to bed, Maxwell boy, then you won't need a woman." "We need a new president, so help me!" "Go back east and leave Wyoming to us, Grantham." "We were here before you came, and you're giving yourself airs as if you were better 'n any of us!"

Grantham waited until the angry catcalls died down. Then he rapped with his gavel and declared, "Say what you like about me; I'm not that thin skinned. But I'm going to stand firm about trying to make peace. I stand ready to talk to any spokesman for the sheep raisers in Wyoming. Between the two of us, maybe we can work something out to please everybody."

"That won't happen until hell freezes over, Grantham! Even if you've got another year as our president, we don't have to listen to you or take your advice." Albert Elston rose to his feet and brandished his fist again. "Let's go to the saloon. Drinks on me for everybody— except you, Grantham. You're not invited."

There were cheers at this, and without waiting for Grantham to adjourn the meeting, the audience broke up and poured out of the hall. Maxwell Grantham, his face drawn with concern, shook his head and muttered, "What damned fools! If they'd only see that in the long run they won't wind up destroying the sheepmen but themselves . . .''

Slowly, he left the stage and walked out of the hall. Glancing up at the sky, he saw an aureole around the moon and scowled. "I don't like that sign. We're in for some heavy snow," he mused. Then, still deeply concerned over the hostility his colleagues had shown, he mounted his horse and rode the long way back to his ranch.

It was midnight when Albert Elston reached his ranch after drinking with his cronies in the Sign of the Steer. After wiping down his horse in the stable, he stomped angrily onto the porch of his sturdy sod-and-wood house. He had come to Wyoming nearly twenty years earlier from Missouri. A bachelor, he currently had as his inamorata a handsome young Mexican woman, who, ironically, had been the common-law wife of a young sheep raiser. The pair had come into the territory a year before, after being driven out of Montana by cattlemen. But six months later, Albert Elston's *pistoleros* had killed half of the young sheepman's flock, and in the ensuing battle in which he had tried to protect his property, he had been gunned down by Jack Nantum, Elston's unscrupulous head *pistolero*. Elston had then slyly persuaded the grieving young woman to come live with him.

Elston entered the house, which was surprisingly luxurious inside, for he had imported Oriental rugs, a spinet piano, upholstered couches and chairs, even a few oil paintings. He was one of the wealthiest cattle ranchers in the Cheyenne area, his spread nearly as large as Grantham's. He poured himself some Maryland rye from a cut-glass decanter on a handsome rosewood sideboard, downed it in a gulp, and then bawled, *"¡Lupe, aquí, pronto!"*

In a few moments, the young Mexican woman emerged wearing a white night shift, her lustrous jet-black hair flowing down just past her shoulders. "I thought you would be home before now, *amorcito,"* she crooned in a soft, husky voice as she came toward him and wound her arms around his neck, arching on tiptoe to kiss him.

Elston chuckled. "I would have been if it hadn't been for that damned Grantham. I want you to do me a favor, Lupe. Put on your robe and go wake up Jack Nantum. Get him over here right now."

When she hesitated, he raised his right hand as if to strike her. "I gave you an order, honey. Don't you know by now you hop when I tell you to?"

Lowering her eyes, Lupe slowly nodded. *"Sí, comprendo, mi patrón,"* she quavered, disappearing for a moment and then returning with a thick woolen robe and her slippers. She let herself out of the house and closed the door behind her. Elston chuckled again, poured himself another shot of rye, then sprawled into one of the thick, overstuffed armchairs.

Soon the young Mexican woman hurried indoors, scurried through the living room, and disappeared into the bedroom. Behind her, with a lascivious smirk, tall, slim Jack Nantum sauntered toward his employer. He wore only his trousers, work shoes, and a heavy leather jacket over his torso. His face was lean and cadaverous, with a small, thin mouth and the coal-black eyes of a cynical killer. "What's on your mind, boss?"

"Help yourself to a drink, Jack, and sit down."

Nantum did as he was told, but not without a sideways glance at the beautiful Mexican woman, who had emerged from the bedroom and was now standing next to Elston's chair.

Elston resumed, "Jack, I want to put a scare into that eastern traitor, Maxwell Grantham. Don't kill him. Just hurt him bad enough that he'll be forced to sell out his ranch. Then I'll buy it. If all goes according to plan, there'll be a bonus for you."

"It'll be a pleasure, boss. I don't like a man that wants to let those damned woollybacks run all over our grassland. Tough enough to keep the cattle fed through the winter without having the damn sheep eatin' everything down to the roots."

"Here, Jack, use my rifle. It's more accurate than what anybody else around here has got."

Nantum finished his drink, got to his feet, then winked slyly at Elston's woman. "You be good now, ya hear?"

Elston rose with a lewd chuckle. "Don't worry, you'll be taken care of *real* good, so long as you do what I want you to." Abruptly, Elston went to the sideboard, put his empty glass down beside the decanter, and then walked to his bedroom, while the *pistolero*, with another soft chuckle, let himself out of the house and went back to his own quarters.

"Looks like the blizzard's holding off for a spell, sweetheart," Hugo Bouchard told Cecily as they finished their breakfast this first Monday in November. Throughout the weekend the sky had been heavy with low clouds, but only an inch or two of snow had fallen, and now the sun was shining. "Anything on your agenda today, Cecily?"

"Maybe a call from Mr. Meridew—his wife's expecting her firstborn."

"I hope you'll get paid for this one. I'd like to buy sturdier windows. Winter is upon us. Last Friday the *Gazette* warned cattlemen and sheepmen to round up their strays now and not wait until the blizzard strikes."

"The worst thing about blizzards is getting to people who need us," Cecily observed. "Otherwise, I rather like being snowbound with you." She looked longingly at her husband.

"Is that so?" Hugo replied. "Darn, there's someone at the door. We'll continue this discussion a bit later." Hugo went to the door and opened it, and a young clerk who worked at the general store, which was next to the telegraph office, handed him a wire. "Thanks, Joe." He closed the door and showed the paper to his wife. "I hope it's not bad news." He opened the telegram, frowned, and shook his head. "That's all we need right now."

"Why, what is it, Hugo?" Cecily rose, her eyes widening with alarm at the tone of his voice.

"Young Paul Bouchard is coming to visit us."

"All by himself?" Cecily asked, surprised.

"Seems so. He says not to worry, that he won't be any trouble."

"Why in heaven's name would he come all the way out here at this time of year? What about school? There's something strange about this. I would have expected his mother to have written to us herself." Cecily shook her head.

"Well, we'll know when he gets here. It's a long train ride, and I don't imagine he'll be here much before the end of the week. I'll be getting over to the hospital. I've got to check on that sixteen-year-old who broke his collarbone and fractured his tibia when he was thrown off a horse. He and his mother arrived two weeks ago from Boston to join the father, Daniel Attenberg, who has that small spread near Mr. Grantham's. I suppose the boy figured he had to prove he was a true son of a rancher by going out with the rest of the cowhands. Well, he's a little wiser now, but fortunately there's no permanent damage. I'll see you later, then, sweetheart.''

"Yes, Hugo, unless I get word that Mrs. Meridew needs me. I'll leave a note on the table if that's the case.''

Hugo walked back to the table, took Cecily in his arms, and gave her a long kiss. "You know what, Dr. Bouchard? I wish we could be snowbound for about a week.''

"Hugo, I love you." She reached her arms around his neck and again they kissed passionately. Then she said, "Now you get over to the hospital and make yourself useful.''

"To hear is to obey, Dr. Bouchard!" Hugo laughed, then quickly kissed Cecily's cheek and left the house.

Jack Nantum saddled his pinto, a small, very fast horse. In the saddle sling, the *pistolero* had sheathed his boss's 45-80-500 rifle, a U.S. Trapdoor Long Range rifle. Jack knew exactly where to find Maxwell Grantham; he planned to find a spot with plenty of cover and hit Grantham with the first shot.

For added protection in case he was pursued by Grantham's men, Nantum belted on the twin holsters for his six-shooters. These were good only for short range, but they could throw a lot of lead in a short time.

He took a back trail toward Grantham's spread, figuring that he would most likely find the rancher rounding up strays.

The thick gray clouds over to the southeast suddenly sent swirling thick flakes into his face. Nantum had a feeling that the expected blizzard had begun in earnest. He was half glad. Although the snow would make his aim more difficult, it would also make tracking him impossible. He took the pinto at a slow pace, because riding hard might draw attention to himself. If Grantham and his men spotted him riding hell-bent for leather, he'd have no chance at a shot from hiding.

His thin lips suddenly curved in a grim smile as he saw far in the distance the outlines of a herd of cattle and the vaguer forms of a few men on horseback riding around them. That'd be Maxwell Grantham and his crew, all right.

He reined in the pinto and rose in his stirrups to survey the surrounding land. Far to the north stood a cluster of pine trees. They were not too tall, but there were plenty of them and they would make good cover. He'd circle quickly from the west and get in there before the herd and Grantham and his men reached the spot.

Crouching forward in the saddle, he gave his horse a harsh kick with both booted heels. With the pinto's speed and agility, Nantum reached the thick stretch of fir and pine trees well ahead of the riders alongside the placid cattle. He dismounted and tethered the reins loosely at the very back of the grove so that after he had completed the task, he could mount up and escape due north at full speed to avoid Grantham's cowhands.

"Stay right there, boy," he murmured to his horse as he unsheathed the rifle, quickly inspected it, and then loaded it. It was a one-shot weapon that had to be reloaded every time, but he was quick enough when it came to reloading.

He crawled on his belly to the front row of fir trees and found a thick bramble bush, an ideal hiding place, took his place, adjusted the rifle to his shoulder, and waited. Soon the riders came into view, the cattle beside them. And, yes, there was Grantham himself, big as you please, with his gray Stetson. Nantum was pretty sure he could hit the rancher and give him a real scare.

The *pistolero* could see that four of Grantham's riders, each with a rifle, were close by their boss. Impulsively, he decided to take the cattleman from the back; shooting Grantham as he approached would give his riders a split-second's advantage in finding where the shot had come from. He'd aim for Grantham's shoulder, so the eastern dude would be in bed for a good long spell.

Sucking in his breath, his eyes narrowed and cruelly eager, Nantum leveled the rifle and, just as the president of the Wyoming Stock Growers' Association rode past, squeezed the trigger. The gray-haired rancher stiffened in the saddle, uttered a groan, and reached back with one hand as he dropped the reins of his horse as if trying to locate the entry point of the bullet. It had taken him in the right shoulder blade.

Crouching as low as he could, Jack Nantum tore his way out of the bramble bush and raced back to the pinto, pulled the reins loose, leaped into the saddle, and kicking his heels against the pinto's belly, urged it to a full gallop, then swerved eastward to outflank Grantham's men. Taking one quick look over his shoulder, a self-satisfied grin transformed his face; he had done it.

"If I could get my hands on the lowdown skunk who shot the boss . . ." Hank Johnson, Grantham's foreman, exclaimed, his handsome face contorted and dark with fury. "Randy, Tom, take him back to the house as careful as you can—I'll ride for Doc Bouchard. The bandage stopped the bleeding, but that bullet has to come out. Dammit all!"

Two cowhands gently lifted a pale but still conscious Maxwell Grantham onto the horse. A third wrangler got on the other side to support the rancher's leg. Randy mounted behind Grantham, put both arms around the injured man's waist, and muttered, "Lean back against me, boss. We'll try to get you there fast." Tom mounted his horse, took the reins of Randy's horse as a lead, and began to trot back to the ranch house.

Fred Caston, the fourth wrangler, approached the young foreman. "Want me to go look for that bush-whacker, Hank?"

"No use. This storm will wipe out his tracks. You go with Randy and Tom and get that cook to heat up some water—I know the doc will need some. See you at the house." With this, Grantham's foreman spurred his black gelding and galloped off.

A quarter of an hour later, Hank Johnson leaped off his lathered gelding and banged on the door of the Bouchard house. As the door opened, Johnson sighed with relief. "Thank God you're here, Doc! The boss took a rifle bullet in his shoulder blade. Can you come with me back to the house?"

"I'll be right with you. You're lucky; I just got home," Hugo said. He grabbed his bag, saddled his horse, and rode with Hank Johnson back to the Grantham house.

After Hank left Maxwell Grantham, the three wranglers had carried the gray-haired rancher into his bedroom and carefully laid him on the bed, with pillows to prop him up. The cook, fussing over his employer, told them plenty of hot water was ready for whenever it was needed, and Randy Evans, a good-natured cowhand who had been with Grantham since he'd come to Wyoming, declared, "Boys, he needs a stiff shot of whiskey more 'n hot water. Where do you keep your liquor, Mr. Grantham?"

"There's a bottle of bourbon in the cabinet on the lower shelf. Pour me one, and you boys join me."

"Thanks, boss. Guess we could all use it. Damn,

what I wouldn't give to get my hands on that skunk!''
When Randy had poured the whiskey, he handed one
shot glass to the rancher, who nodded his thanks and
took a tentative sip.

"That'll do me until the doctor gets here." He took
another sip.

The cowhand and his two cronies stood holding their
drinks, anxiously watching their boss. Randy cleared
his throat. "You sure there isn't anything else we can
do for you?''

"No thanks, boys. You've done a lot. Probably
saved my life.''

A short time later, Dr. Hugo Bouchard hurried into
the bedroom with Hank Johnson, who motioned to the
cowhands to leave. The doctor frowned and shook his
head at the wound. "Yes . . . that bullet has to come
out, Mr. Grantham. I'd say it probably broke the shoulder blade, but there shouldn't be any complications. I'm
going to give you some chloroform. The pain from my
probing for the bullet will be too intense otherwise.''

"Do what you have to, Doc. I've got confidence in
you.'' Grantham smiled faintly.

"Hank, would you go into the kitchen and get a
couple pans of boiling water?''

"Sure, Doc.'' The young foreman hurried out.

When he had returned with the water, Hugo instructed him, "Now then, first I want you to use one of
those pans to sterilize my instruments. Just take the
scalpel here by the handle with the very tips of your
fingers. . . . That's it. Now dip it into the hot water and
turn it around while you count to a hundred. Another
thing you can do is to get some towels that you can
throw away when this is over.''

Hank ran off for the towels. Meanwhile, Dr. Bouchard
administered the chloroform and waited until his patient

was deeply unconscious. By now, Hank had returned with some towels, which he ripped into wide strips. "I want to help, Doc."

"All right, let's turn him gently, the pillows under his chest. That's it, Hank. There'll be some blood—I hope the sight doesn't bother you."

"Nope, I've seen enough of it in my time, Doc. I'm fine."

Twenty minutes later, Dr. Hugo Bouchard straightened, his face damp with sweat. "Well, here's the bullet. The shoulder blade is definitely fractured. I'll repair the damage as best I can, and he shouldn't have too much trouble after the wound heals."

When the final stitches had been taken, Hugo put down his instruments. "That takes care of it. He ought to be able to ride without too many twinges—but not for a while, you understand, Hank."

"You really did a job there, Doc."

"You can give yourself a pat on the back, Hank, for getting him help fast. Now we wait."

"That's better. Now how do you feel, Mr. Grantham?" Hugo asked solicitously.

"Stiff and sore—otherwise all right," Maxwell Grantham admitted. They had laid him on his left side and made certain that he did not roll onto his back and irritate the wound.

"That's natural. You were very lucky, Mr. Grantham. It was a clean fracture, but you'll have to take it easy for a good long while. Relax and let this heal. Those are doctor's orders."

Grantham made a wry face and grudgingly agreed. "I'd give a lot to know who's behind all this. I have enemies, but I don't know anyone who'd shoot me in the back."

"Whoever he was," Hank Johnson spoke up, "he made a clean getaway. We didn't see hide nor hair of anybody."

"I'll tell you one thing," Grantham said, "I'll be on my guard from now on."

"Good idea. I'm sure Hank and the rest of your men will keep an eye out for anybody snooping around the ranch," the young doctor said. "I'll come back tomorrow after I've done my work at the hospital, and see how you're getting along."

Grantham grinned weakly, and he held out his hand. "I'm in your debt, Hugo. Hope you don't mind me dropping the title."

"You call me whatever you want," the doctor said. "Hugo's fine."

Grantham motioned to his foreman. "Hank, get my wallet and open it up. I'd say the doctor's services are worth a hundred dollars or my name isn't Maxwell Grantham. Now you take the money from Hank, Hugo. If a hundred's too much, then let the remainder stand as a contribution for folks who need medical services and can't afford to pay."

"Thank you—that's mighty generous. Enough talk for now. You try to get as much sleep as you can."

Chapter 17

On Saturday, five days after he had been ambushed by Albert Elston's *pistolero*, Maxwell Grantham stubbornly decided to go to the vaunted Cheyenne Club, whose membership was exclusively limited to wealthy cattle raisers. When Hank Johnson reminded him of Dr. Bouchard's orders to rest, the rancher replied, "Just have one of the wranglers hitch up a horse and buggy and take me to town. That way, I can rest the wound and still get out." Then, his face shadowing, he added, "And I just might catch wind of the fellow who shot at me. Besides, I'm looking forward to seeing Count Pierre de Charbouille. He's going to use the new refrigerated boxcars to ship meat to Chicago and St. Louis."

"So he can slaughter cattle here and *then* ship it?" Hank asked.

"Yes. If the idea works, all of us will profit by it. When we send meat on the hoof to the market, a lot of weight is lost in traveling."

Hank shrugged. "I guess if you're driven, you'd be following Doc Bouchard's orders, so I'll keep my mouth shut. Matter of fact, I'll drive you there myself. Anyway, if the man who shot you is there tonight, he's in for a shock when he sees you. Maybe he'll give himself away, and I'll want to be there with you if that happens."

"All right. Have the horse and buggy hitched up and

ready in about an hour. I want to be there just in time for supper. The club serves magnificent food.'' Grantham grinned. "After my diet of beef broth and biscuits, I'm ready for pheasant under glass.''

The Cheyenne Club stood on the plains of the Wyoming prairie like a diamond on burlap. Built in 1880, it boasted the most elegant dining and lavish interiors in the West—but only for the enjoyment of its two hundred members, and even they had to obey the rules: no profanity, no drunkenness, and no untoward behavior.

Hank Johnson helped his boss down from the buggy. "I'll catch me supper in town, boss, then I'll be back. Any idea when you might want to leave?''

"Certainly before midnight, Hank. Dammit, this sling is awkward as hell. It won't be easy to eat with my left hand.''

"Sorry about that, but if you use that arm, boss, it's going to bother your shoulder.'' The foreman shrugged sympathetically, then walked with his boss up the stairs onto the wide oak porch of the Cheyenne Club. Hank looked around, trying to detect any surprise on the faces of the elegantly dressed men who were reading their newspapers. No one seemed shaken by Grantham's presence, however, so he continued through the wide, glass-paneled doors into the main lobby. Here elegantly upholstered chairs were set in groups on the plush carpeting, and gentlemen engaged in quiet conversation, passing the time of day, exchanging news on cattle marketing, and making million-dollar deals. A few faces turned their way, but again no one reacted to Grantham's presence in an unusual manner. Hank took his leave, satisfied that the rancher was in no danger at the club. Grantham himself continued through the lobby to the smoking room, where he was to meet Count Charbouille.

Marie de Jourlet

He passed one of the two grand staircases, and he thought he noticed a startled look from a man walking down the stairs—a man he recognized as having been at the last meeting of the Stock Growers' Association—but the man's eyes were quickly averted, and Grantham could not determine whether or not he had accurately read the expression. *Am I overly anxious?* he wondered. He walked on into the smoking room, where the odor of the finest imported cigars assailed him, mingling with the sweet scent of the best sherry the world had to offer.

"Ah, mon ami, M'sieu Grantham!" A dapper, black-haired man with a waxed mustache sprang to his feet from his leather chair, carrying a glass of sherry. He set the glass on a taboret and began to offer Maxwell Grantham his hand. At the same moment, the Frenchman's eyes widened with surprise. *"Tiens,* what happened to you?"

"I—got in the way of a rifle bullet, shall we say."

"Mais c'est terrible, vraiment! Here, take this chair beside me."

The nobleman beckoned to one of the liveried club waiters who unobtrusively stood by. "A sherry for my friend and another for myself," he said in French.

"At once," the man replied, and hastened to procure the ordered drinks.

Grantham leaned forward, a serious look on his face. "I consider you among my friends, Count, and I—"

"Please call me Pierre, and I shall call you Maxwell."

Grantham smiled. "Pierre, then. Someone wants to kill me, my friend."

"Mon Dieu!" the count exclaimed. "For what reason?"

"You and I have talked several times about my plans as head of the cattlemen's association to bring about a peaceful agreement between cattlemen and sheepherd-

216

ers. So far flocks have been clubbed to death—even dynamited—and innocent sheepherders are shot down like wild dogs. I'm afraid the government will soon send in federal troops, and since we're still a territory, things could go very badly for us. We might be under very vigilant authority by outsiders from that day on. I want to avoid that if I can."

"I agree. There is no need to bring about a war just because one prefers to raise one animal or the other. But, Maxwell, do you know who shot at you?"

"No. At the meeting last Saturday, many ranchers denounced me and threatened to disregard my authority as president. Someone is very angry about my desire for peace—angry enough to shoot me in the back."

"If I learn anything about who did it from my men, I shall get word to you at once."

"You are a good friend, Pierre."

"I am new to your country, and there is much I have to learn. You have always been good to me, Maxwell, suggesting ways I can improve my operation."

"It has been my pleasure. I personally think your idea of slaughtering the cattle and then shipping the meat has a great deal of merit. You must be prepared to take some losses at the outset, before the rest of the country catches on. Folks aren't used to buying anything but carcass meat and having their local butchers cut it up for them on the spot."

"*Oui*, it will be a while before I can expect a profit."

Grantham leaned back, and he and the count savored the fine dry sherry that the waiter had brought them.

"You do very well with the left hand, *mon ami*." The count chuckled as he watched Grantham sip from his glass, keeping his right arm motionless in the improvised sling that Hank Johnson had fashioned for him. "*Mon Dieu!* Here comes a man I do not like."

Maxwell Grantham looked up to see Albert Elston lurching toward them. Obviously quite intoxicated, Elston put out his left hand as if to steady himself on the back of Grantham's chair, then gave the rancher a sudden shove.

"Look out there," Count Charbouille cautioned.

"We ought to kick you out, Grantham!" Elston declared in a hoarse, angry voice. "Hobnobbin' with a Frenchie who don't know a damn thing about cattle. Didn't we make it clear at the meeting last week? Why don't you sell your ranch and go back east where you belong—and take Frenchie there with you!"

Grantham had stifled a groan at the shove, his face paling from the sudden searing pain, but he composed himself. "Mr. Elston, the count and I are talking, and you have no business interrupting us this way."

"Who the hell are you to tell me what to do, Grantham?" Elston clenched his right hand into a fist and struck Grantham hard on the right shoulder. The rancher groaned aloud this time, and his face contorted with pain.

Pierre de Charbouille sprang up from his chair, his lips tightening. "M'sieu Elston, your behavior is abominable! I demand an apology."

"You can't demand anything of me, Frenchie! Who the hell do you think you are anyway?"

"Apologize!" Count Charbouille repeated, his voice growing angrier.

"I will not! But I just might see how bad your friend's wound is." Elston raised his fist, and his mouth formed into a sneering smile.

The count stepped in front of Elston and with a sweep of his arm blocked the drunken rancher's fist.

"Why, you skunk!" Elston erupted.

Several members and waiters were drawn by the disturbance and stood ready to intervene.

"I refuse to be insulted by the likes of you, M'sieu Elston. I hereby challenge you to a duel!"

"Go away, Frenchie, I got no truck with you—" Elston said.

But at the same moment, Pierre de Charbouille had drawn a glove from his waistcoat pocket and struck Elston across the face. "Now then, M'sieu Elston, you've no choice but to accept my challenge or else proclaim yourself a coward before all these members."

Albert Elston staggered back, startled by the unexpected retaliation. Then, his eyes narrowed cunningly and in a sly, slurred tone, he replied, "Well, now, so you wanna duel me, do you, Frenchie? All right. I'll just take you up on it. Tomorrow morning at dawn, in back of the club."

At this moment Maxwell Grantham rose from his chair and laid a hand on his friend's arm. "Pierre, I cannot allow you to do this. I can fight my own battles."

"I am not fighting for you, *mon ami*. You heard what M'sieu Elston here called me. The duel will take place tomorrow morning," Count Charbouille interrupted. Then, turning to Elston, he said in a steely voice, "I shall eagerly await your arrival."

"Yeah, I'll bet you will. Wait now, the feller who gets challenged has the right to pick his weapons, ain't that so, Frenchie?" Elston sneered. "Well, I'll take a good ol' Colt revolver. Let's see if you can beat me with that!"

"*Soit, entendu!* At dawn, then."

Elston turned to some of the members who had witnessed the scene and were amazed that the confrontation would come to this conclusion. "I'll kill 'im for you, boys!" he proclaimed, slapping his chest with his pudgy hand. "So help me, the club'll have a vacancy come Monday." With this, Albert Elston staggered out.

Pierre turned to his friend. "Maxwell, I know what I am doing. The man insulted me, and I intend to teach him a lesson. Have no fear for me—I am an expert shot. I only wish he had chosen rapiers, for then I should have given him a few delightful scars that would mar him for life—though he is ugly enough at present even without those." The count shrugged. "As it is, I intend to cause him some pain and considerable humiliation."

The eleventh of November began as a bleak day, with a few drifting flakes of snow. Despite the early hour, twenty members of the Cheyenne Club had come out, eager to see the outcome of the duel.

Albert Elston had brought as his second his foreman, Cash Agnew, a lean, taciturn man reputed to be one of the best *pistoleros* in Wyoming. The nobleman had asked Jean-Louis Barbeau, his tall, supercilious-looking majordomo, to act as his.

Despite the discomfort of his shoulder wound, which Elston's shove and blow had made throb with pain for hours, Maxwell Grantham had insisted that Hank Johnson drive him in the buggy to witness the duel at the Cheyenne Club. He felt responsible for the risk his friend was about to undertake. If anything were to happen to the Frenchman, he could never forgive himself. On their way to the club, he had grumbled to his foreman, "Dammit all, Hank, I'm just as good a shot with my left hand as with my right. I shouldn't have let him take over for me."

"Boss, you know that the count wouldn't allow that. Beside, I've heard some eye-opening tales about this Frenchman; he'll do all right. Anyhow, from what you said, Elston will have to do a hell of a lot of sobering up to be ready this early in the day."

Pierre de Charbouille, dapperly dressed as was his wont, had asked the president of the club, Philip Dater, to act as judge. Dater summoned the opponents and their seconds, examined the revolvers, and then said, "I want you to know that I frown upon this, gentlemen. I ask you to reconsider—"

"Not on your life, Dater!" Elston answered roughly, sneering at the Frenchman.

"And you, sir?" Dater turned to Pierre de Charbouille.

"My opponent needs a good lesson, M'sieu Dater. I am here to provide one."

"Oh, you are?" Elston jeered. "Hell, we'll soon see about that. I hope that fancy guy you brought along to be your second knows how to measure you for a coffin, Frenchie."

"That will do!" the club president ordered. "Now, at my count, gentlemen, you will walk off twenty paces. When I give the word, you are to turn and fire. Under the dueling code, if either of you should attempt to fire before that word is given, I have the right to shoot the offender down. If you have no questions or objections, you will now place yourselves back to back."

Albert Elston glanced back over his shoulder and muttered, "Say your prayers, Frenchie. Sunday's as good a day as any to die—maybe better. Say your prayers real quick."

To this gibe, Pierre de Charbouille did not deign to reply. Revolver in hand, he waited for Dater to begin counting. After a moment, clearing his throat, the club's president began: "One . . . two . . . three . . ."

Elston appeared to have recovered from his inebriation of the night before, and he was sure that he would kill his opponent. Nevertheless, he was careful to heed

Philip Dater's warning and had no intention of breaking the code.

"Eighteen . . . nineteen . . . twenty!"

Elston turned and with a snarl of rage fired brashly, but the bullet whined past the count's left arm. Unperturbed, the dapper nobleman raised his revolver and carefully took aim. Elston blanched, his eyes widening as he saw the muzzle of the gun level at his head, yet he dared not turn away or fling himself to the ground, for if he did, he would be branded as a coward by all his associates. Ringleader of the mutinous cattlemen as he was, he realized he would have to stand the count's fire.

Slowly, the Frenchman squinted along the sights and then squeezed the trigger. "Jesus Christ!" Elston yelled, clapping his left hand to his ear. The bullet had very neatly taken off his left earlobe.

A chorus of incredulous gasps came from the astonished witnesses, not the least of whom was Maxwell Grantham. Elston staggered back, trying to staunch the blood that ran down his shirt and whimpering from what he had perceived as his near scrape with death.

"M'sieu Elston, let me say now that your earlobe was indeed my target. I could easily have killed you." His tone dripped with sarcasm. "But I will tell you this: If ever again you bother M'sieu Grantham or myself, I shall kill you."

"You—you low son of a bitch!" Elston hissed, his fear turning to anger. "I'll get you for this! Making a fool of me in front of everybody—you'll pay for this, Frenchie!" His foreman came to him now and tried to halt the flow of blood with a bandana, but Elston snarled, "Go bring Doc Bouchard to my place. And don't take your goddamned time bringing him, either.

I'll ride back home now. I'll fix that French bastard, I'll fix him!''

The crowd went their separate ways, and Maxwell Grantham clasped his friend's hand. "That was wonderful, Pierre! What you did to Elston ought to make him think twice—but you've made a deadly enemy."

"Maxwell, *mon ami*!" Pierre replied coolly. "You need not fear for my safety. In your country, a man proves himself by what he does, not by the pretense he makes. The ranchers will think better of me now. M'sieu Elston was all bluff and bluster, full of contempt for me, a silly foreigner. Now I trust he will change his opinion. But come now, Maxwell, let me take you to my chateau. We shall have a celebration breakfast. I know that my wife is most anxious and will be relieved to know how well it all turned out."

Oblivious to the early hour, Cash Agnew galloped off to the Bouchard house, wakened Hugo, and insisted that the doctor waste no time in accompanying him. "My boss's been shot, Doc, and he's bleedin' bad!"

"I'm coming, I'm coming." Hugo tugged on trousers, shirt, and heavy coat, reached for his bag, then kissed his sleeping wife. Then he hurried out to join the impatient foreman.

As they rode toward Elston's ranch, Agnew informed the young doctor what had taken place, and Hugo was surprised to hear of Pierre de Charbouille's marksmanship. He would never have believed that the suave nobleman could outshoot a burly, ill-tempered cattle rancher like Elston.

When he entered the ranch house, he found Albert Elston in bed, both hands pressed to a towel he had applied to his bleeding earlobe. Hugo greeted the distraught rancher, then said, "I'm going to give you a sedative first, Mr. Elston. Then I'll clean the wound and examine it. I'll probably have to take some stitches.''

"Do what you have to do, and be damned fast. Cash, when the doc here's done, you bring your best gunmen in. We're gonna have us a palaver.''

"Right, boss.'' Agnew left the bedroom.

Hugo administered the sedative and then carefully cleaned and swabbed the wound. He had to take nine stitches, and Elston swore at each one. Like most bullies, he was a coward when it came to pain.

"Mr. Elston, you were lucky you escaped with your life.''

Elston glared at him. "Doc, he made a laughingstock out of me. He'll be sorry, you watch and see.''

"Why not let the matter be done with?''

"Don't tell me you're siding with that sissified Frenchie? All right, Bouchard, you've done your work. Now get the hell out of here! Tell Cash I said to pay you off, whatever you charge.'' Elston gingerly groped with a forefinger for his wounded ear, which Hugo had bandaged.

"I wouldn't touch that, and if it does start to itch, that'll be the stitches. I'll take them out when the wound has healed—in a couple of weeks, most likely.''

"All right, all right, you've said your piece, now beat it!'' the rancher shouted, savagely dismissing him.

About fifteen minutes after Hugo had returned to his house, doffed his clothes, and climbed back into bed to resume his sleep, Cash Agnew entered Elston's bedroom with six *pistoleros*. Elston was propped up by pillows in bed, smoking a cigar, with a glass of whiskey in his hand. He glowered at the men as they walked in.

"Hey, boss, what happened to you?'' One of the *pistoleros* smiled slightly.

"Wipe that smirk off your dirty face, Rodriguez, or you won't be working for me anymore. Same goes for the rest of you, too. Anybody object?"

The men cast their eyes at the floor and remained silent.

"Good. Now here's what I want you to do. I'm gonna get even with that bastard Grantham—"

"Grantham? Cash said the count shot you," Rodriguez interrupted.

"If you'd shut your goddamned mouth . . . !" Elston yelled, his face turning red. He tossed down the rest of his shot of whiskey and said in a calmer tone, "The count shot me, right, but Grantham is the one I was after in the first place."

"What can we do, boss?" Agnew demanded anxiously.

"Use your brains, idiot! You're the foreman. Do I have to do all the thinking around here?" Elston raged, shifting his cigar from side to side of his fleshy mouth and glaring at them all. "Keep your eyes and ears open. Let me know anything you hear about what Grantham and the count are up to—*anything*, understand? Something is bound to turn up to help us. And once Grantham's out of the way, Frenchie will be next." Elston chewed on his cigar for a few moments, seeming to savor the idea of revenge. Then he shouted, "Now get out of here and go to work on it! That's all!"

Chapter 18

The same day that Laure Kenniston had received the telegram from Paul saying he was safe and intending to visit Wyoming, she had wired Lopasuta Bouchard in New Orleans, asking him to go to Wyoming and bring Paul back home. She had sent a second wire to Hugo and Cecily, thanking them in advance for looking after her son until Lopasuta could arrive to bring him back safely.

Now, the day after her visit with Jessica Haskins in Tuscaloosa, she wrote a lengthy letter to Arabella Parmenter in Galveston, thanking her for her intervention with Paul. Finally, she wrote another letter, this one to Jessica, thanking her friend for the wonderful reunion and telling her that Paul was safe and would most likely be home in a few weeks.

This done, she knelt in prayer to thank God for the news of Paul's safety and said a prayer for Leland's soul.

Laure's wire was delivered to Lopasuta's house in New Orleans on the evening of Wednesday, November 7. His wife, Geraldine, opened the envelope and quickly read the telegram. She sighed; her husband would have to take the long train ride to Cheyenne. Tonight Lopasuta was having dinner with a client, and she decided to wait up for him.

By now, the children were all asleep. The eldest, Dennis, was now six; Luke was a year younger; and Marta was almost four. Geraldine decided to occupy herself with her sewing, for she was making a dress for little Marta. She frowned, for it was nearly eleven o'clock at night. It was unlike her husband to stay out so late when he had to work the next morning. There were several other cases that Lopasuta and his partner, Eugene DuBois, were handling that were scheduled for hearings on the New Orleans court calendar throughout the month of November. How on earth would her overworked husband find time to fetch Laure's boy from Wyoming? Geraldine sighed and continued to sew.

Benjamin Stoddard was a plump, thickly bearded, gray-haired man in his midfifties, whose wife and daughter were presently concluding their trip to Europe. After treating his attorney, Lopasuta Bouchard, to a superb dinner, Stoddard had insisted on spending a few hours at La Maison de Bonne Chance, the gambling casino once owned by Laure. Leland had sold the casino for her, but stricken by his manic-depressive malady, he had gambled away a good deal of the proceeds of that sale, an act that had helped plunge Windhaven Plantation into its present severe economic straits.

For his part, Lopasuta would have greatly preferred to take his leave of Benjamin Stoddard tonight and return home to Geraldine, but his client would have none of this. "You're my guest, Lopasuta, and I'm in the mood for a game of chance. Now surely your wife can spare you for a few hours. I'm going to win my case against Andrew Drumain, and I don't want to celebrate that victory by myself. Come along now—my carriage is waiting!"

Lopasuta had felt obliged to humor the middle-aged

hotel owner. He was representing the man in a case involving a patron who had tumbled down the carpeted stairs of Stoddard's hotel and brought suit not only for injury but also for ridicule by the hotel employees, who, the patron claimed, had laughed at him as he fell. Lopasuta had learned that the patron had been intoxicated at the time, through no fault of the hotel. The final hearing before the judge was the following Tuesday.

Lopasuta knew that Stoddard was an inveterate gambler and was afraid it would be well past midnight before he returned home. The thought of sending a messenger to Geraldine occurred to him, but Stoddard had given him no time to do so, taking hold of his arm and leading him out to the carriage as he jovially boasted of how he expected to break the bank tonight at the elegant casino, the glittering temple of pleasure.

As Lopasuta Bouchard watched Benjamin Stoddard stack a little pile of chips on a *carré* on the green baize cloth of the roulette table, he took his watch out of his waistcoat pocket, consulted it, frowned, and wondered how much longer Stoddard would go on playing. Well, he couldn't be rude to a client. Stoddard's liking for him had brought him other business in the past.

A pretty attendant wearing a red velvet dress with rhinestone buckles brought him a glass of chilled white wine as he sat in the chair watching his client continue the pursuit of riches. Lopasuta accepted the glass and tossed a coin onto the attendant's tray. She gave him a warm glance, and her full, soft lips murmured, *"Merci, m'sieu!"* as she made her way around the table to serve others.

The tall Comanche lawyer sipped his wine and noticed a man in a plaid waistcoat and trousers walking about slowly, watching the patrons at the various tables.

This man had attracted Lopasuta's attention because he had an appearance that set him apart from the genteel clientele of the gambling hall. The man's light blue eyes were shrewdly shifting, narrow, and appraising, and his lips formed a faintly cynical smile. Lopasuta dismissed the man's expression as insignificant, knowing that he himself, when in a courtroom, had a habit of scrutinizing a strange face to memorize it, searching for character traits that might determine whether that face belonged to a potential enemy or friend.

The man moved out of Lopasuta's range of vision now, and the lawyer finished his wine and turned back to the study of his client's play as Benjamin Stoddard pushed a large pile of chips forward on a *carré* again, stepped back, and watched as the croupier spun the wheel, saying, *"Rien ne va plus,"* thus formally declaring that no further bets would be taken. The wheel stopped at last; there was the sound of the ball rolling back and forth until it came to rest. Stoddard uttered a soft groan and shook his head. The croupier's rake confirmed the outcome, for it removed the large pile of chips from the *carré*.

Stoddard now turned to Lopasuta and, with a shrug, declared, "I very nearly won that time. If the little ball had landed in the next space, I'd have made three thousand dollars. Oh, well. I had amusement for the money I squandered. Let's have a last glass of wine, and then I'll get my carriage."

Lopasuta pleasantly nodded his agreement to this, and Stoddard beckoned to the pretty attendant to get the lawyer more wine and a glass for himself. When she did so, Stoddard lifted his in a toast to the charming young *soubrette*, who curtsied and colored hotly. Then, as a gesture of gallantry and thanks for her service, he fished in his waistcoat pocket for a small bill and tossed it with a grandiose gesture onto her tray. Finishing his wine at a gulp, he set the glass back down on the tray and then turned to Lopasuta. "Now we can be off!"

As he turned away from the table to accompany his client, Lopasuta saw the man dressed in plaid come toward them, quicken his steps, and brush by them as he left the room ahead of them. There was not even a murmured apology on the fellow's part, and Lopasuta frowned. Not everyone could be a gentleman, he reflected.

Once in the street outside the casino, Stoddard looked around for his conveyance and said, "Where's the lazy doorman? Where are my horse and carriage?"

The liveried doorman's face fell, and taking off his top hat, he scratched his head as he strove to explain. "M'sieu, I have dreadful news. Your horse—something happened to it. It had the heaves. The man in charge of our stable said it looked as though your horse was poisoned! I regret it deeply, m'sieu. Your horse will have to remain here overnight. I will try to call you a hansom cab—"

"Damnation!" Stoddard fumed. Then, after a moment's thought, he winked at Lopasuta. "Do you know what I've been thinking, Mr. Bouchard? We're near Rampart Street. And it so happens there's a very pretty *fille de joie* named Lucette, with the most brilliant red hair you've ever seen. I should like very much to visit her. Would you like to accompany me? There are one or two friends of hers whom you might find appealing."

"No, sir. I'll be going home," Lopasuta replied curtly.

"Of course, of course. Well, then, would you be terribly offended, Mr. Bouchard, if I said good night to you? The doorman will find a hansom cab for you."

"I would take no offense. I bid you good night, Mr. Stoddard."

Benjamin Stoddard and Lopasuta shook hands. "I'll leave you here." Stoddard strode down the sidewalk in a northerly direction, turned the corner, and disappeared.

"I'll do my best to find you a cab, m'sieu, but at this late hour, there are not too many drivers who come into this section," the doorman remarked anxiously.

"Well, then, don't bother. Two blocks from here, as I remember, there's an intersection with more traffic than this street. I'll take my chances there."

"Ah, c'est vrai, m'sieu, but do be careful. The surrounding neighbors are not the best."

"Of course. Good night to you." Lopasuta nodded and began to walk down the street.

It was dark, with only the gas lamps flaring at the corners, casting an eerie glow on the storefronts and the buildings of this section of New Orleans. Lopasuta walked out to the curb of the street, but strangely enough no hansom cab was in sight. A haze had come over the moon, heralding an oncoming storm. Another block and he would be at the intersection. If need be, he could walk home, for it was not much more than a mile and a quarter. Geraldine would be worried, for it was well after midnight now. He wished that he had begged off going to the casino, particularly since his host had quixotically decided to end the night with a bout of commercial love.

The air was humid, and Lopasuta took several deep breaths, then quickened his step toward the intersection. The darkness made the distance seem even longer. Suddenly he stopped dead in his tracks; from the ghostly light reflected by a gas lamp across the street, he could see two men come out of the shadows. With drawn knives they came slowly toward him, smirks on their faces, ready for any move he might make.

The two footpads glanced at each other and nodded.

"Now then, friend, why not hand us your money and keep out of trouble?" the older of the two wheedled.

"I have no money for thieves." At this moment Lopasuta remembered a news story in the *New Orleans Picayune*, warning citizens to be on their guard against a clever group of thieves who dressed elegantly and frequented good restaurants, theaters, and casinos to select their victims. "I know who you are—you belong to that gang the *Picayune* wrote about last week. Your leader must be the man I saw in the casino!"

"That knowledge won't do you much good, m'sieu," the younger man said in a low, sinister voice. He suddenly lunged at Lopasuta, but the Comanche nimbly leaped back to the right. The other man now came at him, and even as Lopasuta quickly dodged him, moving backward to his left, the tip of the man's knife dug into the lawyer's right thigh.

Grimacing with pain, Lopasuta clamped his right hand on the older man's wrist and twisted it viciously, forcing the thief to release the knife. It clattered onto the planking of the sidewalk, and Lopasuta swiftly seized it just as the other thief came at him.

"I'll kill you for that, *mon ami*," the thief hissed as he lunged at Lopasuta's breast. But Lopasuta deftly parried with the knife he had retrieved from the other assailant, and a clash of steel rang out as the two men, face to face, exerted all their strength to force down the other's knife arm.

"Kill him! Kill him, Benedict!" the onlooker cried.

Lopasuta suddenly stooped and, lunging right, drove the knife deep into Benedict's left side. The thief uttered a gurgling shriek, drew back his own knife as if to retaliate, and then slumped to his knees. His accomplice, with a cry of terror, turned and fled, disappearing down an alley.

The bloodied knife in his right hand, Lopasuta stood there panting, and glanced down at his leg. His own blood was staining his trousers. He stared at the man called Benedict, but the thief was dead, his eyes glazed and wide, staring up at the dark sky.

The liveried doorman of La Maison de Bonne Chance had been hurrying up and down the street on which the casino was situated, hoping to find a hansom cab for the tall Comanche. Having heard the cry of the escaped thief, he had run like one possessed until he had reached Lopasuta. "*Mon Dieu*, I was afraid of this," he said, panting. "I saw one of them—"

"Yes, there were two. I managed to take the knife out of the other man's hand and use it against this devil. His friend ran off."

"You're wounded, m'sieu!"

"Just in the leg. I can stop the bleeding with my handkerchief. Get the civil guard."

"Surely one of the patrols should come by soon. I am upset that a patron of our casino should sustain this injury—and all because of your friend's horse!"

The doorman went to find a civil guard while Lopasuta waited. Twenty minutes later, he returned with a uniformed patrolman, and Lopasuta gave an accurate description of the thief whose knife he had taken to defend himself. The patrolman took Lopasuta's name and address, then said, "In the morning, m'sieu, it will be necessary for you to come to the Cabildo to make a formal statement."

"Of course."

"I commend you for your courage." The patrolman

looked intently down at the corpse of Benedict. "One less rogue to plague our beautiful city."

After the patrolman had arranged for the removal of the corpse, Lopasuta, despite the lateness of the hour, asked the man to accompany him to a nearby hospital, where he had the knife wound properly treated and bandaged. Then, after promising the patrolman that he would appear at the Cabildo the next morning, he at last found a hansom cab to drive him to his home.

Geraldine had been frantic, and when her husband quietly let himself in, he found her standing in her night shift and robe, her face drawn with anxiety. "Lopasuta, what happened to you? I was so worried, I couldn't sleep."

"It's all right, Geraldine."

"You're walking so stiffly. My God! You've been hurt!" she gasped.

"Don't worry, my darling." He ascended the stairs, trying to maintain a normal step so as not to deepen her concern. "Tonight, my Comanche blood came in handy. I was attacked by two men and disarmed one of them. Unfortunately, I had to kill the other. Tomorrow morning I shall have to make a formal statement."

"Then you're not seriously hurt? Don't try to hide anything from me," she said anxiously, beginning to weep.

He took her into his arms, kissing away her tears. "I have never lied to you, and I never shall. It's only a slight wound in my leg. I went to the hospital to have it treated."

"Oh Lord, I'm so relieved! If anything should ever happen to you . . . Oh, a telegram came for you from Laure this evening. I'll get it for you right away!"

Geraldine disengaged herself and hurried to the bedroom, returning to him at once with the telegram.

He read it quickly, then sighed. "Poor Laure! How worried she must have been! I don't know if I'll be able to go to Wyoming for Paul. I may have to stay in town to testify about the attack. I won't know for how long until tomorrow. I'll wire Laure that I'll go to Wyoming just as soon as this business is over with. Ah, well, let's go to bed, my darling. I must get up early."

"Of course, sweetheart. I'm so relieved." She put a soft palm over his mouth and pressed herself against him. "Dear Lopasuta," she breathed.

After a quick breakfast with Geraldine and the children, the tall lawyer hailed a hansom cab to take him to the Cabildo. The chief of the civil guard respectfully greeted him. "Mr. Bouchard, I have the report that you gave Louis Calteran late last night. Were there no witnesses?"

"No, sir. The street was deserted. In fact, if I had been able to find a carriage or a hansom cab at the casino, this incident would never have happened."

"I must take your deposition and turn it over to the judge of the court, and then there will be a hearing. I do not foresee any trouble for you, Mr. Bouchard. Your fine reputation is known, and you have acted as I am sure any man would who was attacked."

"I have pressing family business that requires some travel. Do you know how long the procedures will take?"

The chief shrugged. "From your own experience, you know that our courts are crowded with civil and criminal suits. Surely in a week or two it can be completed. I will see Judge DuCroix. Rest assured I will do everything I can for you. I think you've rid this city of a cutthroat who has, with his gang, accounted for quite a few thefts and at least two murders. Your deposition says that you are prepared to identify the man who ran away, as well as the one in the casino who you think may be the leader.''

"True. If I can assist you in any way, it will be my pleasure to do so.''

After leaving the Cabildo, Lopasuta went to the telegraph office and sent a wire to Laure Kenniston, informing her that he would leave for Wyoming as soon as circumstances permitted. This done, he went to his office to tell his partner, Eugene DuBois, about the previous night's adventure, as well as Laure's telegram, which would necessitate Eugene's assuming Lopasuta's case load when he left town.

Late on Monday afternoon, November 12, Paul Bouchard got off the train at Cheyenne. Bewildered by his new surroundings, he asked the stationmaster how he could get transportation to the house of the people he had come to visit. The crotchety old stationmaster said, pointing, "The stable is that way. They'll rent you a horse and buggy, or maybe Chet Ames'll send one of his boys to drive you there in style—if you got the cash to pay for it.''

"I can pay my way, mister. Thank you for the information." Paul drew himself up, gave the stationmaster a nod, and walked out of the railroad yard.

He found the stable easily enough, and the owner, Chet Ames, hearing him ask if he might be driven to Dr. Hugo Bouchard's residence, affably replied, "Why sure, son. I'll have my boy Artie take you there in just a jiffy. It'll cost you a dollar.''

"I can pay it.''

Chet Ames inclined his head. "There's Artie now.

Artie, I want you to drive this young feller to Doc Bouchard's place."

By sundown, the horse and buggy was drawing up in front of Hugo and Cecily Bouchard's attractive little house, and just at the same moment, Hugo came riding up on his white gelding. He had been to Albert Elston's house to change the dressing of the wound, which he had pronounced was healing satisfactorily.

"I'll bet you're Paul Bouchard!" Hugo said as he dismounted and tethered the mare's reins to a hitching post.

"That's right. Are you Dr. Bouchard?"

"Certainly am. Good to meet you. You've had quite a trip, all the way from Montgomery to Galveston and up to Wyoming. Come in, come in. Cecily will be back from the hospital in time for supper. I'll bet you're hungry."

"I sure am, Dr. Bouchard."

"Call me Hugo. After all, we're relatives. You and my father are both sons of Luke Bouchard—by different wives. That makes you my dad's half brother. By golly, that means you're my half uncle!"

"Gosh," Paul exclaimed wonderingly, shaking his head. "It's hard to believe!"

"It does seem rather strange."

"Mother's talked about you," Paul said eagerly. "You didn't like being on a ranch, so you became a doctor. That's sort of the way I felt at Windhaven Plantation. All I was doing was farm work. It was awful, and it didn't have any future, so I decided to run away and find out what I could do on my own."

"And give your poor mother fits in the process! Well, come on in and we'll wait for Cecily." Hugo slapped the boy on the back and led him into the house.

About half an hour later, when Hugo had shown Paul to his room and Paul had unpacked the clothes the Parmenters had bought him, Cecily arrived home.

"Paul Bouchard! Welcome to Cheyenne!" Cecily merrily greeted him as she put away her medical bag.

"Do you realize," Hugo said in a mock-solemn tone, "that this wayward youngster is my uncle?"

Cecily laughed. "Welcome, Uncle Paul!" she said. "I'll prepare supper for two hungry men who have just discovered their positions on the Bouchard family tree!"

"Good idea, sweetheart." Hugo clapped Paul on the back. "You'll want to wash up, Uncle," he joked, then added in a more serious voice, "One word of warning—after your mother got your wire about coming to Wyoming, she sent a wire to Lopasuta, asking him to get you and take you safely back home. So enjoy your freedom while you may."

"I will. And I want to talk with you, Hugo. I need your advice. I want to be as useful and helpful to people as you are when I'm your age."

"You will be, with an attitude like that, dear," Cecily said warmly. "Now go wash up properly, or I won't serve either of you a thing except the sharp edge of my tongue!"

On the evening of that same day, Maxwell Grantham and Count Pierre de Charbouille met for supper at the Cheyenne Club. Albert Elston did not grace the club with his surly presence this evening, but one of his new cowhands, Kyle Winger, was there. Winger had just drifted into Wyoming to find work and would not be recognized by the club's members. In order to gain admission, Elston had given Winger a guest pass and told him to "mingle and find out what the goddamn Frenchie and Grantham are up to."

Winger came in quietly, as was his wont. Dressed in

a stiff white shirt and a cravat, he mingled, calling little attention to himself. From one end of the huge room where the members relaxed before dinner, he observed Count Pierre de Charbouille and Maxwell Grantham talking in subdued tones. He sidled closer to them until he was able to make out what Grantham was saying: "At four tomorrow afternoon, a few miles east of Rocky River, I'm meeting with the sheep raisers' leaders. I'll learn what water and grazing rights the sheep owners want, and then I'll tell them what the cattle owners want in return. I'm hoping to take the first steps toward peaceful coexistence."

"If you can accomplish that, *mon ami*, you will have worked wonders," the count answered enthusiastically. "Please come to tell me of the outcome."

Winger blessed his lucky stars that he had been able to intercept that bit of news and earn the goodwill of his new employer. He took a last covetous look around the ornately furnished room, swore under his breath, moved to the exit, and disappeared into the night. Outside, he untied the reins of his horse, mounted it, and rode back at a gallop to confer with Albert Elston.

As soon as Elston had heard the news, he called a meeting of his *pistoleros*. "Boys, tomorrow afternoon at four, some of you are gonna pay a little visit to Grantham's ranch. Grantham's men don't know all of you, do they?"

"They don't know me, boss," Al Murtree, a lanky, towheaded wrangler in his late twenties, spoke up.

"How about you, Jackson?" Elston demanded of Murtree's companion, a stocky cowhand in his early thirties, as efficient with knife and shotgun as he was with a Colt revolver.

"They don't know me from Adam," Ted Jackson growled.

"Good. You boys, Winger and Jackson and Murtree, go see my housekeeper. She'll give you a half dozen bottles of good whiskey. Take it to Grantham's tomorrow afternoon, make friends with some of his men. Get 'em so drunk they can't stand up, then snoop around. While you're there, you're gonna happen to pick up a few things that folks'll recognize right away as Grantham's. We're gonna use 'em to get the son of a bitch in hot water. We'll stage a raid on a sheep raiser's place. After we have what we need, I'll call you all in and give you the plan that'll send Maxwell Grantham to the gallows!''

Chapter 19

There had been a light snowfall early the morning of Tuesday, November 13, a precursor of much more to come. The winter's second raging blizzard, now west of Wyoming, was heading east. The air was crisp and wintry, and hardworking cowhands had ice crystals in their beards and mustaches.

It was about four in the afternoon, and Maxwell Grantham, in a buggy with Hank Johnson and accompanied by two other wranglers from Grantham's outfit, had ridden to meet with the six sheep raisers who owned the largest flocks and acreage—the six who, to most cattle ranchers, represented the strongest threat to their monopolistic control of rangeland and water rights.

Accompanying the owners were their head sheepherders, mostly men of Basque or Mexican descent, loyal to their employers and grateful for their wages, which enabled them to live better than they had in their native lands. These simple men were disturbed and bewildered by the ferocious enmity they and their flocks raised among some cattlemen. Several of the sheepherders' friends had been killed and their sheep slaughtered for no apparent reason. They took pains to keep the sheep inside their employers' borders and were thus baffled by the savage range war.

Peter Ringold, a bearded, jovial Swiss who owned

six thousand acres and a flock of twenty-five hundred sheep, was the spokesman for all the sheep raisers in the territory. He was known to be a gentle, fair-minded man.

There was also Ringold's neighbor, Jasper Cullingham, who owned some forty-five hundred acres and two thousand sheep, an English farmer who had been at the mercy of an inconsiderate landlord until his uncle in New Zealand had died and left him a fortune. He had been in Wyoming Territory for three years now, and his wool was considered to be of prime quality, as was Peter Ringold's.

Besides these two, there was Christophe Desaigne, born in Normandy, the very same province old Lucien Bouchard had been born in. Attracted by the open frontier and prompted by his dissatisfaction with taxes, he, too, with his wife and children, had come to make a fresh start. So had Hans Schweigstrom, a burly, good-natured Silesian; Bernard Westerman, a middle-aged Bavarian; and William Garner, a widower who had raised sheep in the Ohio Valley region and, saddened by the tragic death of his wife and three children in a fire, had sought the vast isolation of this land to forget his sorrow as best he could through the arduous, never-ending work generated by a large flock of sheep.

These six had been the most outraged by the cattlemen's insults and threats, and Peter Ringold had gone from ranch to ranch, exhorting the sheep raisers to form an alliance akin to the cattlemen's, to stand together against the cattlemen's hatred and violence. Ringold had sent a messenger to Maxwell Grantham, the president of the Wyoming Stock Growers' Association, urging this late afternoon meeting.

Above them, the clouds raced across the sky, driven by the approaching storm, which also tugged at the branches of the fir trees and the spruce and the oak. Grantham did not like the look of the sky.

"I'm glad you've come out to meet me, gentlemen," he said. "I think I know what all of you have been through. I propose we form an alliance between our two groups. The senseless slaughter of animals and the harm to sheepherders has got to end."

"You talk big, Herr Grantham," Hans Schweigstrom spoke up, glancing at his companions. "I also would like peace. But I ask you, if we form this alliance that you speak of, how do we know the cattle ranchers won't pretend to work for peace, then shoot us and our animals later that same day?"

"I will do my best to make sure that doesn't happen, Mr. Schweigstrom," Grantham courageously retorted in a loud, clear voice. "Today we should take steps toward a plan we all can live by. I will carry it back to the Stock Growers' Association and try to get the ranchers to agree to it. We have to be content with a suspicious and wary truce at first, but if they would keep their word and you keep yours, gentlemen, some progress will be made."

William Garner, a dour-faced, lean sheep raiser, spoke up. "I will try anything reasonable, but I won't kiss the behind of any cattle rancher. My flocks have been dynamited, and I haven't done anything wrong!"

"But you see, Mr. Garner," Grantham spoke out, "many cattlemen believe that sheep eat the grass down to the roots, leaving nothing for cattle. On the other hand, from what I'm told, sheep require a great deal less water than cattle."

"You have heard right about the water, Herr Grantham," Schweigstrom spoke up. "A great deal less, and we have tributaries of the Rocky River as well as freshwater creeks near and on our land. As for our sheep endangering the grasslands, that is untrue. There is more than enough graze for all our stock.''

"The cattlemen's water needs may be the place for us to start,'' Grantham said. "Most of the cattle ranches in the area have little water, and, of course, their stock needs more than yours. I'm asking a lot, but if I tell the cattlemen that the sheep raisers are willing to allow the cattle to water, I think the ranchers will be taken aback by your generosity. It may inspire them to take the next step toward reconciliation.''

"Herr Grantham,'' Ringold spoke up, "if your cattlemen would agree to a truce, we would willingly give them access to our water. In return, we will make certain our flocks don't graze on their land.''

"That is very fair,'' Grantham said, nodding. "When I tell the ranchers what you've said, Mr. Ringold, they'll understand that you're not trying to take their land from them or drive them out.''

"It is all very well to hear these nice words,'' William Garner spoke up dourly, "but how can we be sure you mean what you say?''

"Mr. Garner, I'm sure you've noticed that my arm is in a sling. Let me tell you what happened. Last week somebody shot me in the back. It probably was one of the cattlemen who doesn't want me to come to an agreement with you. But I'm not the sort of man who backs down from a challenge. I'm going to do my level best to get that agreement between the cattlemen and the sheepherders.'' He looked around at the silent group. Then, with a wry chuckle, he concluded, "If I don't, I'll for sure have more than my arm in a sling!''

"I am glad we had this meeting with you, Herr Grantham. You are an honorable man.'' Peter Ringold came forward to offer Maxwell Grantham his hand, and the gray-haired rancher eagerly shook it.

*   *   *

On this same Tuesday afternoon, Lopasuta Bouchard was at his law office when a message came from the civil guard saying that a hearing had been scheduled before Judge Joel DuCroix for the following morning.

"That's good news, Eugene!" Lopasuta happily exclaimed to his partner. "If we can get it over with tomorrow, I can leave for Wyoming on Thursday. With you acting as my attorney, I anticipate no difficulties."

"Your confidence in me is gratifying—but in any case, I don't think you have anything to worry about."

"I hope not. I know my going to Wyoming will make extra work for you. Thank you for looking after the cases I have on the docket. You're a good friend as well as a good partner, Eugene. I'm very grateful. Shall we go over my testimony for the hearing tomorrow before Judge DuCroix?"

Promptly at nine the next morning, when Eugene DuBois accompanied Lopasuta to the courthouse, they found Judge DuCroix on the bench, with the coroner and bailiff awaiting Lopasuta's appearance.

"Mr. Bouchard," the elderly judge said, "in all cases wherein death by violence has occurred, a hearing must determine whether charges should be brought against the person involved. I have before me your deposition, admitting responsibility for the death by reason of self-defense. I also have the coroner's deposition. This informal hearing will establish for the record the facts of the case, following which I'll give you my decision as to the appropriateness of charges being brought."

"I understand, Your Honor," the lawyer replied solemnly.

The coroner began by presenting his findings in detail, and Lopasuta winced to hear the precise anatomical description of the fatal wound he had inflicted upon his assailant. It was only with difficulty that he reminded himself that he had been acting to protect himself against certain bodily harm.

Eugene placed a comforting hand on his partner's arm and, as the coroner was finishing his testimony, rose to present his client's position in the case, taking care to make mention of the stranger whom Lopasuta had seen circulating among the tables at La Maison de Bonne Chance, whom he believed to be part of the gang that attacked him.

Judge DuCroix listened intently, and when Eugene had resumed his seat, the elderly man shuffled some papers on his desk, cleared his throat, and spoke.

"I have here a report from the captain of the civil guard. Given the criminal record of the deceased, it is highly probable that he would be participating in such activities as you have described. Knowing Mr. Bouchard's reputation—not only as an outstanding citizen but a fine lawyer—I find no reason to hold him for trial. He is hereby cleared of all charges and free to go."

Lopasuta rose and inclined his head toward the elderly judge. "I am grateful to Your Honor."

"I must say, Mr. Bouchard," the judge added, "that New Orleans can ill afford to lose you as an attorney. In the future I hope that you will not leave yourself vulnerable to unsavory characters—it will be quite sufficient if you aid in their prosecution, rather than mete out their punishment."

Lopasuta could not help chuckling. "I shall take Your Honor's advice most seriously. And may I express my gratitude for your concern."

On the same afternoon that Maxwell Grantham met with the sheep raisers, James Weymore, dressed in his very best, drove upriver to the red-brick chateau at Windhaven Plantation. Ostensibly, he made his visit to introduce himself and express his great sympathy for Laure Kenniston's bereavement. In reality, he wished to have a look at this beautiful widow whose property he coveted.

After receiving title to the entire four hundred fifty acres that had belonged to Jessica Haskins, James Weymore moved into the large house on the property. Over a dozen years earlier, it had been virtually reconstructed with new red brick and solid timbers and glass windows.

To live in comfort, James Weymore engaged a staff from Montgomery: an eighteen-year-old stable boy, a widowed cook in her fifties, a majordomo who would also fulfill the role of valet, a foreman, and ten workers. All were white; Weymore considered black workers shiftless and given to bad habits.

As for Flora Alexander, the comely widow who had become his mistress in Tuscaloosa, he had told her that he was going east on business. Although she had been a satisfactory lover, it would be impossible—especially in light of her pregnancy—to have her come live with him near Windhaven Plantation. During their brief affair, he had very cleverly refrained from mentioning any property in Montgomery so that if she felt aggrieved by his prolonged absence from her bed, she would not think of looking there for him and unduly embarrass him.

As his buggy approached the twin-towered chateau, Weymore's eyes glittered with avarice. This was unique indeed! A castle in the middle of rural Alabama—the perfect setting for him! He knew that he must acquire it, and it did not much matter how. Perhaps the widow would need the money badly enough to sell it at a loss.

He stopped the horse, got down, and looked around

for someone to take the reins. Jasper Thornton, a son of the deceased foreman of Windhaven Plantation, came hurrying up to take the reins and to lead the horse and buggy into the stable. "Is your mistress at home, boy, do you know?" Weymore queried, his tone unconsciously taking on a note of contemptuousness, for this was his invariable attitude toward those born with black skin.

"Yes, sir. Miz Kenniston, she's home all right, sir."

"I'll announce myself. Take good care of that horse, now. Don't water him down too much," he curtly ordered as he strode toward the front door and, observing the huge brass knocker, took hold of it and rapped peremptorily.

Amelia Coleman, who was helping Clarabelle Hendry with household chores this afternoon, was closest to the front door when Weymore knocked. When she opened it, he smiled, for Amelia, a lovely octoroon, could have passed for white.

"A good afternoon to you, miss," he unctuously greeted her. "Could you announce me to Mrs. Kenniston? I am James Weymore, her new downriver neighbor, and I wish to pay my respects."

"If you'll come in, sir, I'll tell her you're here."

Weymore entered the foyer, noted the elegant furniture, and seated himself in an overstuffed chair, his hands in his lap, his back straight, his head held high—an individual to be reckoned with.

A few moments later, Laure entered, wearing a white muslin dress. In token of her mourning, a black band was sewn to the left sleeve.

Her visitor instantly rose, respectfully inclining his head, and in a suave voice declared, "Forgive me for intruding upon you, Mrs. Kenniston. My name is James Weymore. I've just moved onto the former Haskins property and learned that I would be your neighbor. I wished to come by and express my deepest sympathy for your great loss.''

''It's kind of you, Mr. Weymore. Jessica Haskins told me that she had offered the property for sale, but I didn't know who had bought it.''

''I was fortunate enough to learn of it from a realtor in Montgomery. I'm looking forward to taking my part in developing this thriving community.''

''I wish you the best of luck, Mr. Weymore.''

''Thank you. I hesitate to intrude upon you, as I say, but I've heard that—forgive me again—that you have had some slight difficulties in the handling of this plantation, none of them, of course, due to your own fine management.''

Laure gave him a quick look, trying to comprehend the motive for this flowery little speech, and then casually responded, ''If by that, Mr. Weymore, you mean that I have had financial reverses, you are quite correct. I daresay that most large properties in this part of the country are suffering now from the general economic setback.''

''Quite true, Mrs. Kenniston. Since you have been astute enough to divine my meaning and—may I apologize in advance for what I'm about to say—since I've fallen in love with this area, you will not be surprised that when I saw your magnificent chateau towering above the Alabama River and looking out over the bluff, I knew it would be a dream come true if I could acquire it. Perhaps if I made you a generous offer, one that would at once rid you of the financial burden—''

But Laure was already shaking her head. ''No, no, thank you, Mr. Weymore. I appreciate your sentiments, but I have no intention of selling Windhaven, not for any price. You may not know that it is the Bouchard legacy, and as such, it is my obligation to restore it and pass it on to the children of my second husband, Luke Bouchard. It is a sacred trust, you see.''

He gave her a low bow, his right hand inside the coat of the elegantly tailored gray linen suit. ''Mrs. Kenniston, I'm touched by your determination to keep the plantation. Alas, in a way you remind me somewhat of my poor wife, who regrettably died several years ago. For she, too, wished to keep our household together, and I think all the work she did killed her. I admire your intention to preserve all this, for it is a landmark. On the other hand, the money would be very handy for yourself and your children, would it not?''

''It would, Mr. Weymore, but not at the cost of sacrificing all that the original founder of Windhaven Plantation did to build this wonderful chateau for future generations to enjoy,'' Laure replied tartly. Those memories touched her, and her vision blurred from tears.

Weymore was silent for a moment, shrewdly trespassing on her obviously retrospective mood. Then carefully he phrased his next words: ''Then perhaps I can be of help in another way. I've been most fortunate in my own economic ventures. Would you allow me to invest in this plantation? I would accept it as collateral. By accepting this offer, you would overcome your financial difficulties—without endangering the legacy. It would be an agreement drawn up and approved by your attorney and mine.''

''That's most kind of you, sir, but I could never consider such an offer.''

Weymore then sought to be his most persuasive self and said forlornly, ''There's yet another reason I wish to do this. We've only just met, but you and I share a similar sorrow. I'm a lonely widower, and you have just lost your husband. We might be of some comfort to each other. We may find that, as landowners, we have much in common. And who knows? That may one day lead to, well, a closer association.''

Laure regarded him intently for a moment. She blushed and stammered, ''Why, Mr. Weymore, we— I—I don't know what to say. I'm most grateful for your kind thoughts and condolences, and I would be pleased to have you call again. But beyond that—well, I think we should leave matters just as they are for now.''

''Very well, then, but permit me to declare myself a friend whenever you are in need of one, my dear Mrs. Kenniston.'' Weymore stood and reached out to take her slim hand and bring it to his lips with the most courtly of gestures. ''It was kind of you to receive me. I hope I have not caused you any embarrassment or annoyance.''

''No, you haven't, sir. I am glad you are my neighbor. Now, if you will excuse me . . .''

''Of course, Mrs. Kenniston. I am glad I came; perhaps more than you can guess. Yes, I do hope to see you again. Good afternoon to you.''

Chapter 20

$\mathcal{A}$lbert Elston stood on the porch of his sprawling ranch house and stared gloatingly at the dozen men who had clustered before him. They included his foreman, Cash Agnew, his head *pistolero*, Jack Nantum, and his new cowhand, Kyle Winger. It was a little before midnight of the same day that had marked the conciliatory meeting between Maxwell Grantham and the sheep raisers.

"You, Murtree, and you, Jackson and Winger, did you get those things from Grantham's like I told you to?"

"Sure did, boss." Al Murtree sauntered forward with a broad grin on his homely face. "We took the whiskey over to some of Grantham's wranglers, and me and Jackson were getting on just fine. Then Winger snuck around the back and found an old glove in a shed. It had a fancy label on it, some shop back east. Has to be Grantham's."

"Fine, Murtree, fine. Anything else?"

"Sure. Ted said he had to go outside and piss, while I kept the wranglers busy playin' poker. He snuck around to the house."

"Get to the point!" Elston snapped.

"I got one of his Stetsons, boss." Ted Jackson now stepped forward, brandishing it. "There warn't any light in the kitchen, so I eases in there, see, and found myself in a hallway, and there, sure as God made little green apples, was a hat tree and a brand-new gray Stetson on it. So I swipes it. Now Kyle put the glove he found into my saddlebags, see, so I just put the hat in there, too, then went back to the poker game. We lost a little money on purpose, so they'd feel good and keep on drinking. Then we said good-bye and rode off, purty as you please.''

"Good thinking. I'll give the three of you whatever money you lost playing poker and a little extra for your pains. Now listen up. You're gonna hit Peter Ringold's flock tonight. Cash, you're in charge. Take my 45-80 along. Yessiree, boys, this is gonna work out real fine.'' Albert Elston laughed, his plump face twisted in hate. "Cash, make sure you kill the head sheepherder, that crazy Basque. And you, Nantum, be sure you plant the glove and the Stetson near the corpse. Grantham, he's gonna get the rope when he's brought to trial for the raid.''

"I gotta hand it to you, boss, that's real clever!'' Winger flatteringly put in.

Agnew took the rifle from his employer, checked it over, then took the box of bullets that Elston handed him, and put one of them into the chamber. "If this was a repeater, boss, I could really spray lead at a good range.''

"You don't need to spray a lot of lead! One shot from my rifle will kill a man from two hundred yards. All right, you know what to do. Just make sure nobody spots you. Wear bandannas, all of you. I don't want anyone recognized and traced back to me. And by God, if that should happen, I pity the man that gets me into it. He'll beg for the rope as an easy death before I get done with him, if I have to go to jail for his stupidity.''

"We've all got bandannas, and we all changed horses, just in case somebody might recognize a roan here or a bay there," Winger said.

"All right, get going."

Abruptly, Elston stomped back into the house, where Lupe, the young Mexican woman, awaited him with a pensive expression on her face. He stared greedily at her, a cruel smile on his sensual mouth, and then snarled, "Get me a glass of whiskey, Lupe, and make it snappy! Then take off your clothes. I'm in the mood for a little fun with you—unless, of course, you'd prefer to wait for Jack Nantum—"

"Oh, no, Señor Elston, I will do whatever you wish. Only, please, not that awful man again—I am so afraid of him. When he looks at me, it is like death," Lupe sobbingly stammered.

Juan Epanisse, the white-haired, sixty-two-year-old head sheepherder of Peter Ringold's large flock, found it hard to sleep. There were signs, all too ominous and unmistakable, of an approaching blizzard, and he was worried about the sheep. He was more conscientious than most employees, but that was because Juan Epanisse could not have asked for a finer employer than Peter Ringold. The man was a gentleman; he was considerate, and he looked upon a sheepherder as an equal.

Because of Juan's high regard for his employer, he was also concerned about the hatred he had seen in the cowhands, for they sometimes came near the flocks and threatened unspeakable things. Why should they hate Herr Ringold when everyone knew that here was a man who never spoke ill of his neighbors and who wanted only peace and the right to earn an honest living?

Juan thought of what Maxwell Grantham had said to the sheep raisers—words from the heart, and Juan believed them. If only they could come true, then he could ask for nothing better in this life than to go on tending these sheep for Herr Ringold. It was a rugged life, true enough, but he felt at peace within himself.

He put on just his woolen jacket, protection enough against cold weather; he was used to it. So long as he kept moving, he would keep warm.

At his belt he wore a sheathed knife, and he carried a heavy club—precautions against predators. When danger was near and the sheep caught the scent, they would bleat, and then the leader with the bell would move anxiously about and Juan would hear the bell and know what must be done.

About five hundred yards away stood a small hut, where Jorge Santurce lived. Juan and Jorge often visited each other when there was no work to be done, to drink wine and talk over their younger days when they had first come to work with sheep. He took a few steps toward the cottage, his eyes narrowing so that he might see better in the darkness.

Suddenly his body grew inexplicably tense. He told himself he was getting old. But then he heard the little bell of the flock's leader, and his pulse quickened. The leader did not move about unless there was trouble. Gripping the club tightly in his right hand, Juan moved forward, wanting to locate the bell so that he could determine what had made the leader restless so late at night.

Then it was that he heard the sound of horses' hooves, and at once he could tell there were many of them. He could see nothing. He should have lit a torch earlier; now there was no time. He quickened his step, moving in the direction of where he believed the bell had sounded.

Then there was chaos, the sound of maddened bleating, the yells and the curses of men riding hard, their horses bearing down on the helpless sheep. Before he could react, Juan heard the sickening thuds of clubs striking the helpless sheep, crushing their skulls, breaking their spines. In panic, some of the flock turned to run, and the bell rang again, again, and again.

"You there! What do you do with my sheep?" Juan cried out.

"That's the bastard! Get him, Cash!" one of the voices called from the distance, and yet in these confusing moments, Juan Epanisse seemed to hear the words clearly, as if they were no more than a few feet away. Then came the shot, and the world ended for him as he fell with an inaudible little moan, the club dropping from his nerveless hand as he sprawled upon the hard ground.

"Nice shootin', Cash," Ted Jackson called. "I'm gonna kill me some more of these lousy woollybacks!" Raising his club, he rode into the frantically scrambling flock, leaning from his saddle to strike and strike again, until the end of the club was sticky with blood and brains.

Jack Nantum, reaching into his saddlebag, took out a stick of dynamite with a fuse nearly a foot long, struck a match on his thumbnail, and lit the fuse. Then he flung the stick toward Juan Epanisse's little cottage, and with a hoarse warning to ride away, he rode off in the opposite direction. The sound of the explosion was cataclysmic in the lonely night, and the cottage was blown into smithereens. Burning debris fell among the fleeing, bleating animals, who, now as frenzied as any herd of stampeding cattle, rushed this way and that in their pathetic attempts to survive the carnage and the hideous noises that beset them from all sides.

Jorge Santurce had been taking a short nap, for he

too had worried about the coming storm and knew that there might be much required of him before dawn. The sound of the attack had wakened him, and he sprang up, tugged on his thick, warm jacket, and hid outside his hut. He was too sensible a man to try to stop the carnage. After his hut was blown up, he knew the attackers would think him dead. He felt safe. He had hardly stood up when a bandana-masked horseman drew hard on the reins of his gelding and then, leveling a rifle at Jorge, pulled the trigger. The sheepherder feebly clutched at his chest, where a patch of blood was staining the warm jacket. Then he fell backward and lay with arms outstretched, face frozen with horrified surprise.

"That does it for the woollyback tenders," Kyle Winger shouted. "Now let's kill off a few more of the goddamned animals before we call it a night!"

In the light from the burning hut, he watched the others shoot down the bleating sheep or use their clubs with hideous speed and effect. Then, drawing a gunnysack out of his saddlebag, Winger directed his gelding toward the sprawled body of the Basque sheepherder, opened the sack, and dropped a gray Stetson near Juan Epanisse's corpse. He rode ten yards farther, then dropped the glove, which also belonged to Maxwell Grantham.

Now he turned his horse back and sat watching the others at their inhuman task while he rolled and lit a cigarette, chuckling with satisfaction when he thought of what he would tell the boss. It had been a good night's work. And it wouldn't be long before the boss took over this nice piece of land and let cattle graze on it for a change. Not long at all . . .

Cash Agnew turned in his saddle and gestured to Jack Nantum. "Light 'em all and get rid of 'em fast. Then let's get the hell out of here before old man Ringold and his boys come to find out what all the noise is about!"

"Gotcha, Mr. Agnew!"

And then the night was hideous again with erupting explosions and the pitiful screaming and bleating of wounded and dying sheep and the sound of horses' hooves galloping off into the distance.

"Sheriff Blaisedale, I am here to bring charges of murder. In all my life, I would not think it would be this man, not after the kind words he had to say to us yesterday afternoon!" Peter Ringold was shaking with anger, and his eyes were red and swollen.

"Now take it easy, Mr. Ringold," the moon-faced sheriff said. "Suppose you start in from the beginning."

Peter Ringold glared at the fat sheriff, then flung his saddlebag onto the official's desk, opened it, and took out a trampled gray Stetson and a glove. "*Ja.* This is the beginning, *mein Herr.* You recognize them, do you not?"

"A gray Stetson . . . yeah, could be Grantham's. He's about the only feller I recall wearing that color out this way. But please explain to me what happened, Ringold."

"Last night, about midnight, my sheepherders, Jorge Santurce and Juan Epanisse, were shot. Cold-blooded murder, it was, Sheriff Blaisedale! Men threw dynamite sticks into my flock and blew up the cottage where poor old Jorge lived. About four hundred sheep were killed and at least a hundred more I will have to destroy because of this! My men found this hat and glove near Juan's body. I say to you, it is dreadful! Herr Grantham talked to us yesterday afternoon. He said that he wished peace between the cattlemen and ourselves. And we believed him, may God pity us."

"This is a serious charge you're bringing, Mr. Ringold. You know that, don't you?"

"*Ja, das weiss ich!* I demand that you arrest Grantham and make him stand trial. We shall see if he was not a liar when he talked of an alliance!"

"Calm down, Mr. Ringold, calm down. Now you say he came to meet you yesterday afternoon?"

"*Ja*, I said that! And here is a hat just like the one that he wore. And that glove, look at the label! That too is Mr. Grantham's."

Sheriff Blaisedale scowled, then grudgingly nodded. "If it's true what you say, I'll arrest Mr. Grantham on suspicion of murder."

"That is all I ask. I leave this to you; I go back to my ranch now for a funeral for my two good men. *Ach Gott,* why do men pretend they come as friends only to cause such horror!" He groaned aloud, and then, putting on his hat and buttoning his jacket, stomped out into the cold air.

A light snow had begun to fall, the beginnings of the predicted blizzard. Sheriff Blaisedale watched Ringold go, then sighed heavily and beckoned to a young deputy. "Sam, you stay here. I'd better get a head start before that snow starts to come down in earnest. I got no choice but to bring Mr. Grantham back here and put him in jail. Dammit all, looks like we've got a range war on our hands."

Young Dr. Cecily Bouchard opened the door and stared out, then closed it and came back to her husband. "I don't like the looks of it, Hugo, but I've got to go out. Ed Meridew's here, and I've got to go with him to deliver a baby."

"You'd best go as soon as you can. I'll be at the hospital on rounds, and I'll look in on your patients for you," Hugo replied.

Ed Meridew stood just inside the doorway, ill at

ease, twisting his hat between his hands. "I'm awfully sorry to take you out on a day like this, Doc," he said, "but Maria is having a terrible hard time."

"I understand, Ed. We'd best hurry. I wouldn't be surprised if we had a foot of snow before nightfall."

"That's about the way it looks to me, Doc," the sheep rancher responded gloomily.

Cecily drew on her warmest cloak and mittens.

The young doctor turned to her husband and said, "Don't worry about me, honey. If I'm snowbound, I'll just stay out there until it's safe to come back home. You just take care of yourself."

"Of course. Please take care." The rancher had tactfully turned his back and was opening the door as the two young doctors embraced. Cecily then followed the man out to the stable, saddled her horse, tied her medical bag to the saddle, and nodded that she was ready to accompany the rancher.

She glanced up at the leaden sky and shook her head. Huge flakes were falling fast. "Tough going for the horses, Ed."

"We won't get there much before noon." The rancher shook his head and scowled.

By the time Cecily Bouchard and the sheepherder reached the isolated little cabin, the sheriff had gone to Maxwell Grantham's ranch house. There Sheriff Blaisedale had explained to the president of the Wyoming Stock Growers' Association what had happened at Peter Ringold's ranch. "I'm going to have to take you in, Mr. Grantham," he concluded.

"Of course I'll go with you, but I swear before God, Sheriff Blaisedale, I had nothing to do with it."

"You'll have a chance to get yourself a lawyer once

you're behind bars. Let's move it. I want to get back while we can still see two feet in front of us."

As the two men stepped outside and headed toward the barn for Grantham's horse, the ranch owner called to his young, freckle-faced foreman, who was standing over by the corral. He briefly described the accusations. "Go see the count and tell him what's happened."

"Right away, boss. This has got to be a put-up job."

"I'm grateful for your support, Hank, but there's no use talking about it now. Handle things while I'm gone."

"You can count on me, Mr. Grantham. There isn't a hand on this ranch who won't stand by you."

Maxwell Grantham's eyes were misty as he gripped the young foreman's hand. "Your loyalty means a lot to me, Hank. Thanks. We'll come through this thing, don't you worry." Then, turning to the sheriff, he said, "I'm ready to go with you now."

They rode back to Cheyenne, and the sheriff asked Grantham whom he wanted to represent him. The cattleman had given Scott Chalmers's name.

"Are you sure you want him? He's a tenderfoot. You could get Mr. Edmundson or Mr. Jenkins—"

"They wouldn't touch my case, Sheriff. They're very hostile toward me—they don't agree with what I've done to bring peace to the range. They'd just as soon see me hang!"

"All right, Grantham, just as you say. I'll send the deputy for Chalmers."

Sheriff Blaisedale sent his young deputy, Sam, to a two-story building about three blocks from the Cheyenne courthouse to find Scott Chalmers, a resident of Cheyenne for only eighteen months, who had received his license to practice law in the territory just two months before.

Chalmers was a pleasant-featured young man three

years away from his thirtieth birthday. He had come to Wyoming to stay with his college roommate and, liking the open range and the more pertinent fact that his roommate's sister was extremely attractive and unmarried, decided to make his home and livelihood in Cheyenne. He and Marcy Kenton were engaged to be married the day before Christmas.

When the young attorney arrived at the jail, Maxwell Grantham gave him a brief chronicle of the events that had led up to his arrest.

"Mr. Grantham, I'm new to the bar here in Wyoming, as I'm sure you know, but I'll take your case. Your glove and hat at the scene obviously pose a serious problem, and the bad blood between the cattlemen and the sheepmen could interfere with your getting a fair trial. But you look like an honest man, and I'm inclined to believe that you're innocent."

The sheepherder's wife had had a protracted labor, and the birth, just as Cecily had suspected, proved to be extremely difficult. Happily, she had been able to effect a successful breech delivery two hours after she had arrived, and the sheepherder's young wife, Maria, whose first child this was, and their little boy were doing well, much to the joy of the husband, who did not conceal his gratitude to the young doctor.

Despite the snowfall, which had grown heavier by the time Cecily had reached the distant cabin, she was eager to return home. She wanted to spend more time getting to know young Paul Bouchard, to offer whatever advice she could to help the boy out.

It was just after three when Cecily began to bundle up for the ride home. Even allowing for the slowdown because of the intemperate weather, she estimated that she could probably arrive home before midnight.

When Ed Meridew realized that Cecily planned to ride back to Cheyenne, he tried to change the doctor's mind. "Doc, why don't you stay here until the blizzard's over? You won't starve either—I'm a pretty good cook."

Smiling, Cecily shook her head. "It's a very tempting invitation, but I really want to get back. We have a young relative in from Alabama who's probably never experienced a blizzard before, and he might be scared. If I start right now, I ought to be able to make it home before it's too late without any problem."

But by the time Cecily had been riding for an hour, the snow was swirling and thickening, the winds rising in their intensity. Her horse was growing confused and frightened as the howling of the wind increased. Suddenly the animal reared. Before Cecily could right herself in the saddle, she was thrown, and her head struck a rock. The horse whinnied and turned around in a circle, growing more and more terrified. Cecily lay still, a startled look on her beautiful face. Her frantic horse had halted now and stood, trembling and whinnying violently and piteously as the fury of the storm seemed suddenly to redouble.

Diego Martinez, an elderly Mexican sheepherder who worked for one of the smaller ranchers, was caught in the blizzard as he tried to round up the small flock of two hundred sheep in his charge. His own hut was not far off, situated in an eight-foot-deep, wide gully, and he was anxious to get the flock back there, for the gully would provide an ideal shelter.

As he made his way, calling soothing words of encouragement to the bleating animals, he heard the shrill whinnies of a horse. He frowned. Who would be out riding on such an afternoon? The sound grew louder and louder as he moved southward toward his hut, and he searched the short distance he could see around him to find the source of the noise. Suddenly he crossed himself and muttered, "*¡Madre de Dios!* Now I understand." He halted his sheep, stooped down, and with an effort pulled the unconscious body of a young woman into his arms. "She will freeze to death, and so will her horse. I must save them!"

He calmed the frightened horse, speaking soothing words to it. Then, taking a coil of rope from the large pocket of his thick, baggy trousers, the old Mexican hefted the unconscious body and, grunting and gasping with exertion, managed to place Cecily over the horse. He swiftly wound the rope under the horse's belly and over the young woman's back. This done, he took hold of the reins, picked up his shepherd's crook, and then called out to the flock, "Now we go, my little ones! *¡Adelante, pronto!*"

Diego trudged down into the gully to the little hut, untied the rope, and carefully lifted the young woman down, carrying her inside and laying her on a pallet. Then, kneeling beside the pallet, the shepherd rubbed the snow off Cecily's face and began to slap her cheeks lightly. He was rewarded by seeing her eyelids flicker for an instant, and he grinned with relief. After wrapping two sturdy wool blankets over the prone body and placing a pot of stew over a fire, he hurried out to make sure that the small flock and the horse had taken refuge west of the house. He looked at the white-gray sky. There was no sign of the storm abating. He crossed himself and reverently prayed that the blizzard would subside soon and that the woman he had found would live.

He fed the woman's horse from a sack of grain and spoke comforting words to the still-distraught animal. It was then that he noticed the black leather bag tied to the horse's saddle on one side. Hoping to learn the identity of his injured guest, the shepherd untied the bag and examined it and its contents. Certainly the young woman was a nurse or doctor, the shepherd decided after peering into the bag, but all he had to go on for a name were the two silver letters attached to the bag near its clasp: C.B. The shepherd brought the bag into the hut.

When the stew was steaming, he ladled it into two bowls and walked over to the pallet, knelt down, and was rewarded by again seeing the young woman's eyelids flutter, then open. "Thanks be to *El Señor Dios*, you are alive, señora!" he exclaimed happily.

"Yes. Where is this? Who are you?" The woman spoke in a halting, quizzical tone.

"I am Diego Martinez, and I tend sheep for the Señor Arneson. I found you out there, and your horse, too, and I brought you back here to my hut. Are you warm enough now?"

"I—I think I am."

"I have something for you to eat. May I ask your name and where you come from? I tell you truly, I did not think I would see anyone on horseback on a day like this."

"Was I on horseback? Oh, my head hurts!" She clapped a hand to her head, where she found a large bump. She also felt dried blood and brought away her hand and looked at it wonderingly, then stared at the old Mexican.

"Yes, I have seen that bump on your head. I think you fell off your horse and struck your head. Who are you?" the shepherd asked again, but the stranger only stared at him in bewilderment. "You do not know your name?" Now the old Mexican's face was twisted in anxiety.

"No, I don't. . . . I don't know why—what I was doing here."

"*Bueno*, you will stay here in my hut until you get back your strength. Fortunately I have enough food for several days, and there will be plenty for both of us. Now you try to sleep. It is a good thing, sleep, and often it helps cure an ailment. And I will say a prayer to *El Señor Dios* that you will be well very soon."

Chapter 21

*T*he blizzard did not end until sundown of Saturday, November 17, and fortunately for Hugo Bouchard, his medical duties had not required him to ride any great distance in the storm. He went to the hospital on Friday and Saturday to care for his few patients and Cecily's, and he found all of them progressing quite well. Paul Bouchard accompanied him, expressing an interest in his work.

When they had returned home and were having supper late on Saturday evening, Paul ventured, "Hugo, I'm sort of worried that Cecily hasn't come back yet."

"That's very considerate of you, Paul. But she's an excellent horsewoman, and a prudent one as well. I feel certain she took the precaution of staying at Ed Meridew's house until the storm was over. Now that it seems to be over, I'm sure she'll be home early in the week."

"I guess maybe you're right, Hugo. In the meantime, can I do anything to help you—starting now, with the supper dishes?"

"Yes, I think I'll let you do that. It makes you feel useful, doesn't it?"

Paul nodded, feeling good because he *was* being useful. Hugo was certainly an important contributor to the Cheyenne community; Paul had witnessed that at the hospital. If he and Cecily could acquire such good reputations in so demanding a profession as medicine at the age of only twenty-two, Paul himself might well be able to embark upon a quite satisfying career by that time, too.

During the evening, Hugo and Paul whiled away the hours by playing checkers. It proved to be a welcome distraction for them both that evening and the next, for Sunday came and went without any sign of Cecily.

On Monday morning, a telegram arrived from Lopasuta, sent from the Santa Fe, New Mexico, railroad station. He was transferred to another train and hoped to arrive in Cheyenne on Thanksgiving. Hugo read the telegram aloud, and Paul's face fell, for he realized that his prolonged and certainly exciting adventure was soon coming to an end. As they were having breakfast, Hugo and Paul discussed Lopasuta's background, and Paul told him as much as he knew of the recent activities of the Comanche lawyer whom Luke Bouchard and his own mother had adopted. "Mother says he's a wonderful lawyer," Paul concluded.

"I only wish he could help Mr. Grantham." At the hospital, Hugo and Paul had heard all about the attack on the sheep raisers and Maxwell Grantham's unfortunate circumstances.

"Do you think he did it, Hugo?"

"Of course he didn't!" he retorted spiritedly, his eyes flashing with anger. "But I'm afraid he'll have a hard time convincing others of his innocence." Hugo gulped the rest of his coffee and then pulled out his pocket watch. "It's getting late. Paul, I want you to stay here. Because Cecily's not back, I have to go out to see Jack Sparling's wife. Her broken arm isn't mending the way it should. Then I have to go to the hospital. I should be back by evening. You can read some books and keep busy that way—a letter to your mother wouldn't hurt, either. I wish I knew when Cecily was going to get back. I'm really getting worried now!''

"Hugo, why don't you let *me* go and look for her?" Paul proposed bravely.

"Oh, no, young man! I'd never let you go out alone on a mission like that! She'll turn up. Maybe there was a complication after she delivered Maria's baby. We can't foresee these things, but they do happen. No, you stay here until I get back.''

Three days later, on Thanksgiving Thursday, the tall, black-haired Comanche arrived in town and was welcomed into the Bouchard home.

"There you are, youngster!" Lopasuta chuckled when he saw Paul. "Safe and sound. If you knew how worried your mother was about you—''

"I know. But I sent her a wire when I left Galveston that I was coming here to visit Hugo and Cecily," Paul interposed earnestly; then, wanting desperately to draw the conversation away from his delinquency, he blurted, "Hugo's wife is missing, Lopasuta!"

The New Orleans attorney looked quickly at Hugo, who detailed the circumstances of Cecily's disappearance.

"You know, Hugo," Lopasuta said after a moment of thought, "I've ridden in trains all week and need some exercise, so if you'll permit me to ride over to this ranch that Cecily went to, I'll see what I can find out. Is there a horse you can lend me?"

"Of course, and I appreciate your offer. I rode out to Meridew's ranch on Tuesday but had no luck. He said Cecily had left Saturday, after the baby was born. That was the day the blizzard began. I've ridden in that direction a couple of times now, but I've had to get back to the hospital, so my searches haven't been extensive.''

"I'll search for your wife while you do your doctoring. That should take pressure off you. And you, Paul, stay here with Hugo."

Hugo smiled gratefully at the other man. "You'll find a very sturdy mare in the stable." Then he gave Lopasuta specific directions on how to reach the ranch.

A few moments later, Lopasuta was riding off across the prairie.

Hugo turned to Paul. "I wonder if Lopasuta would mind helping Mr. Grantham's lawyer. Chalmers is so young and inexperienced, and the evidence against Grantham so strong. Paul, come with me. On the way to the hospital we'll stop at the jail and suggest it to Mr. Grantham and see if he'll agree to Lopasuta's assistance. Chalmers could come over to see Lopasuta this evening." He hesitated and shook his head. "But it's thirty miles to Meridew's ranch and back. Lopasuta may not get here by this evening."

"He's as strong as an athlete and smart, too. I know he'll do it, Hugo."

Lopasuta reached Ed Meridew's ranch that afternoon and learned that he had found no sign of Cecily since she had left for home in midafternoon on the day of the blizzard. Figuring that she would have returned home by the same route Hugo had instructed himself to take, Lopasuta took his time riding back to the doctor's house, searching the area for clues as to her whereabouts, but unhappily he found none.

A disappointed Hugo watched as Lopasuta rode up to the house alone, with no trace of Cecily or her horse. Lopasuta offered encouraging words and promised to gather together a search party the next day to scour the fifteen miles from their house to Meridew's ranch.

"Thank you, Lopasuta. I can't thank you enough for

helping me at a time like this. Being responsible for her patients as well as mine—''

"Don't give it another thought."

"Lopasuta, I have another favor to ask of you," Hugo said, and explained Maxwell Grantham's predicament, then asked if the Comanche lawyer would mind consulting with Scott Chalmers, who had earlier agreed to come to the house later that evening.

When Chalmers arrived, he and Lopasuta enjoyed an immediate affinity.

"I'm considered pretty foolish among the other lawyers in town because I agreed to take Mr. Grantham's case," Chalmers said ruefully. "No one else would do it. The prosecuting attorney is a sharp, experienced man, but I like Mr. Grantham and believe he's the victim of a malicious plot to get rid of him."

"Tell me all about the case. I don't have a license to practice here in Wyoming, but maybe I can help you unofficially."

"I appreciate that, sir. I really believe in my client's innocence."

The young lawyer gave Lopasuta the background and details and concluded, "My personal feeling is that somebody among the cattlemen dislikes Grantham enough to want to see him convicted of murder and hanged!"

Lopasuta nodded his head, considering.

Chalmers drew a sheet of paper from his inner coat pocket. "I found this shoved under the door of my house this morning," he said, handing it to Lopasuta.

He read it quickly. "It's a death threat! *'Grantham's guilty as hell. Stay away from his case—or else you might wind up lynched, too!'* "

He handed it back to Chalmers and said, "I am determined to help your client. I'd help any man whose enemies prejudge him and make death threats to his lawyer.''

"I'd be grateful for any help you can give me. I've never had a case as big or as important as this.''

"It's a challenge we'll accept together, Mr. Chalmers.''

As Chalmers was taking his leave, Lopasuta moved to the door to confer with him in a low voice. "I want to visit Mr. Grantham as soon as I can. But first I have to organize a search party for Cecily.''

"Grantham could help you there, Mr. Bouchard.''

"How's that?''

"As one of the biggest ranchers in these parts, he has a lot of cowhands and wranglers. I'm sure he'd be only too glad to have them look for Dr. Bouchard—and they'd be willing, too. Everyone in these parts thinks highly of the Bouchards,'' Chalmers explained.

"Fine. Then first thing tomorrow morning I'll go to the jail and speak with Mr. Grantham, and if he gives the word, you and I can go out and talk to his men about finding Cecily.''

After Chalmers had left, Lopasuta turned to Hugo. "I'd like to borrow that mare again. Can you tell me where I might find a hotel—''

"You are *not* going to a hotel!'' Hugo interrupted firmly. "We have plenty of room for you here, if you don't mind sleeping in my study. There's a cot in there.''

"Please don't go to any trouble. I'm happy enough to be here.''

"And *I'm* so happy you're here. Your assistance has considerably eased my burden.''

"Mr. Grantham, my name is Lopasuta Bouchard. I'm a relative of Hugo's. He told you about me?''

"Yes, Mr. Bouchard. I can use all the help I can get.

Scott Chalmers is a very capable young man, but the feeling in this town runs strongly against us. Sheriff Blaisedale just told me that my trial is scheduled for November twenty-ninth, a week from yesterday, when the circuit judge arrives in Cheyenne.''

"That gives us time to prepare a very good defense. Before we get to that, I'd like a favor from you. Cecily Bouchard is missing. She was last seen by Ed Meridew, the man whose home she visited. I'd like to organize a search party for her, and I'll need—''

"Mr. Bouchard, say no more. Go out to my ranch and see my foreman, Hank Johnson. Scott, will you go along and introduce them? Hank and the other boys will be glad to help,'' Grantham said.

"Thank you. I'll go just as soon as we have had a chance to talk. By the way, what happened to your arm?''

Maxwell Grantham ruefully looked down at his arm, which rested in a sling. "Somebody shot me in the shoulder blade about two weeks ago, when I was out riding the range. If it hadn't been for Dr. Bouchard, I might not have survived.''

"Your luck *has* been sour! Any idea who might be responsible?''

"I have made many enemies because of my stand in the conflict between the sheepmen and the cattlemen. I have a pretty good guess, though. Albert Elston is the only person who would go so far as to have me shot.''

"Isn't that the same man, Mr. Chalmers, that you said picked a quarrel with Mr. Grantham?'' Lopasuta asked.

"Yes, it is.'' The younger lawyer turned to the cattlemen. "I told Mr. Bouchard all about that incident in the Cheyenne Club, Mr. Grantham.''

"Good. Yes, Elston has been overtly threatening

toward me, Mr. Bouchard. I have plenty of witnesses to testify to that. Did Scott tell you about the duel between Elston and Count Charbouille?''

''Yes,'' Lopasuta said with a slight smile. ''I understand the count shot away part of Mr. Elston's earlobe.''

The rancher could not conceal a look of amusement as he nodded. ''That's right. Nobody expected the count to be such a fine marksman; he could easily have killed Elston.''

''And Elston said that he would get his revenge, is that right?''

''Yes. Again, there are several witnesses to that.''

''Good. We may need to call on them. Now, as to the raid itself. Do you have an alibi?''

''I started for the count's that night but never made it because of a loose buggy wheel. I returned to my ranch and went to bed early. My staff can attest to that.''

''I'm afraid, Mr. Grantham, that your staff could be said to have ulterior motives for seeing you go free.'' Lopasuta rubbed his chin. ''The only evidence against you is that your glove and hat were found at the scene of the raid.''

''Yes, but I have no idea how they got there—except by someone who wants to see me blamed. I had discarded that pair of gloves because one was badly torn, but the hat was brand new. I kept it on a rack near the door.''

''Would anyone in your employ betray you by giving your things to Elston or to anyone else who paid a good price?'' Lopasuta asked.

Maxwell Grantham shook his head. ''Absolutely not. I trust my staff and my men implicitly. None of them would do a thing like that.''

''When did you notice the hat missing?''

''Let's see, I wore my old one to the meeting with

the sheep raisers, but the new one was there when I left. It must have been taken after that time, but I don't know exactly when.''

"I see." Lopasuta paused again. "Mr. Grantham, I'd like to do a little investigating Would you mind if I asked your men a few questions—and maybe took a look around the areas where these incidents took place?"

"Not at all! Hank will be glad to show you around. Just tell him I sent you."

"I'll do that. First I'll see him about that search party."

"Tell Hank to send out all the men he can spare."

"Mr. Grantham, I'll see you again soon—and I hope with good news." Lopasuta shook hands with the tall rancher and then left the jail with Scott Chalmers.

Hank Johnson had picked twenty wranglers to search for Dr. Cecily Bouchard. But he had done so at Chalmers's request, rather than that of Lopasuta Bouchard. When the Comanche had first introduced himself to Hank, the foreman had stared at him with an icy hatred that Lopasuta had come to recognize as racial enmity.

A few minutes later, the twenty men were riding with Lopasuta Bouchard, Scott Chalmers having returned to town at Lopasuta's suggestion to confer with his client. Hank rode at the head of his men, and he took care to stay as far away from Lopasuta as he could. He hated the idea of the Indian accompanying him, but his respect for his boss was stronger than his loathing, and so he said nothing.

The search party reached Ed Meridew's house in the early afternoon, and the young sheepherder told them all he knew about the doctor. Already another storm was brewing; the sky had darkened and was filled with racing clouds, and the wind blew shrilly on the high slopes of the elevated plain. Hank divided his men into two groups, one going north, the other south, but by nightfall they called a halt. They had found no sign of Dr. Cecily Bouchard, and another blizzard was beginning.

That night Ed Meridew provided lodging for the members of the search party, the hands sleeping in his bunkhouse and in the barn, while Lopasuta and Hank shared a little guest room. The tall Comanche lawyer, sensing the young foreman's resentment, did not try to engage him in conversation, nor did Johnson offer any.

That night old Diego Martinez kept his flock in the gully, sensing that another blizzard was imminent. He fed and soothed them, hoping they would not panic during the oncoming storm. He also attended to Cecily, who was fully conscious now but remained weak. She did not yet know who she was or what she was doing in the sheepherder's hut. Hearing the wind and feeling the cold blasts of air whenever the old sheepherder stepped outside to check on the flock, she was aware of the oncoming storm and expressed her gratitude to Diego and her fear for the future.

"You mustn't worry," the old man replied. "The good God will see that you get well and strong, and then you will know who you are. The best thing for you to do now is to rest, and I will pray for you."

After breakfast on Saturday morning, Ed Meridew said, "I know you men want to visit every resident in the area. There's a rancher about five miles or so southeast of here. He's only got a small flock—maybe two or three hundred sheep—but you might try over in that direction. He's got an old sheepherder working for him, and maybe that fellow saw Doc Bouchard."

"We'll try it," Hank Johnson declared. "We're mighty grateful for your hospitality, Mr. Meridew."

"Glad to be of help. There isn't anything I wouldn't do for Doc Bouchard, not after all the good she's done around here. By the way, I've heard about the trouble your boss is in. You can tell him that I believe he's innocent."

"Thanks, Mr. Meridew. I'll tell him when I see him. All right then, we'll be on our way."

The snow was falling heavily now, and it was difficult to see their way, but Hank followed Ed Meridew's directions until at last they came to a gully and heard the bleating of sheep. "This must be the place!" he called out, raising his hand, and then dismounted.

Lopasuta had already dismounted and was striding toward the little hut, which was at one end of the deep, wide gully. He banged on the door with his fist and called out, "Is anyone here?"

The sheepherder opened the door. "*Sí*, it is I, Diego Martinez. How can I help you, señor?"

But Lopasuta had already seen the pallet at the back of the room and Cecily lying on it. "We've found you! Thank God!" Then, turning to the old man, he exclaimed, "We've been looking for this woman, señor. We will take her back home."

"That is a good thing! I have prayed to *El Señor Dios* ever since I found her last week that someone would come for her. You see, señor, she must have fallen and hurt her head, and now she does not know her name, where she belongs, or why she is here." Diego Martinez crossed himself. "I think that once she is home, she will remember everything."

"I am sure that you are right, *mi amigo. Muchas gracias* for all you have done. Her husband will bless you in his prayers," Lopasuta told him. The Comanche turned to Hank Johnson. "I'll put her on my horse."

"I guess that's good enough," Hank answered laconically. "But let's get going. This storm's getting worse. It's gonna be a job getting back to Cheyenne with all this snow and the wind."

Lopasuta bent down and helped Cecily rise to her feet. "Do you think you can ride behind me, Dr. Bouchard?" he asked.

The young doctor gave him a curious look, then slowly rubbed her face with her hand. "Uh . . . yes, I think I can ride a horse. Where are you taking me?"

"Back to your husband, Dr. Bouchard." Lopasuta stared steadily at her. Cecily's eyes were wide and without expression.

"I am married, then." She looked at the ring on her finger. "I'll go with you—yes, of course. This kind old man has given me so much of his food and shared his hut with me, I mustn't take advantage of him any longer."

"We owe him a debt for taking care of you, Dr. Bouchard." Lopasuta was hoping that the repetition of the young doctor's name would help bring back her memory, but Cecily's face retained the blank, wondering look. He heartily added, "All right then, let's get started at once. And hold on tight to me. Are you strong enough?"

"Yes. Will you tell the old man in his own language how grateful I am for all he's done?"

"Of course I will." Turning to the worried-looking old sheepherder, Lopasuta conveyed Cecily's thanks in fluent, gracious Spanish, and the white-haired Mexican grinned and nodded as he retorted, "But I would do that for anyone. I do not need thanks. To share one's food out here where it is all so lonely, that warms the heart. *Vaya con Dios*—I will pray for the señora."

With that the men rode off, trailing Cecily's horse behind them.

Chapter 22

On Friday night, with no word from Lopasuta, Hugo could no longer suppress his anguish, for by now he was certain that his wife was dead. He wept, his head bowed onto his folded arms on the kitchen table, and Paul Bouchard awkwardly tried to comfort him.

By Saturday afternoon, Hugo was even more disconsolate. He had forced himself to go to the hospital that morning, for there were patients he had to see. When he returned from the hospital, he said in a listless voice, glancing at Paul, "I forgot to make lunch for you, Paul."

"It's all right, Hugo. I made my own. Could I heat you a cup of coffee? There's a pot on the stove."

"Yes, thank you. I really am glad you're here, Paul, otherwise I think I'd go to pieces entirely. I'm so worried about Cecily. And now with this blizzard, and Grantham going to trial next week for his life, everything seems to be happening at once." He looked as if he was going to break with tension, and Paul shyly put an arm around his relative's shoulders.

"Hugo, I think I hear horses coming. Yes, lots of them!" Paul suddenly cried.

Hugo straightened and dried his eyes, a look of hope coming into them. He hurried to the door, and a blast of cold air rushed in when he opened it.

"Oh, thank God! Thank God! They've found her. She's riding behind Lopasuta. Look, Paul!" he cried. "Oh, darling! I was so worried. What's wrong, Cecily?"

She stared at him, her face still stricken with a pathetic, wondering look.

"Cecily—it's me, Hugo. . . . Cecily?" He turned to Lopasuta with a frantically questioning look.

"We found her in the hut of an old sheepherder quite some miles away from Mr. Meridew's house," Lopasuta explained quickly. "Apparently she fell from her horse and—"

"Oh, dear God—I'll bet she's had a concussion." He picked his wife up and carried her inside, Hank and Lopasuta following. Hugo carried her into the bedroom. When he came downstairs, he went back outside and said to the men who sat astride their mounts, waiting for their foreman to return, "I'm so grateful to all of you for helping to find my wife. God bless you all."

"I'm glad we could help, Doc," one of the riders spoke up. "Mr. Grantham thinks a heap of Doc Bouchard and you. Sure hope she gets better. You'll get her back in good health soon enough, I reckon."

"I hope I can. Thank you again."

Hank and Lopasuta emerged now, and the foreman turned to the lawyer. "We'll be going back to the ranch now."

"Mr. Johnson, I want to ask you a favor, not for myself, but for your boss."

"What is it?" Hank said almost belligerently.

"After the blizzard is over—maybe tomorrow, if you've about an hour or so to spare—I'd like you to take me to the site where Mr. Grantham was shot."

"Why do you want to go out there?" Hank looked at Lopasuta with narrowed eyes.

"I just want to look around, to see if I can find any clue to the gunman's identity."

"Don't bother. After Mr. Grantham was shot, me and the boys searched around the place, and there wasn't anything to find. It was snowing like hell when it happened, and it's snowed since. You'd be wasting your time—and mine—to go back." Hank turned to walk away.

"Wait, Mr. Johnson. I'm sure that you and your men searched carefully, but nevertheless I'd like to have a look myself. I—"

"Look, Bouchard. You won't find anything, understand? Now let me get back to my job."

"According to your boss, Mr. Johnson, your job is to show me the site where he was shot. Mr. Grantham will verify that if you don't believe me." Lopasuta smiled. "Please, I don't want us to be enemies, but—"

"All right, all right! I'll go." Hank spat. "If this blizzard's over by tomorrow morning, I'll come by for you after breakfast, around eight. That suit you?"

"It does indeed. Thank you, Mr. Johnson."

"For nothing," Hank Johnson grumbled as he left the house.

The next morning, a Sunday, the skies were clear and the blizzard had stopped. The air was bitingly cold, and Hank Johnson turned in his saddle to glare at Lopasuta. "I'm only doing this for Mr. Grantham's sake, understand? I can think of a lot of other things I'd rather be doing than riding around half frozen with all the snow piled up."

"I'm sure Mr. Grantham would rather be back at his house enjoying a steak and a glass of good whiskey than sitting in jail, facing the prospect of the hangman's rope," Lopasuta answered curtly.

The two men rode on, without conversing, into a desolate landscape piled with sparkling white snow, snow that transformed bushes and shrubs into grotesque and gargoylelike figures, petrified in this icy wintry land. The horses snorted, the steam of their breath rising in clouds, as it did from the breath of both men.

"There's the place." Hank nodded toward a clump of trees. "I figure the fellow who shot at Mr. Grantham came around from the back there." He pointed to the left.

"Do you know about where Mr. Grantham's horse was standing when he was shot?"

"Best I can remember," the young foreman scowled and scratched a stubbly touch of beard, "he was about a hundred yards from around the middle of that stretch of trees. He was shot from the back. We'd turned south, heading the cattle back to the ranch, when it happened."

"Must have been a rifle. A revolver shot wouldn't carry as far as that, and it wouldn't be as accurate," Lopasuta mused aloud. "I'm going up to that stand of pines and see what I can find."

"Suit yourself," Hank said, shrugging. He watched Lopasuta spur his horse ahead and grimaced with annoyance. "Damn Indian, thinks he's so smart," he muttered.

Lopasuta tethered the reins of his horse to a snow-laden pine branch at the western end of the grove, then disappeared among the trees. With his keen eye, he marked the approximate place where the foreman said Grantham's horse had been and began to move quickly through the trees. Because of the tall pines' height and density, they had acted as a shelter against the snow, so that while the outer branches at the front and rear edges of the grove were heavily burdened with the downfall, the interior of the grove itself was not thickly covered.

Lopasuta wore a pair of heavy gloves, and squatting down, he began to examine the brush on the floor of the grove.

Hank Johnson, astride his horse at the edge of the stand, continued to scowl as a gust of wind tugged at him. He would not be doing this for anybody except Maxwell Grantham. Grantham had recently promoted him to foreman over men who were much older and who had more experience. He would never forget that. And that was the only reason he was out here now on this frigid Sunday morning, when any sensible cowhand ought to be snug in the house, keeping as warm as he could.

His irritability grew as the minutes passed, and he was about to ride up to the grove and order Lopasuta to abandon this futile quest when suddenly the tall lawyer appeared.

"I've found what I was looking for, Mr. Johnson," he called. "I'll go back with you now. Sorry it took this long."

Hank looked at the Comanche with an open mouth. "I'll be damned. . . ." he muttered to himself. "What the hell could that Indian have found that we didn't spot?"

Lopasuta mounted his horse, and the two men began to ride back toward Cheyenne. Hank kept silent for the first leg of the ride, but soon he could not repress his curiosity. "All right, let's have it."

Lopasuta smiled. "It's the spent casing of a rifle bullet, Mr. Johnson. Bullets are stamped with what sort of weapon they come from. This one's a 45-80. What kind of rifle do most people own around here?"

"An army-issue 45-70," Hank answered.

"Let me tell you a little about 45-70s. The army issued twenty-five hundred to three thousand of them at least. The 45-80 may be something different. I'll go to see a gunsmith in Cheyenne tomorrow. He'll have a catalog of rifles. If the 45-80 is a relatively rare weapon, we'll find out who owns one around here—and maybe then we'll know who had it in for your boss. I have a suspicion that the same man who shot your boss directed the raid on Mr. Ringold's sheep ranch and planted Mr. Grantham's Stetson and glove at the scene of the crime."

"Jesus Christ!" Hank exclaimed. "I remember Mike Norden—he's one of Mr. Elston's hands—was telling me a couple of months ago that his boss had a better rifle than anybody else in this territory and that he could hit a bull's-eye at two hundred yards."

"And from what Mr. Grantham told me, Mr. Elston has no great love for your boss," Lopasuta ventured. "Think you'll see Mike Norden again soon, Mr. Johnson?"

"Sure. Once in a while he drops over to play poker. Matter of fact, he might even come out tonight. There aren't any chores right now on the ranches. Once the cattle are out of the blizzard, you see to it that they've got enough water and feed to last them until you can send them out on the range again."

"Good. Ask Mike Norden as casually as you can if Elston owns a 45-80. And then you let me know—don't say anything to anyone else. Just make sure that you find out for me before the trial next Thursday."

"I won't tell a soul. My Gawd!" There was awe in Hank's voice, and he looked at Lopasuta with grudging respect. "I didn't think there was anything to be found—especially with all this snow. How the hell did you find it?"

"You're forgetting, Mr. Johnson, that I am an Indian."

*   *   *

The same day that Lopasuta Bouchard found the bullet casing, Nils Sonderman decided to visit Laure Bouchard Kenniston. He had called on her twice in the past two weeks, once on his own, and once at her invitation to have dinner with her and Lucien.

Lucien, on his weekend visits to the family, continued to praise his employer in the most glowing terms, and Laure had by now accepted the Swedish architect as a friend in whom she might trustingly confide.

During his previous visits and particularly at the dinner, Laure had learned about Nils's background, and his gentle manner and forthright integrity made her look more and more toward him, though perhaps unconsciously, as a bulwark against the many problems that beset her.

This afternoon, as Clarabelle admitted him into the chateau, she whispered, "I'm glad you're here today, Mr. Sonderman. Laure's been feeling very low. Your visit will certainly cheer her up. She's in the study. I'll let her know you're here."

Clarabelle showed Nils into the sitting room, then withdrew. When she returned with Laure, Nils could see from Laure's reddened, swollen eyes that she had been crying. Solicitously, he turned and said to Clarabelle, "I think your mistress could use a glass of sherry. And I'd like to share one with her—if I'm not being too importunate?"

"You're never that, Mr. Sonderman." It was Laure who answered, and then attempted a laugh, which sounded hollow and unconvincing. "As a matter of fact, that's exactly what I need to settle my nerves. Do bring two glasses, dear Clarabelle."

She served the sherry, then left the room. Nils gently said, "Have I distressed you by coming?"

"Certainly not! I—I just hate to burden you with my troubles, Mr. Sonderman."

"What are friends for if not to rely upon? And I do hope that we are good friends by this time. . . ." Though he said the words lightly, his look was intent. Laure was trembling, but she intercepted his gaze and blushed. Her woman's instinct told her that he might very well be in love with her. The realization disturbed her for two reasons: She still had not rid herself entirely of her guilt for neglecting Leland and thereby causing his death in the Alabama River; and, in the second place, she was beginning to feel more than friendship for him.

"Yes, yes, we surely are friends, Mr. Sonderman, and I'm very glad to have you to talk to. Talk, they say, airs one's worries. I wish I could believe that."

"Why not try?"

"It's many things, Mr. Sonderman. I shan't really be at ease until Paul is safely home and I find out exactly why he ran away. Until then, I'll feel that I've failed as a mother."

"You are too hard on yourself. And I'm sure the boy will be well looked after by Mr. Bouchard on the journey home."

"Oh, yes, that's true. Yet I have other concerns. We are still unable to produce the revenue we need to maintain Windhaven Plantation. Now that Leland isn't here, this burden is entirely upon my shoulders, and I feel utterly exhausted, drained."

"It is indeed a great burden for one woman to bear, Mrs. Kenniston. I only wish I had the right—no, let me rephrase that." He colored, for he had unwittingly come close to revealing his fondest wish: to have the right, as her husband, to shoulder her burdens. "I wish I had the skill of an attorney or a good agronomist to help you find a way to earn more income from this beautiful place. But please believe me—not only because I'm your son's employer but also because I admire you—if I can do anything at all to alleviate your distress, I want you to call on me." He hesitated again. He had made a comfortable living and saved a good deal of money. But out of sheer tact, he knew that to offer her money, even as a loan, might be misconstrued. And he would rather err on the side of caution, not committing himself to what was now foremost in his mind rather than risk offending her in the slightest way.

"I shan't forget what you've said, Mr. Sonderman. I do feel better for your having visited. You're welcome at any time, believe me," she said with a faint smile.

"Then I'm amply rewarded—and will be even more so if I can truly help you. Now I'll bid you good afternoon, Mrs. Kenniston. Let me first tell you that the Marksons' house is coming along beautifully, and you can be proud of your son, just as I am pleased with my own good judgment in selecting him as my apprentice."

She saw him to the door and watched as he climbed into his buggy and drove off. He was a kind, soft-spoken man, she reflected, and she was sure she could trust him. And yet—and yet she could not erase from her mind her feeling of vulnerability.

Now that he was a resident of the area, James Weymore had engaged Montgomery lawyer Oscar Peterman to handle his affairs. Peterman was forty-five, a typically elegant southern gentleman. At their first meeting, Weymore had told Peterman that he wanted very much to own Windhaven Plantation. He told the attorney to research the possibilities for fulfilling his desire. But at their second meeting, Peterman did not have an optimistic report for his client.

"Mr. Weymore, I think you may have to set aside

any plans for the Bouchard property. The deed for that acreage has no flaw in it—I checked it myself at the recorder's office immediately after you first visited me. The taxes have always been paid promptly, without a shadow of any delinquency, which might bring about a public sale for overdue taxes. The only way for you to obtain that land is for the owner, Laure Kenniston, to sell it.''

Oscar Peterman leaned back in his chair, waiting to hear what his client had to say. Weymore's wealth and ambition had impressed him, and the blunt truth was that the attorney was looking forward to a handsome fee for services rendered to this determined entrepreneur.

''You're wrong about that land,'' Weymore said with a chuckle, after having made certain that his cigar was drawing well. ''I have quite another method in mind, but I assure you, sir, equally legal. I'm glad you looked into this, Peterman.''

Without a single word of farewell, Weymore sprang to his feet and strode out of the office.

Upon leaving the attorney's office, Weymore had walked briskly to a florist down the street and there had imperiously placed an order. ''I want the very largest and most beautiful bouquet you can arrange, and I want it delivered immediately. Do you understand?''

''Oh, to be sure, sir, to be sure! Why don't you go over to the desk there and fill out a card?''

''Good idea.'' Weymore seated himself and began to write, pausing from time to time so that he might select each word as a jeweler selects only flawless stones in the arrangement of a prize bracelet. When he had finished, he read it half aloud: ''May these flowers, like your beauty, never fade.'' Satisfied, he muttered to himself, ''Yes, indeed I do have another legal method of making Windhaven Plantation mine.''

*　　*　　*

With Cecily's return, Lopasuta had quickly moved to the hotel on the main street, not far from the Cheyenne Club. Hugo had protested, but he was clearly beside himself with concern over Cecily's continued amnesia, Lopasuta realized.

On this Wednesday morning, Hugo prepared breakfast for his young wife and brought it into the bedroom on a tray. Paul Bouchard remained in the little guest room. The boy found himself in the midst of a distressing situation, helpless to do anything except offer a few words of solace to Hugo. On those occasions when he entered Cecily's bedroom to inquire politely as to her health, Cecily responded with a blank stare and a banal phrase, the only acknowledgments she gave to anyone. The world held only strangers for her now.

"Good morning, darling. I've brought you your breakfast." Hugo affected a bright tone, which in no way did he feel.

Cecily eyed him, nodded solemnly, looked down at the tray, and said, "Thank you, I'm rather hungry today."

"Did you sleep well, Cecily?" Hugo asked. Because she saw him now as a stranger, he had thought it best to sleep on the couch.

"Oh, well enough."

"I'll be leaving for the hospital when you've finished eating. I have to make rounds, you know."

Cecily took a sip of coffee.

"How long have you been a doctor?" she asked.

"Just as long as you have, Cecily." Hugo tried to keep his anxiety at bay when answering such obvious questions. "We attended medical school together in Chicago—Rush Medical College. That's where we met."

"And how long ago was that?"

"We graduated a little more than two years ago, darling. And then we were married and moved here to Cheyenne." Hugo was silent for a moment.

She looked at him with pity. "I'm sorry. You've been so kind to me, but I just don't remember anything. I'm sorry."

Hugo stifled a groan and hurried out of the bedroom, not trusting himself to stay there a moment longer. He wanted to grab his wife's shoulders and shout into her face, "Remember! You must remember!" From what he recalled from medical school, transient amnesia lifted of its own accord, but it could take from a week to a month to even a year to disappear and, the professor had pointed out, sometimes even longer, depending upon the extent of brain damage. Her concussion must have been grievous, Hugo thought, to have so prolonged her memory lapse. All he could do was care for her as lovingly as he could, whether she recognized him or not—and to pray. There were times when medical science was powerless, and this was one of them.

The fateful trial of their good friend Maxwell Grantham was to begin the next day, and in a sense it was Hugo's salvation, for he was forced by it to think of something other than his own plight. He had told Paul that they would attend once the jury selection was completed. He hoped that Lopasuta had garnered enough information to help the young, inexperienced lawyer. Just yesterday Scott Chalmers had received still another anonymous threat, warning him that if he pursued this case, he was skating on extremely thin ice in regard to his own physical safety.

Chapter 23

The courtroom was packed with spectators. Not only were all of the leading cattlemen present—some hoping that Grantham would be cleared, some hoping for his conviction—but also in attendance were many of the sheep raisers and leading citizens of Cheyenne, including the president of the Cheyenne Club. The jury had been impaneled the day before.

Among the first to enter the courtroom this morning had been Hugo and Paul, Hugo having first made certain that Cecily was comfortable at home. He had explained to her the case against Maxwell Grantham and what a friend the cattleman had been to them, and so Cecily was aware of the need for Hugo to attend the trial. Before he had left her, he encouraged her to try to sleep.

The bailiff now called the courtroom to order and bade those present to rise. The traveling circuit judge, Marvin Aspergren, a bespectacled man nearing sixty, entered and seated himself at the bench. He had just come from a town near the Colorado border, where he had ordered the hanging of two cattle rustlers.

The prosecuting attorney, a prominent Cheyenne lawyer named Donald Murchison, had been elated to learn that Judge Aspergren would preside at Grantham's trial. The forty-eight-year-old lawyer had announced glibly to his friends, most of whom were cattlemen, "I happen to know, gentlemen, that Aspergren favors those who raise cattle. In his last case, for example, there really wasn't too much evidence against those two poor devils, from what I've heard, but Aspergren convicted them anyway. We'll have no trouble with him at all. The case against Grantham is ironclad. Everyone knows how Grantham caters to sheep ranchers, and I'm sure Aspergren does, too."

Judge Aspergren settled himself on the bench and then surveyed the crowded courtroom. Clearing his throat, he sternly declared, "Before we begin, I wish to remind everyone that I will tolerate no disturbances. If they occur, I shall clear the court. Now then, Mr. Murchison, if the prosecution is ready, you may proceed."

"Thank you, Your Honor." The prosecuting attorney rose to his feet and addressed his opening remarks to the jury. His dark brown hair was streaked with gray, and elegantly trimmed sideburns framed his saturnine face. Hands in his pockets, he swaggered confidently as he spoke. "Gentlemen of the jury, Maxwell Grantham, current president of the Wyoming Stock Growers' Association, is charged with the first-degree murder of Jorge Santurce and Juan Epanisse. We intend to prove that he called a meeting between himself and the principal sheep raisers of this territory for the express purpose of beguiling them into believing that peace would come, then willfully returned to the scene, under cover of night, to commit murder."

After Murchison had continued in this vein for some minutes, and then had concluded his blistering attack on Maxwell Grantham, Scott Chalmers rose to make a brief statement to the jury that his client was a man who believed in peace and that witnesses would be called to show that Grantham sincerely believed that an alliance between sheepmen and cattlemen was possible. Moreover, he would have no motive in carrying out such a raid, since sheep had never threatened his own property or herd.

The opening remarks concluded, the prosecution called its first witnesses to the stand, Sheriff Blaisedale and Count de Charbouille, whose testimony combined to establish that the glove and gray Stetson found at the scene of the crime belonged to none other than Maxwell Grantham. After the testimony of each man, Chalmers, acting on the advice of Lopasuta—who had belatedly entered the courtroom just as Judge Aspergren was bringing the courtroom to order—waived the right to cross-examine the witnesses.

With a disdainful air, Murchison called two more witnesses, both members of the Stock Growers' Association. While their testimony added nothing material to the case, it did tend to confirm, under Murchison's artful questioning, a growing impression of Grantham as a strong-willed, contentious man who had been quick to anger and slow to forget a wrong done to him. Twice Lopasuta had to forcibly keep Chalmers from leaping to his feet to shout objections to the proceedings.

"All in good time," Lopasuta whispered to the young man. "I'm going to ask you to put me on the stand—and after you've finished questioning me, nothing Murchison says will matter at all. Just ask me where I've been this morning and what I've found." Because the Comanche lawyer had arrived so late this morning, he and his young colleague had not been able to confer.

Finally, Donald Murchison, bringing to a close his questioning, turned to the judge and said, "The prosecution rests, Your Honor." With a supercilious air, he turned to Scott Chalmers and said, "Your turn, Counselor."

The young attorney flushed with indignation at this cavalier treatment, but when he looked at Lopasuta, the Comanche only smiled and shook his head. Chalmers rose and called to the stand his first witness, Maxwell Grantham.

Grantham took the stand and declared that the glove and hat did indeed belong to him, but that he had thrown the pair of gloves out about a week before the date of the raid because one was torn. As for the Stetson, he had last seen it before he had gone to the meeting with the sheep raisers; it had been hanging on a hat tree in a hallway near the kitchen. He didn't recall having seen it since and had instead been wearing an old hat identical to the gray Stetson held for evidence by the court.

Rising to cross-examine, the prosecuting attorney approached Maxwell Grantham, who still wore his arm in a sling. "Now then, Mr. Grantham, let me understand you. You admit to possessing the Stetson and the glove that have already been admitted into evidence. Your claim is that you had thrown out the glove and that the hat was missing, so it could not have been you who wore those items to the raid."

"That's true."

Murchison was silent for a moment, stroking his chin. Then he spoke up. "Mr. Grantham, if you were not present at the raid, where were you that night?"

"At seven o'clock I started out to pay a call on Count de Charbouille."

"And when did you reach the count's house, Mr. Grantham?"

"I never did. The wrangler who was driving my buggy thought one of our wheels was working loose, so we turned around and went home."

"You say a buggy, Mr. Grantham? You didn't ride over?"

"Not with my arm in a sling, I didn't." At this Grantham gave a smile and a nod in the direction of the gallery, where Hugo sat watching the trial. "Doc Bouchard would get after me if I tried anything as foolish as riding with a fractured shoulder," he averred.

Ignoring Grantham's aside, Murchison went on to his next question. "And did you repair the wheel and set out again?"

"No, it was too late for that. I retired to my study and went over some reports from my foreman about the ranch. Then I had a brandy and went to bed."

"So, Mr. Grantham, we are to believe that you spent a quiet evening at home with only your work as a companion, unwitnessed by anyone except the employee who drove your buggy early in the evening. This man will conveniently testify to the facts as you state them. But it is a known fact that the loyalty of men out here in the West is very strong, and that a man who's on the payroll of a wealthy rancher would like very much to keep his job."

"I object to that insinuation, Your Honor!" Scott Chalmers sprang to his feet, this time with Lopasuta's encouragement.

"Sustained. In the future, Mr. Murchison, make statements for which you have produced incontrovertible evidence."

"My apologies to you, Your Honor, and to my learned rival." Murchison mockingly made a slight bow toward Chalmers.

"Mr. Grantham, let me put it a different way. Would you say that your employees are loyal to you?"

"Yes, but—"

"Do they follow your directions?"

"Of course they do, but I would never ask them—"

"No further questions, Your Honor," Murchison interrupted.

There was a loud murmur in the courtroom, and the judge pounded emphatically with his gavel and reminded the spectators that it was within his power to clear the court.

Lopasuta bent to Chalmers and murmured, "I think it's time for me to introduce my evidence. Mr. Murchison seems intent on assassinating Grantham's character. We'd better stop him."

"Whatever you wish. You say you've found something that will help."

"I do indeed. Just give me a chance to tell my story," Lopasuta whispered.

Chalmers rose and said, "Your Honor, I would like to call Mr. Lopasuta Bouchard to the stand."

After Lopasuta had been sworn in and was seated on the stand, Chalmers asked him to give his profession and place of residence in order to establish his identity, then said, "Mr. Bouchard, will you tell the court where you were this morning and what you found there?"

"Your Honor, I object!" Murchison said. "This man by his own testimony is a stranger to these parts. What's more, he's an Indian. He says he's a lawyer, but how do we know that?"

"Objection overruled," Judge Aspergren said. "I assume that Mr. Chalmers has a particular point he intends to make and that it has a bearing upon this trial." To Lopasuta, the judge said, "Answer the question, sir."

"Thank you, Your Honor. Early this morning, just after dawn, in fact, I rode to the Ringold ranch and visited the site of the massacre of the two sheepmen. After searching the area for over an hour, I found a rifle casing, which I have here in my pocket." Lopasuta reached into his pocket, pulled out the casing, and handed it to the judge, who examined it closely.

"The court will hold this as evidence," the judge said, nodding to Scott Chalmers.

The young lawyer looked at Lopasuta as though he wished he could read the Comanche's mind. Finally, divining as best he could the older attorney's intent, he asked, "Mr. Bouchard, have you ever seen a casing like this one before?"

When Lopasuta smiled slightly and answered, "Yes, I have," Chalmers breathed a sigh of relief.

"Will you tell the court when and where you have seen a similar casing?"

"I found an identical casing last Sunday at Maxwell Grantham's ranch."

The courtroom erupted with shouts of condemnation for the cattleman, as well as cries of shocked disbelief, and one man was heard to say, "That about does it for Grantham."

Albert Elston's face, however, was florid with angry confusion, and he turned to the cattle rancher sitting next to him, John Corning, and muttered, "What the hell's all this? I thought Murchison had it all sewn up—you said that yourself!"

"Don't worry, Albert. Everything's goin' great— Grantham was the one who did it, and this guy's helpin' to prove him guilty! What're you complainin' about?"

Elston turned and stared at his friend but said nothing.

Judge Aspergren had to pound his gavel for nearly a minute before he could be heard. "I warn you again! I will have order in this court! Now, proceed, Mr. Chalmers."

"Mr. Bouchard, you say you found the casing at Maxwell Grantham's ranch?" The attorney was perplexed as to the direction in which the testimony was going. "Was it in Grantham's house?"

"No, sir," Lopasuta replied eagerly, trying to convey to the young attorney that he was on the right track.

"Then where, sir?"

"I found the casing at the northwestern corner of Mr. Grantham's property. It was lying on the ground in a small pine grove—the same grove that concealed the man who shot Maxwell Grantham over two weeks ago, wounding his shoulder and requiring him ever since to wear the sling you see on him now."

The spectators in the courtroom murmured quietly, but the noise died before Judge Aspergren could raise his gavel.

Anticipating an objection to Lopasuta's conjecture, Chalmers quickly asked the witness, "Mr. Bouchard, how can you be sure that the ground on which this casing lay is the site from which Mr. Grantham was shot?"

Lopasuta smiled at the young lawyer's fast thinking. "Mr. Grantham's foreman, Hank Johnson, took me to the site of the shooting. From the position of Mr. Grantham's horse—and the fact that Mr. Grantham was shot in the back—there was only one place the assailant could have hidden himself in anticipation of the attack. That is where I found the casing."

"Do you have this casing?"

"Yes, sir." Lopasuta pulled it from his pocket and handed it to the judge.

Judge Aspergren examined the casing and then compared it to the first. "Identical," he said. "Let it be recorded that both casings bear the numbers 45-80-500 on them. Do you know what kind of rifle these casings came from, Mr. Bouchard?"

"Indeed I do, Your Honor. According to the catalogues kept in the gun shop of Mr. Jacob Marsh, these shells were shot from a very rare rifle—only one hundred and fifty-one were made—the U.S. Trapdoor Long Range rifle."

John Corning gasped and turned to face Albert Elston, saying in a loud whisper, "That's *your* gun, Albert!"

"Shut up, you ninny!" Elston hissed. "Close your goddamned mouth or I'll do it for you."

Chalmers walked away from the bench and said with an extreme show of affability, "Your witness, Mr. Murchison."

"I have no questions, Your Honor," Murchison said, a scowl on his face.

The judge excused Lopasuta, and then Chalmers surprised those in the gallery by saying, "I wish to call to the stand Mr. John Corning."

Corning moaned in protest, but after a stern look from the judge, he made his way to the front of the court, was sworn in, and seated himself on the stand, squirming with discomfort.

"Mr. Corning, how long have you lived near Cheyenne?" Chalmers began.

"For twenty years or thereabouts."

"Would you say that you know most of the ranchers who live in this region?" Chalmers asked.

"Sure do!" Corning suddenly came to life. "Why, there ain't a fella in these parts I haven't passed the time of day with. I bet I know more 'n most in this room."

Chalmers smiled at the witness's enthusiasm, then asked, "Mr. Corning, do you know the type of rifles your friends use?"

John Corning's smile faded as he realized what the lawyer was about to ask him. He looked into the gallery and caught the eye of Albert Elston, whose face was pinched into a grimace so threatening that Corning could not maintain eye contact with his friend. He swallowed hard as he said, "Well . . . yes, I suppose I do."

"And do you know, Mr. Corning, who in this area

might own a U.S. Trapdoor—and remember, you're under oath."

Corning lowered his gaze and mumbled something inaudible.

"Louder, Mr. Corning!" the judge admonished.

"Albert Elston owns one of them rifles," he fairly yelled.

Elston was on his feet instantly, shouting, "I object! I object!" as he clambered over the people seated near him, trying to get to the aisle. "Your Honor, that don't prove a thing!"

"There will be order in this court!" Judge Aspergren said loudly. "Order! Mr. Elston, you will contain—"

"But, Judge, I didn't do it! It's my rifle, but that don't prove a thing. It was missing—yeah, somebody stole it. I didn't do it!" He turned on Murchison. "You said this was an open-and-close case, you bastard. I'll get you for this!"

Elston by now was flanked by two law officers, who took hold of his elbows and constrained him. Those who knew Elston were on their feet, their mouths open in amazement. One man, a cattle rancher, shouted, "Elston, you oughta be hanged!"

"Yeah, Elston," another spoke up. "You're givin' us a bad name!"

"Order!" Judge Aspergren demanded, and when the calls had died down, he said, "The court will take a fifteen-minute recess, during which time the gallery will be cleared. This trial cannot be concluded in the midst of such chaos. And, Mr. Elston, I hold you responsible. You are in contempt of court! Officers, escort him to my chambers until we reconvene."

Elston struggled as the guards led him away, and he was accompanied by the boos and hisses of many of his colleagues. As he passed by the witness stand, he glared at John Corning, spat, and said, "I won't forget this, Corning."

Cash Agnew, Ted Jackson, Jack Nantum, and Kyle Winger had been sitting behind their employer, and when Elston was led away, they exchanged worried glances and got up to leave. The courtroom exit was guarded by a law officer who looked to the judge for permission to let the men out. Judge Aspergren read their intentions clearly.

"You men wouldn't happen to be in the employ of Albert Elston, would you?"

The four blanched.

"Sheriff," the judge said to Blaisedale, "please detain those cowhands."

During the recess, Grantham and Chalmers approached Lopasuta with smiles of gratitude. "Lopasuta, I don't know what to say," Grantham said. "I'm sure the charges against me will be dropped. Those cowhands won't go to the gallows quietly. If I know their kind, they'll spill everything they know about Elston to save their own hides. But if you hadn't found those bullet casings, I'd be in deep trouble. Thank you."

"Please, Mr. Grantham, it has been my pleasure."

Scott Chalmers joined in his client's praise for the Comanche.

"Mr. Chalmers, I can't take all the credit. You have a quick and concise mind. I'm sure you're going to become a very successful attorney."

"Thanks to you," the younger man avowed.

Fifteen minutes later, Albert Elston was escorted back into the courtroom by the guards. Judge Aspergren, who climbed to the bench, sat down, and pounded the gavel to resume the trial, began, "Assuming the defense has no further witnesses and both sides rest their cases, I will give this case to the jury. Gentlemen, you may retire for deliberation.''

Those remaining in the courtroom watched as the men of the jury filed out. When they were gone, Judge Aspergren continued, "As for you, Mr. Elston, I have asked the sheriff to place you and your men under arrest for the murders of Jorge Santurce and Juan Epanisse.''

"You can't do that—''

"Oh, yes I can, Mr. Elston. The evidence against you is circumstantial, true, as was the evidence against Mr. Grantham. But it is certainly enough to warrant your being held until you can be brought to trial. Take him away.''

The protesting Albert Elston was removed from the courtroom.

Five minutes later the jury foreman sent a note to the judge that they had reached a verdict. Judge Aspergren had the twelve men ushered into the jury box, where their foreman happily announced their unanimous decision: Maxwell Grantham was found not guilty of both charges of murder.

The judge then turned to Grantham and congratulated him. "I hope you will testify in the trial of Mr. Elston.'' Then to Scott Chalmers, he said, "You have proved yourself more than worthy, Counselor. I commend you.''

Chalmers smiled and said, "Judge Aspergren, I cannot take credit for Mr. Grantham's defense. Lopasuta Bouchard is entirely responsible, not only for unearthing the key evidence but for advising me of what line of questioning to take. He, sir, is truly the one to be commended.''

The judge looked at Lopasuta. "Mr. Bouchard, you are a credit to your profession. This territory could use more men like you, whatever their race. I'd be honored to shake your hand for a job well done.''

Chapter 24

Jubilant over the vindication of his good friend, Count Pierre de Charbouille had invited Grantham, Lopasuta, Paul Bouchard, and Scott Chalmers to a superb dinner celebration at Cheyenne's finest restaurant, the Prime Tenderloin.

Cecily and Hugo had been invited, too, but Hugo had begged off with thanks, saying that Cecily needed to rest and that he needed to tend to her. "In her present condition, she might take it into her head to wander away—and I'd never forgive myself. One of these days, Count, when things are back to the way they should be, you and Mr. Grantham must come over, and Cecily and I will prepare a wonderful dinner for you," he told the Frenchman.

The dinner proved to be a complete success, as the tensions of the past weeks faded and the friends enjoyed each other's company. At the end of the meal, while coffee and cordials were being served, Maxwell Grantham turned to Lopasuta, reached into his coat lapel pocket with his good hand, and took out a check.

"Mr. Bouchard, I want to give you your fee."

Lopasuta unfolded the bank draft. "A thousand dollars! Please, Mr. Grantham, I cannot accept money for doing something of my own accord. My reward is in seeing justice done."

"Look, Lopasuta, you saved my life, not to mention my reputation. What you've done is worth much more than a thousand dollars."

"Please—you embarrass me, Mr. Grantham. I was not your attorney, after all," Lopasuta demurred.

"Don't concern yourself on that account. I'm not neglecting Scott. He has already been paid for a job well done. But I insist that you take the check."

With a broad grin on his face, Lopasuta nodded and pocketed the check. "I accept, but with this stipulation, Mr. Grantham. I will only use it when I can be of benefit to those who are unjustly accused and cannot afford proper counsel. It will pay for my efforts on their behalf."

"Have it your way, then. Well, I'm damned glad this boy here"—Maxwell Grantham reached over and gave Paul a slap on the back with his good hand—"took a notion to come up here to see my friends the doctors. I tell you, if he hadn't, bringing you in his wake, Lopasuta, I might have just eaten my last supper instead of this magnificent dinner."

It was Saturday evening, the first day of December of this momentous year of 1883, and Lopasuta and Paul Bouchard waited on the platform of the Cheyenne railroad station for the train that would take them on the first leg of their journey back to Windhaven Plantation. They had said good-bye to Hugo Bouchard earlier in the day, for he had found it necessary to remain home with Cecily. There was still no change in her condition, and the strain was beginning to show on Hugo.

"She keeps wondering what she should be doing," Hugo had told Paul and Lopasuta in a choked voice after the three of them had visited Cecily in the bedroom. The young doctor had shaken hands with the two travelers, and when they had wished her well, she had politely thanked them, as if they were indeed total strangers.

"I think it may be necessary for me to put her into the hospital," Hugo had told them at the door of the little house. "At least then she will understand that she is being treated for an injury, and it may make her less restless. Also, there will be staff to watch her so I can treat our patients without worrying about her wandering off."

Lopasuta comforted him with an embrace. "You have had great courage, and God has seen this. He knows that you and your wife have led lives of sacrifice for the sake of others," he had solemnly consoled the younger man. "You know, Hugo, it is said that we Comanche have dreams and visions from the spirit world that forecast our destiny, our future. I feel strongly that Cecily will recover and that all this will be remembered only as a bad dream. You are both young and have your lives ahead of you—there will be much joy for you. Of this, I am certain. There is a proverb, 'The mills of the gods grind exceedingly slow, but fine.' This is, I feel, true of your situation. May God watch over you and your wife."

"I shall never forget what you have done for us—and for Mr. Grantham. Perhaps you'll come again someday to visit us, after Cecily is better?"

"I shall try. Now we must go to the train station. Laure is anxious to see her son back home again, and I am eager to see her."

Just as Lopasuta and Paul arrived at the station, a distant whistle sounded, heralding the approach of the train. It would not be long before the young lad would be back safely at Windhaven Plantation. "You've had a most adventurous journey, Paul, more than many men twice or even three times your age have had in so short a time," Lopasuta philosophized with a friendly smile. "How do you feel about going back home now?"

Paul Bouchard thought a moment and then said, "I know I shouldn't have run away, Lopasuta. But you know, I'm glad I did. Just as you said, I've seen more of this country than most people, and a lot of things have happened to make me stop and think—meeting Cecily and Hugo and seeing how much they've done and how much people love them, and then being at the trial and learning how you managed to find out the real criminal. Why, I've even thought that maybe someday I'd like to be a lawyer like you, though I don't think I could ever be as good as you are."

"Now, don't flatter me, Paul." Lopasuta chuckled and gave him a friendly nudge in the ribs. "You can be anything you set your mind to. I think that the goals you've set for yourself during this journey are going to be very beneficial to you in the years ahead. And I hope you'll make your peace with your mother—that was the only really unhappy side of your whole adventure."

"You're right. It was inconsiderate of me to make Mother worry so much, with all the other things she has on her mind," Paul mused. "I will try to make it up to her, and I'm very sorry that I caused you so much trouble—taking you away from your work in New Orleans and coming up here to take me back."

"You mustn't look at it that way," Lopasuta interrupted. "If I hadn't come, who knows what might have happened to Maxwell Grantham? That ruthless man, Elston, might have succeeded in his plot to destroy a kind, generous man. No, we must look for some divine plan in all of this, Paul. It was meant for you to run away, as it was meant for me to come to take you home."

The two stood silent for a few moments, and then the conductor called, "All aboard!" As they walked toward the train, Lopasuta said, "On the way back, maybe you'll tell me some of your experiences, Paul."

"Sure, I will." But behind his back, Paul crossed his fingers. He would never tell about Boxcar Pete—certainly not to his mother, for that would distress her and make her conjure up all sorts of dangers. Nor would he tell Lopasuta, for believing in honor and integrity and decency as he did, the tall lawyer might feel that Paul had been an accomplice to a criminal. The outside world— the sheriffs and the deputies of Alabama, certainly— considered Boxcar Pete as no more than that. No, Paul resolved, that would be his own secret; the memories of the giant mulatto would never fade. For though Pete was not educated and was hated by some for having black blood in his veins, he had tried to right the wrongs done innocent people, just as Lopasuta, with Comanche and Mexican mingled in his veins, had brought justice to a man who had been cruelly slandered and wrongfully charged with the most serious crime a man could commit.

On this same Saturday evening, Nils Sonderman had come to dinner at Laure's invitation. Lucien had driven to Windhaven with him from Montgomery in the architect's buggy so that he might, as usual, spend the weekend with his mother. On the way, Nils had remarked to his handsome young apprentice, "Carl Markson told me only yesterday that his daughter, Angela, is quite smitten with you." Nils turned to eye Lucien with a sly smile. "Am I right in suspecting that my gifted young apprentice is contemplating something permanent in the future? I know that Mr. Markson thinks very highly of you, just as I do."

Lucien flushed and hesitated a moment before replying. Finally, he answered, "It's still too early yet, Mr. Sonderman. She's a very beautiful girl, and interesting, but we're both so young. I think it's too soon to think of marriage. Besides, to be frank with you, I'm not sure I'm an attractive match for any girl right now, not with all the expenses of running the plantation and the debts that remain to be paid."

"I rather think—although I suppose it's really none of my business, Lucien—that difficulties like those can be overcome. You have a fine name and background. Indeed, your future is assured—you've already shown such promise in so short a time in this new profession that I venture to say within a few years you'll be able to go out on your own and earn a very good livelihood."

"That's encouraging to hear, sir. It's very flattering that Angela likes me so much, and—well, to tell you the truth, Mr. Sonderman, it's a little embarrassing sometimes. It might be just infatuation, you know."

"That's possible," Nils replied, smiling. "What will be, will be. Right now I'm looking forward to seeing your lovely mother again."

"Mother likes you very much," Lucien blurted, then flushed again. The conversation about Angela had caught him off guard. He was thinking that his plan to marry for money must still be the motivating factor in his choice of a wife, and Angela Markson certainly had money. He had now steadfastly put aside from his mind all thoughts of Eleanor Martinson. Indeed, the wisest course was to forget all about her and let the affair with Angela progress as it would.

"You can be commended for not acting impulsively," his employer commented as they neared the chateau.

*　　*　　*

Celestine, Clarissa, and little John had come to look upon Nils Sonderman as a good friend, for he invariably related amusing anecdotes of his experiences, aimed at pleasing them and revealing unusual customs of life abroad. Over dinner this evening, for instance, he had talked about a wonderful puppet show he had seen in Paris as a youth, and he mimicked some of the puppets so cleverly that little John, turning at once to his mother, petulantly demanded, "Mama, I'd like to see puppets, too. Can we go see them?"

Nils touched his mouth with his napkin and chuckled. "I fear that I may unwittingly have saddled you with a new problem, Mrs. Kenniston. That was farthest from my mind when I said what I did."

"Oh, please, Mr. Sonderman, don't be concerned," Laure smilingly responded. "I think puppets are charming."

Lucien glanced at his youngest brother. "Mother," he volunteered, "I'll find out if Montgomery has a puppet show. If there is one, I want that to be my Christmas present to John."

Laure smiled lovingly at her eldest child, proud of him for his thoughtfulness.

After Clarabelle Hendry had come to take John to bed and Clarissa and Celestine had left to work on a quilt they were making, Lucien excused himself, tactfully sensing that his mother wanted to talk privately to Nils. He walked down to the riverbank and stood looking up at the tall bluff, reflecting on his life. Lucien felt at peace with himself, for at last he had found some permanence and goals, which were welcome after the abrupt termination of his studies in Dublin and his tragic love affair with Mary Eileen Brennert. He had found a position with a man he admired, who had inspired him to use his own creative processes to adapt himself to a new profession. And now he had proved that he had imagination and ability.

Again he looked up at the bluff, and he felt the strange, compelling attributes of his forebears, a joyous determination to become a man who would one day glean as much respect as the first Lucien and who would save that great man's legacy from ruin. It was a goal well worth striving for, a goal that would channel him and demand the utmost of his resources and his integrity. With this as his purpose, he could be well content.

Laure Kenniston remained in the dining room with her guest and, looking down at her coffee cup, said in a casual tone, "The children really like you, Mr. Sonderman. Your re-creation of the puppet show was just charming."

"I like your children very much, Mrs. Kenniston. They are very fortunate in having such a warm and devoted mother."

She blushed violently, lifted her coffee cup, put it to her lips, and set it down again. There was a long silence until finally she broke it with the remark, "I—I have to be truthful with you, Mr. Sonderman."

"Will you not call me Nils by now?" he implored.

Laure's expression blossomed into a smile. "Nils . . . of course. You've become a true, good friend, Nils. And a friend in whom I can confide."

"And will you let me call you Laure, in turn?"

"Oh, yes." Her intuition again told her that he loved her. She was grateful to him for not upsetting the balance of their friendship by confronting her with an emotional dilemma, which, at the moment, she did not feel capable of solving. So she said in a soft, shaking voice, which betrayed her inward emotion, "Then as a friend, I need your advice, Nils."

"You have only to ask for it."

"This Mr. James Weymore has made a very tempting offer for this chateau and the land. I don't want to accept it, because of my responsibility to the legacy left me by Luke. . . ."

"Must you even consider such an offer?" Nils asked.

"I'm not sure." Laure looked down at her hands, not knowing how much more to say.

Early the previous week, she had received wires from two creditors in Europe demanding at least partial payment of huge debts incurred by Leland, threatening legal action against his estate if some money was not sent to them at once.

Fortunately, a few days before Laure had received these wires from the European creditors, she had finally received word of a small dividend from her shares in the Brunton & Alliance Bank of New Orleans. Even more welcome was a larger check on the life insurance policy that Leland had taken out in New York, naming her as beneficiary. This check she had taken to Montgomery for deposit at her local bank, not wishing a further delay by forwarding it to the Brunton & Alliance bank, where her principal account remained. At the same time, she had sent wires to the factors, informing them that as soon as the insurance check cleared, they would have substantial payments.

That had been a bitter blow, for she had hoped to keep that money in trust for the children's future.

"If I were to tell you that I could . . ." he began in a faltering way. "Laure, I will not insult you, but if you need aid—"

"No, but God bless you for the thought, dear Nils!" she quickly interrupted him. "Fortunately, two days ago I received a check from the insurance company. It was on Leland's life, and by using it I will be able to pay off the creditors—not in full, but enough to satisfy them for a long while. What I fear most, Nils, is the future. Mr. Weymore has proved himself to be a most courteous and considerate gentleman, as well as my close neighbor, but I still do not wish to sell this property. What am I to do?''

''Adhere to your convictions, Laure!'' he said with a fierceness in his voice that was impelled by his own love for her. ''Such resolve only proves how truly you are a Bouchard, how genuinely you respect this historical legacy and the intrinsic honor and loyalty it confers upon you. Laure, if at any time you find yourself hard-pressed by creditors who have no compassion and cannot understand the significance of Windhaven Plantation, let it be me who will give you aid—with no strings or stipulations, let me hasten to assure you.''

''Thank you. You have given me heart and courage.''

''You will see; all will go well for you. I feel it strongly, Laure.'' He rose and made a low bow toward her. ''Perhaps I am being too bold, but I would find it the happiest fulfillment of my life if I could undertake the solution of all your problems.''

There were tears in Laure's eyes as she replied, ''I am honored. Let us wait and see what the future holds. I shall try not to accept James Weymore's offer. You have reminded me of honor, and that has been my creed of life, even in the darkest hours. Once, when I thought I was in the very nadir of hell, I met someone who restored me. That was Luke Bouchard. Now again, after having lost him and then Leland, you appear to give me courage. I will take the lesson to heart.'' She came to him and offered him her hand; he gravely took it, and their eyes met, and perhaps it was a promise of what was yet to come but could not yet be vouchsafed between them.

On the second day of December, shortly before noon, Laure received a telegram from Lopasuta, sent from Cheyenne, informing her that he and Paul had begun their journey back to Windhaven Plantation. She joyfully told the news to Clarabelle, Amelia, and Lucien. "It should take them about a week to reach here," she declared. "Oh, Amelia, we must have a wonderful dinner ready! The prodigal son returns. We'll kill the newly fatted calf."

"Now that we know he's safe and sound," Lucien said, "I'll try to make him feel welcome. I promise that I'll try to make amends with him."

"Lucien, that's good of you. And I've felt that perhaps I'd neglected him as his mother."

"No, you didn't, Mother. He was brokenhearted about leaving New York, and there was nothing here for him to do." He put his arm around Laure's shoulders. "I'm going to be a real brother to him from now on, and a friend—I promise."

"You know, Lucien, you've grown up a lot. I'm very proud of you—and your father would be, too," she said softly, then turned away to hide the tears welling in her eyes.

Shortly after Lopasuta's telegram arrived, James Weymore paid another visit to Windhaven Plantation. As the golden-haired widow entered the sitting room, Weymore promptly stood and solicitously declared, "I've come again, Mrs. Kenniston, wanting to reassure you of my honorable intentions. I want to offer you whatever assistance I can in running this plantation."

"It's most kind of you to think of me, Mr. Weymore. And thank you for the magnificent bouquet you had sent over."

"A mere token of my esteem for you, dear lady. Please consider my offer to extend you a loan. You could bring the property up to its usual yield and hire temporary workers to harvest your crops." He paused and then with an unctuous smile added, "I'm just one neighbor trying to help another. After all, we both want to do well here and keep these beautiful places going." When she glanced at him, frowning a little from his words, he slyly pursued, "A loan—or, indeed, sale of the land—might be just the thing to ensure its careful preservation for the future. If you were to sell to me, you'd still have a home here. Only, I'd work the land and do with it as I pleased. I'd be, in a way, a kind of overseer."

Laure bit her lip. The offer was more than generous, yet once she sold Windhaven Plantation, it would put an end to all that old Lucien Bouchard had achieved within his lifetime. "I—I don't want you to think I'm not grateful, Mr. Weymore, but I simply can't sell this property. If I were a newcomer here, if I had acquired the land by marrying someone who had recently bought it, then I might be more disposed to accept your offer. But you see, Mr. Weymore, it has been passed down for generations. The name of Bouchard is stamped upon it indelibly. Certainly I thank you for your help. I do hope that we shall continue to be good neighbors."

He gave her a courtly bow, reached for her hand, and kissed it. "Dear lady, I could never feel any hostility toward you. It's true that you disappoint me, but that's only from a business viewpoint. I still regard you as a wonderful, courageous woman. I'll say good afternoon to you, Mrs. Kenniston."

He had scarcely left the chateau and climbed back into his buggy to drive upriver to the old Haskins land, which was now his by rightful title and deed, when Laure flung herself down upon a settee and burst into heartrending sobs.

She found herself in an emotional quandary. The day before, Nils Sonderman had shown his sympathetic nature, and Laure knew that he loved her.

But James Weymore both fascinated and puzzled her. His courteous, genial demeanor and respectful behavior were motivated by an attitude she could not fathom, and she was uncertain what he wanted of Windhaven Plantation—and of her. Of course, he was wealthy; he would have to be in order to buy all the Haskins land. And now, when Windhaven revenues were so slight and the debts mounting, wealth represented Windhaven's salvation. That would be the easy way, but it could not be her way now, not with so much at stake.

At least today one ray of brightness pierced her dark cloud: the news that Lopasuta and Paul were coming back home. And for Paul's sake, as well as for that of the other children, she dared not take James Weymore's money and turn Windhaven Plantation over to him—a stranger, when all was said and done.

Chapter 25

$\mathcal{I}$n Texas, on Windhaven Range, Lucien Edmond Bouchard had risen early this Monday. Going into the kitchen, he had asked the cook to prepare a tray for his wife, Maxine, for she had been in bed since Thursday, when she had had a fainting spell. Since then she had been unresponsive and lethargic, spending most of the day asleep. Understandably concerned, Lucien Edmond had summoned a doctor to examine her on Saturday, but the physician had also been puzzled; Maxine seemed in good health, except for her blood pressure being a bit low, but he went on to say that if her condition did not improve in one week's time, she should be hospitalized.

Lucien Edmond, now forty-five and filled with vitality, was content with his life as long as his family was well and happy. He had much for which to be grateful, including a letter from Carla. Lucien Edmond had promptly taken it into the bedroom to show to Maxine.

"Darling, good news! It's another letter from Carla, and she's sent more Paris newspaper clippings."

He had handed the envelope to Maxine, but she turned over and said in a sleepy voice, "Later, dear. Just leave it on the nightstand." With that, she went back to sleep.

Later, as he ate his breakfast, he looked at the morn-

ing's mail. One letter he ripped open right away, for the
return address was from Windhaven Plantation.

The letter was not from Laure, as he had at first
assumed, but from Clarabelle Hendry. Why would the
governess be writing him? Lucien Edmond scanned the
letter, then read it slowly.

Dear Mr. Bouchard:

I'm writing to you because I don't know what
else to do. Things are not good here, Mr. Bouchard,
and Laure, she's too proud to tell you that she's in
trouble. Just the other day, more letters from creditors came, and from what she told me, it sounds
like she may lose Windhaven Plantation if she
doesn't come up with what is owed. Now far be it
from me to interfere in somebody else's business
matters, but I just didn't think you'd want her
going through all this by herself. A man who's
bought property near here has offered to buy
Windhaven, and, Mr. Bouchard, I'm afraid Laure
just might say yes.

Please, sir, don't let her know I wrote you
about all this. I don't want to meddle, but I thought
you'd want to know.

Yours truly,
Clarabelle Hendry

Lucien Edmond was taken aback by Clarabelle's news,
and he pushed the remainder of his breakfast aside.
Windhaven Plantation was the true home of all the
Bouchards—a spiritual home, Lucien Edmond had always thought—and to let it be lost to creditors or sold
to a stranger would be tantamount to forsaking the
family name. If he mailed her a check, she would send

it back. He had to think of a way for the plantation to get back on its feet again; he must not let it be taken away. He had to go to Laure.

But he could not leave. Maxine's condition was too uncertain for him to leave her. He would never forgive himself if something happened to her.

"Here's the tray for Mrs. Bouchard, sir. Don't you want any more?" the cook asked, noticing his unfinished breakfast.

"No, Marie. That'll be all. I'll take this to Maxine. Thank you."

Lucien Edmond, his face somber, took the tray and gently opened the bedroom door. Laying the tray down on the night table beside the bed, he stood for a moment looking at her face in repose, and then he gently murmured, "Maxine, darling, wake up. I've brought your breakfast."

Maxine's eyes opened, her brow furrowed, and then she said, "I'm not hungry right now, darling. I think I'll sleep a bit longer. I'll call for something when I'm hungry." Then she rolled over and fell asleep again.

His worry increasing, Lucien Edmond left the room.

Mara, coming to the house to check on Maxine, saw her brother in the hallway. "Lucien Edmond, what's the matter?"

"It's Maxine. I—I'm really concerned about her, Mara!"

"Is she worse?"

"I don't know. And I've received news from the plantation, which demands my immediate attention there, but Maxine is so . . . so unlike her normal self, I'm reluctant to leave. I don't know what to do!"

Mara Hernandez took the tray from her brother, placed it on a taboret, and put her arm around his shoulders. "Come with me, my dear. Tell me all about this letter, and we can decide what should be done." She led the distraught man to the study, where Lucien Edmond handed her the letter and expressed his deepening distress over his wife.

When she had read the letter and Lucien Edmond had spilled out the concerns of his heart, Mara said, "Lucien Edmond, if you went to Alabama, Ramón and I would take very good care of Maxine and let you know if there was a change in her condition. The doctor has told you she is fine as far as he can tell. She needs sleep, and that is what she is getting. Go to Laure and help her. Please, do not worry."

"God bless you, Mara." Lucien Edmond's voice was choked with emotion.

Later that day, Lucien Edmond joined Mara's husband, Ramón, in the study. After pouring Ramón and himself brandies, Lucien Edmond said, "Ramón, as my partner, I ask your consent to withdraw a substantial amount from our account to give to Laure for Windhaven Plantation. Without a sizable cash investment at this point, I don't think she will be able to hold on to the property. And as you know, the plantation means so much to her—and to all of us."

"Lucien Edmond, you have my consent and also my blessing."

"Would you feel comfortable giving Laure as much as, say, twenty thousand? I hope also to offer her a way to guarantee Windhaven's future survival, although I haven't come up with anything yet."

"Twenty thousand should be fine, Lucien Edmond. Give Laure my warmest regards and stay as long as you need to. Mara and I will take good care of Maxine and the children."

Lucien Edmond smiled at his brother-in-law, then remarked, "I don't feel right leaving you with so many of my responsibilities, Ramón. A sick wife, the children, and of course there's Windhaven Range."

"You must not be concerned, Lucien Edmond. I am glad to have the opportunity to repay your many kindnesses."

Early the next morning, arriving in San Antonio, Lucien Edmond procured a draft at his bank for twenty thousand dollars and, finding out that his train east would not depart for another two hours, occupied the time in sending off cables to his children, Carla and Hugo, telling of Maxine's illness and his trip to Alabama. Then he wrote a lengthy letter to each. To Carla's letter, he added that he hoped she would return to the United States to visit them and that they loved her very much and were proud of her.

By Thursday in the late afternoon, having made excellent train connections, Lucien Edmond arrived in Montgomery and, hiring a horse at a livery stable, rode to the red-brick chateau, arriving there at about seven o'clock in the evening. As he entered the courtyard and dismounted, his eyes were filled with tears. Here he had been born, in this very chateau, and in this same area he had courted Maxine, who had come from Baltimore to visit her uncle Ernest Kendall. Here was where it had all begun, and now fate had designated him to save Windhaven Plantation from what might well be an ignominious oblivion.

Before he knocked on the front door, he turned to look up at the towering bluff just beyond and said a silent prayer for his father, who had so ingeniously directed him to court Maxine.

He crossed himself, bowed his head, took a deep breath, and then lifted his hand to the great brass knocker to announce his return to Windhaven.

*   *   *

"Lucien Edmond—oh, dear Lucien Edmond! What a surprise!" Laure was visibly flustered as she came to meet her mature stepson in the foyer after Clarabelle Hendry had admitted him and then hurried into the dining room to inform her mistress of his arrival.

"I should have wired you, I know, Laure. But I decided to come at the last minute."

"Well, I am certainly happy to have you here, whatever the reason. But we'll have to wait until later to catch up on things. You see, James Weymore, the man who bought Andy Haskins's land downriver, is here for supper."

"I apologize for bursting in on you."

"No, no, it's very fortuitous. You'll meet Mr. Weymore, and I'll value your advice about an offer he's made me."

"Of course, I'll be glad to help. In fact, that's what I'm here for. Let me just freshen up a bit after my journey."

"Certainly, dear. Clarabelle, would you show Lucien Edmond to a guest room? I'll go back in and tell the children and Mr. Weymore that we've a very special guest for supper." Laure squeezed his hand and then, with a sigh, turned and went back into the dining room.

As tall blond Lucien Edmond entered the dining room fifteen minutes later, James Weymore, elegantly attired in flowery cravat and an imported tweed waistcoat and trousers, got to his feet with an amiable smile on his plump face. "Mr. Bouchard, sir, a pleasure to make your acquaintance," he said as soon as Laure had made the introductions.

"And yours, Mr. Weymore," Lucien Edmond responded courteously. Before seating himself, he greeted the children. "I hardly recognize any of you. Celestine,

Clarissa—you're very lovely young ladies. And you, John, you're a fine, sturdy young man indeed!''

At this Laure's youngest replied, "Thank you, sir," and his face broke into a smile that would light up a night sky.

Laure said to John, "Lucien Edmond is your half brother."

"Half? Mummy, where's the other half, then?" the boy demanded.

James Weymore guffawed and then unctuously said, "Mrs. Bouchard, that boy of yours is indeed a charmer—just, indeed, as you are, ma'am."

Lucien Edmond shot him a veiled look of amused appraisal as Clarabelle began to serve the dinner. Amelia had prepared baked catfish and sweet yams, with ears of late fall corn liberally buttered and salted. As Lucien Edmond sampled the first bite of catfish, he gave her a boyish grin and remarked, "I haven't tasted this since I left for Texas, and it's even better than I remember."

"I'll tell Amelia you said that. She'll be very flattered," Laure returned.

"That's right, Mrs. Kenniston told me you're from Texas, sir." James Weymore patted his sensual mouth with his napkin and eyed Lucien Edmond speculatively. "I understand you've a big ranch down there. Must be doing pretty well with all the big-city demand for beef these days."

"Reasonably well, thanks," Lucien Edmond replied casually.

Clarabelle came round the table to fill Weymore's wine glass with a mild Médoc, and the land speculator lifted his glass to toast Laure, then the children, and finally Lucien Edmond, seated across the table from him. "Health and good fortune to all," he proposed genially. After a sip, he repeated, "Yes, to all of you, health and good fortune." Then, setting down his glass, in a confidential tone to which he added his most ingratiating smile, he resumed, "Perhaps you know, Mr. Bouchard, that I've recently acquired the Haskins property downriver from here."

"Yes," Lucien Edmond replied, "so Laure said."

"I'm very taken with this part of the state, especially this riverfront land—good and fertile, it is, with lots of possibilities for profit. Wouldn't you agree, sir?"

Lucien Edmond eyed Weymore, then said blandly, "Yes, of course."

"Naturally, though, to make profits on any land, you must put money into it. Yes, lots of money, wouldn't you agree, sir? And that's why I'm so excited about my purchase, because I have more than enough capital to get the land into top-yielding condition." Weymore imperiously waved his glass in the direction of Clarabelle, and he held it high as she filled it with more wine. "Of course, Mrs. Kenniston here is fortunate to own the most desirable piece of property I've seen in a long time. And I know, ma'am, that you've cared for it as best you could. Times are bad for agriculture, no doubt about it. A good shot in the arm would help this place, I'm sure." Weymore lowered his voice and leaned conspiratorially toward Laure. "You just keep that in mind, my dear Mrs. Kenniston."

Laure blushed slightly that Lucien Edmond should not have heard the idea of selling Windhaven Plantation from her.

Lucien Edmond was quick to notice Laure's chagrin, and he caught Clarabelle's eye and smiled. When she had answered his knock, he had profusely thanked the loyal governess for sending him word of her concern for

Windhaven's troubles. Now he knew that her concern was valid.

"Perhaps you know, Mr. Bouchard, that I've made Mrs. Kenniston a very handsome offer for her property. Thus far, regrettably she hasn't seen fit to accept it. But I do hope she'll reconsider. Hailing from Texas, you may not be aware that crops are failing to provide decent revenues for most landowners in these parts. And as I told Mrs. Kenniston, even if she agreed to sell the land to me, I'd respect her wishes and permit her practically all the control she now enjoys over her tenants. It would be, you see, Mr. Bouchard, a kind of helpful partnership, eliminating her debts and enabling her to realize the golden future I'm sure she plans for this magnificent stretch along the Alabama River."

"Your sentiments do you credit, Mr. Weymore," Lucien Edmond answered. "But I must tell you that in no way will I try to influence her. By the terms of my father's will, she and her eldest son are co-owners. Laure lives here, and the decision regarding the land must be made by her alone."

"Oh, to be sure, to be sure, Mr. Bouchard, sir," Weymore avowed effusively, again favoring Laure with an unctuous smile and lifting his half-empty wine glass. "I have the utmost respect and regard for Mrs. Kenniston, and it is only in the spirit of neighborly helpfulness that I have approached her with this offer. I'm sure you understand."

"Of course," Lucien Edmond replied noncommittally.

"Mr. Weymore," Laure spoke up, "if you don't mind, I'd rather not discuss business matters right now. Let's enjoy the wonderful supper Amelia has prepared for us."

Weymore inclined his head. "I bow to your wishes, dear Mrs. Kenniston." Then, after finishing his wine, he turned to Lucien Edmond. "Do you know, sir, I've always been interested in cattle. In my opinion, it's the coming investment for long-range profits. Would you mind, sir, telling me something of your operation?"

After James Weymore had taken his departure, Laure and Lucien Edmond retreated to the study, at last to catch up on the happenings of the far-flung Bouchard family members. Lucien Edmond told about Hugo's flourishing medical practice and happy marriage, and about Carla's success as an artist, and Laure related Lucien's promise in the field of architecture and Paul's troubling disappearance. When Laure asked about the other members of his family, her stepson explained Maxine's puzzling illness but that Ramón and Mara were caring for his wife and that they promised to notify him if there was any change in her condition.

Then he began the speech he had rehearsed all the way from Texas. "Laure, doesn't it make sense that one Bouchard should help another and thus solve any problems within the family?" he reasoned. "Mr. Weymore has a way of making his offer sound attractive, but have you considered the ramifications of selling Windhaven Plantation?"

"Of course I have, dear Lucien Edmond, and I have hesitated on that account. But Mr. Weymore said that the children and I could remain here and that everything would continue as normal. He gave me his word—"

"I'm afraid that *that*, dear Laure, is just the problem. I don't trust the man, and I can't say that I would take his word—especially on an important matter such as this."

"You mean he might be lying?" Laure seemed genuinely surprised.

"Did you notice how inquisitive he was about

Windhaven Range, Laure? Mr. Weymore is worried—
and justifiably so—that I have come to offer you assistance, thereby eliminating your need to sell the plantation.
He seems most intent on acquiring this property, Laure,
and I fear that he would promise almost anything to get
it."

Laure looked down at her hands folded in her lap,
and was obviously distressed.

"You mustn't worry, Laure. I'm here to help." He
reached into his jacket pocket and withdrew a long
envelope. "This bank draft is my investment in the
heritage of the Bouchards, so it will continue without
blemish or obligation."

Nonplussed, Laure opened the envelope and stared at
the check. Finally, she said, "But it's much too much,
Lucien Edmond. I can't accept it," she protested.

"Laure, listen to me," he said gently. "This was my
childhood home, and where Maxine and I were married. I've been thinking of ways to turn this beautiful
property into a source of continuous revenue for you
and the children. And I think I've hit upon a pretty
good idea. Everyone in the state knows the Bouchard
history, knows the beauty of this magnificent chateau on
the bank of the Alabama River. Why couldn't we transform it into a summer resort for vacationers? I'm sure
there are plenty of wealthy people from the North who
would like to visit the South and see the gentle and
scenically beautiful traditional life that existed before
the Civil War. Why, we could hire a first-class chef,
and some of the workers here could act as guides
throughout the area. We could even arrange for boat
tours along the Alabama River and for picnics and
such."

Laure's lovely face brightened, but then she frowned.
"Lucien Edmond, you're forgetting one thing. I don't

have the resources to purchase the materials needed to transform this plantation into a resort, not to mention—"

"I'm not forgetting anything," he interrupted forcefully. "What *you're* forgetting is that I'm a part of the Bouchard family and that Windhaven Plantation is my responsibility, too. The extra money in this draft, which I suspect will more than clear your indebtedness, will be a start toward the new enterprise. And since Windhaven Range is doing much better, I fully intend to finance the entire transformation. No, let me finish, Laure! I have my own children to think of, you know. The investment I can make here will profit you as it will profit me, and it will keep the property safe and untrammeled by any debt or lien. Think of the possibilities! Thanks to the wisdom of Luke and my great-grandfather, this land was never abused by cotton and tobacco, so it's still fertile and productive. You'd be able to raise much of the food you'd serve, and you could sell your surplus fruits and vegetables to the local markets. You'd have a good income, and the onerous duties of raising crops and livestock would be greatly eased."

"Oh, dear Lucien Edmond, I—I don't know how to thank you . . . for the check and for your wonderful idea! Just imagine, the chateau would come alive again with all the old activity. How kind you were to come here, especially with Maxine so ill."

He put his arm around her shoulders and kissed her on the cheek. "Laure, being here has helped me more than you know. There's been nothing I can do at home to help Maxine."

Laure squeezed his hand with loving gratitude.

The two of them spent the rest of the evening discussing the new plan. Seating himself at his father's escritoire, Lucien Edmond drew up a rough draft comprising all the ideas that he and Laure discussed. When he had finished, he told her, "Tomorrow you and I will write to the editors of northern newspapers, and we'll tell them that you plan to turn this great chateau, with its hundred-year history, into a tasteful and elegant resort for those who want to see the traditional beauty of the Old South. We can ask Lucien's employer to make detailed sketches of the chateau and the property, and those sketches can be sent to the newspaper editors, who can make woodcuts of them and run them as illustrations in the stories. I'm certain the publicity will draw many interested and wealthy Northerners.

"Yes, and this magnificent building certainly has room enough to house quite a few guests, and in the utmost luxury such as can be found in the finest European hotels. But best of all, it will be run in a spirit of love, not so much commercialism, though for the sake of practicality we must consider the commercial benefits as well, Laure."

"Lucien Edmond, it's a miracle that you've come at this time, when I had just about given up hope," Laure exclaimed. "Tomorrow I'll have Ben drive us to Montgomery. We'll tell Mr. Sonderman about the idea for the sketches. Oh, Lucien Edmond, I don't think I'll be able to sleep tonight, my mind's so full of ideas—all because of you. God bless you."

It was late on Wednesday evening when the concierge hurried up to Carla Bouchard's atelier with the cable from her father. Carla herself answered the elderly woman's knock while Henri Courvalier discreetly moved into the kitchen so that the gossipy old woman would not see him.

"*Je vous remercie, madame,*" Carla politely thanked the woman, fumbling in the pocket of her smock and

328

drawing out a *vingt-centime* piece. *"C'est bien soucieux de vous."*

"What is it, *ma chérie*?" The mature vintner came to Carla, putting his hands on her shoulders and kissing her neck.

"A cable—it must be from home." Carla tore open the envelope. "It's from my father. Oh, no! My—my mother is very ill, but Father is going to Alabama to help his stepmother. Why would he leave her? Wait." She read on. "Oh, God, Windhaven Plantation may be sold! Henri, I must go home at once."

"Wait a bit, *petite*." He kissed her cheek now and held her close. "What can you do at home that you can't do here?"

"I can take care of Mother, that's what."

"Carla, *ma chérie*, would your father leave your ailing mother without proper care? Would he leave her at all if she were desperately ill? Of course not! Besides, in the time it would take you to travel home, she is most likely to recover."

"I suppose you're right, Henri," Carla said uncertainly.

"Of course I am, my darling girl!" Henri gave her a playful hug. "Why don't you wait for a week or two and see how your mother is feeling then? Your father will surely inform you if your mother gets worse, will he not?"

"Yes, I suppose so," Carla said.

"Good. If she is not improved by then, I will be more than happy to pay your fare home. Is that suitable, my Carla?" the Frenchman asked.

Carla smiled shyly. "Yes, Henri, that is fine."

He kissed her lightly on the mouth and said, "Good! Now, tomorrow the second exhibition of your paintings takes place, and in a far larger gallery than that of M'sieu Vertrier's. But there is one thing you do not yet know, and it is that I have arranged for the most important art critics in all France to attend."

"Henri—no, you didn't tell me!" Carla turned to him, wide-eyed.

"If they like your paintings—and I know in advance they will, for what you have done since we have been together is the finest of all your work—believe me, then your future as an artist will be assured. *Ma mignonne,* you see that it is very important for you to attend this exhibition tomorrow."

"Oh, dear Henri, you're so thoughtful. I'm very fond of you, *tu sais.*" She turned to him and put her arms around his neck. "Who would have thought it could begin by your coming from that bistro to visit Giles's gallery?"

"Let us say it was destiny for both of us, *ma belle aimée,*" he responded gallantly.

Chapter 26

The train that Paul and Lopasuta Bouchard had taken at Cheyenne had been delayed nearly a full day in Denver because of a ferocious blizzard. On the morning of Saturday, December 8, the train they had ridden for the rest of their trip pulled into the Birmingham station. "We'd best get out and stretch our legs, Paul," Lopasuta proposed genially.

As they left their seats, a porter hurried up to them. "You gentlemen kin mosey around if you like. The conductor, he say we gonna stay here half an hour."

"I wonder why that is," Lopasuta mused to his young companion after the porter had moved on.

As they descended the steps of the passenger car, they saw beyond them an enormous crowd. Mystified, Paul said, "Look at all the people. What do you suppose is going on?"

"Let's find out," Lopasuta proposed.

Most of the people seemed to be congregating at the far end of the station—and there were hundreds of them. As Paul walked toward the crowd, his eye was drawn to a sign at one end of the station: "See Boxcar Pete Brought to Justice!"

"Oh, my God!" he said to himself in a low voice. An icy shiver of fear coursed through him. "Wait a minute, Lopasuta, I want to find out. Please wait here for me.''

"If you like,'' Lopasuta said genially, then called after, "but don't be long!''

Paul pushed his way through the crowd, sickened by the thought of what he might find, and a fat man angrily turned to him. "Who the hell you think you're shovin', bub? You wait in line like everybody else. Cost you two bits to see that nigger bastard!''

"I—I beg your pardon. We came all the way from Wyoming, sir. I don't know what this is. We're on our way to Montgomery,'' Paul faltered.

"So, you wanna know what this is? Ever hear of Boxcar Pete, boy? He's a nigger thought he'd start a real ruckus down here in Alabama, but we sure as hell put a stop to him! A sheriff down south and his deppities, they cornered him in a store—sent him word a friend was sick, and when he showed up, they filled him full o' bullets. Leastways, that's what I heared tell. They've roped off his worthless, robbin' hulk. It's on a table over there, and you gotta pay two bits to see him. Yes, they finally caught up with him, and they riddled him full of bullets, that dirty black crook!''

"My God!'' Paul felt his stomach lurch.

The fat man grinned at him and winked. "Sure, sonny. They're showin' him off in jist about every train station in 'Bamy, that's a fact. I already seen him in Mobile, paid my two bits like everybody else, and then I come up here to spend the week with my sister Hetty, and here he is again, the black bastard. Whoever's totin' him around is sure makin' a pile of cash, I'm here to tell you!'' The fat man's laugh sounded evil to Paul. Then the man leaned over and said in a low voice, "Tell you what, sonny, since I already seen the bastard once, you kin git ahead of me in line, if you wanna.''

"No—no thanks, mister," Paul quavered.

"He's laid out real nice on a sheet, his arms over his chest. And everybody comes up there and spits at him and laughs at him and tells him he didn't amount to so much after all. Don't you wanna do that? Hell, I'll even stand treat for you, sonny. Be a good lesson fer ya, when you grow up. Niggers is poison, take it from me, 'n' I'm Caleb Joshaway. Got the biggest dry goods store in Selma, that's a fact!"

Paul fought the tears that nearly blinded him. "No thanks, mister. I have to go to Montgomery. I'd better get back on the train. Thanks for telling me."

The fat man snorted in derision, and Paul turned away and walked slowly back toward Lopasuta. After he was apart from the bulk of the crowd, the boy closed his eyes and thought, *I'll never forget what a friend you were to me, Pete—never. You helped me grow up. I'm so sorry you had to die because of a crooked sheriff and a lot of people who thought the way he did.*

He ground his teeth and sniffled, trying hard to clear his tears before he returned to Lopasuta. He took several deep breaths and then, forcing a smile to his face, walked up to the tall lawyer. "Seems they're charging admission to see the body of some criminal they caught, Lopasuta. Let's get back on the train."

Lopasuta nodded gravely. "Perhaps this is a good lesson for both of us, Paul. Some people say that Indians are savages. But even at our worst, we never displayed the bodies of our enemies to gloat over them. Come, we'll be back home very soon."

They reached Montgomery at about nine o'clock that same evening, and Lopasuta proposed that they rent horses from the livery stable and see who could race back first to Windhaven Plantation. Paul was grateful for this challenge, which drove from his mind the agonizing memory of the Birmingham station, where so many faces were twisted in hate, reveling in the death of a man who, though he was a criminal, had done so much good for others and selflessly sacrificed himself for their sake.

"Oh, my God! Paul!" Laure cried out almost hysterically as she hugged her young son, while Lopasuta, smiling at the reunion, stood beside him. Still clutching Paul to her, she said to Lopasuta, "There aren't any words for how grateful I am to you for bringing him home safely, dear Lopasuta!"

Lucien, who had been reading in his room, had heard the sound of the knocker and hurried downstairs to greet his younger brother. "Paul, it's great to have you back!"

"I'm glad to be home, Lucien." Paul sheepishly held out his hand to his older brother, who eagerly shook it. "I think we ought to have a celebration," Lucien said.

"Let's go out into the kitchen, and I'll do the honors," Laure, smiling through her tears, now proposed. "How good it is to have both of you back with me. Paul, you must tell me everything that happened. I was so worried about you!"

"I know, Mother. I didn't mean to cause you all that worry, truly I didn't. I want you to know that I'm ready to return to work so I can help around here. I mean it."

"We'll talk about that later," Laure said as they entered the kitchen. She gave him a quick hug and went to the cupboard and began to fix a late-night meal as the others seated themselves at the table. "I've got wonderful news to share with you all. First, Lucien Edmond is here from Texas—he's in Montgomery for a few days, seeing to some business for me—and he's had the most marvelous idea. I'll tell you all about it once the food's on the table. My gracious, it's almost like old times having everyone here—you, Lopasuta, Lucien, and Lucien Edmond, and of course you, Paul.'' She smiled warmly at her son, who colored slightly.

After Laure had prepared pancakes with honey and some strong coffee, she sat and looked fondly at her two strong sons and at Lopasuta. ''There's so much I have to tell you,'' she repeated.

''Don't hold it back another minute,'' Lopasuta teased. ''You can tell us while we're busy eating. That way you won't be interrupted.''

Laure laughed and then began, ''First of all, Lucien Edmond has paid the debts that threatened this property.''

''That's wonderful, Mother!'' Paul exclaimed.

''Don't talk with your mouth full,'' Laure said woodenly, and they all burst out with hearty laughter at her automatic response. She went on to explain Lucien Edmond's idea of transforming Windhaven Plantation into a posh resort and his generous contribution to be used in effecting the necessary changes in the red-brick chateau. She was pleased with the enthusiastic response of all three, and she gave a silent prayer of thanks when Paul showed an eagerness to help out with the resort.

They discussed the idea for an hour, then Laure and Lucien listened to Lopasuta's and Paul's adventures in Wyoming. By this time Paul's eyelids were growing heavy, and Laure turned to her younger son and with a mock-stern expression on her lovely face said, ''Young man, you're going to bed. You're obviously exhausted.''

''I guess I am, but I'd like to take a hot bath first.'' He rose from his chair and walked around the table to Laure. Putting his arm around her, he said, ''Mother, I won't ever cause you any worries again, I promise.''

''Things will be different between us, you'll see, dear,'' Laure promised.

A few minutes later, after Paul had gone upstairs,

Laure turned and clasped Lopasuta's hand and said, "You've been a tower of strength. I know what an inconvenience it must have been—"

"It was the least I could do, Laure," the tall Comanche said. "You know, I think his journey may have been the best thing that could have happened to him. From what he has told me, he was feeling pretty aimless before he left. Meeting Cecily and Hugo seems to have made a big difference. When he saw all that Hugo has accomplished at such an early age, it inspired him to make something of his own life, I believe."

"I do hope Cecily will regain her memory soon," Laure said. "Poor Hugo! What a burden he has."

"Yes, but he's a strong man. He was a tremendous help to Paul."

"He does seem older somehow," Laure said. "When I start to think what terrible dangers he might have experienced . . . Well, now I want to forget it all."

Lopasuta rose and kissed Laure on the cheek, then said to her and Lucien, "It has been a long day, and I think I'll retire now, if you don't mind."

When Laure and her eldest son were alone, she said, "Lucien, I'd very much appreciate your inviting Mr. Sonderman for dinner when you ride into Montgomery tomorrow. By helping us with the sketches, he'll be part of the plans for making Windhaven into a resort. Just think," she said, sighing, "we won't ever have to worry about money again, God willing."

Lucien chuckled. "Am I wrong in thinking that you and Mr. Sonderman have become good friends, Mother?"

"You're not wrong." With a flash of her former vitality, Laure primly added, with the hint of a smile lurking around her sweet mouth, "But, young man, we are just that—friends—and nothing more. And now it's time for me to go to bed, too. It's been such an exciting day!''

"Mother, before you go," Lucien said, placing a restraining hand on her arm as she rose, "I think it's time I told you that Mr. Markson says he wouldn't object to my marrying his daughter, Angela. Her parents are very wealthy, as you know, and maybe I can help out that way. The resort may take several years to show a profit."

"Now just a minute, Lucien," Laure began sharply. "You're not going to jeopardize your career or your life by marrying someone you don't care for!"

"Don't worry, Mother. She's a beautiful girl, and I happen to know that she cares for me a great deal. Maybe she can be my salvation, after all I lost in poor Mary Eileen," Lucien said as he rose from the table. He came to her and kissed her. "Good night, Mother. We'll talk about it more in the morning."

Chapter 27

It was Tuesday, December 11, a week before old Lucien Bouchard's commemorative birthday, a birthday which, had he been alive, would have been his hundred twenty-first. Today was the last day of Carla Bouchard's exhibition, and Henri Courvalier had escorted her to the gallery and, after that, to a private party for a celebration. The critical notices had been laudatory, and Carla had found it hard to keep from having her head turned by all the lavish praise heaped upon her by visitors to the gallery as well as the Parisian art critics.

As they left her atelier to go to the gallery Henri stopped at the desk and, noticing a letter in Carla's mailbox, gestured to the old concierge to let him have it. He took it, acknowledged his thanks, and then handed it to the beautiful young brunette, bowing low and smiling at her.

Carla examined the letter and saw that it was from her father and postmarked from San Antonio. She panicked momentarily, apprehensive of its contents, but then realized it must have been mailed at the same time the cable was sent. She once again felt a stab of guilt for not having gone back home to care for her mother. Yet there was no time for that now, and she turned, composing her face into a winsome smile as she offered her arm to the vintner to take them to the carriage that awaited outside.

Once there, however, her curiosity took over and she tore open the letter, excusing herself to her gallant escort.

In his letter Lucien Edmond went into long detail over his proposed trip to Windhaven Plantation, and he revealed that he had an idea that could help Laure put the Bouchard property back on an excellent financial footing. Then, to her own chagrin, he related how grateful he was to his daughter for having written Maxine and him about terminating her affair with James Turner, as well as telling Carla what pride Maxine felt for her daughter's artistic success.

Carla's face was shadowed, for to this date she had not yet told her family of her alliance with Henri Courvalier. As the vintner took her hand and kissed her gently on the cheek, murmuring how much he loved her, she wondered—and not for the first time—whether her growing fame in the art world would be so great if she were not romantically involved with this influential man. Then she dashed any such thoughts from her mind. How could she despair at a time in her life when romance, fame, and success were courting her?

The weather was unexpectedly sunny and unseasonably warm on this Tuesday, the eighteenth day of December, 1883. Laure, her sons and daughters, Lopasuta, and Lucien Edmond as well, had ascended the gentle slope to the top of the towering bluff. Once again, they came, this time to pay tribute not only to the founder of the dynasty whose name had been a legacy of honor and justice, but also to Luke Bouchard and to Leland Kenniston.

It was late afternoon, and the setting sun of the short

winter's day touched the slope with red, as it had on that burning August day when Laure had laid Leland to rest. The mistress of Windhaven felt a wave of sorrow, recalling all that had been lost, and yet the year's end had brought new hope for the future, new glory for Windhaven in years to come.

She knelt down beside each of the graves, saying a brief prayer, coming at last to old Lucien's burial place. "Sleep in peace, Grandfather," she said, "for Windhaven's salvation is being achieved, and its spirit will never die. What you bequeathed to the Bouchards, I shall not let perish so long as there is goodness and decency in the hearts of men, regardless of their race or creed or color. It was you who taught this credo to your beloved grandson, Luke, my revered and adored husband and the father of my children. I shall cherish it, and I shall never forget it, and all those who have the Bouchard name will uphold it in the days to come."

Paul Bouchard knelt beside his elder brother. He turned to Lucien and squeezed his hand as he whispered, "Amen."